Oh Jesu, what was happening to her?

Her heart began to beat hard in her chest, and the inner voice said: *This is wrong. This is wrong, stop it now.* And yet she could not seem to pull away from him. Not even to save her life could she break away from the grip of whatever had her as its prisoner. Deep inside she knew she did not even want to.

And then Henry made a sound very like a groan of pain, and dipped his head and kissed her.

Henry's mouth was hot, while his lips were cold. The combination was astonishingly delicious. Jenova, at first too surprised to move, found her own mouth responding, found herself kissing him back. He was so familiar, and yet so different. He was Henry and yet he was not the Henry she knew, had thought she knew. Someone she had imagined to be very familiar seemed to have altered beyond all recognition.

But he was still Henry.

SARA BENNETT

KISSING THE BRIDE

AVON BOOKS
An Imprint of HarperCollinsPublishers

HarperCollins*Publishers*
77-85 Fulham Palace Road
Hammersmith
London W6 8JB

ISBN: 0 00 775079 X
www.avonromance.com

This edition published 2005
First Avon Books paperback printing: July 2004

Printed and bound in Great Britain by Clays Ltd, St Ives plc

Thank you to R for his love, support and belief in me through the years. I honestly couldn't do it without you.

Prologue

London
Winter, early 1075

*L*ady Jenova requests that Lord Henry of Montevoy
come to her at Gunlinghorn . . .

Lord Henry sighed as the messenger, an earnest young
man in baggy breeches, carried on in a piping voice.

*. . . come to her at Gunlinghorn as soon as his duties
at court allow him.*

It was not that Lord Henry of Montevoy did not want
to come to Lady Jenova at Gunlinghorn, he thought as he
sent the messenger off for refreshment. He had known
Lady Jenova forever, and he was very fond of her. She had
once been wed to the king's cousin and was now a widow.
Even if the king had not favored her, that marriage had
made her important. No, it was not that Lord Henry did
not want to visit Lady Jenova. It was just that, at this particular moment, he had other things on his mind.

King William was not currently in residence at court in London; he was across the Channel, dealing with rebels in Le Maine and attending to his affairs in Normandy. But many of the great men of England were there. There was intrigue afoot, stirrings among the barons, jostlings for more land and more power. Greed had awoken, lifting its head and casting a glance about to see who was watching.

Lord Henry did not like the tension he felt in the air these days.

It was not just the thought of leaving this simmering pot unattended that concerned Henry. He told himself he had always preferred to be in the thick of things, to know what was going on and with whom, to use his intelligence to untangle the problems of the realm. Henry had never been much of a one for the isolation of the country, and Gunlinghorn was four days' ride to the southwest.

And, of course, he enjoyed partaking of civilized pursuits. More particularly, good conversation, fine wine and beautiful women. With his clear blue eyes set in a face almost perfect, Lord Henry was often called the most handsome man in England. Henry had always treated the title with good humor—especially now, at the age of thirty-four. His handsome face hid a keen mind, and any man who at first glance dismissed him as just a face was soon put aright. Henry was an integral part of King William's council, and as such the powerful barons saw him either as a shrewd friend to look to in times of trouble, or a man to be wary of if they were involved in anything detrimental to the king.

The women saw him differently. Henry was also famous as a lover, and few ladies could resist so handsome a trophy to show off to their friends.

Jenova was the only woman he'd ever known who was

unaffected by his handsome face. She didn't see him as a pretty trophy, or a shrewd adversary. That was one of the reasons Henry liked her, and why he felt so at ease with her. He could be himself with her, he could be *Henry*.

If he remembered rightly, the last time he had visited her, she had sent him home with an indulgent smile and with the admonishment to be good. Henry had laughed and kissed her fingers, then left her without a backward glance. Had he been "good"? In his way, he supposed he had, but Henry knew he had done things that Jenova would quibble over. What did she expect? She looked upon him almost as if he were a troublesome mortal and she a goddess on high: a man struggling to rise to the dizzy heights she expected of him and yet never quite reaching them. Still, she accepted his faults. She accepted *him*.

Such a friend, be they man or woman, was truly a rarity.

Henry sighed again. Of course, he would have to go to her. Jenova would not have asked if she had not needed to see him, and if he left at dawn tomorrow he could be in Gunlinghorn in four days, assuming the weather held. That would give him a few hours to tie up any business he had at the court—his trusted second in command, Leon, could keep an eye on matters and report to him if or when it became necessary. That would leave this evening free for Henry to visit his current mistress, Christina.

He could not expect to find someone like Christina at Gunlinghorn, nor would he feel comfortable preying upon Jenova's women. She was always, to his mind, overly strict when it came to visiting lords defiling her ladies—especially when some of those ladies seemed most eager to be defiled.

He turned the message over in his mind. It was a

strange relationship, the one between Jenova and himself, and yet it was a comfortable one. She had loved her husband, Mortred, and had been grieving for him now for two years. When Mortred died, Henry recalled, the glow had left Jenova's green eyes. As if night had come to her soul.

Their son must be five years old. Henry tried to remember what he looked like and could not; beyond a pat on the head and a vague greeting, Henry never took much notice of the boy. In truth, children were of little interest to him; there was no place for them in his life. And as for having any children of his own . . .

Henry shuddered. He did not want the responsibility. Not after what had happened to him when he was a boy.

Shrugging off his dark thoughts, Henry let himself wonder what Jenova could want of him that required his swift attendance upon her. Was her son ill? Was *she* ill? But she would have said so, surely? Perhaps she needed his advice? But no, Henry smiled mockingly at his own thoughts, to Jenova he was and had always been *Henry*, whom she treated with a combination of amusement and indulgence and irritation, but never took too seriously.

That wasn't strictly true, Henry chastised himself. When he gave Jenova advice on important matters, matters to do with land and the running and defense of her manor, she usually took it—she had always trusted him to know the best paths to follow in the murky waters of King William's England. But once, when he had tried to tell her that a red gown suited her better than a yellow one, she had laughed until she'd cried.

"Are you a lady's maid now, Henry?" she had asked him at last, her green eyes brimming. "Mayhap I should ask you for reports from the court as to what is in fashion. Mayhap you will wear a likeness of the latest headwear for me." And she was off again, bubbling with mirth.

Henry had tried not to take offence. They had known each other since they were children, and to Jenova he would always be that boy who followed her about, who was to be tolerated in a fond sort of way.

He found her attitude frustrating, but at the same time oddly comforting.

Jenova was not like other women, and he had never treated her so.

"Reynard!" he called suddenly.

"Yes, my lord?" Reynard, come last year from Lord Radulf's household to serve Lord Henry, looked up from where he was slumbering by the fire. At the moment he had the appearance of a large, disheveled hound, his deceptively sleepy dark eyes fixed on Henry. But Henry knew Reynard was far from being the idle man he looked.

"We will go south to Gunlinghorn at first light tomorrow. Prepare, will you? I do not expect our stay to be a long one."

"Who is at Gunlinghorn, my lord?"

Henry smiled. "An old friend," he said. And realized that he was looking forward to this journey, after all. It had been too long since he had last seen Jenova. Far too long.

Chapter 1

The weather had not been altogether bad. South beyond London, the Forest of Anderida had enclosed them like a green ocean, but Henry had arranged for a guide to lead them through its timbered vastness. Snow had fallen, but not heavily, and not enough to slow down his troop of men.

Henry, huddled in his thick, fur-lined cloak, had thought wistfully of Christina, her long, dark hair covering the smooth, pale skin of her back as last evening she'd poured him wine from a jug. Her movements had been graceful and languid, and as she had turned to him, she had smiled. Aye, she had made a tasty picture, dressed only in her ebony locks.

He did not love her, any more than she loved him. Theirs was a relationship of convenience, and love was not something that was part of the contract between them. For Henry, women like Christina were a necessity—a necessary pleasure. If she was not the greatest conversationalist, and her intelligence was shrewd rather than deep, what did it matter, when she more than satisfied him in bed? And as for Christina, the daughter of an ambitious minor noble, she was more than happy with her comfortable rooms and fine clothes and jewels.

"I have to leave tomorrow," he had told her, sipping the wine.

She had blinked. "Go where, my lord?"

"To the Downs in the southwest, Christina. To Gunlinghorn."

Her eyes had widened. "Oh, my lord, I would not like to go outside London! There are savages in the countryside!"

Henry had grinned. "Then it is as well you are not going, Christina. You will stay here until I return."

She had been relieved, Henry thought now with wry humor. Christina had had no desire to share the perils of Henry's journey. She liked him, or at least she liked the luxuries he could afford to give her, but that was as far as it went. She was glad he was going alone.

Why were women so fickle? They couldn't wait to get into bed with him, but none of them sobbed more than a few false tears when it was time to part. Was it something to do with him? Did he not please them in some way? Henry knew that wasn't so—his women were always well pleased. When their relationship had run its course, and they left, they nearly always took with them a mutual fondness. Nay, the problem lay elsewhere. And Henry had lately begun to understand that something was missing.

But what?

As clever and handsome as he was reported to be, Henry did not know.

In younger days he hadn't felt the need to dwell on such puzzling and incomprehensible matters. Then all he had wanted was a lusty woman in his bed. But now . . . *I must be getting old,* he thought in disgust. Or maybe it was seeing Radulf and Lily, and Gunnar and Rose, and Ivo and Briar, all so happy, all content with exactly what they had, all so much in love. . . .

It was ridiculous, but it made Henry feel lonely.

Love?

In his heart, Henry held a dark fear. Love would mean sharing all his secrets with another person and trusting them to understand. It would mean giving more of himself than he was prepared, or perhaps able, to give.

Henry had been more or less orphaned at the age of five, and at thirteen he had been a man well and truly. He did not look to love as a reason to survive.

What does it matter if I haven't found a Lily or a Briar? he asked himself angrily. He had what other men envied. He was well favored in looks and fortune, he had the king's ear and any woman he wanted. It was no boast, but honest truth. Women never turned Lord Henry down.

Love!

He had no time for love; it was the least of his concerns. He admitted to himself that that was why he preferred the lighter intimacies of women like Christina; it was less trouble. It was *safer.*

Henry and his troop of men rode on, into the wintry forest, through the fertile Weald and onto the windswept Downs. Here the Gunlinghorn River was born in the chalk downs and grew wide and strong, leading them into the Vale of Gunlinghorn. Winter rains had turned ponds into small lakes, and the water meadows were full of life despite the weather. Henry watched a long-legged waterbird fly low across the gray surface, momentarily surrounded by a flock of smaller linnets. Gunlinghorn had always been plentiful in its harvests of both land and water. Before the Normans came, life here had been fortunate, bountiful, and under Lady Jenova little had changed. In that regard, Gunlinghorn was truly a small slice of Eden.

The castle stood upon a tall hill, overlooking the Vale. From the highest point of the keep, one could look out over the cliffs on the coast of England, to the very sea the Normans had sailed across to make their conquest.

The keep itself was constructed of timber cut from the woods surrounding the Vale of Gunlinghorn. The strong wooden ramparts encircling the keep were currently being remade in local stone, with the grim-looking gatehouse already completed. Jenova was ferocious when it came to protecting what belonged to her, and Henry had suggested stone the last time he'd been here. Now, seeing with his own eyes that she had taken his advice, he felt an unexpected rush of pleasure.

Gunlinghorn's heavy gates opened easily to his name. Henry led his men into the bailey, casting an eye over the busy castlefolk, and nodding in reply to the many cries of welcome. He was known here. Liked, too, he thought. It was almost like coming home. With an odd catch in his chest, Henry realized that Gunlinghorn was probably the nearest thing to a family and a home that he had ever had.

In the great hall, several servants bowed low, their voices hushed to murmurs. Henry hardly noticed them. The warmth and welcome of Gunlinghorn embraced him, laced with the aroma of roasting meat from the kitchen. Henry felt himself begin to relax, the tensions easing out of his shoulders like loosening knots. He never relaxed in London—it was neither safe nor prudent to do so. And yet now, at Gunlinghorn, the need to be constantly watchful was being replaced by a sense of well-being.

Henry could not help himself: He smiled. Making his

way to the roaring fire, he accepted mulled wine from one of Jenova's servants. He gulped it down, feeling instant warmth spearing through his chilled body, and then set about stripping off his heavy gloves and stamping the snow from his boots. Several castle dogs snuffled about him with friendly curiosity.

"Henry!"

Her familiar voice rose above the bustle. Henry did not realize how much he had missed her until he heard it. Or how the sight of her warmed his heart, he thought, as he turned.

Lady Jenova was coming toward him. Her moss green gown and the hem of her creamy chemise swirled elegantly about her legs, while a jewel-decorated, golden girdle rested low upon her shapely hips. Rings sparkled upon her elegant fingers, and her silken white veil drifted about her head and shoulders. Even from the far end of the hall, Henry could see the smile glowing in her green eyes.

Surprised, Henry wondered why he had never noticed that her skin was as creamy and as smooth as milk. And he knew the brown hair beneath her veil to be lush and curling, perfect for a man to tangle his fingers through. Her eyes, a haunting deep forest green, were set within long dark lashes and topped by slim, arching brows. Such eyes . . . they were really quite remarkable. Would they darken with passion when she was in the arms of a man?

With her wealth there must have been many suitors hoping to win her approval. And not just because of her riches, either. Jenova was an extremely good looking woman.

Although he had known many very beautiful women, Henry realized there was *something* about Jenova . . . something unique, something he had never noticed until now.

"I did not expect you so soon," Jenova said.

"I did not think it worth sending your messenger with a warning I was on my way—I would have arrived before him."

She gripped his hands firmly with her own cool fingers and smiled straight into his eyes.

For a moment, a single moment, he felt as if she had reached into his chest and squeezed his heart. And then Henry blinked and shook off his strange abstraction. He raised her fingers to his lips, enjoying the scent and taste of her, surprising himself yet again. When he looked up, there was a twinkle in her green eyes.

"I thought that you might be otherwise occupied at court, Henry. Too busy with your intrigues to get away."

"Nothing could ever be as important as your wishes, Jenova," he said blandly, and for once he meant it.

She laughed. Jenova never took his compliments seriously, Henry thought irritably, but in another moment he was smiling at his own foolishness. This was Jenova, after all. Why should it suddenly matter to him whether she believed his compliments or not?

"You are looking well," he said.

She was tall for a woman, for she stared into his eyes at almost the same height. "I *am* well," she replied. "Come, Henry, and sit with me a moment. As soon as my sentries came to tell me they had seen you, I told the cook to prepare food, and I know you will want a hot bath, so there will be one waiting, when you are ready for it. You see, we are not complete barbarians here."

"I am pleased to hear it."

She pulled a face at him and turned away. Henry followed her. Her skirts swayed gently as she walked, and the line of her back was straight and graceful. The sight of her was to be enjoyed, but Henry told himself that what he really enjoyed about it was that he felt absolutely no desire. None at all, he insisted to himself. There was no urgency to bed her, and to make her his. It was actually quite restful. He had not fully appreciated it before, but being with Jenova was really very soothing.

Jenova led him to an alcove, partially hidden behind an embroidered screen. Gracefully, she sat down, arranging her skirts about her, and Henry sat beside her, smiling as he watched her fuss. She seemed to be avoiding his eyes. What had she done that she could not tell her oldest friend?

"You sent for me and here I am. Now, tell me, Jenova," he said with a slight impatience. "What is it?"

She looked up, and her green eyes shone with both excitement and trepidation. "Henry, oh Henry, I am thinking to marry again."

Henry stared. For such a practised lordling who was never at a loss for a quip or a joke, he suddenly found himself with nothing to say. And worse, inside his chest a mixture of very intense emotions writhed like serpents.

Was one of them dread? But why should he feel thus? And was another disappointment? Now it occurred to Henry to wonder why he was so surprised by her news. She had loved Mortred, aye, but he had been dead two years, and there must have been many ambitious barons who had set their sights upon her since. True, she had told Henry soon after Mortred had died that she did not intend to wed again, and because of her kinship with the king, it had been possible for her to honor her vow. The king's fondness for her had worked in her favor, and Jenova had remained a widow, ruling her own lands, doing just as she'd wished. Indeed, thought Henry with an inner smile, when had he ever known Jenova to do otherwise?

Henry tried to clear his thoughts, tried to shrug off the

strange mood that had come upon his normally cold and rational self. Mayhap he was just concerned for her well-being? That must be it, he thought with relief, as he looked at her.

Jenova was frowning at him, a tiny wrinkle between her arching brows. "You do not seem overjoyed, Henry," she said with a bite to her tone. "And I have not even told you his name. This does not bode well, does it, for your attendance at my bride ale?"

Henry managed to laugh, though it took more effort than he would have believed possible.

"I am sorry, Jenova, but it was a shock . . . a *surprise*. I had no idea. . . . You have been a widow so long, I am used to your single state. I did not realize you wanted to alter it. Who is the fortunate man?"

"I have not decided to say aye to him yet, but the man is Baldessare."

Henry kept the smile on his face through sheer strength of willpower. Jenova gave him a sharp, searching glance but seemed satisfied with what she saw. Relaxing a little, her cheeks faintly flushed, she proceeded to tell him about her chosen husband.

But Henry wasn't listening. He did not need to hear anything about Lord Baldessare. Henry knew him. Twice Jenova's age, warstruck and truculent, how could such a man attract the attention of the Lady Jenova, let alone her affection? For, aye, there was affection in her voice.

It was beyond his comprehension.

" 'Tis all very well, sweeting," he said patiently, interrupting the flow of her lilting voice, "but isn't he a little *old* for you?"

Jenova stopped, blinked and stared. And then she laughed aloud. "Oh Henry, you fool! No, no, not the father! I am thinking to marry the *son*. Alfric. He is not too old, in fact he is younger than me, and very amiable. I am certain we will get on very well together."

"You mean he will never forbear you anything you ask for, and you will boss him about unmercifully," he retorted.

Jenova had the grace to look a little ashamed. "Well, mayhap. But I would not want a man who ruled me, Henry. I am too used to my own way, and more so now, when I have run Gunlinghorn for so long, alone. I fear I would not take kindly to interference."

That last sounded like a warning. Had she asked him here because she wanted him to say "aye" to everything she asked of him? Well, he thought with a sudden spurt of anger, he'd be damned if he'd come all this way just to flatter her.

"My sweet Jenova," Henry began, careful to sound as friendly and helpful as he could. "I do not mean to criticize, but to marry with the expectation of treating your husband like one of your serfs does not bode well for your future happiness."

Jenova smiled coolly and narrowed her intriguing eyes. "And of course you are all knowledgeable when it comes to marriage, Henry."

"Nay, you know I am not, but I have witnessed many others falter, or end in misery."

"Henry, I do not marry for love," she explained to him in a patient voice. "I honestly do not expect to find anything more than companionship, and if I wed a man who bows to all my wishes, I will certainly be the happier for that."

But Jenova deserved so much more, Henry thought, and felt sadness for her sake. She seemed to believe herself unworthy of genuine happiness. Unworthy of the sort of love that Henry's friends had discovered. Perhaps, he thought, she didn't know such a love was possible? Perhaps, like Henry, she had never experienced it? But no, that could not be, for she had loved Mortred, or at least the man she had imagined Mortred to be. Henry had made very sure that she never learned the sordid truth about Mortred, and he believed he had succeeded—after all, Jenova had sworn not to remarry when her husband died.

So what had changed her mind?

He opened his mouth to ask her and then stopped himself. It was not his business. He was here to give Jenova practical advice, not to take on the role of bridegroom finder. She would laugh at him, or mock him, and deservedly so. Jenova, he reminded himself firmly, was a clever and intelligent woman. She knew what she wanted, and if she wanted young Baldessare for her husband, who was Henry to deny her her heart's desire?

And perhaps it is her heart's desire. Perhaps, despite her protestations, she has fallen in love with him.

The thought slipped slyly into his head. He gave Jenova a searching glance. Her cheeks were still flushed, her eyes glowed, her lips had curled into a sly little smile. . . . She looked well, very well indeed. But was she a woman in the throes of a lusty love? Henry did not think so, but mayhap that was because he didn't *want* to think so. He admitted it to himself. There was something about believing Jenova in love with Lord Baldessare's son that turned him unpleasantly cold.

Jenova tried to hide her smile. Henry looked grumpy. He didn't approve of her marrying again, but he was trying to hide it. Had he and Mortred been close friends, she might have understood his lack of enthusiasm. But they hadn't been. Henry must have been well aware of the lie that was Mortred.

Jenova's smile faltered. Why had he never told her? Why had he let her wallow in her grief never knowing the truth? For two years! Had Henry kept her in ignorance because he saw naught wrong in Mortred's behavior? Or because he sought to protect her from a knowledge that would wound her?

Knowing Henry so well, Jenova favored the latter explanation. Aye, she had known him since they were children and he had been sent to live with her family, claiming some tenuous kinship with her father. "Henry has been abandoned by his own mother," Jenova remembered her father saying, as if it had been a serious fault in Henry's character. As if the abandonment had been entirely Henry's doing.

Sometimes, now, the boy that he had been still crept into her heart like a little ache, and sometimes the man he had become irritated and yet intrigued her in equal measure. Most of the time she tended not to take him too seriously—she had known him for too long—but he did offer good advice some of the time, and some of the time she was inclined to take it.

As for her possible bridegroom, Jenova admitted to herself that Henry was partially right. She had chosen Alfric because he would deny her nothing, and she was well aware she could order him about. A woman would be a fool to give herself to a man who would not put her first.

But there was more to her sudden decision to remarry.

Vengeance. Aye, there was that, if one could take vengeance against a husband who was dead. The fact was, Jenova felt foolish for mourning so long for a man unworthy of her grief. But over and above these things, there had grown a strong sense of lacking, of loss, of *loneliness. . . .*

Aye, she was lonely.

What would Henry know of that? Jenova asked herself irritably. It was doubtful he was ever lonely. From the rumors Jenova had been privy to, and her own observations, she knew that Henry didn't lack for female companionship. He would not understand her loneliness, her taking the weight of Gunlinghorn upon her shoulders and making a success of it, and then having no one with whom to share her triumphs. She had no one to laugh with, to weep with, no one with whom to spend the long nights, to hold her in the darkness, and to wake with in the morning light.

More than anything, though, Jenova knew she missed the companionship and the closeness she and Mortred had once shared. *That* was what she wanted from Alfric—someone to smile at her and hold her hand and lead her to the table, someone to kiss her and hold her when she was feeling low. It didn't need to be wild passion; she didn't really think she was capable of wild passion. Jenova just wanted someone who cared—or did a good job of playing the part!

She shook off her melancholy thoughts. Usually she had no time for such self-indulgence—the running of Gunlinghorn left her with very little time to ponder her solitary state. And if she wed Alfric, there would be no need to ponder it at all.

"I hope you will treat Alfric with courtesy," she said, giving Henry a long, censorious look. "I do not want him to feel as if you are judging him."

Henry cast up his bright blue eyes, and the smile he gave her was a touch mischievous. "I won't intimidate him, sweeting, if that is what you mean."

Jenova studied him a moment more, trying to make him out, but of course it was impossible. If Henry did not wish you to read his thoughts, then you couldn't. It was one of the most infuriating things about him. On the surface he was charming and easygoing, but there were hidden depths to Henry. Well, she would just have to take him at his word.

Jenova relaxed into a smile of her own. "Thank you, Henry. Now, there was something more. . . ."

"Oh?"

"It concerns Lord Baldessare, Alfric's father. He sent his scribe, who is also his priest, with a request . . . nay, a *demand,*" Jenova's eyes glittered, "that the marriage contract include my agreement that, in the event of Alfric's death, he himself would become guardian to *my* son, and protector of Gunlinghorn."

Henry frowned. "Guardian to your son? If you were a feeble female, I suppose I would understand it, but you are not. And protector of Gunlinghorn? You have had no protector thus far, why would he imagine you needed one?"

"That is what I ask myself," Jenova said, pleased to see he was as put out by Baldessare's demands as she. "Perhaps you can discover what notions are wriggling about like worms in that man's head, for I fear he is beyond me."

Henry smiled at the image, but he still looked uneasy. "He is a tough old warrior, I grant you. Perhaps he thinks all women are weak and unable to care for their lands, and there's an end to it. Perhaps if we persuade him you are as capable and clever as you are beautiful, he will desist."

His praise pleased her. "Well, I will not agree to his terms, and there's an end to it. If I wed Alfric and anything were to happen to him, I would rule alone, as I do now, until my son is old enough to see to his own inheritance. I do not want interference from strangers who know nothing of Gunlinghorn, and care less."

"Is Alfric sickly?" Henry was still worrying at the problem. "Mayhap the father knows something you do not."

Jenova tapped a slim finger against her cheek. "I would not have thought so, no. He appears hale and healthy. But you must make your own judgment on the matter, Henry. I'll warrant you know more than I of the lies and tricks powerful men like to play."

Henry wondered if she meant that as a compliment. If not, then what was she implying? She was the only woman he knew who could confuse him like that. "My feeling is that Baldessare is simply too greedy to allow the possibility of Gunlinghorn falling out of his grasp."

"But it is not in his grasp. If I marry, I will be marrying Alfric."

"And Alfric is a man you can rule, Jenova. But think on this; if you can rule him, then so can others." He stood up. "I will bathe, and change my clothing, and see you and your bridegroom anon."

Jenova smiled, and then watched as he strode across the hall, calling to his man as he went. He looked very handsome, despite the dust of his journey, but then Henry had never been anything *but* handsome. It was ungenerous of her, she knew, but sometimes she wished he could look just a little worn or frazzled. A little less than perfect.

Henry's big, swarthy servant, Reynard, fell in behind him. He wore Henry's emblem on his tunic, the phoenix surrounded by flame. The two of them, Henry and Reynard, vanished up the stairs into the keep's upper reaches.

Jenova knew that in her heart she was glad she had asked Henry to attend her. He may be famed for his honeyed tongue at court, but she knew that in such a situation as this he would give her an honest opinion. Even if she did not agree with it, she could rely upon him to be sincere. That was something she missed when he was not here—a man who told the truth to her. Alfric tended to flatter her, telling her what she wanted to hear. And while it was very nice, and he seemed to mean it, Jenova preferred the brutal truth.

You are as capable and clever as you are beautiful.

The words echoed in her head. Did Henry really think her beautiful? She imagined he was used to flattering women, and doing other things to them that made them gasp and squirm and beg for more. An image of his naked, well-muscled shoulders and back, his body almost entirely covering the female form beneath him, his hands and mouth touching, caressing, his chestnut hair curling at his nape . . . *her* fingers tangling in it as she felt his lips, warm and teasing, moving over the plump curve of her breast toward its center. His hot mouth brushing her so that she gasped. His tongue circling, and then his lips closing over her and she . . . she . . .

Jenova stood up abruptly. Shocked. What on earth was she thinking? Henry's women were naught to do with her. She was sometimes curious, aye, but for some reason just now that curiosity had gotten out of hand. Her cheeks felt quite hot. And it wasn't just her cheeks.

Jenova took a deep breath and pushed all such thoughts firmly out of her head. Enough. That was quite enough of that. She had Alfric to dream of, hadn't she? Henry was her friend and that was all. Even to begin to imagine such a situation was dangerous and foolish and a sure way to get herself hurt.

When she was quite certain that she had regained her composure, Jenova went to attend to her own appearance.

Chapter 2

Alfric, son of Lord Baldessare, arrived on a snowy horse at the head of a troop of grim-faced men. He was dressed in a fine woollen tunic of woad blue, with soft, dark leather breeches. The spurs attached to his boot-heels shone like stars. He was a good-looking young man, with hair fairer than Henry's, and with eyes of a deep, melancholy brown. As Jenova came to greet him, the gaze he turned upon her was more like a hound's toward its master than a future bridegroom's toward his bride.

Henry sighed inwardly. If Jenova wanted a man who was her slave, then she had chosen well. While he stood back and waited to be introduced, Alfric was busy kissing her fingers and whispering preposterous compliments to her, his puppy-dog eyes full of meaning. Reynard, who was standing behind Henry, murmured something derogatory under his breath.

"Now, now, Reynard," Henry said in mock reprimand. "We cannot all be men of intelligence. And the lady seems to be enjoying his attentions." Indeed, Jenova was quite flushed. "Perhaps that is a lesson for you and me—be not clever or skilled if you want to succeed with the ladies. They much prefer stupid men."

"I need no help when it comes to the ladies, my lord," Reynard replied with some arrogance.

Henry turned and looked him up and down. Reynard was a big man, more like a bear than a man, but with his rugged good looks, women seemed to cluster about him. Even Christina, when she thought Henry wasn't watching. Mayhap Reynard was right, and he did not need instruction from Alfric. Or Henry.

"Lord Henry!"

Jenova had finally managed to fight free of her aspiring bridegroom, and now her gaze was fastened meaningfully upon him. It was time for him to play his part, outwardly at least. But, as Henry strolled forward, full of his usual smiling confidence, he felt anything but amiable toward Alfric, son of Baldessare.

"Lord Alfric," Jenova introduced him, "this is my oldest and dearest friend, Lord Henry of Montevoy."

Alfric looked up. His eyes widened at the sight of Henry, and then as quickly narrowed. There was no mistaking the gleam of jealousy in them. He tightened his mouth. In a heartbeat he had turned from a handsome, charming young man into a small boy who has had some bauble taken from him and doesn't know whether to scream or cry.

Was Alfric really so lacking in trust for Jenova that he would be jealous of an "old friend"?

Or was it just that Lord Henry's reputation with women had followed him all the way to Gunlinghorn?

Still, Henry did not allow his own smile to falter—he

was doing this to please Jenova, not Alfric. He gritted his teeth and made his brief bow and spoke of his pleasure at meeting Alfric. Then, for good measure, he added, "As Lady Jenova has mentioned, she and I are very old *friends,*" stressing the word.

Alfric's demeanor brightened a little, although he still didn't appear altogether comfortable in Henry's presence. "L-lord Henry," he stammered. "I have heard of you, of course. Your name is well known throughout the-the land."

Henry raised an eyebrow. "Indeed? You flatter me, Lord Alfric."

"No, no, I do not! You are known t-far and w-wide. My father has often spoken of you. Indeed, once at court, when h-he claimed a parcel of land to the west, you—" But Alfric came to an abrupt halt. His face flushed a deep and ugly red, and he glanced away, swallowing audibly. "That is, he-he met you once, in London, at court. That is all I-I meant to say."

Reynard snorted rudely, turning it into a cough. Henry ignored him. "Of course you did," he said evenly. "And I do remember your father." *And the matter you speak of,* he thought, but did not say it aloud. Alfric already looked as if he was about to explode with embarrassment, or terror, or both.

Jenova appeared confused, as well she might. Her glance slid over Henry's innocent expression and narrowed, as if she blamed him for Alfric's state—most unfair, in Henry's opinion. Then with a brilliant, determined smile, she took Alfric's arm and, speaking softly to him, led him within the keep.

Henry followed, his smile genuine and no longer polite. He remembered the incident at court well enough, although he had forgotten it until Alfric reminded him.

The father had claimed some land that was not due him, and the king had asked Henry what he thought. Henry had said he had seen the land himself and had joked that he wouldn't mind having it, and the king, more as a rebuff to Lord Baldessare's presumption than to reward Henry, had promptly given it to him. Baldessare had left in a rage, swearing vengeance.

He must have thought better of it, for the vengeance had never eventuated, but it was clearly still on his, and his son's, mind. Being acquainted with the truculent and bitter Lord Baldessare, Henry could well imagine that the slight, and the loss of the land, had never been allowed to be forgotten.

The meal was succulent and well prepared, and there was even a juggler to add to the occasion. Jenova was excelling herself to please her would-be bridegroom, and young Alfric seemed willing and eager to be pleased. Now and then he would cast a nervous glance in Henry's direction, and his stammer was more pronounced when he spoke to him, but otherwise the occasion went off without further incident. Henry was able to converse with some of Jenova's household, her ladies and steward and Sir John, the knight in charge of her garrison.

Gunlinghorn impressed him tonight, with its elegance and grandeur, as it had never done before. It was the sort of place he might have dreamed of living in, as a child. An abandoned child, he reminded himself wryly. A son of the minor nobility, Henry had been technically an orphan by the age of five, when his devout mother had decided to enter a religious house and spend her remaining years within its walls. She had wanted to be a nun from girlhood but had been prevented by her family and forced to marry. With her husband dead and a son she looked upon as the product of a sin rather than her own flesh and blood, she had followed her inclination.

Alone and abandoned, Henry had been passed from relative to relative, no matter how tenuous the connection. He had lived in many different castles and keeps throughout Normandy, reliant upon others for his well-being—or lack of. He had looked upon it as an adventure, suitable training for the tough knight that he one day planned to become. And then he had been taken to a castle like no other. He had been drawn into the shadows—swallowed whole with no hope of escape. Henry had been thirteen when he'd been released from that hell, and he had taken the chance he'd been given. Like a phoenix he had risen anew from the ashes and four years later had been knighted for his bravery in a small skirmish. He had not looked back.

Aye, he was proud of what he had become, the life he had made for himself, the man he had molded from the boy. He preferred the present. The past was full of dark corners. Memories he did not revisit often. Shadowy recollections he preferred not to dwell upon.

Much better to remember when William the Bastard had set out to conquer England, although he had claimed at the time it was rightfully his. Whatever the legality of the matter, Henry had known it was his opportunity to make good. He saw that he could use William's ambitions as a lever to raise himself higher. So it had been. He'd been there with William at Hastings and had helped him to victory. Ever since that day, the king had enjoyed his company and found his clever tongue useful. And he had certainly been well rewarded for his efforts.

Not that Henry was complacent. He was well aware that his circumstances could change quicker than King William's moods. His position would always be precarious, and he could never be too careful. One of the reasons why, despite his trust in Leon, his second in command, he preferred not to be away from court for too long. Allegiances shifted, favorites fell, wheels turned full circle, and Henry did not intend to be one of the casualties.

Mayhap I shouldn't have come, Henry thought now, uneasily. There were stirrings at court and about England; some of the Anglo-Norman barons were intent upon securing more land than they deserved. It had been Henry's job to keep an eye on these rumors and plots, and to put a stop to them if it became necessary. Leon would send word if matters became dire, he knew, and yet. . . .

But Jenova had asked for him, and because she was his friend, and he wanted to please her, he had come. Although, he thought grimly, if pleasing her meant allowing her to wed a weak fool like Alfric, then he might do better to displease her. Was that what she really wanted? A husband who would gaze at her as if he was witless and do exactly as she told him? Then Alfric was perfect for her.

Besides, who was Henry to judge!

He, himself, had never looked for more than a compliant mind and body when seeking a new mistress, and that could not be much different for a wife. Certainly the last thing he had ever wanted was for his heart to be engaged. Christina was pretty and amiable, and she cared no more for him than he cared for her. The perfect situation, surely? Why should Jenova be any different in her choices, and why should Henry want her to be?

"Well?" Jenova demanded, when at last Alfric was gone and they were alone again. Her cheeks were flushed, her eyes were bright, and a strand of hair had come loose from her veil and lay against her temple. She looked like a young girl again, rather than a mature woman who had been wed and borne a son. Henry had an urge to reach out and brush the strand away; he squeezed his hand into a fist to stop himself.

Suddenly, touching Jenova did not seem like a good idea.

"Well?" she asked again, impatient with him now. "What do you think of Alfric?"

"What do I think of Alfric?" Henry pretended to ponder. "Does it matter what I think?"

Jenova poked her finger into his arm. "Stop teasing me, Henry. I want to know your opinion of my future husband."

"Very well. I think that Alfric is smitten with you, Jenova, and as long as his love lasts, he will be easy enough to manage." That was the truth as Henry saw it.

Jenova, who had begun to smile, froze. " 'As long as it lasts'?"

"No love lasts forever, but some last longer than others. I don't know whether the fact that he is jealous of me is a good sign, or a bad sign. Mayhap good."

"*Jealous!*" Jenova declared, green eyes narrowing. "What do you mean, Henry? Alfric has no reason to be *jealous.*"

"Didn't you see the way he looked at me when we met? He was jealous, Jenova. He thought you and I are . . ." Her eyes had narrowed even more, like a cat, and Henry bit his lip on the less than polite word he was about to use. "Let us just say, sweeting, that he believes we are far more than friends."

Jenova broke into a peal of laughter. "You cannot be serious! You and me, Henry! I will have to explain to Alfric that if there are two people in all of England least likely to be lovers, then 'tis you and me!"

For some reason Henry did not feel amused.

What *was* so amusing, anyway? What was wrong with him? Was he less of a man than Alfric? Henry felt the stirrings of a strange anger deep inside himself. He was a better man than that cow-eyed youth, and he knew it! Why did Jenova find the notion of him and her so laughable? It was enough to make him want to prove her mistaken.

Henry inwardly shook his head at his own shortsightedness. Such a step would be both foolish and cruel. He was not a cruel man, and he was certainly not a fool. If Jenova had hurt his pride, then it had been unintentional. She was his friend. Surely having such a friend was far, far better than making her his lover for a short time, and then, inevitably, having nothing.

But, just for an instant, a heavenly vision came to him. Of Jenova, her creamy skin uncovered and her brown hair loose about her lush body. Her green eyes, sleepy with desire, lifted to his and her arms held out toward him.

Just for an instant, and then it was gone, and Henry could breathe again.

Jenova was combing her hair. The long, heavy tresses fell over her back and shoulders, curling up at the ends, shorter strands tickling her face and neck. She often thought her hair dull, but the firelight brought out the many different colors to be found in it—gold and mahogany and red. They gleamed and meshed, making the dull glorious.

She thought of Alfric and smiled. He might seem young, but he would mature with time and some careful tutoring from her. Henry was right. Although she had not liked to admit it, Alfric was uncomfortably jealous of other men. That, Jenova decided, was the fault of his youth, and of his overbearing father. With time his confidence would grow, and he would no longer be quite so insecure.

He was not Mortred, she reminded herself. He did not have Mortred's easy self-confidence. But then she did not want another Mortred. She had loved her husband, mourned him, and he had betrayed her. Men like Mortred, men like Henry, found it too easy to manipulate a woman's gentle heart and willing body. She wanted no more of them.

Jenova took a deep breath.

Wasn't that one of the reasons she was marrying Alfric? To take revenge upon Mortred's memory? But that was her secret. Not even Henry must know the true extent of her hurt—he would not understand. Henry never allowed emotion to interfere with business, and what was marriage but a business contract?

She drew her comb through her hair, remembering Henry's face when she had laughed at the idea of him and her. She should not have laughed. It had been impolite of her. But the thought of them together had struck her as so bizarre that it was amusing. They were so totally unsuited, so unlikely a couple! For a moment there he had looked . . . hurt, before his good humor had reasserted itself. That was one of the wonderful things about Henry; he was so even tempered that very little upset him. He had been a sweet boy, and he had grown into an amiable man.

Jenova knew she was lucky to have Henry as her friend. And so much better to be his friend than his lover. She had always felt a little sorry for his women, although they did not appear to resent the experience. There were always lots more of them willing to take the place of those who had gone before.

Is he really such a good lover?

The curious thought had hardly entered her mind when it was followed by an image of Henry. Golden skin and blazing violet-blue eyes, rising above her, his handsomeness all for her. She shook her head, uncomfortable with herself. No, no, not again, that would never do! Henry was her friend, one of her *few* friends, and she did not want to ruin such a fortunate relationship. Once, when they were hardly more than children, they had kissed one afternoon in a meadow, and it had been very sweet, but that was long ago. Such things were best forgotten.

If she had really hurt his feelings by laughing at him, then she would make it up to him tomorrow. She would take him out riding! Although the Vale of Gunlinghorn and the surrounding hills were white with snow, the ride would be a bracing treat. Henry had always loved to ride around Gunlinghorn.

Jenova was well aware that he would already be missing the court, with its verbal maze of rumor and gossip, the constant stimulation of his mind and his senses. Henry thrived upon such things; they were his life. It was important that while he was here, she keep him entertained with all the pursuits he enjoyed.

Aye, tomorrow they would go riding.

Just the two of them.

The Gunlinghorn countryside was white, the fields covered in a crisp layer of snow, the water meadows and marshes half-frozen, while ice and snow hung heavy from the bare branches of the trees in the woods. Beyond the cliffs to the south, the sea was gray and sullen, while some brave gulls floated in a sky that was just as gray.

Jenova had risen early, washing and dressing in her warmest gown and fur-lined boots, and hurried down to the hall. Henry, who was already risen, as she had known he would be, smiled at her over his mug of ale and morning meal of bread and cheese. Jenova hesitated as she reached him. That was odd. Why had she never noticed before how white and strong his teeth were? And how the little lines by his blue eyes creased up so attractively when he smiled?

For a moment her thoughts were confused, and she found herself wondering what she had been about to say, but she quickly shook off her strangeness. It wasn't as if she had never seen Henry before. And yet, just for a moment there, he had been like a stranger. A handsome, desirable stranger.

"I thought we could go riding this morning, Henry," Jenova said, a little breathlessly, striving for normality. "I have not been out for weeks, and although 'twill be cold, I believe the weather will hold for a few hours."

Henry's smile broadened. "I would enjoy that very much, Jenova." He hesitated. His smile remained but lost something of its ease. "Alfric will be coming?"

Jenova shook her head. "No, not Alfric. We will go together, Henry, just you and me."

Henry nodded, and then hesitated, as if debating something, before launching into what sounded to her like a prepared speech. "I have been thinking about your marriage, Jenova. The king may not approve an alliance between you and Baldessare. Mayhap you should wait until he returns from Normandy and see what—"

Jenova held up her hand. "No, Henry. Not today. We will speak of my marriage, but not this day. I intend to forget the Baldessares, all of them, and enjoy myself. Please," she added.

Henry paused. It was true, he had been mulling over

her marriage during the night, and the more he mulled, the less happy he became at the idea of *his* Jenova aligning herself with that family. And perhaps more importantly, the less happy he believed King William would be. But she was right, such things could keep until later.

"Of course," he said genially and rose to his feet. "Let us ride together."

"Mama, Mama, can I come?"

The boy running toward them had hair that curled wildly about his head and neck and was the same color as Jenova's. He came to a halt against her skirts, buffeting her, but she laughed and hugged him to her. *What is his name?* thought Henry. What was Jenova's son's name?

"Raf, you grow stronger every day," Jenova pretended to scold, solving the problem for him.

Raf gave her a broad grin and then turned his gaze on Henry. There was a slightly wary look in his eyes now, as if he was well aware that Henry did not willingly seek the company of children. Henry had a suspicion that Jenova herself may have told her son not to bother their guest, and he was grateful.

"Good morning, Raf," he said in a falsely jovial voice.

The boy bowed carefully. "Lord Henry, I pray you are well in mind and body."

Henry's lips twitched despite himself, while Jenova bent and murmured something in the boy's ear. For a moment Raf looked mulish, but then with a resigned sigh he nodded. A plump young woman waited anxiously farther down the hall, clearly waiting to ferry him away. He turned and, slightly dragging his feet, returned the way he had come, but not before he cast another glance at Henry. This time the look in the boy's eyes was pleading, and Henry had an uncharacteristic urge to call him back, to say that of course he could go with them. He stifled it.

Boys like Raf reminded him too much of his own young and innocent self.

He supposed he *had* been that innocent, once. Or nearly so. Life had sometimes been difficult, and he had been much alone, but he had been brave and strong and determined to make the most of his opportunities. How was he to know he would fall in with such evil creatures?

Jenova's warm fingers brushed against his, startling him from his reverie. "Come then," she said gently, almost as if she had read his mind. "Let us go while the weather holds."

The horses had not been exercised for some time, and they were as eager as Henry and Jenova to be out in the brisk morning air. For a while they simply rode, Reynard and the troop of men-at-arms spread out behind them. When they reached the top of Gunlinghorn Hill, they stopped, breathless, and gazed at the view before them. On such a crisp and cold day, it was possible to see for many miles. Henry looked with satisfaction upon the rich Vale of Gunlinghorn, with its wide river and meadows and, overlooking it all, the stark bulk of the protecting castle. This may not be London, but, to Henry's mind, it was the next best thing. If he had to live in the country, if he was ever forced to become a live-in landlord, then he would choose Gunlinghorn.

Then he remembered. Soon Alfric, with his brown, melancholy eyes, might be master here, and Henry would no longer feel welcome. The idea of that sulky boy at Gunlinghorn was suddenly so repugnant to Henry that he determined that if the marriage went ahead, he would never visit again.

With that realization came another. Henry had never understood just how much he would miss Gunlinghorn.

And Jenova.

He glanced at her, wondering if she was thinking the same thing, if she realized this might be one of their last days together. But Jenova was smiling as she gazed over her domain, her thoughts clearly very distant from his own. Jenova caught his eye, and there was a wildness in hers that he remembered from when they were children. "Let's ride to the sea," she cried and, with a laugh, kicked her horse into a gallop. She flew down the hillside, and into the woods, the hood of her fur-lined cloak falling back from her hair. She didn't look back, she just expected him to follow her. And so he would; so he always did. With a laugh of his own, Henry set off in hot pursuit.

They spent the next few hours simply enjoying themselves, in a manner they had not done for years. They reached the sea at Gunlinghorn Harbor, the village that straddled the mouth of the river where it spewed into the sea. Jenova received revenue from the trading boats that came and went from her harbor, and because it was a relatively safe, though small, anchorage along an often dangerous coastline, she was never short of vessels putting in. Dwellings and hostelries had grown up around the timber wharf, catering to the seamen, merchants and traders, with their packhorses, who came to carry the goods to market elsewhere.

"My lord." Reynard nodded toward one particular building, where a sign painted with the image of a black dog was propped against the wall. "My father's sister lives here. Her name is Matilda. Have I your permission to visit her? If you wish"—he glanced at Jenova—"she will serve us with food and ale. I have heard this inn is well known for its good service."

Henry raised a brow. "I did not know you had blood relations here, Reynard."

"My father was a builder of boats, my lord, and lived here for a time under the reign of the English king Edward, called the Confessor. My father's sister married and stayed after he returned to Normandy."

"Thank you, Reynard," Jenova said. "I would be glad to partake of your aunt's hospitality. I know Matilda, and you are right, this inn has a fine reputation."

Reynard's aunt Matilda was a small, plump woman with wiry dark hair, and when she hugged Reynard, her head only came to his armpits. She fed them well, and Jenova sat by the fire, warming herself, and enjoying the informality. 'Twas not often she allowed herself a day away from the endless tasks that befell her at Gunlinghorn. She glanced across at Henry and found him watching her in an oddly intent manner, his eyes half closed. Almost at once he smiled, sharing the moment.

"It is long since we sat together like this," he said. "As I recall, your mother would never let you sit idle for long. You had to learn to be a great lady."

"And you a brave knight," she retorted.

"She did not like me," Henry said matter-of-factly. "She was afraid you would grow too fond of me."

"All the girls were in love with you, Henry. 'Twas the fault of your handsome face."

She was teasing him, and he laughed, but there was something at the back of his eyes. Something she did not recognize.

"But you did not, did you?" he said at last. "Fall in love with me, I mean. You made me run errands for you, and fetch and carry. And I was only too willing to do so."

"You could have told me nay, Henry."

He smiled at her again, and his smile made her feel hot. "I'd never tell you nay, sweeting, you know that. I am yours, body and soul, to do with as you please."

The picture he made for her was not at all calming. Suddenly she was too close to the fire, or she had eaten far too many of Matilda's pastries. She felt uncomfortable and a little feverish. She wanted to wriggle on her bench and fan herself with her hand.

Jenova found herself looking at him, really looking at him. His violet-blue eyes, his wide mouth, his masculine throat, his broad chest and narrow hips and his strong legs, stretched out before him. His hands, long-fingered and scarred, resting elegantly upon his lap. And she found herself wondering what it would feel like to have those hands on her bare skin.

Luckily, before the rogue thought could progress any further, their cozy interlude was interrupted.

"My lady?" One of the men-at-arms was standing before her, a note of urgency in his voice. "A boat has run aground on a sandbar inside the river mouth. They are asking for help to pull her off."

"What boat is this?" Henry asked with interest.

"From Bruges, my lord. They say they are carrying wine and oil and some bolts of cloth. We can attach ropes from the shore and pull her free. The tide is on the turn, so that will make things easier. Have we your permission to help?"

Henry opened his mouth and then stopped and looked at Jenova. She could see the quick remembrance in his eyes. This was her harbor, her village, her river. The decision was hers. His consideration pleased her—not many men would have remembered that it was not their place to give orders, and if they had, not many men would have cared.

"Of course you must help," she said briskly. "Use all the men-at-arms and as many of the villagers as you can find."

The soldier left, and Henry rose to his feet, stretching,

and held out his hand to Jenova. "Come, we had best take a look at this boat from Bruges."

Outside the air was cold, and the wind tossed their cloaks and made Jenova catch her breath. A craft lay stranded upon a narrow sandbar, tipped to one side and being washed about by the incoming tide. The boat was rather squat, with a combination of deck and tarpaulin to keep her cargo safe and dry. Several crew members were busy tossing ropes to the men upon the shore, while Reynard pointed and shouted and generally took charge.

"I doubt we are needed here," Henry said, glancing at Jenova's huddled form. "Are you cold?"

Jenova nodded her head. "I am, but 'tis not that. I have much to do. I think 'tis time for me to return to the castle, Henry. I can ride alone; I have done it before. 'Tis perfectly safe. Mortred long ago rid our lands of any brigands."

"I will come with you. Reynard can manage here."

The swell of pleasure she felt at his offer seemed excessive, and Jenova forced her voice into more moderate tones. What was happening to her? She had been alone with Henry before, many times. This agitation was new.

Jenova glanced at the sky. There were dark clouds edging it to the north, but they seemed far away. She considered the danger and dismissed it in her eagerness to ride with Henry.

"Very well. We can ride east, along the cliffs. You will like that, Henry. It is a wild and dangerous place."

"Then we will enjoy them together," Henry said with a smile that made his eyes bluer than ever. "We will be wild and dangerous together, Jenova."

And why, Jenova thought, as Henry helped her onto her mount, did that sound like a threat?

Or a promise.

Chapter 3

The cliffs were dizzyingly high, and below them the gray sea prowled and snarled. Henry and Jenova set their horses at a gallop over the tufts of grass, startling the birds and a few egg-gathering villagers. The wild setting reminded Henry of Jenova's family home, in Normandy, where the same sea also crashed against cliffs. Perhaps, thought Henry, that was why she loved Gunlinghorn, and perhaps that was why she was so content with her life here.

Although not completely content, he reminded himself as he paused to catch his breath. Not if she wished to remarry. Mortred's image shimmered in his mind, half forgotten, dark-haired and light-eyed, his face scarred from smallpox. In character, Mortred had been a little like Henry, confident and clever and brash. But his passage through life had been far easier; he had grown up under King William's shadow and protection and had not had to battle against Henry's odds.

Jenova's mother had wanted her daughter to marry Mortred when she was still very young, but Jenova would not have him. Mortred had married elsewhere, but the woman had died without any children to show for their union. So Mortred had cast his eye about again, and this time Jenova had decided to be more amenable. She had fallen in love with him, and so she married him. Henry had had no doubts at the time that Mortred loved her, too. He had even believed that Mortred would be faithful to her—or mayhap he'd just hoped so.

But of course he hadn't been.

During their marriage there had been other women, lots of them, but at least Mortred had kept the knowledge of them from his wife. How could she, safe at Gunlinghorn, have known what her husband had gotten up to elsewhere? There had been times when Mortred's careless behavior had angered Henry, and he had struggled hard to hide the facts from Jenova. It had been she he'd thought of every time he'd lied or tidied away Mortred's mess. Not Mortred.

And would you have behaved any differently? the voice in his head mocked him. *If you had been wed to Jenova, would you have been true to her and only her?*

Possibly not. *Probably* not, he corrected himself. But then he would never have allowed himself to be placed into a position where he could hurt her, would he?

A gull soared above him, screeching, and then diving, sending his thoughts tumbling along with it. The sea air blew cold against his face, stinging his eyes, tugging at his clothing, and yet he felt very much alive. And carefree. Here at Gunlinghorn there was nothing to do, no one to see, no rumors to track down or unravel, no plots to untangle, no assassins to fear. It had been a long time since Henry had felt so unfettered by worldly cares.

He was not sure he trusted it.

Jenova was also deep in her own thoughts, though hers were more prosaic. In her head, she was counting up the carefully packed barrels of salted meat in her storerooms, and wondering if they would last through until the spring. She did not doubt they would, not really, for she was a careful housekeeper. But winter was a season for taking stock of what they had, and what would be needed for Gunlinghorn in the year ahead. Jenova had a great many souls dependent upon her good management, and she did not mean to fail them.

Mortred had never understood that, or perhaps he just had not cared as much as she. He was like Henry, preferring the life and liveliness of court and the king's company and, she had discovered, the easy women to be found there. Domestic bliss was not for Mortred, it seemed, and yet she had been too besotted and trusting to see it. Never again. She would never place herself in such a position again.

The wheeling gull caused her to look up, too. And as she did, a snowflake fluttered down and melted upon her cheek. They had ridden far today, almost to the farthest edge of her lands, and suddenly she realized that the weather was closing in. The threateningly dark clouds she had seen earlier were almost upon them. Already a thick mist hung low over the hills to the north, lapping at the forest that lay between them and the safety of the Vale of Gunlinghorn. Soon the storm would be surging in to cover them all. She had been so lost in dreams that she had failed to notice the approaching danger.

"We must go home," she said sharply and glanced over her shoulder at Henry. "There is snow coming, and lots of it."

Henry too was frowning at the heavy clouds. Snow

was beginning to fall more quickly now. "Hurry then," he replied and met her eyes. "Lead the way, Jenova, and I will follow."

She gave a brief nod and, without another word, headed into the forest.

The air grew swiftly colder, and as hard as they rode, they could not outrun the snow. Thick, blinding snow. Jenova felt her body growing chilled, her feet turning to ice, and feared that soon they would be unable to continue. That was when she saw the old tree, the gnarled and twisted oak, rising tall above its younger brethren. And she realized she was much closer to Uther's Tower than she had been aware.

Uther's Tower was a place used mainly in the warmer months by the woodsmen who cared for the Gunlinghorn forests. However, there were times when her people used it for shelter in the winter, so it was kept in good order all year round. They would be safe there, and surely it made sense to wait out this storm in relative comfort.

She felt a tingle of doubt. As if she was about to make a decision that would have far-reaching consequences. . . .

"Jenova?" Henry was behind her, his face grim and white with cold, his eyes narrowed against the weather. "We cannot stop here," he shouted. "We must find shelter!"

Henry was depending upon her, Jenova reminded herself. He trusted her to get them to safety. He was following her, just as he had promised to do. She owed it to him not to fail.

"There *is* shelter. There!" she called back, and pointed through the stark trees. Henry nodded to show he had heard, and urged his tired horse after her, ducking his head beneath the bare branches, once again letting her lead the way.

Uther's Tower rose stark before them. A squat tower gave the building its name, and attached was a solid cottage structure, made of a mixture of timber and stone. It looked as if it had simply sprung up from the ground. There was already a thick coating of new snow upon the jagged roofline, and more piled up in front of the low door.

Henry dismounted, quickly using both his hands to clear enough of the snow out of the doorway so that they could open the door and enter. He looked back at her. "Come on!" he said, with a frown. "You'll freeze to death."

He was right, she knew it. And yet she had a sense of risking all, of burning her bridges, of stepping into the unknown. . . .

Jenova followed him inside.

It was hushed out of the storm. For a moment Jenova blinked, seeing only darkness, and then slowly her sight grew accustomed to the gloomy interior of the building. There was but a single room, with an earthen floor and some clean straw tossed into a heap against one wall. Wood had been piled neatly, and while Henry stabled their horses in the lean-to at the back of the tower, Jenova began to make a fire.

Her hands were frozen now, as well as her feet, and when the wood finally caught with a lick of flame, she sank down beside it with a grateful whimper. By the time Henry returned, his cloak heavy with snow, the wood was well ablaze and giving off some heat.

"I did not pay enough heed to the weather," she confessed, giving him an apologetic look as he fastened the door. "I saw the storm approaching, but I was enjoying myself too much, and I thought we had time—"

He untied the laces of his cloak and swung it off, laying it over the woodpile to dry. "So was I. Enjoying myself, I mean." Henry came and stood by the fire, looking across the flames at her. He seemed to be searching her face, reading her thoughts, and then he gave a wicked smile. "We were the same when we were children, remember? Riding out together and forgetting ourselves. Your mother was always scolding. We are equally at fault, Jenova, but we are safe here now. And in such luxurious lodgings. What is this place?"

"Uther's Tower. We don't really know who Uther was, but legend says he was a long-ago king of this part of England. I think he was a Briton, holding his lands against the Romans. He built this tower as a warning to them not to come any farther. One of the stories tells of his love for the wife of a captain of a Roman Legion. This may even have been where the lovers met."

Henry raised his brows. " 'Tis not very romantic."

"Aye, it is," she retorted, refusing to be annoyed with his skepticism.

"I could think of better places to meet," he went on, glancing about. "There isn't even a comfortable bed."

Jenova shook her head at him in disgust. "They were *in love,* Henry. 'Tis a state of mind."

"Like lunacy?"

She tried to smile, but suddenly she was just too cold. Even though the fire was now crackling pleasantly, she couldn't seem to get warm. There wasn't enough heat to counteract the intense cold that had already entered her body and was still seeping into the building from the snowstorm raging outside.

With a frown, Henry moved to kneel by her side. "Are your feet cold?"

"I cannot feel them at all." Despite her furs, Jenova shook and shivered.

"Here, then." He reached to take her boots in his hand, swiftly removing them and arranging them by the fire to dry. Her stockinged feet were very cold, and his hands were so warm. . . . They felt wonderful. He set about rubbing each of them to warmth, toes, heel and instep. Next he set to work on her hands, pink with cold beneath her gloves.

His face was creased with concentration as he performed his task, and his touch was impersonal and thorough, yet gentle. He was doing what needed to be done, but Jenova did not feel like an object, far from it. She felt cherished; there was something very agreeable in his touch, something very comforting, almost sensuous. . . . Jenova was aware of her whole body relaxing, growing languid with the pleasure of Henry ministering to her.

"Thank you, Henry," she said softly. "You are very good to me."

Henry looked up at her, the firelight dancing in his blue eyes. "Why wouldn't I be?" he mocked. "We are old friends, are we not?"

He looked very appealing. And very handsome. Why, thought Jenova in surprise, he is like a stranger! If she had not remembered this was the man she had known forever, her childhood companion, she would have been as foolishly attracted to him as any other woman. Jesu, she *was* attracted to him. . . .

A warm trickle of an unfamiliar sensation ran through her cold body, a stirring she had not felt for a long time. Jenova shivered.

"Are you still cold?" Henry demanded, a crease of worry between his brows. He reached again to clasp her hands, his fingers strong and sure. There was a crooked white scar on the back of one of them, and suddenly she thought; *I do not know how he came by that scar.* And at the same time she realized that there were many things she did not know about Henry. In her arrogance she had believed she knew everything there was to know about him. The truth was, she didn't. She couldn't. And mayhap it was not safe to do so.

"Jenova?" He was watching her, waiting for the answer to his question, and puzzled by her silence.

She turned her thoughts away from this new, dangerous direction, and managed a pale smile. "I am still cold . . . that is, a little."

His frown deepened. Was his annoyance with her or the weather? Before she could ask the question, he lifted her cloak so that it enfolded them both, his arm sliding under the furred lining. He drew her in, close, to his side, and pressed her head gently down onto his shoulder. Surprise kept her from protesting, and then, when he tightened his hold about her, pleasure stopped her from moving away. Aye, she was enjoying it, enjoying being completely enclosed. By Henry.

"You will soon be warm," he murmured, and his breath stirred her hair, brushed against her skin. Her heart quickened within her breast, and her blood seemed to melt, turning her insides into a river of heat.

Jenova heard her inner voice sound a warning. *Run for your life!* it said. She ignored it, just as she had ignored the danger of the storm clouds. Henry was her friend, her oldest friend, but as she listened to his voice rumble deep in his chest, and the easy beat of his heart, her usual equilibrium tottered into a quivering mess. The truth was, she liked his body, so hard and warm against hers, and the strong band of his arm about her waist.

Jenova shivered again, but it was no longer from the cold. Nay, she was getting warm, far, far too warm, and all from touching Henry. Indeed she was ready for marriage; until now she had not realized how her woman's body had missed the contact of a man. . . .

"Jenova?" Henry sounded concerned. She lifted her head from his shoulder and looked up. He was watching her, staring down into her face. Their gazes tangled, played games. Jenova slid the tip of her tongue along her upper lip, meaning to moisten its dryness, but instead the movement made him catch his breath. In an instant he was alert, his body tense. She knew he could see something of her feelings in her face. She was sure her need was writ plain in her eyes.

Oh, Jesu, what was happening to her?

Her heart began to beat hard in her chest, and the inner voice said, This is wrong. This is wrong, stop it now. And yet she could not seem to pull away from him, she could not seem to stop it. Not even to save her life could she pull away from the grip of whatever had her as its prisoner. Deep inside she knew she did not even want to.

And then Henry made a sound very like a groan of pain, and dipped his head and kissed her.

Henry's mouth was hot, while his lips were cold. The combination was astonishingly delicious. Jenova, at first too surprised to move, found her own mouth responding, found herself kissing him back. He was so familiar, and yet so different. He was Henry and yet he was not the Henry she knew, had thought she knew. Someone she had imagined to be very familiar seemed to have altered beyond all recognition.

But he was still Henry.

Jenova pulled back with a shaken laugh, putting her fingers to her lips. He was staring down at her, breathing fast, and behind the confusion she saw in his eyes, mirroring her own, was desire. Hot, burning desire.

It shook her to the core of her being. It jolted her back

to the here and now, and out of whatever fantasy she had just strayed into.

"I don't know what is happening, Henry," she said in a trembling voice, and it was no more than the truth.

"I kissed you," Henry said and turned away, moving to throw more wood upon their fire.

Jenova felt chill with the lack of him. Her body still trembled, but was that cold or something more? She no longer trusted herself to know the difference. Her senses had betrayed her.

"I cannot believe you have never been kissed before, sweeting," Henry added, and his familiar mockery stung.

Jenova forced a husky laugh. "Is that all it was? A kiss between old friends? It felt like more." That sounded like a question, and she immediately wished it back.

But Henry was busy with the fire, and there was nothing in his manner that confirmed what she believed she had seen in his eyes. *Desire? For me? No!* She had been mistaken. Henry did not desire her, why would he? They were friends, nothing more, and he had plenty of women to sate his needs. The simple truth was that she had probably looked so cold and miserable that Henry, being the kind man he was, had kissed her to warm her up!

Henry arranged another cut of wood on the fire, concentrating on it as if his life depended upon it. Behind him, he could feel her puzzlement and her uncertainty, and he cursed himself. *Why* had he kissed her? The fact that she had looked so kissable, so delectable, should not have had any effect on him. He had never desired Jenova. She was the one woman he had always felt safe with, the one woman with whom he had never felt a need to prove himself.

Why in God's name had that suddenly changed?

But it hadn't, Henry insisted to himself. Nothing had changed. It had been a momentary aberration, and now it had passed. He glanced at her over his shoulder, noting her wet, straggling hair and cold, pinched face. *See, not a flicker of desire,* he told himself proudly.

And then he looked at her again.

She really was soggy. Her gown was soaked and clinging to her, her arms were wrapped about her body with her fingers tucked under her arms, as if seeking warmth. Her feet in their damp stockings were as close to the fire as she could bear them.

"You need to take off your wet clothes," he said matter-of-factly. "My cloak is almost dry now. You can use that to cover yourself until your own dries."

Something deep in his mind was jumping about, waving its arms and shouting, but he didn't heed it. A warning? What warning? He needed no warning. This was Jenova, remember? Jenova needed his help, and he had never failed her before.

Jenova cocked her head to one side, as if she heard the warning too. "I don't know, Henry. . . ."

"You will freeze to death, Jenova. You do want to get home to Gunlinghorn, and eventually wed your Alfric, do you not?"

Perhaps it was mention of her bridegroom that did it, or perhaps it was the matter-of-factness in Henry's tone. Jenova felt herself relax as her fears receded. Henry was right. Of course he was. Jenova knew it. It was just that, after that kiss, she felt a little uneasy with him. Another sensation she had never experienced in Henry's presence before.

Don't be silly. This is Henry. I need to get warm or I really will get ill. It is foolish to be prudish with a man I have known most of my life.

With a shrug, she reached under her cloak and began to unfasten the damp laces at the neck of her gown with stiff, uncooperative fingers. Henry watched her sideways, pretending he wasn't. When he could bear her fumblings no longer, he sighed loudly and, crawling across to her, pushed her fingers aside and quickly unknotted the laces. He undid the cloak, too, and pulled it from her shoulders.

"There. Now take your things off, and I will fetch my cloak for you." But again he hesitated, eyeing her damp feet, then he began briskly to remove her stockings from where they were tied above her knees. He pretended the legs he was uncovering were not slim and very attractive; he sensed that if he stopped for a moment to consider what he was doing he might well be in trouble.

"Now," he said, as she thanked him gravely, "take off the rest."

He went to fetch his cloak, bringing it to her before laying out her own cloak and stockings on the woodpile. Then he returned to the fire and sat with his back to her. Very soon a bare arm stretched out and dropped the remainder of her garments beside him. He noted them. Her gown and a warm woollen chemise and another, silken one, to be worn close to her skin. Henry proceeded to deal with them as matter-of-factly as the rest. If his fingers noted that the last chemise was soft and clinging, and retained the scent of her skin, he told himself not to dwell upon it. And if his head felt a little dizzy, as if he were becoming intoxicated, he told himself it was the smoke.

When at last he had finished his task, and found the courage to turn again to Jenova, she was sitting on her side of the fire, small within the folds of his much larger cloak, her hair spread over her back and shoulders to dry. *Her* side of the fire? When had it become necessary to separate them like this? When had he needed to put distance between them? This was Jenova, his friend, his sweeting . . . and her hands were shaking as she held them to the flames.

And yet he hesitated. He played for time.

"We are still like children," he said, and smiled. "Too busy playing our games to notice the weather closing in."

"We always were a b-bad influence on each other." Jenova's teeth were chattering now, though she strove to keep them still. "R-remember how my mother was always trying to s-separate us?"

"She never could. We always found a way to sneak past her watchful eyes." His smile turned grim at the memories—perhaps his recollections were different from Jenova's. It was true, her mother had never liked him, she'd had a way of pursing her mouth when she'd looked at him, as if he'd reeked of some odor only she could smell. But Jenova had been indifferent to her mother's threats and warnings, preferring to make up her own mind. In those days she'd believed Henry could do no wrong, and in repayment for her loyalty he had led her into much mischief. He would not have blamed her if she had abandoned him to his own company, but she never had. Jenova had remained his loyal friend.

"You were always very kind to me, Jenova. Probably far kinder than I deserved."

She looked at him in the firelight, and her green eyes glowed with golden lights. "Oh Henry," she said softly, "you were such a sweet little boy. I could no more have given you up than . . . than my best pony."

He chuckled at the comparison, but his heart swelled. She had loved him, and he her, there was no denying it, but time had moved on and they had grown. He had done things he would not wish her to know about, lived a life far beyond her world, while she had in turn become a wife and a mother to Mortred's son, and the Lady of Gunlinghorn. They were as far apart as the moon and the sun, but still that long-ago bond remained, tying them together.

She was his lodestone, he realized, his center. He needed her to remind him of his origins, of who he really was. He needed to see the warmth and admiration in her eyes to continue to believe in himself.

With lithe grace, Henry stood and moved back to her side of the fire. It was fate, he told himself, what happened next. It was not up to him, or her. Perhaps it was this place, this Uther's Tower. He slipped his arm about her, and drew her in against his body and his warmth. She was shaking, and he murmured in sympathy, and put his other arm about her, so that he could hold her tight against his chest. When she still shook, he lifted her onto his lap, and held her there, curled within his arms. Her damp hair tickled his nose and he burrowed into it, enjoying her fragrance.

"Am I still sweet?" he asked her at last, more for something to ease the awkward moment than because he needed to know.

Jenova managed a giggle, and he felt her icy fingertips creep up and flutter against his cheek. "Of course, dear Henry. You will always be s-sweet. To m-me."

He looked down at her with a raised brow.

She smiled, her face pale and naked within the heavy mass of her hair. Young. Vulnerable. Defenseless. And yet her body was so soft curled against his; he could feel her breasts through the cloak, where they pressed against the arm he had wrapped about her. The nipples were hard little nubs from the cold. He wanted to warm them with his mouth.

He closed his eyes, but that was no good either. He could feel the soft roundedness of her bottom resting upon his groin. In a moment she would feel him growing hard. But he couldn't help it. He should move away from her, but he didn't want to. She felt so good, and he didn't want to.

"Henry?"

She sounded uncertain. He opened his eyes and found her gazing up at him, and now Henry understood what the warning deep inside him had been about. And realized also that he should have heeded it. But it was too late.

Jenova knew it too. Her green eyes clouded as they gazed into his, and she opened her mouth to speak. To tell him nay? Henry did not know. He was already bending down to claim her lips.

If she had been about to refuse him, she had changed her mind, because before he reached her mouth she had lifted her own. When they joined their lips together, it was mutual.

And this time there would be no stopping.

Chapter 4

Henry's mouth was firm, yet tender, persuasive as his lips urged hers to respond, to open. Jenova needed no urging. She felt dizzy, not herself at all, and again the warning pealed in her head. Surely this was sheer lust. The need of her body, so long without a man, to find a mate. In her heart she knew it, and yet the knowing didn't seem to make a scrap of difference.

She wanted him, and want was enough.

Somehow her hands had crept up to his shoulders and around his neck. Her fingers were tangling in his hair, tugging him closer. She felt his hand slip inside the cloak and close with tender possessiveness upon her breast. A groan leaped from her throat, and she felt him smile against her lips.

"Henry . . ." she whimpered, but he would not let her say more. He bent his head and took her nipple in his mouth. Jenova let her head fall back at the sensation of his warm tongue against her sensitive flesh. The pleasure

57

shot through her like an arrow, and she stared with dazed eyes at the rough timber beams of the roof. The urge to push him away, to stop this now, still remained, but with each touch, each kiss, it was growing fainter.

At least she was no longer cold.

Her fingers trailed across his tunic, and then impatiently tugged at the ties at his throat. Henry shifted back and pulled the garment over his head, and with it his shirt, carelessly tossing both to one side. Now when Jenova touched him she found only warm, smooth, muscled flesh. He was tawny, like his hair, his skin warming to the reflection of the firelight. She discovered a scar here and there, and a line of hair running down to his belly. She followed it. Over the hard flesh of his stomach, down further still, disappearing inside the tight breeches.

Her fingers followed.

He groaned and leaned back, propped up upon his arms, bare chested, with his head thrown back, as if to give her complete access to his body. As if he were hers to do with as she willed. Jenova feasted upon him with her eyes. He was not a giant of a man, but he was well muscled and strong, and there was no fat upon that lean, hard body. So handsome, so well-made, so perfect. No wonder the women of the court pursued him.

Her eyes dipped lower.

There, beneath the firm dark cloth of his breeches, between the long, hard muscles of his legs, was the steep rise of his manhood. Henry was most definitely aroused. Delicately, fingers trembling now, she reached out to brush her hand over him. And then to smooth them against the rigid, thick length that was hidden there. He caught his breath; his arms shook. And yet he did not pounce upon her, he did not rip open his breeches and take her as she half thought he might. He let her move the moment along at her own pace.

Jenova was grateful for that. It had been a long time, after all, since she had had a man to herself. Carefully, she began to unlace the top of his breeches, loosening them enough so that she could begin to tug them down over his narrow hips and well-muscled thighs. His manhood sprang free, and she sat back, trying not to stare.

It *had* been a long time, but surely her memory was not that fuzzy? Surely she would remember if a man's part was that big? Why—she reached out—her fingers could not even reach around it! Mayhap if she squeezed. . . .

His breath caught sharply and he sat up, catching her hand in his where she still grasped him. His eyes blazed, as if he were afire. "Slowly, sweeting," he said in a deep, husky voice. His manhood quivered in her hand, and she wanted to stroke it better. Tentatively she stretched out a finger, smoothing the velvet flesh, and he let her, his eyes glazed. "Jenova," he groaned, "I do not want to spend until I am inside you. Deep inside."

Now it was her turn to catch her breath. Henry slid his arm about her waist and slowly, using his strength to support her, he eased her back onto the ground. The hard ground, when he had declared that lovers needed soft beds. But although the floor beneath her was firm, his big, thick cloak cushioned it, made it almost cozy. Above her, Henry's body moved into place upon hers, keeping her from the cold. Now she was completely cocooned in *his* warmth.

And *her* desire.

Her hands ran over him, all bare flesh and curved muscle. It had been a long time since she had felt a man's passion, and known it was for her and her alone. Her fingers sought again that hard evidence of his desire for her, and she smiled when Henry moaned softly, pressing his lips to her skin in tiny, urgent kisses.

"I should stop," she whispered, but her fingers kept exploring, gently squeezing. She couldn't seem to make them stop; she didn't want to.

"Don't stop, Jenova," he murmured. "Not now, not now . . ." He bent to her breasts, caressing the full, creamy flesh with his tongue, lathing her nipples until it was almost pain, and most certainly pleasure. She arched up against him, making soft noises of encouragement, and felt his erection against her inner thigh. His hand followed, cupping her hot flesh, his thumb sliding up and down the swollen cleft. She was wet with need, wanting him, aching for him. It had been so long, so long. . . .

Henry kissed the base of her throat, making a trail up the arch of her neck and finding her mouth. Gentleness departed now, and he kissed her with passion, his tongue tangling with hers. Between their bodies his knee parted her thighs, widening them. The head of his erection brushed against her soft curls and she felt her legs tremble. Wanting him. Needing him. Her skin was on fire, and everywhere he touched a new blaze sprang forth. Her body throbbed with the need to find fulfilment, and she had long ago ceased to care for the consequences of what they were doing.

This was dangerous, far too dangerous.

He pushed inside her, just a little, as if to test her. If he expected her to resist, then he was mistaken. Jenova pushed back, wrapping her thighs about his hips, clasping him in her arms. He sank in deeper.

Now it was Jenova who pleaded with him not to stop, moving restlessly beneath him. But Henry had no intention of stopping. He doubted that he could, even had he wanted to. The feel of her, the sensation of being inside her, the scent of her, was pounding relentlessly at his senses. Had he ever felt like this before? He could not remember it, and if he had, then it was a long time ago. Aye, he felt more than a man. This was more than just a releasing of the tension in his body, the pleasing of himself with a willing woman, far, far more. . . .

He felt like a god.

Henry eased more of himself inside her, experiencing the slight resistance of a woman who has not had a man for some time. The knowledge gave him immense satisfaction. He did not want that mooncalf, Alfric, to have her. Henry wanted to be *the one*. The one to take her, to make her weep with pleasure, to make her beg for more, to make her forget all other men.

Jenova was moving her head restlessly from side to side, her soft hair loose and tangled about them. The fragrant scent she used filled the air as her body warmed. He buried his face in those tresses, and pushed that last little bit, deep into her body. And stopped, his own body shaking with the need to go slow, his chest rising and falling with each heavy breath.

"I'm not hurting you?" he asked, in a voice husky with tension.

She laughed, almost a sob, and closed her arms even more tightly about him. "No, Henry, you are not hurting."

"Not even if I do this?"

She groaned at his movement, trembling with the pleasurable sensations he was causing. He moved again, and she cried out, lifting her hips to allow him greater access. And he drove deep, once and again, suddenly as mindless as her in his need to find release.

As the wave of pleasure swept over them both, Henry was aware of an edge of frustration. He had planned to do so much more! He had hardly had a chance to explore her creamy flesh, to tease her into a state of heightened passion, to run his fingers and tongue over every swell and curve of her. . . . Where had his mastery gone, his self-control? It had deserted him. And now, even as he rode that long, wondrous wave of repletion, he wanted her again.

It was not ended, and he wanted her again.

How could that be?

Finally they lay still, clasped in each other's arms. With his palm still on her breast, he could feel her heart beat, feel it slowing, her body languid with pleasure. For a moment all was quiet and well, all was perfection. In the midst of the storm they were at peace.

And then with a jolt, her heart began to pound and her body stiffened, and Henry knew that memory had returned. And with it, realization.

Jenova felt crippled with returning knowledge. *What have I done? How could I have been so foolish?* Both confusion and wretchedness beat at her like hard fists. Henry was her *friend*. What they had done had complicated that fact terribly, mayhap even destroyed their friendship forever. How would she ever look him straight in the eye again? How would she ever again turn to him with ease and trust? How could he ever look at her again without remembering how she had turned into a wanton in his arms?

Jenova felt tears sting her eyes.

She should have said no. Made a joke of it. Put an end to the situation before it had begun. She could have done that. She was well able to manage all manner of awkward situations. But Jenova knew why she had failed in this one. Because she hadn't wanted to end it. She had been just as caught up as Henry in what had been happening between them. Maybe more so. She hadn't been able to think of anything but the pleasure he'd been giving her. Nothing else had mattered.

She had never felt like this before, not even with Mortred, whom she had believed she'd loved and whom she had lain abed with many times. But never like this; it had never been like this. As if her body were awash with feeling, alive with need, as if she might do something wild and completely against her nature. As if a caged creature she had not known existed inside her had been set free.

She frowned. Of course, then there was the fact that Henry was a practiced seducer—he had had more women than there were trees in Gunlinghorn Woods. Aye, she *had* been his willing partner, but he would have known exactly how to play her body, how to dull her doubts, how to make her forget all her fears. If she was another type of woman, she would blame him totally for what had happened between them, accuse him of forcing her to desire him against her will.

But Jenova was a just woman, and she knew her accusations would be unfair. Besides, she was certain Henry did not want these complications any more than she. He might be a fine lover, but in this instance he had been as much a victim of their unexpected passion as Jenova.

It had happened, but it was over. Time to move on.

With determination, Jenova pushed Henry aside and stood up, holding the cloak about her like a shield as she moved to fetch her clothing from where it lay drying by the fire. The cloth was warm, and although not completely dry it was far better than before. She picked up her chemise and clutched it, and her courage, in both hands, before she turned back to face him.

Henry was sitting very still, naked, watching her. He

seemed very much at ease with himself, at ease with his body and its perfection. Although, she remembered now, it wasn't so perfect after all. There were scars upon that golden flesh, ridges of white where weapons had cut and slashed, where other men had tried to harm him. He wasn't perfect, he was just a man.

His face was unreadable. He was waiting for her lead, she realized. Patiently waiting to agree to whatever decision she made. Jenova swallowed, pleased and yet dismayed by the power he was handing over to her. Whatever road she took now must be the right one, for both their sakes.

"This must never happen again, Henry," she said quietly. Her voice was flat and serious, and she realized it sounded just like it did at the manor court, when she passed judgment on her wayward people. She reached up to push her long hair over one shoulder, and found that her hands were shaking. "We have been friends for so many years. To believe we could be more than that is ludicrous. Ridiculous. This was an aberration, and I am certain we will both be very relieved to put it from our minds."

Henry watched the emotions flitting across Jenova's face. She had never been able to hide her feelings—she had never had to. He could see she regretted what they had done, and that it confused and frightened her. Obviously she did not want him to trespass upon her further than friendship. She did not think him capable of more.

Henry knew, in that deepest secret part of him, that he was not worthy of more.

Nay, he wasn't worthy of Jenova; he didn't want the complications that would now plague them. But he could not help but wonder whether she would have felt more at ease with what had happened if it had been Alfric with her here, alone in Uther's Tower. Henry could offer her advice on fortifications and help her sort out her problems with Baldessare, but he was denied the joy of being her lover. And yet she had let him into her body; she had near swooned with the pleasure of it. *Would Alfric have been able to give her ecstasy like that?* Henry asked himself a little arrogantly.

At once he stopped himself.

He was being unfair.

Jenova was thinking to wed Alfric, not Henry. Jenova was the one woman Henry had always felt at ease with because she was the one woman he did not physically desire. He did not feel he had to live up to his reputation as a master of seduction with her.

And now? How could he ensure that their friendship survived this moment of madness and did not simply deteriorate into a brief affair? Jenova's friendship meant more to Henry than any physical pleasure, and it did not matter that he had found a pleasure with Jenova that he had never felt in his life before. He did not intend to lose it.

"You are right, Jenova, this must never happen again." He repeated her words back to her firmly, evenly, and he meant every one of them. And wondered why those same words suddenly felt like a betrayal of them both.

Henry reached for his breeches, hurriedly dressing, ignoring Jenova doing the same. Now he wondered, guiltily, if it had actually been his intention, when they'd ridden out alone from the harbor, that matters go this far. He had said it was fate, but now he remembered the mixture of jealousy and frustration he had experienced when Jenova had told him she was thinking of wedding a poor excuse for a man like Alfric, when he knew she could do so much better. Was he really such a devious fellow that he would take her just to show her what she was missing?

Henry knew he was devious, and he had done things best not spoken of aloud, but Jenova was special. He would never purposely hurt her. *Never!* But despite his sincerity, his protests sounded like weak posturing, because he *had* hurt her. He had hurt them both, and their friendship might never recover from it.

"Henry?" Her voice was tentative, and when he looked up from putting on his boots, he saw that her green eyes were full of tears.

Something in his chest gripped him—an urgent need to reach out and take her in his arms and comfort her.

He did not dare.

Impatiently, she brushed at her cheek, wiping away the moisture, and then blinked hard. "Do you think we could go back, Henry? Or have we rent our precious friendship asunder? Oh Henry, I do not want to lose you. . . ."

His chest ached, but he held tight to his self-control. Slowly, deliberately, he reached out a hand to touch her damp cheek. Her skin was warm and soft, and he wanted more. He could not have it, he would not allow himself to have it, and there was a bittersweet triumph in his self-denial. It was not often Lord Henry of Montevoy denied himself a woman.

"How can it be spoiled?" he asked her with gentle mockery. "We have been friends since childhood, Jenova. We will be friends until we are in our graves. We will forget this moment, I promise you. We will put it behind us. We will never speak of it again."

Jenova's smile was sheer relief, brightening her forlorn face like sunlight through the storm. Her voice in reply was breathy. "Aye, we will never speak of it again,

Henry. You are right, it will be forgotten, and everything will go on as it did before."

Their eyes met and held. His so blue and hers deep green, tangling, touching hidden places, remembering, and already beginning to imagine the possibility of a next time. It was like a caress. Her happy smile faded, and his grew cynical. The words were a lie, and now they both knew it. There was no feasible way in which they could go back in time.

Everything had changed forever.

Abruptly they both glanced away, denying the truth, and continued dressing in silence, while outside the hut the storm began to ease.

Chapter 5

The great hall at Gunlinghorn was pleasantly frenetic. A log as big as a man burned in the massive fireplace, making the air warm and smoky. Fortunately, the table on the dais where Jenova and Henry were seated was close to the heat, for even such a fire as this failed to reach all the corners of the great hall. Outside, above the noise of the feast, the wind howled. The foul weather had closed in again soon after they'd reached Gunlinghorn Castle, and now snow was falling in silent swathes across the land. Despite the many candles' brave and bright light, the gloom of winter encompassed them.

Henry could not have returned to London even if he had wanted to. Strangely, for one so much a part of the court, he did not. His gaze rested on the people crowding the hall about him. At one of the tables, Reynard hunched over his food, the rest of his men close by. As he allowed their chatter and noise to wash over him, Henry found himself idly wondering what was happening beyond Gunlinghorn. As Jenova bent to smile at something one of her ladies said, her veil drifting about her shoulders and disclosing a lock of glossy brown hair, as a servant moved to pour more red wine into Henry's silver goblet, he let his thoughts drift northwards. To the concerns that had kept him busy before he'd received Jenova's missive.

While King William was occupied with his troubles across the Channel, his barons were bereft of his strong, checking influence. Archbishop Lanfranc, who sat upon the throne as Regent, did his best, but some of the younger barons lacked either good sense or caution, or both. Henry was beginning to believe that Roger, Earl of Hereford, and Ralph, Earl of Norfolk, were talking treason. Talking was not the same as doing, and they were clever enough to keep their intentions well hid. Henry wished the king would return to knock some sense into them before it was too late. William's mere presence would be enough to still such restless talk.

"Keep an eye on my kingdom," the king had said to him before he'd left. "I trust you, Henry, to do what is necessary *if* it becomes necessary."

King William knew that behind Henry's handsome smile was a ruthlessness that could be relied upon in times of crisis. Henry would crush anyone who rose against his king; he had done it before. There were some things he would not do, but not many.

Henry had long ago put aside his conscience.

But that didn't explain why he felt so miserable and confused when it came to Jenova and their moments together this afternoon. It didn't explain why he couldn't just take what she'd offered and enjoy her and shrug aside regret. He had to admit to himself she was his one weakness, his Achilles' heel. His conscience. Aye, mayhap, if he had any part of a conscience left at all, then its name was Jenova. . . .

"My Lord Henry?"

Henry turned his head and found Jenova's son beside him. Earlier he had noticed the boy seated by his mother at the other end of the table, being petted by Jenova's ladies. But now here he was. At Henry's side.

Henry stared at the boy uneasily—he had rarely spent more than a moment or two in his company. He was a small boy, with a narrow, piquant face and great green eyes. Perhaps he was sickly? Children often were—only the strongest lived to adulthood. Perhaps that was why Lord Baldessare had put Alfric forward. Did he see an opportunity for himself through Jenova's misfortune?

"My Lord Henry?" This time the boy tugged at Henry's brown velvet sleeve, with its crimson embroidered cuff. Henry, who was renowned at court for his style, smoothed the slight crease and forced a smile.

"Yes, uh . . ." What was the child's name? He had forgotten it again. But the boy didn't seem to notice or care—he prattled on regardless.

"You must come and see me ride tomorrow, Lord Henry. Mama says I am too small to ride, but I am strong. I am five, you know."

Henry did not think he looked strong. In fact, the boy looked as if a mild puff of air would blow him away. His wrists, poking from his sleeves, were like twigs, and his breeches hung on his skinny legs.

"Will you come and watch me ride?" Raf's voice had risen—that was his name, Raf.

Henry was not about to argue with a child. "Of course," he said politely, having no intention to do so.

He didn't understand why Raf would want him to come and watch him ride anyway. What was he to Jenova's son? Perhaps the boy had confused him with someone else—Alfric, mayhap? Although Henry could not recall Alfric paying any special attention to Raf when he was last here.

"I will come and fetch you when it is time."

Henry blinked. "Time for what?"

"To watch me ride!" Raf grinned, as if it were a game between them.

"I'm certain that is not necessary—"

"*I* will fetch you," Raf repeated firmly, and his devilish grin turned into a smile. A sweet smile. His whole face seemed to come alight and alive, to actually glow with happiness. Again Henry blinked, taken aback by the brilliance of it. Surely that was Mortred's smile? More innocent, of course, but still Mortred's smile. Mortred, before he took to spending his days and nights in the stews.

And then, before he could say another word, Raf was gone, scampering on his skinny legs back to his mother's side. Henry watched the boy tugging at Jenova's sleeve much as he had done with Henry's, and Jenova dutifully bending her head to listen to what her son had to say.

When had her profile become so perfect?

He had meant to watch her reaction to her son's words, in case she was cross with Henry for promising something he had no intention of fulfilling. But now he became distracted by the curve of her mouth, the soft swell of her pouting bottom lip and the gentle arch of the upper one. He wanted to press his mouth to hers, to follow its shape with the tip of his tongue—last time he'd kissed her, she had tasted of wild, sweet berries. He wanted to taste those berries again.

Heat burned in his blood. She was at the other end of

the table, but now it was as if he could smell her scent. His groin tightened, hardened, and he clenched his jaw. This was madness! Why torment himself like this when there was no chance of his having her again? He took another sip of wine, trying to wash the sensations away. His moody glance about the hall showed him there were plenty of other pretty women and some real beauties. What was it about Jenova that made him blind to all the others? He had sworn never to think of her in that way again, never to touch her, to sink himself deep inside her and watch her lips part as she gasped with pleasure. . . .

Henry gulped at his wine again, draining it. As he lowered the goblet, he realized that Jenova was looking at him. Her hand was resting on her son's shoulder, and whatever it was Raf had said to her, she did not like or else she had read his mind. Those beautiful green eyes were anything but friendly. They burned into him. He raised his empty goblet to her and wondered how long it would take him to turn her cross mood into panting desire—if he had not promised not to touch her.

Jesu, he should never have come to Gunlinghorn!

If he had not come, then he would not have lost control and taken Jenova, complicated everything, turned everything that had been familiar between them into foreign territory. And now he had to pretend it had never happened.

Henry had thought he could do it; he had been determined to do it. He was a man to whom kings came to have their problems solved! Nothing, no puzzle, was beyond him. Except now he realized something new and very worrying; something that had never happened to him with a woman before.

He could not put the thought of Jenova out of his mind. He did not want to. She sat there in her russet gown with the forest green sleeves, the color a perfect match for her eyes, and he knew in his heart that to put her out of his mind was as impossible as stopping breathing. He wanted her again. He wanted her as many times as he could have her, and there was an utter recklessness in the thought that was completely foreign to cautious Henry's nature.

Jesu, how he wanted her!

If possible, his body went harder. He couldn't have stood up, despite the covering of his tunic, or everyone would have noticed his predicament. Henry looked about him at the great hall and the merriment of the castlefolk, and instead saw Uther's Tower. The deep shadows and the snow outside and the flicker of firelight on Jenova's creamy skin. Her little sighs and soft moans, and the way she'd drawn his body against hers and opened herself to him. The tremors inside her as she had pleaded with him not to stop. . . .

Henry took a ragged breath. *Enough*. Surely he had more self-control than this, and he had promised. He had *promised*. . . .

Jenova was laughing. He found himself watching her avidly as she pointed to the juggler, saying something to Raf with a gentle smile. In addition to the juggler, there were acrobats and singers and a tiny man who pretended to fall over. He fell over a great deal. Jenova found it all very amusing, and her melodious laughter rang through the hall this night, bringing smiles to the faces of all those around her.

Henry didn't watch the entertainers. He watched her. His gaze brushed the flush in her cheeks, the smooth, high line of her brow, the stubborn tilt of her chin. The manner in which the russet cloth clung to her breasts, outlining their round, firm shape until he swore he could feel their softness filling his palms.

Henry only just managed to stop himself from groaning aloud.

This was ridiculous! He was behaving like a boy in his first passion, a lovesick knave with all his thoughts centered between his legs. How was it he could want her so badly? He had had her once, and usually, for him, once was enough. Once proved he had conquered her; he had won her, she was his. It proved he was no longer that snivelling boy, abandoned by his lady mother, good enough only to be passed from relative to relative and used by them when it suited. It proved he was an attractive and powerful man who needed no one.

Then why was this occasion so different? Why did it *feel* so different?

He had never wanted the intimacy of one woman. As a child, Henry had rarely had that intimacy, and he had certainly never experienced the close confines of such a life with his own family. His father had died fighting with other Crusaders, and his mother had shortly afterward deserted him for God. When she had left him for her monastery, Henry had sworn never to give one woman such power over him again.

And now that he had made his life just the way he wanted it, he had no intention of handing over, to another proud and selfish lady, the ability to hurt him.

No, that wasn't right, he thought. Jenova was not proud and selfish. She was his friend. Once he had felt relaxed in her company because he had had no need to prove himself with her. Had that changed now? Had Jenova joined the ranks of all those other women he had seduced over the years? But no, Jenova was still different. She was still his friend, despite the fact that she had become his lover. His friend *and* his lover.

The idea terrified him.

And yet even that did not stop Henry's wanting her. With a torturous, aching want that seeped into the deepest parts of his body and soul. Aye, he wanted her, and until he had had her again, Henry doubted he would get any peace at all.

Jenova clapped her hands, caught up in the antics of the entertainers. She turned and smiled at Henry, looking to share her innocent enjoyment, forgetting for a moment their newfound wariness of each other. Whatever she saw in his face caused her eyes to widen, and slowly the laughter drained from her face. Her hand crept to her throat, as if she were suddenly struggling for air, and her long lashes fluttered over her green eyes. She turned away, but not before Henry saw the tremor in her fingers and the way her teeth tugged at her full bottom lip.

Then Henry knew that, just like him, she was remembering making love in Uther's Tower. And, like him, she was torn between the urge to run and the longing to do it again.

Jenova was wishing it had never happened. Or at least, she was wishing she *could* wish it had never happened. She had sworn to herself that she would put the matter from her mind, set it aside like a spent barrel of wine. She had believed she was managing so well, playing her part so well.

Until now.

When the little tumbler fell down, she had glanced to Henry to share the joke, and instead she'd found him watching her with an expression she could not mistake. Desire had been in the tense line of his jaw, in the burning blue of his eyes. Desire and lust. She knew it—read the signs. Because she felt it, too. And now her body was heating up.

She knew why she could not pretend.

Because she didn't *want* to forget what they had done in Uther's Tower. She wanted to think on it, linger on it, close her eyes and squirm with pleasure at the thought of those hot, blissful moments they had spent together. She wanted to dwell on each and every glorious detail.

I have been too long without a man, Jenova's practical voice informed her. *That is all. It has naught to do with Henry; he was simply in the right place at the right time. Any man would have done. I could have been trapped with . . . with Alfric and the same thing would have happened!*

It was clear she needed to set matters in motion for her wedding as soon as possible, then she could escape this fix. Mayhap Alfric could take pity on her and wed her immediately. Surely if she let him know it was urgent, he would set aside his father's absurd demands and do away with the formalities.

Jenova had to bow her head, hiding her smile as she considered herself upon her mare, riding madly through the snow to Alfric's door, demanding he wed her without delay, crying, "For who knows what man I shall bed with next if you do not!"

Her smile faded, and her eyes grew bleak. It was all nonsense. She did not want Alfric, or just any man, to bed her. It was not Alfric who had made her body sing. It was Henry, and there was not another man in the whole of England who could take his place. Something had happened between them; it was as if a spark had been lit that could not now be extinguished. And Jenova, widow and mother and lady to the manor of Gunlinghorn, did not have a clue what to do about it.

"Mama, look!" Her son was pointing and laughing at the jugglers, and gratefully Jenova allowed him to distract her. Raf was a good boy, a fine boy, and she had great hopes for him. As a babe he had been sickly, but he had fought, and she had fought with him, and he had survived. Now she recognized that his thin, wiry frame belied his strength. Raf might look as if he were fragile, but in reality he was tough, he was a survivor. He was her son, and he would make the best of whatever fate threw at him.

Earlier, she had seen Raf seek out Henry. Henry, as she well knew, did not care for children; Henry could be a vain and selfish man in many ways. That did not detract from his abilities as a soldier and a loyal subject of the king and a basically good man—oh, yes, he could be charming. Jenova had felt the tug of his attraction more than once in the past, but she had laughed and marveled and shrugged it off. Henry the lover was not for her. She had much preferred Henry the friend. And she had come to depend upon his unencumbered affection, knowing that if she ever needed him, he would come to her.

Well, so he had, but how could she have known that *this time* it would all be so different?

Jenova lifted her head and allowed her gaze to settle once more upon the object of her confusion. Her heart gave a great thud, a terrible mixture of fear and joy. He was watching her, too. Not slyly, not with the hope that she wouldn't notice. No, not Henry. He had turned fully in her direction, his hair a dark halo in the candlelight, and his blue gaze was fixed deliberately upon her. Assessing, lingering, seducing—eating her up with his eyes. Jesu, had he decided not to honor their vow after all? Because it looked very much to Jenova as if he wanted more of her and was letting her know it.

Jenova gasped, and color warmed her cheeks. Like a simpering maid, she thought in disgust, but still she could not stop the blush. Aye, he was devouring her with his eyes, and she, who knew him so well, could not mistake the set of his shoulders, the tilt of his head. There was fire in the blue, a blaze of passion and remembrance and longing.

Jenova turned away jerkily, lifting a hand to shield her face. One of her ladies, Agetha, asked her what was wrong, but Jenova smiled and said she was tired. She did not dare turn to Henry again. She did not trust herself. She, who had always been so sure and practical, who had always done what was right, could not trust herself to behave in a manner appropriate to the Lady of Gunlinghorn.

"Appropriate" never stopped Mortred, did it?

The thought made her stiffen. Mortred had lied to her, treated their marriage—and their love—with contempt. Mayhap it was time for Jenova to do the same? She had meant to marry Alfric, but wasn't that just more of the same "appropriate" behavior? *Jenova,* Mortred had said to her once, *you are always so predictable.* Now Jenova wondered if there wasn't another, more reckless, manner in which to take her revenge and at the same time indulge herself in this new and unexpected passion.

Like a lightning flash in the darkness, she knew that making that vow of abstinence with Henry had been a mistake. In denying them both, she had only made it more difficult to forget. Mayhap, she thought feverishly, if she were to wallow in her madness, saturate herself in this newfound passion, then she could revenge herself upon her dead husband and wear out her folly at the same time? The end result would be the same, but the getting there would be so, so much more enjoyable. . . .

"My lady?" It was Agetha again, her slightly protruding blue eyes watchful, disapproving. "You seem distracted."

" 'Tis nothing, Agetha. I was puzzling over a problem, but now I have made a decision on it. I have chosen my path."

Agetha fingered the jewel at her throat and looked as if she would like to ask more, but Jenova turned to call one of the servants to refill the wine jugs. She did not want to talk about what that decision was to anyone; it was no one's business but her own.

And Henry's.

Henry lay awake in the darkness. He could not sleep. And although the reason he could not sleep lay in a chamber below, he could not seek her out. He was a guest in Jenova's castle; he could not destroy her trust in him by coming to her bed like a rutting boar. He should not have looked at her like that at the table. She might have been ignoring him, but that was no excuse to give her such a blatantly sensual stare.

He had wanted to shatter her pretended calm. Force her to remember what he could not forget.

For a moment there, he had almost believed he'd seen reciprocation deep in her moss green eyes—a flicker of need as hot as his own. And then it had been gone and he'd been left doubting his own senses. Well, that was a first! Henry the great seducer, the conqueror of women, the master lover! Henry, who always boasted he could have any woman he wanted! Except that the woman he wanted this time was the one woman he could not have. Whom he had sworn not to touch again, ever.

Henry groaned and turned over in his bed, restless and uncomfortable. Just thinking about Jenova aroused him, and knowing he couldn't have her was only increasing his longing. He could send Reynard for a whore, but he did not want a bought woman; for the first time in his memory he would rather suffer unfulfilled passion than be comfortable.

The sound of the door opening was slight, but in a moment Henry had bent and snatched up his sword, within easy reach beside the bed, and thrown back the covers. He rose up, entirely naked, feet apart, ready for any intruder.

Candlelight wavered through the narrow opening the door made, and with it came an ethereal figure. Long, brown tresses hung to her hips, the silken strands catching the light in a myriad of colors. A sheer shawl, wrapped loosely about her form, was more an enticement than a covering. Henry could see the shadow of her body through it, and, as she stepped softly into his room and half turned to close the door, he realized he could see more than just a shadow. His eyes feasted on the delicious curve of her waist, the warm pink of her nipples, and the rich brown curls at the apex of her thighs.

"Jenova?" His whisper sounded harsh. "Why have you come?"

"Why do you think, Henry?"

"I hope to God you do not expect me to be strong and send you back to your room, because I can't do it. I do not have that much strength."

She drifted closer, the candle flame spluttering, and he became aware of her womanly scent. Instantly his body went rigid, his head spun, his mouth went dry. "Jenova . . ." he groaned. "Please."

"I do not want you to be strong," she said matter-of-factly, as if she had no idea what she was doing to him, how dangerously close he was to grabbing her and throwing her upon the bed. "You have started a fire in me. I thought I could deny it, but . . ." She took a trembling breath. "I see now it will not be easily put out, and I see now that to deny these feelings would be foolish as well as cruel. We should allow them free rein, indulge ourselves. Only then will we be rid of the fire, only then can we go back to being as we were."

What she said made sense, but Henry suspected some other matter lurked behind her green eyes, something she wasn't telling him. He tried to think clearly, but he was dizzy with the knowledge that Jenova was giving him leave to sate himself upon her body. Quickly, before she changed her mind, he held out his arms to her. She smiled and blew out the candle, and then she was moving into his embrace, soft and warm and perfect. Jenova was his, and this time Henry did not mean to make any foolish vows denying himself the pleasure of her.

Chapter 6

No turning back now, Jenova thought. Even had she wanted to, she doubted Henry would let her. His erection butted against her belly, urgent, eager, and she reached down to stroke him. With a soft moan, Jenova raised her mouth to his, and he plundered it, kissing her with wild passion. Sucking on her lips and her tongue, his hands tangling in her long hair.

It wasn't enough, she thought feverishly. She wanted more, and more, and more. . . .

How can Henry, my familiar Henry, stir such wild wantonness in me?

Even after her decision in the great hall, Jenova had lain in her bed, fighting the need to go to him. *Wait until the morning,* the voice in her head had ordered her, that proper Lady of Gunlinghorn voice. *Tell him of your decision in the morning . . . if you must!*

But somewhere between the tossing and turning, between pacing her floor and wrestling with her feelings, she had come to the conclusion that there was no need to wait. What had happened between them in Uther's Tower had changed her, and she no longer had the willpower to resist. She wanted him now, she needed him now, and for once in her life she would live for the moment.

Henry's hands slid down her back, cupping her curves through the thin shawl, holding her hips against his, lifting her a little so that his manhood could slide between her thighs and rest against her. She moved against him, pleasure spiraling through her at the friction this caused.

With a groan, he eased back, trying to slow their passion. He brought his hands up to cup her breasts, gently molding the soft flesh into his palms. Jenova arched into his touch, gasping when his thumbs brushed across her sensitive nipples, her hands twining in his hair and drawing him closer. Henry paused, resting his scratchy cheek against her breasts, his breath a warm, reverent murmur against her skin.

"You are so beautiful. Why did I never realize you are so beautiful?"

His words surprised her. "You are very handsome," she said at last, "but I always noticed that."

He laughed a little harshly and rubbed his cheek against her, abrading her soft breast as if to punish her. "But you were never overwhelmed by it," he replied with a hint of mockery. "Were you, sweeting?"

"If you mean did I ever feel like swooning at your feet, then nay, Henry, I did not. I am not the swooning type."

"Not even when I do this?" he teased, and in the darkness his blue eyes fixed on hers as he eased slightly away from her body. And then she felt his fingers, his clever fingers, caressing her, sliding down over the swell of her belly to the downy curls, slipping through them to find the warm opening between her thighs.

"Not even then," Jenova managed, but her voice had grown husky and less certain.

He smiled, his fingers moving, stroking. "You are very hot, lady," he whispered softly. "You are right, there is a fire in you that has been lit. I fear . . . I fear it will take a strong and lusty man to put it out."

"And that is you?" Jenova retorted, but already her head was spinning, her legs trembling so badly that she did not know how much longer they would hold her. He bent to nuzzle against her neck, nipping her flesh with his teeth, not hard enough to hurt but enough to send tingles of excitement skipping across her skin. She rested her hands about his hips, her fingers moving against the firm, hard flesh that covered him, finding the curve of his buttocks. A soldier's body. He may dress as a smiling courtier, he may pretend to be a gentleman, but in essence Henry was a warrior.

"Ah, here 'tis, the heart of the fire," he was saying in that rough-tender voice. He cupped her, his forefinger slipping inside while his thumb brushed against the aching nub. She moved against his hand, her breath sighing between her lips, turning to a gasp when he bent his head to take her nipple in his mouth.

"Henry," she managed, reaching to clasp his head, her fingers tangling in his hair, holding him closer. His mouth was a torment, but it was a torment Jenova knew she could not do without, and she pulled him closer still.

"Come, lady, and lie down upon my bed. There is much, much more." He was easing her back onto the bed, using his strength, kneeling over her. Her shawl fell open, and her skin glowed like pearl.

Should I be letting him do this? Jenova asked herself feverishly. *Should I be allowing him to enslave me like this?* But he was already rearing over her, his hands sliding up her thighs and curling over them, to open them to his perusal.

And then he leaned forward and took her in his mouth, and Jenova lost all awareness of herself as her senses mastered her entirely. All she yearned for now was to find release from this aching pleasure. His tongue flicked against her, and she arched up like a bow, gasping and crying out, beyond caring who heard her. And then, before she could begin to gather and put back together the scattered pieces that were Jenova, he entered her with one deep thrust, his mouth and hands scattering her once more.

Jenova found herself climbing that pleasure staircase again, moving with him, driving all doubts before them. There was nothing but the awareness of his skin, his body, his mouth. There was something magic in him, something pagan, that spoke to a part of her she had not known was there. She was simply a woman named Jenova.

And Henry took her to a place she had never known existed.

When at last she lay quiet in his arms, she tried to make sense of it. "I think," she said, "that because I have never found pleasure like this before, now I cannot stop. Oh, I have had my joys and my sorrows, 'tis true, but not pleasure like this, Henry. Not even with Mortred. You have secrets that no other man knows. You can cast spells. That is why I cannot resist you."

Henry laughed softly, his body hot as a furnace against hers. "If that is what you want to believe, sweet Jenova, then so 'tis. I am a sorcerer."

He began to kiss her again, rolling her over so that he

was atop her. The length of his manhood slid between her thighs, and although she was a little sore from him now, she didn't care. She wanted him again, just as he wanted her.

"Nay, I have no secrets, Jenova," he whispered his confession against her lips. "I can cast no spells. The magic you feel comes from you and me, together."

"Then it will wear itself out?" Was that disappointment in her voice? She was not a child, she should not fear the truth. And Jenova knew in her heart that he was far more experienced in these matters than she.

"Of course it will wear itself out, Jenova. 'Tis a short-lived thing, the fire of new passion. Soon, it will cool and we will tire of each other."

Grief assailed her, but she swallowed it down. "Then we must enjoy every moment?"

"Aye, Jenova, for as long as it lasts."

His mouth covered hers, gently at first, and then with a rising desire. As if he wanted to devour her. Jenova was more than willing to be devoured. His palms cupped her bottom and drew her up, teasing her, entering her only slightly. It was Jenova who thrust upwards, impaling herself fully upon him, making them both groan, and starting the dance all over again.

Morning broke. He had slept without one of his nightmares, and that was always a good thing. The pale light crept through the slits in the shutters, making bars on Henry's bed and on Henry himself. He squeezed his eyes tighter shut, thinking it was this that had awoken him. Until he felt the touch of a small, warm hand burrowing into his and tugging. Who would dare to wake him, after a night of such wild passion? He was wrung out; he wanted to sleep. But the tugging wouldn't stop, and at last, blearily, he opened one eye, glaring at the owner of the offending hand.

A small boy stood by the bed, his green eyes bright with excitement and his mouth set in a familiar line of stubborn determination—he had seen Jenova's mouth look just so.

"Lord Henry," he said in an overloud whisper. "You told me to wake you so that you could see me on my pony."

Had he done such a ridiculous thing? Surely not? Henry closed his eyes. There was a vague memory, but that had been before Jenova had come to his room like a siren, and left him exhausted, washed up like a shipwrecked sailor upon his bed. The remembrance brought a smile to his lips, and the boy mistakenly took encouragement from it, tugging harder.

"Lord Henry," he insisted, "come on! You promised!"

With a deep sigh, Henry opened one eye and then the other. He was certain he hadn't promised, but mayhap he had given that impression. At any rate it was clear he was not going to get any peace until he did what this small, persistent creature wanted. Reluctantly, he rose from his bed and reached for his clothing.

It was early, very early. There were few of the castle-folk about as Henry and Raf descended into the great hall. Outside in the bailey, the air was brisk, stinging color into the boy's pale cheeks, and making Henry's eyes water. He asked himself again why he was allowing this boy to urge him along on a mission he had no desire to undertake, when he'd much rather be back in his warm bed. Thinking of Jenova.

A farrier leading a horse nodded respectfully at Henry, then glanced down at Raf, his old, lined face folding into a doting look. A couple of serving maids, their arms full of laundry, giggled and ducked curtseys at Henry but cooed at Raf. Henry smiled despite his bad humor—clearly Raf was a favorite at Gunlinghorn, a good sign for a future lord of the manor. With a long-suffering sigh, he let himself be tugged along into the musty stables.

They passed the stalls of numerous horses, and Raf named them all, informing Henry of who was most likely to ride each beast and how often. His knowledge seemed a little extreme for so young a boy, but Henry let it pass. He, too, had haunted the stables as a child, although he could not ever remember waking guests at dawn.

"*This* is my pony!" Raf said proudly, as he finally drew Henry to a stop at a stall at the further end of the building.

Henry blinked. Raf's pony was a grandsire at the very least. The creature looked placid enough, but he was nothing like the ponies usually ridden by the children of the wealthy and powerful. If Mortred had been alive, Henry was certain he would have found something rather more spirited for his son and heir. Jenova was possibly afraid her sickly son might be hurt on anything less docile.

Raf was watching him, green eyes old far beyond his years. Henry tried to compose his face, but it was already too late.

"You don't like him," Raf said dully, and his lip wobbled. The big green eyes filled.

Henry felt a wave of sheer terror wash over him. *Don't cry,* he thought. *In God's name, do not cry!*

"No, no, 'tis not so! This is truly a fine animal, a . . . a loyal animal. Nice and . . . and . . . *quiet*, I'll wager."

The boy gave him a suspicious glance. "He *is* very quiet," he agreed. "Is that a good thing?"

"It can be. And is he slow?" Henry ventured.

"Mama says there is nothing wrong with being slow, and that even a lord has to grow up a little before he can ride a fast horse." The boy said it dutifully, but the gaze that now strayed toward Henry's stallion was wistful.

A memory came to Henry. Himself as a child, gazing longingly at the destrier that belonged to the current lordly relative he was living with. He would have given much to be allowed to ride that beast. He came every day to lurk about the stables, dreaming, obsessing. No one noticed, no one seemed to care. His obsession grew, until one day he found himself alone with the destrier. It was a fateful moment, and Henry was unable to resist temptation.

In a moment of sheer, youthful foolhardiness, he climbed up onto the stall and leaped, trying to straddle the huge beast with his skinny legs. The destrier, bad-tempered and far too strong for him, crashed through the stall door and took Henry, clinging to its mane, on a wild ride around the castleyard before depositing him in a particularly foul midden. Henry was humiliated, a laughing-stock, but the lord of the castle still beat him black and blue for his temerity.

Strange, he had not thought of that for a very long time. It was not one of his better memories, but it was not one of his worst ones, either. It had the effect of reminding him that once he had been a young boy, like Raf, believing he was invincible, wanting to grow up all too quickly. If the lord of the castle had been a kindly man, or the grooms had been more observant, Henry might have been allowed to ride the destrier, safely seated behind an experienced handler. Mayhap Henry would then have been satisfied, or at least content enough not to try it on his own.

He could have been killed, not just humiliated and bruised.

Henry narrowed his eyes, watching Raf as the boy watched the stallion. Was it really worth taking the risk that history might repeat itself with Jenova's son? Mayhap he could do now for Raf what the lord of his childhood had failed to do for him?

"Would you like to ride my horse?" The words came out of Henry before he could stop them. In response, the boy's face lit up like a beacon, and it was already too late to bring them back.

"Oh yes," Raf whispered. "May I? May I really?"

If Henry had been inclined to change his mind, the expression in Raf's eyes stopped him. How could he say no when the child was so excited and so grateful? And surely Jenova would not mind too much? If he remembered aright, Jenova had been as wild as Henry in her youth, and had ridden her father's horses fearlessly, much to the poor man's dismay. But then Jenova had been a beloved daughter, and much had been forgiven her. Matters had been far otherwise for Henry.

"Come on then," he said gruffly and led the way toward the stallion's stall.

The horse moved forward to snuffle Henry's hand with its whiskery jaws, searching for a treat. "What's his name?" Raf asked softly, gazing up in wonder at the big, horsey face.

Henry smiled down at him. "I call him Lamb."

"Lamb?" the boy repeated, frowning. "That does not sound very frightening, Lord Henry. I thought a horse such as this would be named something more . . ." He stopped and glanced quickly at Henry, as if suddenly realizing he was on the verge of being impolite. "Why do you call him Lamb?" he asked quickly instead.

"Because he can be as gentle as one, when he wishes to

be. The rest of the time he is more like a wolf in sheep's clothing."

Raf thought about that. "Do you think he will be gentle now?"

"I'll make certain of it."

Raf nodded, perfectly trusting. The knowledge that he was looked upon in such a light made Henry feel anxious and slightly sick. He did not want to be anyone's guardian angel, and he certainly did not want to keep watch over Jenova's son. He was hardly suited to such a position, and he did not desire the responsibility. And yet that was what he had just done, in the matter of the stallion. He had taken upon himself the mantle of Raf's guardian uncle, if not quite angel. No, definitely not an angel. . . .

Henry smiled. Lord Henry of Montevoy as an angel? Now there was an amusing thought!

After instructing Raf in a no-nonsense voice to stand well back where it was safe, Henry saddled the stallion and led him out of his stall. Lamb had decided to abide by his name this morning and plodded from the stable placidly enough, only half rearing once, when he spied a basket full of kittens to one side of the door. The mother cat hissed and arched her back, but they were already out into the yard, and Lamb pretended not to notice the insult.

Raf followed them with wide-eyed expectancy, careful to stay at a safe distance from Lamb's enormous, feathery hooves. Henry lifted the boy onto the saddle, chuckling as he slipped and had to cling with both hands to save himself. Not that he had been in any danger—Henry would have grabbed him if he had started to fall.

"Now hold tight," he warned, and led the stallion a few gentle steps.

Raf's grin of delight threatened to split his face in two. Had the boy really been so lacking in male companionship that he found a round of the stableyard on Henry's stallion so exciting? In truth, this was tame stuff, and Henry was sure they could do better. He glanced about and noted that the bailey was still nearly empty. The weather and the early hour had made the castle servants reluctant to begin their day. He didn't see the harm in taking the boy out under the gatehouse and then back again.

Henry slipped his foot into the stirrup and swung himself up behind Raf, wrapping one strong arm about the boy to hold him close.

"Are you ready?" he asked calmly.

Raf nodded, his brown hair flopping, and he turned excited green eyes up to Henry.

Henry smiled and, with a gentle tap of his heels, set Lamb at a trot toward the gate.

"He is very big," Raf said, his voice jumping up and down with the movement of the horse.

"Very big."

"He is very fast."

Henry smiled again. "Yes, very fast. Too fast for you, Raf. But when you are older, then you will have a horse just like this."

The green eyes turned speculative. "Do you swear it, Lord Henry?"

Instantly, Henry wondered what in God's name had possessed him to say such a thing. He couldn't swear to give the boy something over which he had no eventual control. This was Jenova's son, and naught to do with Henry. Alfric would have more influence over this boy! And yet Henry wanted to say yes, he wanted to make Raf smile, he wanted to give Raf something he himself had never had. And suddenly that selfish desire meant more to Henry than any trouble he might cause himself later on.

"I swear it."

Raf's smile was stunningly brilliant. Henry had never realized before what joy there was in making a child smile. Mayhap he had been wrong in having no children of his own, in thinking they would only bring him pain. Mayhap there was even something healing in spending time with the very young.

Some time later, Jenova paused in the stable doorway, her heart giving a sudden, hard thud. She had been seeking Henry all over Gunlinghorn Castle, and here he was, sitting on an overturned barrel by the brazier in the stable with her son. Their heads were bent close over something or other, Raf leaning his body trustingly against Henry's side.

Who would have thought it? Henry had never seemed the least bit interested in Raf. Jenova, although she loved her son fiercely, had accepted Henry's indifference, just as she accepted his other shortcomings. She had never sought to change him. Not even now.

Gathering her wits, she began to walk toward them. Outside, the snow had stopped and the sky was clear and blue, but the wind was bitter. Even in her wool cloak and fur-lined hood, she shivered. Was Raf warm enough? What if he were to catch a chill? Jenova quickened her step.

"Raf?"

He looked up and instantly gave her a cheerful grin. Her heart turned over, as it always did when she looked upon her son. He was her life, and she would never do anything to jeopardize his future. That was why, in her marriage contract, she would make certain that Lord

Baldessare could have no power over them, even if Alfric should die young.

"Mama, see!" Her son pointed in excitement at whatever Henry held in his hands. "Raven has had babies."

Jenova raised an eyebrow as she drew closer. Henry was holding several squirming, mewling bodies in his cupped hands, and at his feet, watching intently, was Raven, a large, fluffy black cat.

"So she has," she managed, feeling strangely dizzy. Henry looked up at her and smiled wryly, as if he were mocking himself, while Raf hopped about madly beside him, overcome with excitement. The picture they made, the man and the child and the kittens, was such a strange and unexpected one. It made her heart ache.

Jenova forced away the odd emotion and took a breath. "Are you warm enough, Raf? The air is bitter."

"We have been riding," he piped up and then glanced swiftly at Henry, as if he was afraid he had said something he should not.

"Riding?" Jenova demanded sharply. "On your pony?"

"No." The boy looked at Henry again. "On Lord Henry's stallion. He goes much faster than my pony. His name is Lamb, but he isn't always as gentle as one. That is why I must never ride him on my own. But one day, when I am grown, I will have a horse like Lamb, Mama."

"Will you?" Jenova asked blankly, her head spinning again. What on earth had they been up to? How had so much happened in so short a time? "Agetha wants you to come and eat now, Raf. Go and find her."

"But Mama—"

"Now, Raf. Raven's kittens will still be here when you are done."

His lip drooped, and as he walked away his steps dragged, but he went. Henry lifted his handful of kittens and began to settle them back into their warm basket by the brazier. Their mother received them irritably and began lapping at them with her tongue, washing away his offending scent.

Jenova continued to watch him a moment in silence, trying not to be softened by the fall of his hair over his brow and the rough, unshaven line of his cheek and the curve of his firm mouth. It was all very well to see Henry like this, in a completely different light, but he was still the same man he had always been. He had not suddenly changed overnight because they were now lovers. Jenova knew she must not deceive herself into believing Henry would become the perfect man for her, and the perfect father for Raf. In that direction lay much heartache.

"You should have sent Raf to me if he was bothering you, Henry."

"It was no bother."

Jenova tried to read his thoughts, but he was still dealing with the kittens, a crease between his brows as he carefully laid the last one in with its brothers and sisters. Giving in to temptation, she reached out a hand and pushed back the truant lock of hair. He glanced up with a surprised smile, and then reached out an arm to draw her closer to his side. He was warm, and she could smell the male scent of him. Just like that, desire uncurled inside her, making her shiver.

"You are cold?" Henry demanded. Their gazes met, tangled, were reluctant to let go. She saw the spark in his eyes, too, turning the blue brighter and fiercer than it had been before.

"A little."

Henry rose gracefully to his feet and pulled her fully into his arms. Jenova held her breath. They were alone in the stables, only the horses' soft nickers to keep them company, but there was always the chance someone would see them. Did her reputation, her position, mean nothing to her? The Gunlinghorn servants, particularly Agetha, would be shocked if they knew their lady had taken a lover. And what of Alfric, what would he say? Suddenly it all seemed too difficult.

"What will we do, Henry?" she whispered.

Henry stroked her cheek with one long finger, as gentle with her as he had been with the kittens. "It will run its course, sweeting, you will see."

"Do you know that for a fact?"

"Lust burns itself out eventually."

Jenova wondered if that were so. She had never been afflicted with lust before, never desired someone so desperately as she did Henry. But perhaps he was right, perhaps this would vanish as quickly as it had appeared. Mist before a sea breeze. She really should trust Henry, he must know—he had more experience, after all.

He was stroking her neck now, his fingers warm and insistent. She leaned into him, lifting her face, and he kissed her. Their breaths were white in the chill air. Her senses were afire with the same urgency she had felt yesterday. Madness. Sheer madness.

"Will you come to me later?"

Henry smiled. "Wherever and whenever you wish, my lady."

Jenova kissed him again, wondering if she would have the strength to break away, and then she pulled out of his arms and ran, back toward the keep, hardly noticing the cold wind at all.

Chapter 7

Lord Baldessare and his family were to come to Gunlinghorn, to a feast that Jenova had arranged in their honor. They would be remaining at the castle overnight and returning home the following morning. It was an event that had been planned for some time, and although Henry wished he could lock and bar the gates against Alfric and his relatives, and deny them entry, he knew he could not. Even the weather conspired against him, the day dawning bright and clear instead of with the blizzard he had hoped for.

On a day like this, he and Jenova could have ridden for miles. Just the two of them. They could have returned to Uther's Tower, reliving that first time. Instead it was to be wasted on the Baldessares, and Jenova had already wasted two days now on preparations. She had been bustling about, dealing with food and wine and entertainment, making the lives of her servants a misery. Henry had hardly seen her.

Well, apart from one very interesting tryst in the still-room.

Henry remembered it now with a satisfied smile. He had come upon Jenova in that secluded, sweet-smelling place, surrounded by syrups and preserves, with bunches of drying rosemary, fenugreek and sage hanging from hooks in the ceiling, and upon the shelves, pots of such winter remedies as white horehound mixed with honey for coughs, and goosegrease for chilblains.

The room was cool and dim, the lighted candle wavering on the table where Jenova worked. Her sleeves were rolled up, and she was grinding dried chamomile leaves with a mortar and pestle.

Henry simply watched her for a time, enjoying the movement of the muscles in her arms and shoulders, the jiggle of her breasts, the little murmurs of effort. It was cool and dry in here but she wore no cloak, and she had left off her veil, so that her hair lay in a thick plait to her hips.

"What are you doing, sweeting?"

She jumped, despite the quiet timbre of his voice, and turned to stare at him. "Henry?" She wiped an arm over her brow, as though conscious of her disheveled state. Tendrils of hair clung to her damp skin, and she looked flushed and adorable. "I'm making a medicine for Lord Baldessare. Alfric says his father has painful headaches." Jenova turned away after another uncertain glance.

Henry thought he knew the reason for Baldessare's aching head—the heavy burden of his conscience—but he did not say so. He let her work a moment, simply enjoying the sight of her, and then he moved. Jenova turned her head to look at him again, doubtfully, as he slipped his arms about her waist.

He began by nuzzling her neck, kissing the soft, vul-

nerable flesh there, gently blowing on the fine tendrils of her hair. She gasped, leaning back against him, and soon the pestle and mortar were forgotten as his hands moved over her breasts, finding her rigid little nipples through the wool cloth.

"Someone will come," she whispered huskily, turning her face so that she could lick at his ear.

"Not before you, I hope," he said, and began to ease up her skirt. His fingers slid over the long, shapely line of her thighs, finding their way between, where she was warm and damp and ready.

"Henry," she gasped, arching against his invasion and welcoming it at the same time. He pressed his fingers deep inside her, at the same time brushing against that eager little nub. She shuddered, her head falling back against his shoulder. "Henry," she whispered again.

"Hush, sweeting," he murmured against her hair. "Relax and enjoy what I can give you. Let yourself feel. . . ."

Her body moved to the rhythm of his fingers, anointing them with the wet evidence of her pleasure. Henry, with one ear open to any sounds beyond the stillroom, brought her to completion, holding her as she cried out and shuddered in his arms.

His own body was aching, demanding his own release, but he ignored it and instead kissed her mouth gently, allowing her to catch her breath. Giving her pleasure, watching her pleasure, had been enough. In a strange, unnerving way, Henry was happy with that. It was the first time he had ever been content to give without expecting something in return.

Remembering the moment, Henry knew a tremor of unease. Why had it been enough? Because he had known that, as they'd stood together among the herbs in the fragrant silence, Jenova had been his. Not Alfric's, and not Mortred's. It had been Henry who had made her gasp and plead, Henry whose expertise had drawn from her the cries of a woman complete.

What is wrong with that? Jenova wants this as much as me. Maybe that was so, but in Henry's experience, passion was finite. Jenova had told him she was prepared for that, but Henry wasn't sure he was. But he was certain of one thing. With such thoughts churning in his head, he was in no mood to spar with Lord Baldessare.

Jenova had arranged a sumptuous meal, and the tables groaned with bounty. The great hall had been decorated with mistletoe and other winter plants, giving a welcome touch of greenery, while the fire burned bright. The setting was perfect, but the guests within it were less so. Within a few moments of the feast's beginning, Henry was fervently wishing himself elsewhere.

The older lord clearly wanted to vent his spleen on Henry, but he did not have Henry's finesse. When Henry smiled at Baldessare's barbs as if they were jests, failing to respond in kind, Lord Baldessare's muttered insults turned more reckless.

"The king has grown weak. He lets his favorites rule the country and turns a blind eye to their greed," he blustered rudely.

Henry raised an eyebrow. "He rewards loyalty and endeavor, Baldessare. Do you call that weakness? I would call it common sense."

"There are many loyal men who never receive the rewards they deserve. How can they remain loyal when they see other, lesser men continually taking what should rightfully be theirs?"

Lord Baldessare was short and thickset, with gray hair shaved almost to his skull, and a leathery, bitter face set with hard gray eyes. He looked like a man who was never happy with what he had, and who was always looking beyond to his neighbors.

"Mayhap those so-called loyal men would do well to think hard and long about what they had done to displease their king, rather than let themselves be consumed with envy," Henry said thoughtfully. "If such men took the time to think before they opened their mouths, we would all sleep easier."

Baldessare snorted in disgust. "Aye, you have a pretty face and a pretty tongue, Lord Henry. The king enjoys your witticisms, no doubt, at the expense of plain speech. Mayhap he should poke around in your past a little more, and see what foul things he brings up."

Henry felt himself go cold. He hid it, or hoped he did, facing Baldessare with a slight smile, bluffing before those cold, sharp eyes that were cleverer than he had thought. Or mayhap Baldessare was just fishing in the hope of catching something he could use in his campaign to hurt Henry. Aye, that must be it. Best he did not know just how accurate that last hit had been.

"Father, do you not think Lady Jenova's son has grown? You may not know, Lady Jenova, that my brother Alfric is very fond of children, and they of him."

Lady Rhona's pleasant voice was as out of place at such a tense moment as children's laughter at a hanging. Henry took a long drink from his goblet and watched as Lord Baldessare shot his daughter a withering look. She pretended not to notice, smiling and nodding as Jenova made the appropriate response. Agetha, her eyes flicking back and forth, reassured Lady Rhona that Raf was a very obedient boy and would cause Alfric no problems, earning herself a sharp glance from Jenova.

Raf, close by his mother's side, peeped out at Henry beneath her arm like a prisoner through his cell bars. The boy grinned, rolling his eyes, and as Henry grinned back, he knew just how Raf felt. He, too, would do anything to escape the feast and find solitude. Somewhere to settle his thoughts, to shove the dark phantoms from his past, which Baldessare had inadvertently set loose, back into the depths they usually inhabited.

Jenova was watching him, a puzzled expression in her eyes. "Henry?" she said, making it a question. "Is aught the matter?"

She had obviously seen something in his face, read something. He had told her about the land Baldessare had coveted and the king had given to Henry instead, but now he wondered if their new intimacy had made her more aware of his inner emotions, or whether he had lost the knack of cloaking his true feelings.

"My lady, you must forgive Lord Baldessare and I. We grew too . . . involved in reminiscences of London."

Baldessare made a noise like a snort.

Jenova shot him a glance but did not comment. Instead she frowned at Henry. "London is far away, Lord Henry. Mayhap you would do better to concentrate on the here and now."

Henry bowed his head, lips twitching at her rebuke. She would not be so stern if she knew it only made him want to kiss her lips to smiles again.

But perhaps she did know, for as Jenova turned to Alfric, her cheeks were slightly flushed.

Henry winked at Raf, making the boy giggle and incurring Agetha's displeasure. The young woman did not like him, the only one of Jenova's ladies who did not. Did she know that he and her mistress were lovers? Mayhap she did not approve, or mayhap she preferred Alfric, if the doting looks she was casting upon him were anything to go by. Henry put Agetha out of his mind and turned back to the table at large. That was when he realized that Lady Rhona was watching him.

More than that. She was flirting with him. Making promises with her eyes.

Henry took another sip from his goblet and wondered exactly what it meant, and whether he should do anything about it. If he was at home, at court, he would have made an assignation with her. Possibly. Probably. In an hour or so he would have had her naked, in his bed, that pretty golden hair spread about them. But that was at court, not here, not at Gunlinghorn. Here at Gunlinghorn she was just another complication.

Henry eyed her moodily through his lashes.

Rhona closely resembled her brother, Alfric, and they were both of them far prettier than their father. Perhaps they took after their mother, poor woman—Henry had heard she'd died as a result of Baldessare's brutal temper. But of the two, the son and the daughter, Henry believed the daughter to be the one who had inherited her father's shrewd intelligence. Alfric preferred to get his way through melancholic glances and pouting lips. At any other time Henry would have been amused by Alfric's sulking whenever Jenova smiled at Henry. Tonight he was not in the mood to be amused.

Rhona's dark eyes were still fixed upon him. Slyly, over the rim of her goblet. They tilted up at the corners, more so when she smiled, and she was smiling now. Smiling into her wine. Aye, she had a look with which Henry was all too familiar. The experienced I'm-yours-if-you-want-me look Henry had seen many times before in the faces of court ladies.

Lady Rhona was not wed, it was true, and it was more usually the wives who sought his services, perhaps bored with their husbands or simply looking to see whether Henry was as good a lover as everyone said he was. But mayhap Baldessare was not as protective of his daughter's honor as he should be. She was pretty enough, with her dark eyes and pale skin, and the body under her richly embroidered clothing was firm and rounded. If Henry had met her in London, then who knows? But they were not in London, they were at Gunlinghorn, and the simple fact was, he didn't want her.

Henry didn't want her.

It was a strange admission from a famous seducer. And yet it was true. He felt no need of her, no need to experience the conquest—not that it would be much of a conquest, when she was clearly so willing. Was he getting old? No, he had proved to his and Jenova's satisfaction that he was as virile as ever. Did his dislike of the father interfere with his interest in the daughter? But surely his enmity with Lord Baldessare would make the taking of the daughter all the sweeter?

No, the reason Henry did not want to pursue Lady Rhona, although she was giving him plenty of evidence that she was willing to be pursued, was Jenova. Now that he had had Jenova, other women paled into insignificance. Jenova filled his mind and his senses to overflowing, and there was simply no room for anyone else.

And that acknowledgement was disturbing indeed.

Rhona shot her brother a look of disgust. Instead of doing as she had instructed him—flattering the proud

Lady of Gunlinghorn and making himself indispensable to her—he was sitting silent and sullen. In short, sulking. How could he be so foolish? She wished she could shake some sense into him: If they had been alone, she would have had no qualms about doing so.

Lady Jenova was a mature and experienced woman. She was not a woman who would be interested in indulging Alfric's childishness, at least not for long. Oh, she seemed fond of him, but she was not by any means deeply in love with him. This was not, Rhona told herself, a lady whose heart would ever rule her head. Alfric needed to show some maturity of his own if he was not to lose her.

" 'Tis that worm, Henry of Montevoy," Alfric had grumbled on their journey to Gunlinghorn. "He's the problem, sister. You wait and see."

Well—she let her eyes linger on Lord Henry—she could see what Alfric was nervous about. Henry was far more worldly than her brother, far older in experience, if not in years. And he was very handsome, with a certain air about him that could not help but intrigue and attract every female eye in the hall. Was he really the best lover in England? Rhona had heard it said so, and glancing between Jenova and Henry she could not help but wonder if they were more than friends, despite their exemplary correctness toward each other. Rumor had it that Jenova's husband, Mortred, had been Henry's good friend, and when Mortred had died Henry had continued to care for and protect his widow.

But there was something. . . . Mayhap it was the way their eyes lingered overlong when they happened to meet, coupled with the fact that Lord Henry had not given Rhona more than a cursory glance since she arrived. It had been Rhona's plan to divert his interest, leaving the way free for her brother to ensnare Jenova, but it was now quite clear that Lord Henry had no interest in her.

Rhona knew she was pretty, and most men would be flattered by her blatant invitation. Rhona was not a wanton—she did not entice men to her for the pleasure they could give her. She had never felt that pleasure other women spoke of. She used men to get her own way, she used the looks and intelligence God had given her for her own and her brother's advantage. She knew of nothing else a powerless woman could do in a situation such as theirs. And she had hoped to use Lord Henry of Montevoy tonight. Mayhap, she thought now, with a little frown, she was too countrified for Lord Henry. Mayhap he preferred the sophisticated women of the court. Why, oh why had her father never exerted himself to send her and Alfric to London?

But she knew why. Because Lord Baldessare did not enjoy the court himself, he did not wish to expose his children to it. All he wanted was land, lots of it, and then he could sit upon it like a giant, fat spider and weave his plots. And his children were his counters in the games he played, to be put forward as bait, to draw richer prizes into his web. Aye, he ruled them with hatred and fear, and he'd done so for as long as Rhona could remember.

Her narrowed gaze settled upon her father, and Rhona quickly composed her face back into a polite smile, hoping no one had read her real feelings. The baron was not watching her, for he too was staring at Lord Henry, and although his thin lips smiled, his orbs were as cold as ice spears. Lord Baldessare had hated Lord Henry since the time he'd returned from London without the large estate in the west of England he had hoped for. The king had handed it to Lord Henry, and they had both laughed long and heartily about it. Rhona's father had left in humiliation, determined to have his revenge.

How many nights this past year had she heard the baron ranting to his scribe and chaplain, Jean-Paul? How often had she heard Jean-Paul's soothing tones, promising the baron that all things come to those who wait? The marriage of Alfric to Lady Jenova had been Jean-Paul's idea, with Gunlinghorn as the prize. Rumor had it that Jenova's young son was sickly, and once he was dead, Gunlinghorn would belong to Alfric and his father. For what could a lone woman do against the might of Lord Baldessare?

None of them could have known that Lord Henry would hasten so quickly to Jenova's side. Rhona had not even been aware that Henry and Jenova were friends, and she was certain her father had not either. Another of his plots turned sour. Rhona well understood his anger—land was power in King William's England, and Baldessare still had ambitions to become one of her most powerful men.

Rhona, for her part, feared her father and loathed him for what he was and what he had done to her, but she was fully aware of his strength. Although in private she sometimes railed against him, she would never take that extra rebellious step that would set him against her as her full-blown enemy. He would crush her as easily as he would an insect, she had no doubt of that. Jean-Paul had instructed her often enough that it was God's will that she obey her father in all things, and he was a priest after all, even if one she did not entirely trust. But she did not need Jean-Paul's advice to know it was in her best interests to stay on good terms with her father.

Aye, Rhona knew well enough that if she and Alfric

were to remain comfortable and healthy, if they were to continue to enjoy their favored place as the baron's children, then they must strive to please him and do his bidding. Alfric must stop his sulks and do as she said, and then they might both of them come out of this with their father's approbation rather than his truly frightening displeasure.

Rhona leaned closer to Alfric, her voice a whisper. "Smile, brother! Our father is watching!"

Alfric glanced nervously at the grim-faced man further down the table, and he forced a smile, swallowing his mouthful of roasted pork with difficulty. Rhona patted his arm. That was better. There was no denying her brother had a winsome look when he wanted to use it. All was not lost, she insisted to herself with an optimism she was far from feeling. Lord Henry, she reminded herself, was only here for a visit; his real life was in London. He would be gone soon, and when he was, her brother could resume his wooing of Lady Jenova without interruption.

Rhona caught her brother's arm as they moved toward their sleeping quarters—there were guest chambers partitioned off at the further end of the great hall—and drew him into the shadows by the wall. "What is wrong with you?" she whispered angrily. "I thought we agreed you needed to charm her, win her to you, not play at being a sullen child!"

Her brother pulled away from her grip. "She looks at him too often," he grumbled, for all the world like the sullen child she had just accused him of being. "There is more there than friendship, I feel it, Rhona. Do you see the way she *looks* at him?"

Rhona tossed her head as if it mattered not. "They have known each other for a great many years, Alfric.

You heard them speaking of their childhood together? I thought Lord Henry was Mortred's friend, but 'tis Jenova he cherishes. Don't be so foolish as to accuse them of deeds they have not committed. And even if they have . . ."

She had his attention now, and she made use of it.

"*Even if they have,* it is none of your affair. Lord Henry will be gone soon, and you will still be here. In her loneliness, you are the one she will cleave to. In fact, you may turn it to your advantage. Why not wait awhile by the turn in the stairs to Lord Henry's chamber? If the lady decides to pay him a visit, you will be well placed to remind her of the consequences of her actions. Do not berate her, mind, but treat her compassionately, as if you understand and are willing to forgive her her small weakness."

"So even if she is going to another man's bed, I must pretend not to care?" Alfric said mutinously.

"Of course not! You care, but you forgive her because you love her despite her faults. She will think you a better man for expressing such sentiments. Now is that plain enough, foolish brother of mine?"

He grunted, but nodded with reluctant agreement.

"Good. Then play your part, Alfric, or we must both face the consequences of your failure. You know what will happen if we displease our father."

Her brother glanced around sharply, as if expecting to see their father standing there. They both feared him, but whereas Rhona seemed able to charm their father into leniency and herself out of trouble, Alfric could never win any concessions. The baron considered him a failure—Alfric could never live up to the tough and bloody image their father so admired in a man. Gentle Alfric was a complete disappointment to him, or had been, until now. Lady Jenova and her rich lands had given Alfric a chance to show his quality, and Rhona meant to make sure he did.

For all their sakes.

Her gaze shifted. Suddenly she noticed the large, swarthy-skinned man who had just stepped out from the alcove nearby. He was well within listening distance of their conversation, and judging from his stillness, he'd clearly been taking full advantage of that fact.

"Hush!" Alfric had seen him, too, and was tugging urgently at his sister's sleeve. They had both been spied upon too often by their father's creatures not to be wary of any listening.ears. There was very little privacy in the Baldessare household. Even Jean-Paul, who often professed to be their friend, had repeated confidences when it suited him.

Rhona straightened her back, lifting her chin with a show of bravado. She had never allowed any of her father's men to see her fear, and perhaps that was why they respected her far more than they did her brother. Besides, there was something about the eavesdropper that irritated her, be it his unkempt shaggy hair and big, solid body, or the way he refused to lower his dark eyes in the respectful manner to which she was entitled.

Rhona fixed him with a disdainful look. "Why should I care if he hears us?" she said loudly and curled her lip. "He is just a servant. He is nothing. He is the mud under my boot."

Alfric laughed nervously. "Come, Rhona," he said and pulled her away toward the sleeping chambers.

She went with him but turned her head and found the big man gazing after her. There was something in his face that caught and held her attention. Servant he might be, but that was arrogance in the tilt of his head and a single-minded determination in the set of his thick jaw. Rhona had an uncomfortable feeling that her hasty words, far from discouraging him, had acted as a bait to this shaggy bear.

Nay, she told herself impatiently. *He wouldn't dare!* She was a lady. Servants, no matter how attractive, could look, but that was as much as they could do. If he tried to go further, her father would kill him—if she did not do it first.

Reynard stood, watching them go. He had followed the two Baldessare siblings down the great hall and successfully secreted himself in the alcove, but it had been difficult to hear their whispers, and he had edged too close. From what he had overheard, it seemed the girl was advising her brother on ways to ensnare the affections of Lady Jenova. Also, they were afraid of displeasing their father. He could hardly blame them for the latter; Lord Baldessare looked like a mean old ogre.

The girl was beautiful. Small, but voluptuous, everything in its right place. He would have to pick her up to kiss her, but it would be worth the effort. From his more lowly position, Reynard had been watching her tonight, watching the manner in which she'd glanced about her, taking everything in, and the way she had ogled Henry. At first he had been surprised, and then amused. Henry wasn't interested in her—Reynard thought he knew why that was, too—and some instinct told him the girl wasn't really interested in Henry, either. She had been putting on a show, trying to draw his attention. It had been tried before, and by women far more skilled than Lady Rhona.

What did she hope to achieve? Reynard guessed she wanted to leave the way open for her brother to continue his clumsy wooing of Lady Jenova. If Alfric had any spine in him, he could do that on his own, not use his sister as a whore. She deserved better. . . .

Reynard shook his head in disgust. Disgust at the girl, and at himself. He should not care what she did. She was no concern of his. She had made it clear enough what she thought of *him*. He was *nothing*. He was *mud under her boot*. He remembered again the sight she had made as she'd walked off, the sway of her hips beneath the red gown, the arrogant toss of her head. Aye, she was certainly a fine lady . . . or at least she *thought* she was.

She was also a lady who needed a lesson in manners.

And Reynard knew he was just the man to give it to her.

Chapter 8

〜〜⟨♦♦⟩〜〜

In her own chamber, the solar above the great hall, Jenova could not sleep. Before the feast this evening, she'd been visited by the captain of the ship freed from the sandbar by her men and the villagers of Gunlinghorn Harbor. He had been grateful, anxious to thank her, but he had also been eager to do business. He had, he'd told her, some bolts of cloth he wished to show her. Alas, he could not give them to her for nought, although he wished it were so, but he could do her a very favorable deal, if she were so inclined . . . ?

The cloth was exquisite, particularly one bolt. White velvet, the rarest and most beautiful of materials, and so difficult to attain. Velvet was uncommon enough in England, but the color white was beyond price. Jenova had stroked it, hardly breathing, an unfamiliar sense of avarice taking hold of her. "How much?" she'd asked bluntly, and she'd closed her eyes in dismay when he'd told her. The captain had gone on to insist this was a fair

115

price and that he had intended to ask much more. Jenova sighed. The velvet would make a beautiful gown for her marriage to Alfric—she had thought to wear her red wool, but this was so much more fitting for the Lady of Gunlinghorn.

Henry's blue eyes will blaze if he sees me in this.

The thought had been unexpected and somewhat shocking. Jenova knew she should not be thinking of Henry and her marriage to Alfric in the same breath.

"Very well," she had said, trying not to think how much better such a sum of money could be used elsewhere. "I will have the white velvet, Captain. All of it."

The man had hardly been able to contain his glee.

Jenova glanced at the trunk now, where her precious cloth was contained, and felt slightly sick. Not because of the cost but because she was beginning to have second thoughts.

She felt as if something inside her had shifted, subtly but emphatically. Matters about which she had been so clear and certain had now changed. Tonight when Alfric, with his hopeful brown eyes, had continued to flatter her—a little desperately now, she thought—the words she had once enjoyed had seemed hollow and meaningless. She had wanted him to stop, to leave her alone. If only, she had thought, she could find peace and quiet, mayhap she could order her thoughts again, make some sense of them.

Not long ago she had been looking forward to Alfric becoming a part of her life. But now . . . Those dreams were becoming faded and vague; nothing seemed clear to her anymore. And aye, she admitted it to herself, she was having great difficulty imagining Alfric as having any part in her life at all!

It is Henry's fault.

He had done things to her body and mind. Now all she could think about was Henry, Henry, Henry! And when next she might have him alone with her. Even today, amidst the feast she had planned and hoped to make perfect, she had been impatient for the Baldessares to be gone. Just so that she and Henry could be together. She had dared not look at him too often, in case she gave herself away to the people around her, in case her desire glowed like moonlight in her eyes.

Jenova shivered, but she wasn't cold. She was remembering the moments in the stillroom when he had held her and brought her to her peak, and she had been like a wild thing, pressing her own hand to her mouth so as not to scream. Her body ached for his. How could that be right? How could that be just? How could she go on into the future she had planned when her every waking thought was for *him*?

Henry had said their passion would fade, and she had been sorry for that, but in a way she had been relieved, too. Henry had no part in her future— at least, not in the major role he was playing now. But Jenova had not seen any sign of her own passion fading. If anything it had grown hotter, more desperate—her familiarity with Henry had only made her want him *more*, not *less*.

And that was very disturbing indeed.

With a restless sigh, Jenova rose from her bed. Outside her window, the snow fell in silent beauty, coating the bailey in white and turning the world beyond into a dreamlike landscape. This was her land, her place, and she had always felt as if she knew what was best for it and herself. She *was* Gunlinghorn. Now everything had changed, and she was no longer sure—she was adrift. She did not know what she wanted. The future no longer seemed comfortable, or perhaps it was just that the path she had chosen no longer felt like the correct one. Not because she had seen another, better path—she told herself she accepted there was no future for herself and Henry—but simply because Henry had turned her ideas of happiness upside down.

How could she wed Alfric and live here with him now that she knew what she would be missing? How could she be content with affection now that she knew the hot ache of real passion? It would almost have been better if she had remained in ignorance. She could have been content then, blindly, foolishly content.

And what made it worse was the possibility that this situation might be nothing at all out of the ordinary for Henry. Henry might not be overwhelmed by it at all. For all Jenova knew, she was just another body to him, another woman with whom to pass the time.

Not so for Jenova. She felt as if he had taken her from her comfortable, familiar world and then torn it asunder. She could never put it back together the way it was. *She* could never be the way she was.

Oh Jesu, what am I to do?

Mayhap there was still hope that it could all turn out as Henry said—that this passion, this desire, would burn itself out? If she was no longer afflicted with the heat and the longing, she might learn to be satisfied with someone like Alfric, she might learn to accept a more lukewarm passion.

Please, please let it be so!

And if it was not, if she found herself no longer able to be Alfric's bride under any circumstances? Jenova rested her cheek against the cold wood of the window in despair. Lord Baldessare would not be an easy man to dissuade once he had set his sights on something. And, as she was all too well aware, he had his sights set on Gunlinghorn, even if it was only through the compliance of his son. Alfric's character was not strong, and he would always be ruled by someone. Jenova had planned to be his master, but she had known she would have to make her position very clear to his father. Lord Baldessare would have had to learn very early on that, once Jenova and Alfric were wed, he would no longer have a part to play.

Jenova had had no doubts as to her own ability to handle Alfric, rule him firmly but gently, and at the same time keep his father at bay. But if she now turned around and spurned Alfric altogether ... no, Lord Baldessare would not be happy with that.

If she had not known exactly what sort of man he was before, she knew now. During her specially prepared feast there had been little appreciation for her efforts in the baron's demeanor, and he had not once complimented her, or even shown the most rudimentary good manners. The chief emotion she'd sensed in him was a smoldering bitterness. Even when she had presented him with her headache medicine, he had looked at it as if it were poison. No thank you, no gratitude. Just cold dislike.

And Jenova did not think it would take much for Baldessare's dislike to spill over into rage and violence. He was not the sort of man who should ever be crossed. Jenova did not believe Lord Baldessare would ever forgive a transgression, imagined or otherwise, and he was definitely not the sort of man to kiss and make his peace with his enemies.

Jenova told herself firmly that she did not fear him. She was the Lady of Gunlinghorn, widow of the king's cousin, and the king himself was fond enough of her to allow her to arrange her own marriage. No, she did not fear Baldessare. He would need to be a brave man indeed if he were to attempt to harm her in some manner.

Or a desperate one.

Jenova straightened and moved away from the window. The rug beneath her feet was soft and warm—a relic of her father's travels to the East. He was dead now, as was most of her family. Her mother, too, was gone, but she had died happy in the knowledge that Jenova had outgrown her rebelliousness and had made a good marriage. She was alone, and although that did not bother her usually, it did tonight. It would have been pleasant to have had someone who was close to her, someone of whom to ask advice.

Of course, there is Henry.

Jenova tried not to hear the sly note in the thought. Aye, she told herself briskly, she could seek Henry out in his chamber. Talk to him about Baldessare, ask his opinion again. The last time, he had seemed lukewarm on the matter of her marriage to Alfric. Was that because he disliked Baldessare, or did he have some other agenda? She should ask him, she should discuss it with him.

But it was no good, Jenova could not lie to herself. That wasn't the real reason she wanted to see Henry—a warm tingle across her skin, a melting heat in her blood. She needed to be held close by him, to be kissed and loved by him. She had resisted long enough. Her guests would be abed now, there would be no one to see, and she needed him so.

Feeling dangerously reckless, Jenova drew her fur-lined cloak over her thin chemise and slid her feet into her slippers. She reached toward the door.

Would he be alone?

With repugnance, she remembered again the table on the dais and the greedy Baldessares taking their fill of her good food and wine. And the lovely Lady Rhona, with

her dark gaze fixed firmly upon Henry, as if she fully expected him to fall in love with her on the spot.

At first Jenova had been a little shocked by such a blatant display. And then she had been angered. Women,
more particularly wellborn ladies, did not behave so in
her hall! Was this what happened while Henry was attending court? Were women always giving him sugges-
tive looks? And did he always take advantage of them?

Is she with him now?

Jenova took a breath and tried to think clearly. Rhona's
come-hither look, though very shocking, had actually begun to turn a little stale before the meal had ended. Henry
had not seemed to be aware of it, or if he had been, he had
not responded to it. He had spent his time bickering with
Baldessare or staring into his wine goblet. Indeed, she had
rarely seen him so out of sorts, but then Jenova knew she
was not quite her usual self either.

If she had been Rhona, she would have come to the
conclusion that Henry wasn't interested. That, young
and beautiful as Rhona may be, *she* was not the woman
Henry wanted in his bed tonight.

A swell of happiness filled her heart.

Buoyed by the thought that soon she would be in his
arms, Jenova slipped out into the cold stairwell. Henry's
chamber was above hers, up another flight of stairs with
a torch in a wall sconce at the top. Jenova had begun the
climb when a figure stepped out of the shadows behind
her so quietly and abruptly that he made her gasp.

"My lady?"

It was Alfric, his brown eyes catching the light, his
manner a little hesitant, like a child caught out of bed after curfew.

"Alfric, what are you doing here?" Jenova demanded,
more sharply than she meant. She kept her eyes on his

face, although she had the urge to glance up the stairs to see if Henry was standing there. What would she have done if they'd been caught? If Alfric were to discover their secret, it would be horribly embarrassing for them all.

He reached for her hand, and without thinking she gave it to him. His lips were warm against her cold skin, and he squeezed her fingers as if he was trying to tell her something. Alfric seemed far more aggressive in his wooing during this visit—she even sensed a certain desperation in his flattery. He had lost his light touch. Jenova did not like him like this. She supposed he sensed her slipping away from him and at the same time didn't understand why. She should feel sorry for him. Instead, the more desperate Alfric became, the more she wanted to distance herself from him.

Secretly gritting her teeth, Jenova allowed him to finish kissing her hand and then hastily withdrew it from his grip. "What are you doing here, Alfric?" she asked him again. "Is there something amiss?"

"I-I could not sleep," he said slowly, watching her. "I thought to take a walk about the castle, and then I heard your door open. Can-can you not sleep either, my dearest lady?"

Alfric stepped closer, making full use of his melancholy gaze. But there was something intimidating in his movements that Jenova did not like, something almost predatory. She edged back, attempting to put space between them, but he came on, crowding her against the wall, his body a menacing shadow against the torchlight. She had never thought of him in such a way before, but he was Baldessare's son, after all. She seemed to have forgotten that until now.

"Was that the case, my lady?" he said quietly, accusingly. "*Were* you taking a midnight walk? Or had you some specific destination in mind?"

He knows! she thought frantically. Or he had guessed. . . . Her back was hard to the wall now, she couldn't go any farther, and besides, there was nowhere to go. Jenova put her hand against his chest to keep him back, feeling the fine velvet of his tunic and the sharp cut of a brooch fastened at his breast.

"You are frightening me, Alfric," she said, only just managing to keep the tremor from her voice. "It is no business of yours where and when I choose to walk about my own castle—"

"No b-business of mine?" he sneered, his lip curling. His face loomed over hers, and her palm could no longer hold him. "I am your husband! Or will be . . . How can it be no b-business of mine who you spend your nights with, *Lady* Jenova?"

Her heart was thudding so loud that it deafened her, but she forced fear away; showing him how affected she was would only incite him further. This was a side to Alfric she had never seen before, and she knew with a cold, hard certainty that she never wanted to see it again.

"No, it is no business of yours, Alfric. I am not going to marry you. I am sorry to tell you in such a brutal way, but it is best if you know now and do not allow your hopes to continue any longer."

His bravado fell from him like the pretense it was. He stared at her, his eyes huge, his mouth dropping open. He made a strangled sound.

"Now, I am weary," she went on levelly. "I need to go back to my room."

"Nay!" he said, his voice cracking with emotion. "Nay, lady, please, oh please, do not say that. I-I will be good, I swear I will never . . . never . . . I beg you to reconsider! Lady Jenova, please!"

He was distraught, and this was no act. She tried to push him away, but he had gripped her shoulders and was holding on far too tightly.

"You can g-go where you like, sleep with whom you like, I don't care, I don't care, only don't say you will not m-marry me, Jenova—"

"Alfric!" She pushed him, hard, and he finally seemed to realize that he was frightening her. He swallowed, blinked, took a step back. In the torchlight his face was deathly pale.

"Forgive me," he whispered, and tears sparkled in his dark eyes.

Oh Jesu, let him not cry! Jenova could not bear it if he cried.

"Just . . . do not make a decision yet. Not yet. Wait until the morning. I will do whatever you ask of me, anything, but please, please, reconsider."

Jenova steadied her own breathing, watching him closely, wondering if he might lose control again. But, thankfully, he seemed to have pulled himself together. "Very well, Alfric. I will make my decision in the morning."

He nodded, a smile trembling on his mouth. "Thank you," he managed. "Thank you, my lady—"

"Now let me pass. I wish to retire."

He stumbled back, and she hurried by before he could change his mind. The chamber door closed firmly behind her, and she barred it. Only then did she feel truly safe.

She wouldn't marry him, not now. If she had loved him, then perhaps they could have worked through his problems, but she had never loved him. Jenova knew the situation was partly her own fault, and she was sorry for it, and for Alfric, but she would not allow her pity to trap her into making a disastrous mistake.

If it hadn't been for Henry, she may indeed have tied herself to that boy. How could she have so lost her way as to think Alfric would make her a good husband, that an alliance with the Baldessares was a suitable one? Well, the wedding would not now go ahead, but the matter was still a complete mess. One she needed to sort out as soon as possible. In the morning she would confront Baldessare and his son and explain matters to them.

She had changed her mind, that was all. Other people changed their minds all the time, and women were renowned for it. Baldessare probably expected it. He might curse her all he wished in private, but there was not much he could do to her face.

After all, Jenova had the king's favor, and that, she told herself, ensured her safety.

Climbing back into her bed, she closed her eyes. Her decision was made, and she would follow it through to the bitter end. But, although she was a practical woman, she was also a woman, and Jenova could not help a pang at the thought that she would never now wear the white velvet.

"Rhona!" The harsh, whispering voice would not go away. Rhona sighed and, glancing at the quietly snoring servant on the floor beside the bed, threw back the covers and padded, shivering, toward the door.

"Alfric, is that you?"

"Aye, 'tis me. Rhona, I did as you s-said. I w-waited near her d-door and-and—I m-must speak with you!"

Dear God, now what? Rhona thought, but she didn't bother saying it aloud. Quietly, hoping not to wake the servant, she opened her door a crack and peered out at the pale, tear-streaked face of her brother.

Her heart sank.

"She s-says she isn't going to marry me n-now," Alfric said, his voice trembling. "What will I do? Father will kill me for this."

Rhona made soothing noises, patting his cheek, but she felt her own heart thud with dread. Lord Baldessare had had his greedy eyes turned on Gunlinghorn for years; if he were thwarted now that he was so close to having it, she and—more likely—Alfric would pay a heavy price.

"The lady may be having doubts, Alfric, but that does not mean—"

"I persuaded her to p-promise to wait until the morning, to make her decision then, but I am n-not hopeful. She only promised so I would leave her alone. She hates me n-now, Rhona. I-I saw it in her eyes."

He should not have set a deadline for her decision, Rhona thought. Better to let matters drift—there was always a chance Jenova would change her mind back again—but to hedge her into a corner like that. . . . She sighed. She should have known Alfric would mess things up. She shouldn't have trusted him. She should have realized that he could not do anything without her standing behind him telling him what to do. Well, it was done now, and they must prepare to face their father's anger and, if they were clever, talk their way out of it.

And if they could not? The usual bruises, she supposed, the usual punishments and threats. Of course their father might go further this time. He might do more than threaten. Rhona shuddered, remembering. From somewhere she found her voice again, as well as the necessary words to soothe her frightened brother.

"Go to bed. I will be ready in the morning. I will think of something, don't worry."

"Maybe we should use the potion."

Their eyes met, fear in the depths of both. The potion was a secret between them. Once, in a moment of bravado, Rhona had purchased a sleeping potion from an old woman at a market. It was hidden in her chamber. She and Alfric always swore that, if things grew too terrible, they would use it on their father and then, while he was sleeping, they would run away. But how far could they get before he awoke? Rhona thought it would probably never be far enough.

"Nay, Alfric. I will think of something else. Go to bed."

Alfric, his glazed eyes fixed on hers, struggled between his blind belief in his sister to make all right, and justified fear for his own safety. After a moment he gave a jerky nod and turned away. Rhona closed the door behind him, leaning her brow against it and closing her eyes. If only she had been born a man, *she* would not have failed! Jenova would be hers! But Rhona suspected that she would not have been able to get away with half the things she said and did if she had been a man. And besides, she enjoyed being a woman, enjoyed the power she wielded and the admiration she saw in the faces of the men around her.

There had been admiration in that man's face tonight, the big man who had been trying to overhear what she and Alfric had been saying. Rhona frowned, her mind working. It must have been his fault Jenova had scorned Alfric. He must have repeated what he had heard. But no, she did not really think so. Rhona had a feeling that Jenova's doubts stemmed from someone else, someone who had far more influence over her than a servant. Mayhap she could still seduce Henry of Montevoy away from Jenova?

Rhona knew she must not give up yet, and she did not

intend to. Before she allowed her father's fury to roll over them like the violent storm it was, she would do everything in her power to stop him. Would Jean-Paul help her? He had helped before, but, she suspected, only when it suited his own agenda. Their chaplain was a puzzle to her. He had come to their household a year ago, and since then he had slipped into the role of their father's close confidant. It was a position that ensured his wielding much power over Baldessare and his household.

She did not trust him.

She did not trust any man.

Men were weak and greedy and used their strength to oppress. Rhona supposed good ones existed, but as far as she was concerned they were few and far between, and she was not about to gamble her life on the hope that one day a chivalrous knight would come riding to her rescue.

No, if she and Alfric were to be saved from their father's wrath, then they must save themselves.

Chapter 9

The next morning Jenova descended the stairs with her speech prepared. She was pale and weary, but determined. The servants were already up and busy, and she cast a practiced eye over the preparations under way for the midday meal. Feeding the number of souls in a castle the size of Gunlinghorn required much careful planning and strategy. It was a job Jenova had been trained for since girlhood and one that gave her pleasure and a great sense of satisfaction.

In the kitchen, a boy grinned at her as he sat behind the protective screen, turning a spit of roasting meat over the flames so that it wouldn't burn. The smell of fresh baking bread mingled with that of pies coming from the ovens. The cook, a man with a round belly and a wooden spoon in his hand, gave her a respectful nod as he went about his business.

Nothing to be done here. Nothing to cause her to linger. No excuses. Jenova knew she was being a coward, but the thought of facing the Baldessares was turning her into one. Well, best get it over, then!

With a deep breath to bolster her courage, Jenova made her way to the great hall. There were any number of her household already up. Some of them were seated at the trestle tables, involved in conversation or games of dice or chess, while others took their fill of yesterday's bread and ale, which served to break their fast before the midday meal.

"Mama!"

It was Raf, his arms warm and tight about her legs as he gazed up at her with sparkling green eyes.

"We are going to find Raven and her babies. Do you want to come with us?"

Us? Jenova turned and found Henry close behind her. He gave a self-mocking smile, as if she should disapprove of his attachment to her son, when it was one of the things she loved about him. And one of the reasons she knew she could not marry a shallow man like Alfric.

"I would, sweeting, but I have something I wish to discuss with Lord Baldessare," she said to Raf, but she was looking at Henry.

He must have read the tension in her face, because his expression sharpened and his blue eyes narrowed. "Do you want us to wait?"

Sweet Jesu, yes! But Jenova swallowed down her weakness and fear. Raf's open, smiling face was still turned to hers, and looking down at him she knew she did not want him to be privy to the scene she was about to put into motion. Better he was with Henry and far away from Baldessare's displeasure.

"I-no, Henry, no. Find Raven and her babies. I will manage Lord Baldessare."

Henry nodded, still watching her. He stepped closer,

near enough to say, "Be sure you insist on proper terms for your marriage contract. Favorable for you and Raf, rather than my lord Baldessare."

Jenova realized then that Henry thought she meant to talk with the Baldessares about the marriage. He would not know, he could not know, that she had changed her mind completely. She sensed that he would not like the complications this brought to their own relationship, or the expectations.

"Lord Henry, you must come now," Raf insisted, impatient to be gone. Henry took the boy's hand in his but continued to look at Jenova. She forced a reassuring smile.

"Yes, go, Henry. I will be all right."

He hesitated a moment more, then gave a brief bow and left her.

Jenova closed her eyes and took a deep breath before turning again to the great hall.

At once her eye fell upon Lord Baldessare, standing by the dais, slapping his gloves impatiently into his palm. His two fair haired children stood close by, staring at Agetha, who was attempting to engage them in conversation. Jenova knew that Baldessare had already been up and about the stables—one of the grooms had told her—complaining about any number of things that were none of his business. He seemed to think Gunlinghorn was already his.

Jenova felt relief dilute her apprehension. She was doing the right thing in refusing Alfric. She still believed she could have kept Lord Baldessare at a distance, but it would have been wearing on her patience and her temper. The man was a bully, and Jenova did not like bullies. Her resolve strengthened—she was weary of Baldessare, with his cold stares and barely contained contempt.

Better if he never set foot at Gunlinghorn again.

With more confidence in her step, Jenova moved toward the little group, nodding at Reynard as she passed him. Lord Baldessare turned with a frown, returning her polite greeting with a brusque nod of his head. His daughter, her prettiness clouded by a pale, tired face, echoed the greeting in a subdued voice. Beside her, Alfric bowed and said nothing, his shadowed eyes and white face indicating that he, too, had had very little sleep.

Not a happy gathering, then.

"My lady," Agetha smiled, but her eyes were watchful. Agetha would not be pleased when she discovered that Jenova meant to sever all ties with Alfric—he was a great favorite with her. Well, Jenova could not live her life to please her ladies.

"Agetha, would you leave us for a moment. I have something to say to Lord Baldessare."

The other woman gave her a questioning glance but nodded and retreated reluctantly further down the hall.

"My lord," Jenova began in a brisk voice, "would you be seated a moment? There is something I must say."

They were isolated enough that they could converse in private, yet her household was still close enough that Jenova did not feel as if she was under any threat. It was indicative of her change of heart that she even thought of such things; that she was actually considering herself to be in possible danger in her own hall.

"Your servants are disrespectful," the baron informed her as he sat down heavily on a chair, swirling his cloak about him.

"Agetha is no servant, she is the daughter of—"

"Not that silly little girl. I reprimanded your groom for being too slow with my horse this morning, and he gave me a surly look. Your people need a firm hand; you are too lenient with them. I have found that women always are."

"Indeed?" Jenova hid her anger, taking her own seat on one end of a bench, while Baldessare's daughter and son placed themselves at the other end, together, giving the impression that they had formed an alliance against their father.

"Aye, indeed," Baldessare retorted. "Alfric can help you there, at least. He will know how to deal with your servants, and if he doesn't, then I will show him."

The arrogance of the man amazed her. Did he really believe she would allow him to give even one order at Gunlinghorn? He must think her a dolt indeed. Any remaining doubts were fast being replaced by certainty and a sense of relief. She was doing the right thing, and she had best get it over with. Jenova folded her trembling hands firmly together in her lap.

"My lord, I have something of importance to tell you, and I will speak plainly. I cannot wed your son. 'Tis not because he has done or said anything to cause me a dislike of him—never think that. 'Tis just that I have discovered in myself a dissatisfaction with the whole idea of marriage. I do not want to wed again. I do not want to be a bride. I am not yet ready for it, and mayhap I never will be."

Jenova had been staring into Baldessare's gray eyes as she'd spoken. She saw comprehension spark, a tiny flame in the familiar coldness, and then it caught and flared and exploded into a truly terrifying blaze of fury. The air about him seemed to hum like a violent, gathering storm.

As her words stumbled to a close, a hushed silence fell. No one spoke, not Alfric and not Rhona. It was as if they were waiting.

The storm broke.

· Baldessare sprang to his feet, his face the color of over-ripe plums, and he began roaring with anger. "What is this? What worm have you in your head, you stupid woman!"

Jenova jumped, her breath catching in her throat. She glanced sideways at Rhona and Alfric, but they had their heads bent, sitting still and silent, as if by doing so they could prevent their father's anger from settling upon them. Clearly Baldessare was used to getting his own way. Well, thought Jenova, he will not rant and rave here in my hall—he will behave himself or he can leave!

"Do not shout," she said sternly and also rose to her feet, although her knees were trembling. She was a tall woman, and now she drew herself up proudly. From the corner of her eye, she saw that Reynard was standing, too, his hand resting upon the hilt of his sword. The knowledge that he was there gave her added strength.

"You will marry my son! You have promised to marry him and you will do so!" Baldessare was beyond reason. His anger was a scalding wave, flattening all within reach.

He took a step toward her. Jenova wondered if it was possible he would strike her, or snap her neck, before her men could stop him. Despite that possibility, she refused to move back. Her own voice lifted, with her courage, to the challenge. "I did not promise any such thing! I did not give my word, and I have signed no marriage contract. I will not marry your son, and you cannot make me."

"You have lied to me, you bitch, you—"

"I have lied to no one. I have changed my mind."

Lord Baldessare was so close that she could feel his body shaking with his fury, and his face was mottled with it. "Be very careful, my lady," he said, his breath heaving in his chest and whistling through his teeth as he attempted to control himself. "Be very careful what you do and say. No woman has ever denied me. I am Baldessare and I will triumph."

"Are you threatening me?" Jenova demanded, still refusing to step back, although every muscle in her body was screaming at her to do so. "You forget, the king is my friend. If you hurt me, you hurt him. That is treason, my lord."

Baldessare's gray eyes narrowed, and he withdrew slightly. His face lost some of its hideous color, and cunning tempered his ardor. Alfric and Rhona remained seated, quaking, leaning against each other as if to gain strength, and even in the throes of her own fear, Jenova found something pitiable in the sight of theirs.

"Jenova?"

Henry! He had come to her after all, and the sound of his voice had never been so welcome. His hand closed on her shoulder, heavy and warm, giving her vigor, assuring her without words of his protection.

Lord Baldessare's eyes grew hard and savage as he looked beyond her to Henry, but this time the feeling was contained. Slowly, he nodded his head. "Aye, I see how 'tis," he said between gritted teeth. "Once more Lord Henry steals what is mine for his own gain! But this time I will not allow him to get away with it. Beware, Lady Jenova, if you put your trust in this man! He is a liar and a thief, and worse. No matter how grandly he dresses himself and how many jewels he acquires, the filth that sticks to him will always befoul the air around him. And those who would be his friends."

Baldessare gave Henry a final, fuming look, then he turned away, his cloak snapping after him, and strode from the hall.

With a mournful glance at Jenova, Alfric jumped to his

feet and followed. Behind him, her chin held high, Rhona also retreated. In the length of time it took Jenova to take a couple of restorative breaths, the Baldessares had left the great hall of Gunlinghorn. Now once again there was silence, but this time no one seemed willing to break it.

It was done. It was over. Her betrothal to Alfric was no more. Jenova was free.

The warm hand on her shoulder was removed. Henry. How could she have forgotten Henry? Jenova turned and found his blue eyes bright and frowning behind her, his handsome face tight with anger.

"Sweeting? I commend you. What lucky thing have you said to cause the rout of the Baldessares?"

Jenova gave a shaky laugh, but the tears shining in her eyes were not happy ones. "Oh Henry, Henry, have I done the right thing? I have told Lord Baldessare that I cannot . . . I *will* not marry his son."

Henry went still.

Jenova was sure she could actually see the calculations turning in his mind, the cogs wheeling furiously behind the sudden blankness in his eyes. She was not certain she wanted to know what he was thinking, what his clever brain was plotting. She needed him now as an ally and a friend; she did not want to scare him off with the idea that she expected more of him than he was willing to freely give.

"I told Baldessare my reason was nothing to do with Alfric," she went on carefully. "I told him that I had decided I did not wish to wed again, not yet, not now, not to anyone."

"And is that true?"

He was watching her, scrutinizing her, wondering whether or not to trust her. What had she expected? she wondered wildly. A declaration? An offer from him to step into Alfric's place? Had she really believed Henry would do that? Was she such an innocent fool? It seemed that she must be, because Jenova knew that one of the reasons she did not want to wed Alfric was that he could never compare to Henry.

But for her own sake, and the sake of her pride, Henry must never, never know that she had considered, even for a moment, whether he might make marriageable material.

"Of course it is true," she said, meeting his eyes without blinking. "Yestereve, I saw Alfric and he . . . he frightened me, a little. I realized then that he wasn't the man I wanted by my side here at Gunlinghorn. Or standing in lieu of a father to Raf! Better to remain a widow than to take the risk of aligning myself with someone who will do me and my son harm."

"I know that no man can ever replace Mortred."

His eyes were so blue, reaching into her mind, searching her heart. In another moment she would blurt out the truth, and Jenova could not bear that. She had to escape. Hurriedly she turned and began to walk away. Let him think she was overcome with grief at the memory of her husband. Better that than the truth. . . .

"You said Alfric frightened you, Jenova? In what way?"

Henry was following her! Of course he was; he would not let her go that easily. He knew her too well. He knew she was keeping something from him, although he seemed to have settled on her encounter with Alfric rather than Mortred.

Jenova walked faster. "He was so intense, so angry, and then the next moment he was almost in tears. He was so afraid of what his father would say if I didn't wed him. His fear far outweighed any concern he might have had for me." Briefly she glanced over her shoulder, noting Henry's frown. "I think that for Alfric our marriage was simply a way to please his father. As I lay in my bed last night, I realized that I did not want a husband who cared only for pleasing his father, Henry. I wanted a man who cared about pleasing *me*."

"I see."

Jenova wondered if Henry really did *see*, and prayed not. She managed to throw him a smile as she reached the door to the kitchen. "I have matters to attend now, Henry. We can discuss these events later, when I feel calmer."

He halted, and although he returned her smile, it was missing its usual warmth. He looked away from her, beyond the door, and there was something bleak in his face that she had not seen there before. Something that caught at her heart and squeezed.

She hesitated, on the brink of escape.

"Henry? Surely you do not take any notice of what Baldessare said? When he called you a liar and a thief? And the rest? He is a vicious pig, flinging mud at whoever is in his path. I cannot believe you would let the words of a man like that wound you. . . ."

His eyes had returned to hers, and now there was a gentleness in them that warmed her more thoroughly than any fire could. "If you do not believe him, then that is all that matters to me, sweeting. In truth, I was thinking of what I would like to do to him, but that will wait. Go and see to your household, and I will find your son. After he has played with the kittens, I promised him a trot about the bailey on Lamb, and I am sure Lamb is stomping with impatience."

She gave another shaky laugh. "I am sure he is. Thank you, Henry. You have been very . . . kind to Raf."

Henry lifted his eyebrows. "Lord Henry of Montevoy 'kind'? Mmm, mayhap. In truth I do find Raf amusing company. He is not at all like Mortred, you know. Oh, in looks he is a little, and his smile, but his character is all his own."

"I know, and I am glad for it!"

Henry's frown returned. "Jenova?"

Jesu, she had said more than she'd meant, and now he would ask her more questions! She waved her hand at him as she turned away, saying she must go and ignoring his call. But as she hurried toward the kitchen, Jenova felt his curious eyes burning into her back, and she knew in her heart that she was only forestalling the inevitable.

Henry wondered what Jenova could have meant.

I know, and I am glad for it?

Did she not want Raf to resemble his father? But she had loved Mortred! Hadn't she? Henry well knew that she had mourned him and refused to marry again. She had refused even to contemplate it, until now. He had hoped that her love for Mortred had been the real reason she had rejected Alfric and caused such a scene. That she had suddenly been struck by a realization that Alfric was not, and never could be, Mortred.

Her other explanation, that she had had an abrupt change of heart, was plausible enough but very unlike her usual self. Jenova did not sway like a tree in the wind—she was a practical woman of fixed opinions. Surely she must have known what Alfric was like when she'd first set eyes on him? She was certainly not blinded by love for him; the reasons for her marriage, as she had recounted them to Henry, had been clear and precise. How could the scales have fallen from her eyes when they'd never been there in the first place?

No, there was another reason. Something else had happened to change her mind. If she had not refused Alfric because of Mortred, or a sudden realization of what he was, then what?

Henry was aware of a shaky feeling inside. A niggling, fearful doubt. He recognized what it was, that dark worm tunneling its way through his heart. He was afraid that Jenova had refused Alfric because of him. Because of what they had done together in Uther's Tower; what they were still doing, whenever they had the opportunity.

Did she, somewhere in her secret woman's heart, hope that Henry would ask her to marry him? That they would, somehow, despite all the odds against them, live happily ever after?

If that was the case, then she was doomed to be disappointed. Henry knew he would not make any woman a good husband, especially not a woman he cared about as much as he cared about Jenova. He was far too concerned for her happiness to place himself in a position where he could hurt her. Oh, he wasn't sorry she had refused Alfric and sent Baldessare off in a fury. He had never believed Alfric was the man for Jenova.

But neither was Henry.

And yet Henry knew, with a sickening clench in his belly, that in the circumstances, his jubilation that Jenova was no longer planning to wed Alfric was excessive. And it was not just because he did not feel Alfric was good enough. It was because now he, Henry, would not have to stay away from Gunlinghorn just because Alfric was here. He could visit just as usual and see Jenova. He would still be able to take Raf up upon his stallion, enjoy the boy's admiration and smiles, and make him extravagant promises. For Henry, life could go on much as before.

He was happy with an outcome that had made Jenova

unhappy, and he despised himself for it but could not seem to help feeling it.

Baldessare was right. He was not a good man. He was a liar and a thief; a man who reeked of unwholesome secrets. And if that reek did not quite contaminate his friends, friends like Jenova, then his secrets would certainly cause her to eye him with disgust were she ever to discover them. She would turn her back on him and never speak to him again.

Does Baldessare know?

The question was the one he had asked himself last night and dismissed, as he did now. Baldessare was the sort of man who, if he had something to use against Henry, would use it immediately. He was impulsive—not much of a plotter or a planner. It was one of the reasons Henry did not consider him particularly dangerous—he had more bluster than substance.

Threats like those Baldessare had thrown out would not hurt Henry. He must do better than that, Henry thought as he turned about, only to bump into someone standing directly behind him.

"Reynard!" He pushed his man impatiently aside and continued back across the great hall, with Reynard now in pursuit of him.

"My apologies, my lord," Reynard said without a hint of it in his voice. "I was worried for Lady Jenova. Lord Baldessare was like a man possessed of more than one evil spirit."

"Aye." Henry paused and glanced at him with a frown. "Do you think his anger will cool?"

"I think he is the sort to build on it, adding twigs, until it blazes all the brighter."

"Very lyrical, Reynard," Henry mocked. "So you do

not think Baldessare will sit wringing his hands over this matter?"

"Nay, I do not."

"Then you do not believe we should return to London just yet?" he went on thoughtfully, as if it was something he had been considering. "I was thinking it was time to go back to court. There is the matter of the earls and their plotting. . . ."

Reynard met his eyes, and Henry saw the full knowledge there. Reynard knew a lie when he heard it, and knew what was expected of him in return. "Leon would send for you, surely? I think we should stay at Gunlinghorn as long as we are needed."

That was the answer Henry wanted. Very good. Then why was the churning sensation in his belly increasing, and why were his muscles rigid and tense? Henry knew it was in his own self-interest to leave now, return to the life he excelled at and understood, the life he had mapped out for himself when he was thirteen years old. Then he had been the phoenix rising from the ashes.

Did he really want to burn again? To lose all he had gained by stepping back into the flames?

"You are right, Reynard," he said with a sigh. "We should stay at Gunlinghorn. As long as we are needed."

"Lord Henry?" Raf's warm little hand slipped into his, and Henry looked down with a smile. "Can we ride Lamb now?"

"My apologies, Raf. Come then, let us not keep Lamb waiting any longer."

As he began to walk away with the boy, Raf said, "I heard you tell that big man you would stay here as long as you are needed. Does that mean forever?"

Those green eyes, so like Jenova's, met his with a shy

hope in them that made Henry wish he had kept silent. "No, Raf. It means as long as I am needed."

Raf nodded, but he looked doubtful. "And is it a promise? Mama always says that a promise cannot be broken, that one must be very careful about making one, because then you are bound by it forever and ever."

"Your Mama is right, Raf. A promise is binding forever."

"So is it a promise? Will you stay here with us?"

There was no escaping it, Henry thought bleakly. He had never known anyone, man, woman or child, as stubborn and determined as Raf when it came to having an answer.

"I promise I will stay as long as I am needed," Henry said.

Raf opened his mouth to argue further, but he must have seen a warning in Henry's eyes, because he suddenly changed his mind and began to talk about the stable cat's kittens.

Just as well, thought Henry. He would not lie to the boy in this matter, but neither did he wish to hurt him. It surprised him to realize that he had been kinder to Raf than himself. *I am becoming a better man,* he told himself with some mockery. *Jenova has turned me into a saint.*

"Why are you smiling, Lord Henry?" Raf demanded.

"'Tis naught, Raf. I have just thought of something amusing."

"Tell me then."

"No, no, Raf. You wouldn't understand. I hardly do myself. . . ."

Chapter 10

Lord Baldessare was far from pleased. As he strode into his hall at Hilldown Castle, he thought of Gunlinghorn, with its borders abutting his own land, the rich pastures and meadows of the Vale of Gunlinghorn, and its harbor, which could take trading ships with goods from as far away as Venice. Aye, it was a jewel worth having!

And Baldessare wanted it. He had almost had it in his grasp—and completely within the law, too!—only to have been thwarted by a silly woman and a pretty, prattling fool. He felt infuriated, bereft, but he also felt all the more determined. He was not a man to give up his possessions without a fight, and in his own mind Gunlinghorn already belonged to him.

He *would* not give up.

"She will marry you, whether she wants to or not!" he turned and shouted at his son.

Alfric, who was following behind him, cowered. "I did n-nothing t-to—" he began in a shivering voice.

"Be silent!" his father roared.

Alfric glanced wildly at Rhona. Thank God, he thought, that Rhona was there! She had always come to his aid, ever since he was a child. She had always done her best to protect him, sometimes even taking the thrashings that had been meant for him upon herself. He knew well enough that of the two of them, she was the stronger one, the braver one. If anyone could turn their father's foul mood about and into calmer waters, it was Rhona.

"Father, you know this is not Alfric's fault," she said now in soothing tones. "He has done everything you asked of him. 'Tis that bitch, Jenova, who is at fault. She has a fickle nature and is easily influenced by her friends. *One* friend in particular."

Her father's face lost none of its hideous color. He stamped about in front of the fire, sending terrified dogs scattering for safety in the corners and terrified servants close behind them.

"If he had done what I told him to do, then she would still be marrying him!" he said through gritted, discolored teeth. "I finally find a use for Alfric, something as simple as bringing a woman to heel, and he fails me. The boy is feeble and useless, and always will be, but by God he will do his duty to his family with Lady Jenova! Even if I have to bring her to the priest at the point of my sword!"

He stopped, breathing hard, realizing he had said far more than he'd intended.

Rhona was watching him, a spark of intelligence in her dark eyes that was sadly lacking in her brother's. "Well, it may come to that, my lord," she said matter-of-factly. "The king is out of the country, and there is no one to stop us. Apart from Lord Henry."

The baron dismissed Lord Henry with a savage curl

of his lip. "Aye, well, I know things about *Lord Henry* that will persuade him to put a hold on his tongue, if he does not want the whole of England to learn his sordid secrets."

"Do you indeed, Father," Rhona murmured, wondering just what it was her father knew. Never mind, she would discover it eventually, she always did. "That may be, but for now the lady has her gaze fixed upon Lord Henry. Did you not note it, Father? They are lovers, I am certain of it. They have the look of lovers. Their eyes cling at every opportunity. The point of a sword is all very well, but perhaps we should begin with something less barbarous."

Baldessare frowned, his cold eyes narrowing as he gazed upon his daughter. Rhona held her breath, awaiting his decision. Her father had four possible ways of dealing with Rhona's suggestion. He could shout at her for her impertinence, he could strike out at her and bruise her face in his fury, or he could punish her brother instead in the same violent and brutal manner he had often used in the past, though it was a misguided attempt to make a man of him, as if beating Alfric had ever changed him into anything other than a frightened, sobbing mess! Or her father could accept what she said and listen to her advice as he had begun to do more often of late.

His voice broke the stillness. "Mayhap you're right, Daughter. Lovers, you think? Your eyes are sharp. Very well," he said, and although the anger was still there, simmering under the surface, Rhona knew that violence was no longer imminent. "If what you say is so, what do *you* suggest we do?"

"We bide our time," she said promptly. "Lord Henry is a creature of the court, 'tis well known. His life is there, and he will begin to miss it, if he is not already. He will not linger much longer at Gunlinghorn, but will return to London, and Lady Jenova's bed will then be empty. She is a widow now long past her girlhood, while my brother is young and handsome. 'Tis not likely she will find another one such as Alfric so handy to her needs. Lord Henry's going will leave her . . . unsettled. Her body will burn and ache for him, or someone who might replace him. She will look about her, and there will be my brother. You will see, Father. She will be unable to resist him."

" 'Tis true, Father, she will not!" bleated Alfric.

Rhona hurried on before Baldessare could do more than throw him a threatening scowl. "Let Alfric return to Gunlinghorn in a day or so, apologizing for the abrupt manner of our leaving. At the same time he can subtly remind Lady Jenova that Lord Henry will soon be returning to London, and that when he goes, she will be all alone. He might also remind her, again subtly, that she is no longer a young woman. No woman wants to be old and lonely. I am certain Alfric's hints will begin to stir in her mind, and she will realize her mistake, and turn to him with gratitude."

Lord Baldessare grunted at her, but Rhona did not flinch, keeping her eyes fixed upon his face as if she had absolutely nothing to fear. Abruptly her father smiled, but it was not a sight to inspire joy. Inside, Rhona trembled, and she felt her brother move closer to her. Their lives depended upon pleasing their father; it was a fact they had accepted long ago.

"Your idea has possibilities, Daughter, but if it fails, then we will use force. One way or another Alfric will wed that bitch, and by the time King William the Bastard returns to take her side it will be too late. The Baldessares will hold Gunlinghorn. If William does not want to create a scandal for the lady, then he will allow himself to be pacified with some of Gunlinghorn's considerable riches. William is a practical man; he never allows sentiment to influence him over much. He will see the sense of letting sleeping dogs lie."

"Or sleeping Baldessares," Alfric murmured.

Rhona held her breath as their father turned his cold eyes upon her brother. For a moment she was certain he would clout him across the side of the head, but then his mouth twitched, and he gave a bark of laughter.

"Very good, boy, very good."

Rhona smiled, more with relief than amusement, allowing her tight muscles to ease. "What is it you know of Lord Henry, Father?" she asked curiously.

Her father eyed her with something approaching benevolence, but she did not let down her guard. She had learned over the years that it was never wise to trust her father, even when he appeared to be in a good mood.

"You ask a great many questions, Rhona. Do you have a fancy for him yourself?"

The joke was heavy-handed, but she made herself smile. "Nay, father, he is far too pretty for me." A memory of tousled dark hair and piercing dark eyes threw her momentarily off balance. She caught herself, her words barely faltering. " 'Twas only that I thought Alfric could use the knowledge, whatever it is, to drive a wedge between Lady Jenova and Lord Henry. A word, a seed of doubt, and before Henry knows it, she will be treating him like her enemy."

Her father nodded thoughtfully. "Your reasoning is sound, Daughter. I cannot tell you all—the knowledge is in the keeping of another. For now it is enough for you to know that Lord Henry and I have a mutual . . . friend." He gave an unpleasant smirk. "Have you heard of *le château de Nuit*?"

Rhona shook her head, bemused. "The castle of Night?"

"Aye, that is it. Have Alfric mention that name to the lady, and tell her that Lord Henry may have a choice to make very soon. Lady Jenova will not know what he means, but she will repeat those words to him, and he will understand he is in danger of being exposed for what he is. She will ask him questions and he will not want to answer them. If anything will hurry *my lord* back into his hole in London, then 'twill be his fear of the truth." Baldessare grunted a laugh, his eyes gleaming savagely.

"Very well, Father," Rhona said, with a meaningful glance at Alfric, trying not to see the mixture of hope and terror shining in his face. It was rare for their father to be in such good spirits, especially after he had just been routed by a man he hated. The knowledge he held must be damaging indeed. Damaging enough that if Lord Henry felt his position at court to be in danger, he could be worked on, mayhap even frightened away. In Rhona's experience men always put themselves and their interests first. And with Henry gone, then Alfric might actually have a chance.

Pray God this turned out in their favor, thought Rhona, for if they failed. . . . It didn't bear thinking. Her father had not yet broken her spirit, as he had Alfric's, but she feared that the time was close.

For some reason Rhona remembered again the big man with scruffy dark hair who had overheard her and Alfric and who had also been in the hall at Gunlinghorn this morning. He had looked at her in a way she had understood, in a way she might be able to use. Aye, he might come in useful, the stranger with dark eyes.

Reynard.

His name had been Reynard. Rhona shifted uncomfortably. How had she known that? Had her ears pricked to the sound of it when someone had called to him? She was not normally interested in such men. . . . They were not the sort to further her own ambitions and those of her father, but for some reason this Reynard made her feel wistful. Surely such a man as he would never allow his woman to be broken by her bully of a father? She had seen the way he'd stood behind Lady Jenova while her father had ranted, protectively, ready to step in. . . .

"My lord Baldessare, a successful journey?"

The husky voice brought all their heads around. Rhona's thoughts scattered, as they always did when confronted with the scarred and disfigured countenance of their chaplain.

"Jean-Paul! I did not see you there." Baldessare shuffled awkwardly, as if he were embarrassed. Like a squire caught gossiping about matters he had been told not to mention. It seemed completely out of character, and Rhona stared from one to the other, trying to understand what it was that was between them. Ever since Jean-Paul had come to their home, their father had deferred to him. Sometimes, remarkably, he even seemed to be in awe of him, but in a grudging way.

Jean-Paul, in his somber robes, strolled down the great hall toward them, a little smile twisting his thin lips. "I have only just finished my prayers," he said, explaining his late arrival. "Lord Alfric. Lady Rhona."

Rhona responded to his greeting, her eyes slipping away from his. It was always so. The hideous sight of his destroyed face on one side, and the unmarred perfection on the other. Two sides of a coin. It was shocking and disturbing, and she wondered, as she always did, how he bore it without wishing himself dead. She was sure she would never have survived such a disaster, nor would she have wanted to. Sometimes she thought that Jean-

Paul almost reveled in his ugliness, enjoying the effect he had upon them all. Sometimes she thought it gave him satisfaction.

"So, am I soon to join together Lord Alfric and his fair lady? Is the marriage to take place in the spring, as we agreed?"

Alfric cast him a melancholy look. "She has decided she prefers the bastard Montevoy, Jean-Paul."

Jean-Paul shook his head slowly, making Rhona stare as the two views of his face shifted from side to side—the perfect and the destroyed. "Bastard, indeed, Lord Alfric. I have heard stories of this Lord Henry of Montevoy, and I do not like what I hear. He is not to be trusted. Can you not open Lady Jenova's eyes to the truth, allow her to see him for what he really is?"

"She likes him," Alfric replied, as if he could hardly believe it himself. "They have been friends for a very long time."

"So your father has told me, Lord Alfric. Since childhood. I think that our Lord Henry considers Gunling-horn his second home. His . . . sanctuary, hmm?" He smiled, and Rhona stared, fascinated, at the charming smile on one side and the twisted travesty of a smile on the other. "We must see if we can't destroy that for him, make Gunlinghorn feel unsafe. Set fire to his sanctuary and burn it to ashes, and then see what he does."

"Burn Gunlinghorn?" Alfric gasped.

Rhona dug her fingers into his arm before he could make a fool of himself. "Jean-Paul is speaking in metaphors, Alfric. He does not mean to actually set fire to Gunlinghorn, only to destroy Lord Henry's enjoyment of it so that he no longer feels able to stay there in safety."

Jean-Paul met her eyes, his pale blue good eye gleaming with amusement, the other one milky and half closed.

He looked as if he were winking. "Very clever, my lady. That is what I mean."

Rhona wondered, as she had many times, why she felt as if Jean-Paul was their equal, rather than a priest under their authority. What was it about him that gave him that air of command, of control? And fear, for she feared him, too, and not just because of his damaged face. It was fear that prevented her from treating him with the contempt she sometimes felt he deserved.

No, he made Rhona uneasy. Jean-Paul might pretend to be their friend, often championing them to their father, diverting his rages and turning his foul moods to fairer ones. But he did it for his own benefit, not theirs. Alfric did not agree with her—he saw Jean-Paul as some sort of savior—but Rhona had seen and heard things about the priest.

He was known to strike the servants for no reason Rhona could fathom—she had seen him knock the kitchen boy to the ground and walk off smiling, as if he had enjoyed inflicting the pain. The only thing he appeared to love and prize was his horse, a black stallion more suited to a king than a mere priest. Cruelty was not unusual in the Baldessare household, indeed not, but whereas Rhona's father might hit out in rage, Jean-Paul's anger was cold and controlled. And all the more worrying. But if Rhona had suspicions, she was determined not to let Jean-Paul know.

A servant had come with ale. Baldessare lifted a mug to his lips, taking a thirsty gulp, and the brew seemed to return to him some of his familiar bluff confidence. "I know what I'm about, Jean-Paul. Lord Henry will be punished. You will see, you will have your wish granted soon enough. And I will have mine."

Rhona schooled her face into a sweet smile. "And

what is your wish, Jean-Paul? For I know that my father's is to hold Gunlinghorn."

Jean-Paul watched her a moment, his body very still within the dark robes. "My wish is to be allowed to marry Lady Jenova to your brother, my lady. What else?"

What else, indeed?

Why, then, didn't she believe him?

Raf laughed, the joyful, innocent sound ringing throughout the castle bailey. A trader with a heavily laden mule grinned, his teeth white in his swarthy face. Others, servants about the castle or villagers coming and going, paused in their daily routines just to smile.

Jenova, too, smiled from her sheltered seat by the stable wall. She sat, bathed in a burst of winter sunlight, and Henry let himself enjoy the sight of her as he took Lamb on another turn about the yard. Her happy face and her shining eyes gave her all the appearance of a young girl. Henry had seen much of that girl in Jenova of late, and far less of the staid matron and sensible lady of Gunlinghorn Castle. It was as if their lovemaking had set her free, and now she reveled in things she had thought put aside long ago.

"Faster, Henry, faster!" Raf's excited voice brought his thoughts back to the here and now.

"If I go any faster, Lamb might carry us all the way to London, and what would your mother do then?"

The boy thought about that, and then gave Henry his brilliant smile. "Mama could come, too," he announced, pleased he had the solution. "We could all go to London!"

Henry managed a strained smile in reply but found that his quick tongue seemed strangely sluggish. Jenova in London? It was not something he could even imagine, let alone consider seriously. She belonged to Gunlinghorn, to the countryside, to this secret life into which he had been transported. But London? London would mean showing her to the world; it would be like announcing to everyone that he and Jenova were lovers.

A pair.

A couple.

Bound together by bonds stronger than friendship.

People would look and whisper, point and stare. Gossip could be cruel, and the court thrived on gossip. Henry told himself he didn't want her to suffer that. Besides, the voice in his head blustered, the king would not like it. He would be displeased with Henry for bringing his cousin's widow's reputation into disrepute, and Henry had worked too long and too hard to throw away his own life's ambitions in such a careless manner. For a woman? No, no! His existence at court must remain separate, and when he left Gunlinghorn and returned to London, as he knew he must, then the affair would be over. Jenova would go back to being what she was, the Lady of Gunlinghorn, and mother to the heir, and he would go back to being Lord Henry of Montevoy, friend of the king and lover of many women.

You're a liar, Henry.

Henry sighed. He *was* a liar. His excuses were just that, and deep in his heart he knew it. They meant nothing, and all of them could be overcome if he wanted to overcome them. The real reason he didn't want Jenova in his life, the honest reason, was that he was afraid. Jenova did not know the truth about him, she did not know how unworthy he was. If they were to become a couple, a pair, then she would ask questions, she would dig around in his past, until she found out.

Like some fearful fairy tale, she would open the creaking door onto his soul and see the real Henry. No one still living had ever seen what was behind that door, and he broke out in a sweat at the thought of Jenova being privy to what had occurred at *le château de Nuit*.

You've forgotten about Baldessare. You cannot leave her to face that man's tender mercies all on her own. She has thrown aside a marriage, probably because of you, despite her claim to the contrary. Coward, does that not present you with an obligation where she is concerned!

It did, but Jenova could look after herself. She preferred it that way, always had. She was the Lady of Gunlinghorn, and she reveled in ruling her people and her lands. Besides, Baldessare would not dare to make too much of a fuss. He knew she was a favorite of the king, and even Baldessare was not stupid enough to cross King William.

Was he not?

Lesser men have died for such transgressions.

Aye, Henry admitted to himself reluctantly, lesser men still attempted to get away with thievery and treason and murder even when well aware that the king could order them to be put to their deaths. They were too greedy or stupid to care. And though Baldessare was not stupid, he was certainly greedy.

He could use Baldessare as an excuse to stay, if he needed one. In truth, despite Leon's competence, Henry knew he should have returned to London a fortnight ago. He could not seem to drag himself away. He *wanted* to stay here. With her. He was happy here, with her, happier than he had been for a very long time. Oh, it would not last. Of course it would not last, and he did not expect it to. But all the same he couldn't bring himself to sever the cord, not just yet, despite his sense of unworthiness.

Leave it a little longer. Just a little. Mayhap the affair would end of its own accord, and then he would not have to leave with such a heavy heart. Or Jenova might tell him to go, send him off with a flea in his ear, and he would not have to make the decision himself.

But there were no signs yet of their affair cooling, and he seemed to be melding into other areas of her life, places he had never been before.

Yesterday, she had asked for his attendance at a meeting with a merchant from Gunlinghorn Harbor. "I need your advice, your thoughts," she had said, as if they'd mattered to her. This had not been unusual in itself—Jenova often asked for his advice—but rarely on the day-to-day running of her lands and its people.

Henry had attended the meeting, prepared to offer what advice he could and stave off boredom. Gunlinghorn was hardly London, after all. These matters were not likely to affect the future of the kingdom.

But before long, Henry found himself actually intensely interested in what was being said. He found it stimulating in a way he had not expected—certainly had not expected outside the machinations of the court. He was surprised at himself, and curious as to why he was so engaged in the business of Gunlinghorn.

Was it because of Jenova?

Aye, but it was much more than that. It was because he cared. Henry admitted it at last, uneasily. He cared deeply about this place and its people.

The merchant had come to ask Jenova to consider giving her harbor to him as a fief: He would pay her an annual rent, and in return she would allow him to command the trade in the harbor as he wished and keep the profits. At present, the harbor was part of Jenova's Gunlinghorn estate, and therefore hers to do with as she willed.

"A good, honest man like myself, my lady, would be more than happy to remove the worries of such a matter from your already overburdened shoulders. I heard that a boat ran aground lately? You do not want to be troubled with problems like that. It would be my pleasure to spare you from them in any way I could."

Jenova had glanced at Henry, a sparkle in her eye, ignoring his grimace at the flowery language. "Would you really, Master Will? I had thought that bearing heavy burdens was part of being the Lady of Gunlinghorn."

The merchant had continued to flatter and chatter, but it had been very clear to Henry that he'd had his eye on the prize. Gunlinghorn Harbor. With the increasing number of ships arriving there and the prospect of more trade, the man had seen a way to being rich. He'd planned to seize it, and he had not wanted to share. A feeble and lazy lady might have taken his offer, glad to be rid of the "burden." But Henry had known such a move would not have been in Jenova's interest.

"You say that a boat lately ran aground," he'd said, cutting through the flummery. "The harbor is beginning to silt up, then. What will you do about that, Master Will? Have you any plans? Will you put some of your moneys into repairs?"

Master Will had hemmed and hawed, but it had been clear he'd had no intention of doing anything about such long-term problems as the deep channel becoming too shallow to take the larger ships. His plan had been to make his money and go.

"Some things are simply God's will," he had ended piously.

"No, they are Lady Jenova's will, and she is more than capable of overseeing her harbor and the ships that come into it. She is also clever enough to keep her harbor from silting up." Henry had spoken with deceptive mildness.

Master Will had eyed him with dislike. It had been clear he'd wished Henry back in London that very instant, and the knowledge had amused Henry. Poor Master Will had believed it had only been Lord Henry preventing Jenova from caving in to his wishes. Clearly he had not known the lady very well, and it had seemed that Jenova had been quite content to have had it so.

"Lady Jenova is a fragile and beautiful woman, my lord," he had replied, a little desperately. "Women should not be burdened with the troubles of commerce. They do not understand such things. It is for men to help them, and I would not like to think I stood by and watched her sufferings, when I could so easily have relieved her of her troubles."

"*Relieved her of her troubles?*" Henry had snorted. "I'll warrant you would like to! And line your pockets with her profits at the same time. Be gone, Master Will. We have heard enough of your self-serving nonsense. Lady Jenova has made her decision; she will be keeping her harbor."

"My lady," Master Will had blurted, his face falling. "It was not my intention to—"

At that moment Jenova had stepped in and smoothed his ruffled feathers, and eventually she had eased him from the door. Her smile, when she had turned again to Henry, had been broad and filled with genuine amusement, and something more. Pride. But of whom had she been proud?

"Next he will be wanting to open a market every week on the quayside," she had said, "to take advantage of the cargoes arriving so frequently. We will have traders and buyers coming from all over southern England to purchase wares."

"So you will," Henry had teased. "Let me guess, Jenova. You are thinking of doing that yourself."

"But of course. That was why I did not want to relinquish control of the harbor. I would be a fool to do so."

"So you didn't really need my advice after all?"

He had known she was no fool, but still the idea that she had not needed his counsel had wounded him.

"Oh, but I did," Jenova had insisted. "I needed you here in person, Henry. If you had not been here to send him away, he would never have gone. You see, I did not want to insult him—he is useful to me—but you could insult him for me. It is fine for him to be at odds with *you*, but *I* have to remain the saintlike Lady Jenova. Such men as Master Will prefer not to believe that their lady tallies up her profits before bed—it spoils that image of fragile feminine weakness. And that image comes in very useful, Henry, when I want something done."

Henry had laughed. "So I played the devil to your saint?"

"You did indeed. We made a perfect pair."

Her pride had been in him, in Henry.

She had been looking at him as if he had exceeded all her expectations.

Under her gaze Henry had felt himself grow a little taller—some parts more than others. But now, when he thought about the incident, he began to wonder if Jenova hadn't been trying to teach him something else entirely. Had her lesson been that Gunlinghorn wasn't as boring as he thought, that his presence here would actually be of use to her? The harbor, for instance. It would be a challenge to keep the channel deep enough for larger vessels.

Such a challenge appealed to Henry.

Was that what Jenova was saying to him, in her own devious manner? That fundamentally there was nothing to be found in London that could not also be found here?

The memory faded; Henry blinked and found himself once more in the bailey at Gunlinghorn. He urged Lamb to hurry up, smiling at Raf when the stallion tossed his head and snorted impatiently. He used to think he was a clear-thinking man, a pragmatic man, but now he didn't know what to think. Worse, he didn't know what to do! To one side stood Baldessare and his oblique threats, as well as Henry's satisfying life at court; on the other side stood Jenova and her son, and Gunlinghorn. And in between both was Henry, with his dark secret and his desire for Jenova, and his very real fear that he could never be the man she wanted. The man she deserved.

He would fail her.

She just did not realize it yet.

Unaware of Henry's churning thoughts, Jenova drew her warm furs closer about her and watched him and her son, seated upon the big stallion, trotting so steadily around the castleyard. The animal, with his enormous feathery hooves, took cautious, surprisingly light steps. Henry had complete control, and she wasn't afraid for Raf. Besides, he was enjoying himself so much that she very much doubted any command of hers would be heeded.

She had never thought of Henry as a man with a fondness for children. He had never taken much notice of Raf before, and indeed she had sensed he was grateful she had not pressed him on the matter. Jenova was not sure she fully understood his current change of heart. Henry, in her past experience, never did anything without expecting something in return.

Is he trying to please me to gain my favor?

He already had all he wanted from her—she denied him nothing these days. Last night they had lain in each other's arms, their bodies joined, delirious with pleasure. He had brought her to her peak again and again, making her cry out, uncaring who heard her. And she had wondered, as she always wondered at such moments, how much longer it would last.

Jenova told herself to stop trying to see into the future. She should just enjoy it, take it moment by moment. Soon Henry would go, back to London and his real life, and she would be alone again. Alone without even a husband like Alfric to look forward to. But she would still be the Lady of Gunlinghorn, loved and looked up to. Surely there was something to sustain her in that?

Raf laughed and waved one hand. "Mama, we are riding to London!" he shouted. Henry smiled and shook his head at her, while she smiled back. She knew Raf wasn't riding to London, she knew that neither she nor Raf would ever ride to London with Henry. He did not want them there. London was where his real life lay, and Jenova suddenly knew, with a cold shiver in her heart, that he did not want them to be part of his real life.

Well, what did you expect? she asked herself impatiently. *Enjoy the moment, as Henry is fond of saying. Take what you can, and savor the memories. You have made your bed, Jenova, now sleep in it!*

Chapter 11

Jean-Paul closed his eyes, trying to still the ache in his head. The pain was elusive, not yet the pounding agony it would soon become. The headaches were part of what he was now, and he had grown to accept them. Just as he had grown to accept the ruination of his body and face.

That did not mean he had to like it.

God taught forgiveness, but Jean-Paul did not forgive. He could never forgive what had been done to him that night, when the fire had come and he'd been abandoned to this half-life. He had survived, dragging himself away from the charred building, lying half dead in some peasant's hovel. But he had survived.

The people of the village had claimed it was a miracle, that God or one of his many saints had stepped in and taken up Jean-Paul for His own. It had suited Jean-Paul to allow them to believe that, to let himself be persuaded into the monastery, and to learn the ways of the holy men there.

But it wasn't true.

The thing that had kept Jean-Paul alive during those early dark days, and all the days that had come afterward had been revenge. It had been as simple and as complicated as that. Someone would pay for what had happened to him; it was only just. God taught justice, as well as forgiveness. An eye for an eye. A tooth for a tooth. A life for a life?

Yes, someone would pay, and that someone was Henry of Montevoy.

The ache in Jean-Paul's head intensified. Henry had abandoned him when he'd needed him most, left him to die, and worse. Henry deserved all that was coming to him. Despite the pain, Jean-Paul smiled. He was going to enjoy himself in the weeks ahead.

The bath was placed in one of the rooms off the great hall, small but private. Henry lay back in the steaming water with a sigh and closed his eyes amidst the rather feminine scent of violets—Agetha had provided him with the soap.

Henry had a fetish for cleanliness, which was always a source of amusement to his friends. When they made him the subject of their jokes, he would shrug and laugh and tell them that he preferred not to carry around the filth they preferred. But it was more than that—he knew in his heart that his past had much to do with the need to cleanse himself so often. To scrub and scrub at a stain that only he could see and that could never be removed.

Henry shook off such grim thoughts, moving restlessly in the water. Lady Agetha had offered to scrub his back, as good manners required, but he had refused her, to the relief of them both. Now, if it had been Jenova . . .

When he was with Jenova, nothing more mattered. She

would probably laugh if he told her that and think he was teasing her, or begin to make plans for the future. Henry did not trust himself that far. His future had never consisted of remaining with any one woman longer than a month, but even that alarming thought didn't make him want to pack up his belongings and ride northward.

He sighed again, sinking deeper into the water, his well-muscled body a golden blur beneath its surface, while his head and shoulders rested against the side.

The muffled voices from the great hall faded, soothed, and for a time he dozed. He dreamed of forests and the moon sailing in a dark sky and evil things abroad. And blood. Warm, warm blood. It was the sensation of more hot water being poured carefully into the side of the bath that brought him to his senses. Henry blinked and looked up. Reynard was pouring the water, concentrating upon his task, wearing his bland servant's face.

"Is it late?" Henry asked, stifling a yawn. "I fell asleep."

Someone stirred near the door, the whisper of skirts. "So late that I came to see what you were up to, my lord. Reynard led me to you."

It was Jenova. She came forward, looking angelic in pale yellow, her hands clasped before her. But her green eyes held an expression that was anything but saintly. Henry slid further into the water, hoping to hide what she did to him.

"Bathing again, Henry?" she teased gently. "You must allow me to help you wash."

"I have already refused Agetha."

"But you will not refuse me, my lord. It is customary in noble households for the lady to assist her guests at their bath, as you well know. I would not wish you to think me impolite."

Henry glanced at Reynard. Jenova had never done this before, and even though she was perfectly correct, his manservant was not a fool. He must know there was something else afoot here—he had probably known from the first. Henry hoped he would know what was required of him now.

Reynard didn't disappoint. "I will wait in the hall, my lord," he said without inflection. "If someone comes looking for you, I will be sure to let you know . . . in plenty of time." The door closed behind him.

"Henry?" Jenova rested her cool hand upon his shoulder.

He lifted her fingers to his lips, enjoying the feel and scent of her. "Of course I will not refuse to let you help me wash. I will revel in it."

She smiled and stooped to kiss his cheek. "Mmm. You smell of violets."

"Agetha provided the soap."

Jenova's eyes sparkled with laughter. "Ah. Forgive her. She is very fond of Alfric."

"Then she is a woman of little intelligence. Alfric does not want you for yourself, Jenova, only for what you can bring to his father."

He had spoken the truth without thinking, and although Jenova gave another smile, the sparkle had gone from her eyes.

"You think not? Well, I suppose he is like all men. If a woman has property or fortune and she has breasts and the ability to make children, then she will do. What does it matter what she thinks or feels, if she is happy or sad?"

Henry sat up straighter. Suddenly the water felt a little chill, although Reynard had just heated it. He had sensed this strangeness in her before, when Mortred had been mentioned in the great hall, after the Baldessares had left in anger. Then, he had thought her unease had been because of his questions about Alfric, but now . . .

"This is about Mortred, is it not, Jenova?"

She stared back at Henry as if she could not look away.

"Jenova, did you know—" He shook his head, thinking that it was wrong to hurt her after all this time if she was unaware. Mortred, the king's cousin, a man who drank to excess and frequented the brothels, and cared little for his wife and son, far away at Gunlinghorn. Henry had despised him even as he'd kept Mortred's secrets, believing that his silence was protecting Jenova from the hurtful truth. He was still protecting her.

"Did I know?" Jenova laughed softly, but there was a terrible bitterness in her. Frowning, he searched her face, noting the little crease between her brows, the straight line of her mouth, the flush of heat in her cheeks. "Aye, I did know, Henry. I discovered quite recently that my husband was a liar and a cheat."

Jesu! She knew about Mortred after all. He had believed he had saved her from that pain. Henry had even hoped that because Mortred had strayed only when he'd been away from home, Jenova would not have guessed.

Her eyes narrowed and her gaze grew hard and accusing. "*You* knew, didn't you, Henry? About Mortred? All along, you knew, and said nothing to me!"

"What would I have said? I could not hurt you—"

Jenova gave another bitter, humorless laugh. "Hurt me? Nay, Mortred did enough of that. I did not even know until he was dead, after I had wept for him and mourned him and wished myself at his side in the tomb. So then I felt doubly ridiculous, as if I had been cheated of his memory as well as his love. I had mourned a man who had made a fool of me. Who swived every woman he saw or met or knew. He had one of my own ladies, here in my keep, you know."

She wiped a tear furiously from her eye, as if she did not want to waste them on her dead husband.

"He betrayed me with one of my own ladies! I found out from her very mouth, before she left Gunlinghorn last year. She took pleasure in telling me, lingering on the detail."

"Jenova." But he had no answer.

"Why?" she demanded of his silence, and her voice broke with the depth of her humiliation and misery. "Why go out seeking other women time and time again, when I was willing to give him everything I had, be everything to him? How could he do that to me?"

The tears rolled down her cheeks, but she no longer seemed to notice them.

Henry wished he had Mortred here, beside him. It would have been a grim joy to make his nose nice and bloody. But Mortred was dead and gone, and it was Jenova who concerned him now.

"Jenova, he was unworthy of you."

She shook her head, bewildered, and anger glinted in her eyes. "You knew, Henry. You *knew*. You should have told me. I cannot forgive you that you knew and did not tell me."

"Sweeting—"

"No, there is no excuse. Better to wound me with the truth than leave me to mourn a man like that, Henry."

He had thought to protect her, but instead it seemed he had caused her more pain. Henry sighed. "I am sorry," he murmured.

But Jenova was too angry to listen. "I wished I could have taken a lover while Mortred was alive. I wanted to hurt him as he hurt me. But he was dead, so instead I thought marrying Alfric would show them all—all those who knew the truth and pitied me—that I no longer grieved for a man who had never loved me. I wanted to feel again, Henry. I wanted my revenge, even though it was too late. And now I have no Mortred, no Alfric . . . I have nothing."

Henry lifted his head and sat up straighter in the bath. A spark lit his eyes. "You wanted to take a lover, Jenova? You wanted revenge? Then take your revenge. Use me to take your vengeance upon Mortred. Here, now, show him you no longer care."

She blinked, but she didn't pretend not to understand what he meant. "Here?" she asked, and glanced over her shoulder at the door.

"Here. The water is still hot."

"But . . . now?"

"Reynard is watching, we are private. You can do as you wish."

Henry watched her bite her lips as she thought, saw her gaze drop to his body beneath the water. "Take your revenge on Mortred," he murmured, "and chase him from our lives."

She met his gaze again, and now her green eyes shone and her face was flushed and young. She was the girl he had known long ago; the wild girl who would do anything he did and more. And he had loved her for it. Aye, Henry admitted, of course he had loved her then, she had been everything to him. But his life had taken him elsewhere, and they had grown up apart, and Jenova had wed Mortred. . . .

Slowly, her eyes on his, Jenova began to disrobe. Her fingers were trembling, and Henry could read her self-consciousness, though she was pretending hard not to feel that way. She peeled off her yellow gown and the clothing beneath it, revealing a body that was firm and smooth and beautiful. Her breasts full, her raspberry nipples making his mouth water, the slim line of her thighs and the curve of her waist, the rounded flesh of her bottom and the dark curls below her belly.

He wanted her, all of her, with a need that went beyond lust and desire, and seeped into his very soul. He had never felt like this before—it could not be love. Henry was sure he could not love. For with love went trusting, and Henry, abandoned by his mother, hiding his past, found it difficult to trust women. He did not want to open his heart to someone who might break it; he had survived too much to risk himself in that way. Love was such a chancy thing, after all.

Jenova let her chemise slide in a puddle about her slippers. It was not her best one, but she did not think Henry would care or notice. He was gazing at her now as if he truly would eat her up. Revenge, he had said. The notion had taken root in her, and she felt alive, invigorated, powerful.

Henry reached out a hand.

"Nay," she said, her voice breathy. "Do not touch me. This is my vengeance, remember. You are my lover, and I have brought you here to seduce you, to show Mortred that he means nothing to me. You must not touch me, Henry. I will tell you what to do."

He did not like that so well, but Jenova didn't care. Henry had lied to her. Reluctantly, he nodded.

She stepped free of her remaining clothing and stooped over him. Her soft breast brushed his cheek and he groaned, turning to take her in his mouth, but she moved away. Her hands slid over his shoulders and chest, slowly, a little tentatively, and then with increasing eagerness, exploring him as if she had never touched him before. Her palm slid down, below the water, over the hard plane of his belly. He caught his breath and she smiled. His erection nudged against her fingers and she stroked him, and his hips bucked.

"I'm dying," he groaned. "Jenova, let me touch you."

She hesitated, unwilling to relinquish control, but her skin was tingling and flushed by the need to have his response.

"Very well, but you must stop when I say so."

Henry turned, rubbing his freshly shaven face against her belly where she leaned over him, then he reached to caress her breasts, gently squeezing before finally enclosing first one nipple, and then the other, in his warm mouth.

For a moment Jenova felt quite dizzy. She clung to the sides of the bath, awash with feeling. His hand slid up into her hair, tugging her face down to his, and her lips to his lips. He ran his tongue around them, tasting her, and then he devoured her mouth in a long and passionate kiss.

Another moment and Jenova knew she would be unable to think at all. Already she felt his fingers warm against her inner thigh. With a gasp she pulled away and stood, panting, glaring at him. He made as if to rise from the heated water, but Jenova stayed him with a hand to his shoulder.

"Nay," she said, and smiled. "I want you to remain, Henry. I want to . . . to ravish you."

To his credit he did not smile back, but his blue eyes glinted before he lowered the long lashes over them. "Do it then," he said in a harsh voice. "No more games."

"You mean like the games you and Mortred played with me?" she retorted. Once again the powerful sense of anger gripped her. Before she could change her mind,

Jenova stepped into the bath, uncaring for the danger-ously swishing water. With one foot on either side of his hips, she lowered herself, her body sprawled across his. His erection brushed her swollen flesh.

He groaned, his fingers white as he gripped the rim of the bath. She lifted herself, then lowered herself again, al-lowing him limited access before withdrawing. His hard length prodded her swollen, secret layers. She gasped and moved forward, allowing him to suck at her breasts, murmuring encouragement.

"Jenova," he groaned. "Please . . . please . . ."

Mercilessly, Jenova lowered herself onto him again and again, teasing him. But each time it was more diffi-cult to pull away, and in truth she wanted to sink herself fully upon him. It was not in her nature to hold back, and this was Henry, her Henry. She wanted to enjoy him and let him enjoy her.

"Now," she gasped. "Touch me now, Henry."

He did more than touch. He caught her hips in his hands and pushed up, deep, so deep inside her. Jenova felt her body go fluid, and a great shudder then overtook them both. She was flying toward the sky—a clear mid-night blue meadow strewn with gleaming stars—and the world vanished below her.

When it was over, she lifted her head from his chest, her damp hair curling about her, a pulse still fluttering in her throat. "You are not like Mortred," she said, and there was a new certainty in her voice, and a kind of wonder. "I have been telling myself that you were, but you aren't like him at all."

"No," he agreed, making a joke of it. "I am like Henry."

But there was an expression in his eyes, a combination of joy and fear, as if she had found him out.

"Do you forgive me? For keeping the truth about Mortred from you?"

Jenova leaned forward across his chest, their bare, damp flesh sliding together, and looked into his eyes. She saw contrition there, and warmth, and the desire to comfort her and make her happy. "Aye, Henry," she murmured, touching a finger to his lips, "I forgive you." She traced the shape of his mouth. "I think I would forgive you almost anything. . . ."

Henry caught his breath, and something flashed in his eyes, startling her. But before she could ask him what was the matter, he drew her up against him, and his mouth closed hard on hers, drowning her in passion.

Chapter 12

Once again Alfric and Rhona came riding into Gunlinghorn. Alfric's spurs were shining, his tunic of fine brown wool was brushed smooth, and his fair hair was neatly cut. He looked like the handsome young lord that he was—a widow's dream.

Any other widow but the one keeping watch from her chamber, the one who did not want to see him and stated so aloud.

"But you must, my lady!" cried Agetha in dismay, her blue eyes wide. " 'Twould be very ill mannered if you refused him access to you, and after you said you would wed him not so long ago."

"I do not want to elevate his hopes again, Agetha."

Agetha stabbed her needle into the cloth she was embroidering, her mouth pursed. She had always favored Alfric; Jenova had not realized just how much until she had rejected him. Now Agetha alternated between singing his praises in the hope Jenova would change her mind, or grieving for the loss of the handsome young man. Jenova did not know which was worse, hearing a dozen times a day how perfect Alfric was, or listening to how she could expect to be full of regrets in her dotage over the fact that she had not snapped him up when she'd had the opportunity.

Jenova wished she could be as blind in love as Agetha desired her to be, that she could believe in someone as wholeheartedly as Agetha did Alfric. But Jenova was older and wiser by far, and she told herself she had been hurt too badly by Mortred to ever trust blindly again. . . . Her mind drifted to the evening before, and lying in Henry's arms in the warm, fragrant water. She found herself smiling for no particular reason.

"Poor Lord Alfric," Agetha muttered, hauling the needle through her embroidery and tugging it tight. "He must be feeling so confused and bewildered. His feelings must be so hurt. He is *so* sensitive. How can he bear it if you now refuse even to see him when he has come all this way—"

"It is barely two hours' ride from Hilldown Castle to Gunlinghorn," Jenova retorted. "And I can bear it very well."

Agetha's lips tightened. "The Baldessares are your neighbors, my lady. One day Alfric will stand in his father's stead. Does that not make you anxious to be on good terms with him?"

Agetha was right. In these dangerous times who knew when it might be necessary for her to call upon his help. Jenova felt her heart sink. Aye, she would see Alfric and listen to him, and refuse him. But, she vowed, it would be the last time.

"Very well, Agetha," she said. "I will see him, but in the great hall. I do not want to be alone with him."

Triumphantly, Agetha tossed her ill-treated embroidery aside and went tripping down the stairs. It crossed Jenova's mind, not for the first time, that Alfric would be far better off with Agetha as his wife. She was sweet and pretty and certainly loyal. 'Twas a shame the girl had little in the way of dowry to offer the land-greedy Lord Baldessare.

When Jenova reached the great hall, she saw that Alfric and Rhona stood by the fire, waiting, their heads close together, as if they were plotting against her. Jenova, pausing in the doorway, thought that perhaps they were. Rhona, in particular, was cunning enough for anything—Jenova had never trusted her. And Alfric was too gentle and easily led to be trustworthy beyond Gunlinghorn's boundaries. Wed to her, living here with her, he would never have disobeyed her. Away from her, he would be like a leaf blown by whichever breeze was stronger.

She was well rid of the pair of them.

"My dearest l-lady!" Alfric spotted her as she approached. He strode to meet her and took her hand, pressing a fervent kiss to her flesh. Jenova struggled not to jerk her fingers free. Despite his greeting, his brown eyes were cautious, anxious, as if he were uncertain of her reaction. She could not blame him for that—if she had a sire like Lord Baldessare, she would be anxious, too.

Jenova suddenly no longer found it difficult to smile and say, gently, "Alfric, I am truly glad to see you. I would like us to be friends again. For us to put aside the unpleasantness that occurred the last time you were here. However, I must tell you that if you have come here thinking to persuade me to change my mind in regard to your wish to marry me, then you have wasted your journey."

Alfric's mouth quivered, his eyes filled with tears. "But, my lady—"

"My brother *does* want to persuade you to change your mind, my lady," Rhona said evenly, her cool tones slicing through what threatened to be an impassioned plea from her sibling.

Jenova turned to her with relief. She did not want a scene. "Then I am sorry, but—"

"Surely you do not want Alfric to lie, and declare otherwise?" Rhona went on, clearly intent upon saying what she must. "I am very sure, Lady Jenova, you abhor lies as much as I do. But be assured, my brother will not embarrass you over this matter, he will not make you uncomfortable. Alfric will bide his time, and follow your lead. He is young, and he can wait until you are ready to look upon his love for you in a more favorable light."

Clever words, thought Jenova, looking from one to the other. The Baldessare siblings were very alike in demeanor, with their fair hair and brown eyes. A handsome couple, neither of them having inherited their father's rather bucolic looks. Whatever sort of father he was, he had seen that his son and daughter had been well taught in the ways of the Norman aristocracy.

"My lady?" Rhona's eyes shone with an inner intelligence and determination, while Alfric's were more like a child's, begging for some sign of her affection, for some spark of hope. She hated to think what their father would say to them if she turned them out without the least sign of hospitality. And yet if she were cruel, was it not sometimes kinder to be so? It prevented one from having false hope. It was better to allow Alfric to suffer one short moment of pain now, and save himself a later, longer suffering by remaining blindly hopeful that she would change her mind.

"Alfric is young and handsome; he will soon find himself another wife," Jenova said, although not quite as coldly as she wished.

Rhona's eyes flashed, but at once she disguised her anger with a smile, hiding it well. In contrast, Alfric looked even more likely to burst into tears.

"There, now, that is the worst of it," Jenova continued on, more rousingly. "We have stated our positions, and put our differences behind us. Let us take some wine and be friends again. Tell me, how is your father?"

"He is well, my lady," said Rhona, "but if you will excuse me, I prefer to take a stroll in your gardens while you and my brother speak privately. There are still matters he wishes to broach with you, if you will be good enough to hear him?"

Jenova did not want to hear him, but Alfric was watching her pleadingly, like a puppy that expects to be beaten. She was not normally a hard-hearted woman. She had stated her situation, but it could not hurt her to listen to what he had to say, although she feared it would only be more of the same. She would be kind and then send him on his way.

Jenova nodded brusquely. "Very well."

Rhona smoothed her saffron-colored skirts, her fingers heavy with jeweled rings. The Baldessares were wealthy, and it seemed that when it came to his offspring, their father did not stint upon clothing and decorations. Only upon his love and affection.

"Thank you, my lady. I will leave you alone then, briefly."

Jenova watched the younger woman cross the great hall, her back straight and her head high. There were many rumors about Rhona, but Jenova had never inquired into their truth or otherwise. She did not consider her a close friend—Rhona was not the sort to unburden her heart to another or allow anyone to get too close to her. She kept her distance. Until now, Jenova had never wondered why.

"My lady?" Alfric was holding a chair for her, his expression eager. Jenova nodded to a servant, who stood with a tray upon which was set the wine jug and best goblets.

"Will you take some wine, Alfric? It is very good."

"It cannot be as good as you, Lady Jenova."

Jenova tried not to roll her eyes. She glanced about a little desperately and caught sight of Agetha, hovering by the dais, her eyes fixed upon her hero. At least Agetha did not see his feet of clay. . . . An idea suddenly occurring to her, Jenova beckoned her over. "Agetha, please come and join us. I am sure Alfric will not mind."

Alfric looked as if he minded very much indeed, but he could hardly say so. It would have ruined his portrayal of a perfect gentleman. In contrast, Agetha looked as if she might burst with the pleasure of being in the company of her hero. Jenova began to pour the wine, satisfied that she had made the best of a very awkward situation.

Rhona wandered about the flower borders, shivering from the cold despite her fur-lined cloak. Nothing green was growing at this time of year, apart from the winter stalwarts of holly, ivy and bay. A sprinkling of snow lay upon the ground, and every now and then a fresh flutter of flakes would fall about her.

It had been necessary for her to leave the great hall so that Alfric could be alone with Jenova, despite the fact that Rhona could see it was all a pointless waste of time. The lady had made up her mind. Her brother had not measured up to Lord Henry, and angry as she was, Rhona could understand why. Poor Alfric, 'twas not his fault he was weak and frightened and so willing to please. Lady Jenova would eat him alive if they ever did marry. But Rhona knew in her heart that they would not.

Jesu, she was not about to tell her father that! Instead she would spin some tale about Jenova still being undecided, and that Alfric was gradually whittling down her defenses. That there was still *hope*. . . . With luck, Rhona's lies would hold his rage in check until she came up with a better plan. And to come up with a better plan, she needed information from inside Gunlinghorn Keep: She needed a spy.

That was the other reason Rhona was walking out here despite the bitter cold; the real reason she had come to Gunlinghorn on what was clearly a fool's errand.

He had been in the castleyard when they'd arrived. *Reynard*. He had been striding from the direction of the stables, crossing the path of her mounted entourage. Most certainly he was just as arrogant and rude as she remembered, because he had not troubled to lower his eyes from hers. His gaze, dark and amused, had slid over her like a touch, making her shiver from more than the cold.

Rhona had stared back at him, but it had been she who had dropped her eyes first.

He was a stranger and a servant, she reminded herself. Rough and uncouth, ill-mannered and unkempt. Although mayhap not quite as unkempt as she had first thought, for this morning he had appeared quite well turned out in a Lincoln green tunic and brown breeches, with a studded belt fastened about his hips. She had even spied a ring upon his finger—the jewel in it had flashed yellow in the wane light as he'd pushed his dark hair out of his eyes.

Rhona took a steadying breath. Why did he disturb

her so? What was it about him? She had manipulated many men, teased them into doing as she'd wanted and, occasionally, when it had been absolutely necessary, gone further. Her body was but a counter that she used to play the game, and hopefully win it. She did not allow her feelings to interfere in such matters; her father had taught her that when he had callously offered her maidenhead in return for land. Her purity as a Norman lady for a portion of the Welsh Marches.

The experience had not been as unpleasant as she had feared—she remembered her own sniveling terror and the man's kindness. But Rhona had learned a lesson from that; she had learned that she had a very strong stratagem if she wished to use it. And if the use of her body would mean the difference between winning or losing, the difference between her father's rage and his smiles, then Rhona felt she had no choice.

It did not matter anyway. It was just flesh. Those men might hold her and mold her to their hands, but they could not touch her heart or her soul. She remained free, she remained Rhona. At least that was what she told herself over and over again. Until she almost believed it.

This particular game she planned now was probably the most important of all, the most desperate that she had ever played. If Alfric failed, then her father would likely kill him. And Rhona did not think she could bear to be at Hilldown Castle all on her own. . . .

"Surely 'tis too chilly out here for a fine lady like you."

Ah, he had found her.

Rhona wiped the smug smile from her mouth and turned to face him. Jesu, he was bigger than she had thought! But then Rhona herself was small. Many people, particularly men, underestimated her for that very reason.

"And who are you, churl?"

His onyx eyes glittered a moment. Rhona couldn't tell if her rudeness annoyed him or amused him.

"My name is Reynard, my lady. I am Lord Henry's man, his servant. Before that I was a mercenary, and before that I worked with my father, who was . . . well, you do not want to hear about the life of a churl."

Rhona lifted a thin, dark brow. "Why would I not want to hear? I am curious about all manner of creatures, great and lowly, kings and churls."

He shifted on his feet, settling himself. The cold did not seem to affect him, while Rhona could barely contain her shudders. "My father was a shipwright in Brittany, and then here at Gunlinghorn. His ships sailed for ports as far away as Genoa. He always said his work would live on, long after he died, and so it has. His ships still follow the trade routes. Few men can claim that, my lady, be they kings or churls."

The pride in his voice surprised her, threw her off balance. She had little pride in her own father, and certainly no love. For a moment she was actually envious of him, this servant with the intense gaze.

"Then why is his son a servant to Lord Henry of Montevoy?" she asked him coolly, hoping to sting him into a retort.

His dark eyes narrowed, but he was only considering whether or not to answer her question. She could see the exact moment when he decided nay—she had had practice herself in telling lies. Strangely, she was disappointed, which was plainly foolish. Why should he tell her the real story of his life, and why should she care?

"He pays better," he said with a shrug of his big shoulders and took a step closer. His body gave out heat and the rare scent of cinnamon, such a pleasant combination it made Rhona want to move closer. Snuggle up against him. There was something about Reynard that made her feel safe.

To feel safe is dangerous. There is no safety in men. They are all of them out for what they can steal. And if they steal a woman's self-respect, her pride, her virtue, even her life, so much the better. . . .

"*I* can pay you, Reynard," Rhona said quietly and gazed directly into his eyes. He was watching her now with rapt attention, and that was good. In a moment she would have him in the palm of her hand.

"In what coin, and for what purpose would you pay me, lady?"

"In whatever coin you wish, and for the purpose of passing on news from Gunlinghorn."

He snorted. "Spying, you mean."

"No, sharing what you hear. I need to know the situation between Lord Henry and Lady Jenova. My brother"—she sighed, and cast up her eyes in pretended despair—"he loves her still, and he wants to continue to woo her. At the moment she spurns him, but there will come a time, I am sure, when she will view his person with more favor."

He watched her, reading her, and she awaited his answer as if her breath had not quickened and her heart was not tapping urgently against her ribs.

"Do the men you ask usually agree to your demands?" he said quite coldly.

Surprised, Rhona raised both slim eyebrows. "Usually, Reynard. Do you object to me asking? There is no law that I know of to stop me asking. And whatever answer you give is entirely your own."

He ignored her measured response. "So money is enough for them?"

"Of course."

He looked away, across the snowy ground to the wall that surrounded the garden. She thought he did it to gain time, so she held her peace, waiting, wondering what he was thinking. Some men found it more difficult than others to be bribed, but it was rare for any to refuse her. She tended to choose her victims well.

"I prefer my payment in flesh."

Her breathing stopped, and then restarted with a gasp. "*What* did you say, churl?"

He was staring down at her now, a burning expression in his eyes that made her feel quite dizzy. "You said you would pay me in whatever coin I wanted. I want *you*, my lady. I will spy for you, aye, but only for the payment of my choice. For each piece of information I give to you, I want your body in return."

Rhona gave a laugh, but it had a forced sound. "You are a servant, Reynard, and I am a lady. Do you not see something amiss in your request?"

"I see a man and a woman."

"With a great chasm between them. Our positions, our birth, Reynard. There is no comparison."

He ignored that as if it had no bearing. " 'Tis said that you are no maid."

Heat burned her face, and her hands trembled violently as she gripped them together beneath her cloak. She meant to berate him, to answer him with anger. Instead she heard herself say in a small voice, "Do they?"

" 'Tis said your father used your maidenhead as payment for some land on the Welsh border. He would have sold you as a wife, but the man was already wed to some other woman."

Rhona felt cold, colder even than the air around her. The fur lining of her hood brushed her cheek as she drew it closer, trying to feel warm again. Jesu, how had he heard that? It was supposed to have been secret, something never to be spoken of, hardly ever to be thought of. And now Reynard was stating it out loud, as if it was common knowledge. That her father had bartered her maidenhead when he could not use it in marriage, all for the price of some land on the Welsh Marshes. . . .

"I wonder then that you want me at all," she managed, her voice husky with repressed emotion, "if you believe such lies about me. Not that it matters what you believe!"

He took a step right up to her. That heady scent of cinnamon again filled her senses. Tugging at them in a way she had never felt before. She was no longer sure she was in control of herself or the situation.

"I do not care what you have done, or what you have been, Rhona. Such things do not matter to me. I want you, and I will tell you all my secrets, and Lord Henry's, too, if you will pay me as I ask."

His voice was quiet and compelling, and she found herself believing him. Almost. But he was a servant. She shouldn't even contemplate granting his request. Men of wealth and power and breeding were different, and she had bartered herself more than once to get what she'd wanted. It had meant nothing to her, she had told herself, and she had felt nothing. Another arrow in her quiver, that was all—she repeated the well-worn phrase. But suddenly it did seem so tempting for her to tell Reynard yes. Her cool, scheming mind was in a great deal of conflict with the emotions she kept locked up tight inside her.

It is because he is a servant.

The words repeated in her mind. She had never stooped so low before—to sleep with a servant to gain what she wanted. And yet, as Rhona looked up into Reynard's strong, handsome face, it didn't feel like stooping. It felt like want, like need. There was a sensation inside her, warm and liquid and pleasant. It felt like desire.

Rhona had never desired a man before. She had never allowed herself to do so. Far too dangerous. But now she wanted to smooth her fingers over his skin, brush back the untidy lock of hair at his brow, lean into his big, strong body and feel his arms close about her. She wanted to taste his mouth and have his hands cover her breasts. She wanted to have him naked in her bed.

For the first time in her life she wanted a man in her bed for her own pleasure rather than for the sake of some cold, calculating scheme.

"No," she said and stepped back, putting distance between them. "No, I will not pay you in such a way. It is coin or nought, make your choice."

She had lost him. She knew it the moment she spoke. He would not bend, he would not change his mind. His way was the only way. Well, so be it! There were plenty of other servants in Gunlinghorn.

But none others so well placed.

"Well? What is your decision?" she asked coldly, pretending indifference when her body felt as tense as a harp string.

Reynard stood before her, big and bold, the look in his eyes telling her he was his own man and not hers. She had thought to bully him into doing her will; she had thought a smile and a gold coin would be enough. It always had been before with such men as he.

"Nay, Lady Rhona. I will not sell myself for money. The deal can only be struck if both of us give up something that matters. Something that is part of ourselves."

"You are handing me information, Reynard, not the keys to paradise!"

"I am handing you my soul, my lady. You must give me something comparable in return."

"My body?" she said, louder than she meant. "Where is the glory in that, churl?"

His black eyes slid down her and back, and he smiled. A shudder ran through her, and this time it was definitely not from the cold. "Oh, there would be glory, my lady. Do not doubt it."

"The answer is no, now let me pass."

He did not move, continuing to stand in her path. Just as Rhona thought she would have to back down and step around him, he moved aside with a low, mocking bow. Rhona hurried off, her cheeks hot and pink despite the winter's day.

Churl! She would find someone else. He was not worth the effort. How dare he . . . how dare he. . . . Rhona lost the thought halfway through. Her anger was keeping her warm, but beneath it something else lay, cold and hard as ice. Regret. For a moment she had so wanted to say yes.

Reynard watched her go, his gaze lingering on the furious sway of her hips, the arrogant tilt of her head. She was a little beauty, no mistake, and it was a shame she had refused him. That she was also a liar and a cheat, and wanted to bring down Lord Henry and Lady Jenova with her manipulating ways, bothered him not at all. He could see past that to the possibilities that lay deep in her heart.

He had looked into her brown eyes and seen something proud and stubborn and wounded. It had made him feel almost protective. He did not want to hurt her, but he could not allow her to hurt others. He hadn't really believed that comment about selling her maidenhead, although the man

who had told him had been one of Lord Baldessare's former grooms, now come to work for Lady Jenova.

What father would do that to his daughter?

Evidently Baldessare would—there had been no mistaking the dismayed acknowledgement in her lovely face.
Probably that was where she had gotten the idea that she
could have anything she wanted if she was prepared to
offer herself in return. To men of breeding with plenty of
money, that is. The groom had also been keen to impart
other gossip, tales of Lady Rhona's activities, which,
even if exaggerated, still caused Reynard to wonder if she
was truly the lady she pretended to be.

But Reynard had seen enough of the world to know
that sometimes, out of desperation and despair, people
found it necessary to act in a manner they would not otherwise have contemplated. Mayhap Lady Rhona was desperate? Or mayhap she despaired?

Or mayhap she just enjoyed men?

Reynard remembered how she had looked at him, as if
she had certainly enjoyed the thought of him and her, together. She had made much of the fact that he was a
churl, but he did not think that would have mattered if he
had held her in his arms.

He shook his head to clear his mind. She was entan-
gling him in desire and he hadn't even had her yet! But he
would, oh he would. Although Reynard considered himself an experienced ladies' man, and with justification, he
knew when to take a step back. His senses were giving
him that warning right now.

Lady Rhona had an air of danger about her. She
thought she had his measure. Reynard smiled. She was an
apprentice compared to him. He could read her as his father the shipwright had read the weather. She had said
nay to him for now, but she would be back.

Chapter 13

The great hall at Gunlinghorn rang with merriment. The castlefolk ate, drank, chattered and enjoyed the entertainment. Raf cuddled close to Jenova, sleepy-eyed, his little warm body reminding her of how fortunate she was. And how fortunate Raf was, never to grow up with a father like Baldessare!

She glanced at Henry where he sat contentedly, listening to something Agetha said. He had made Jenova blush once tonight already, with his praise of Agetha's violet soap. His charming smile and words had been all for Agetha, but the hot glint in his eyes had searched for and found Jenova.

I will never be able to smell violets again without growing hard, he had told her after their bath together. Jenova had laughed and retorted that next time he must try her own rose-scented soap. As if he would be with her a long, long time. As if they had forever.

He was not like Mortred, she admitted that now. In

her heart she had known it all along. He was honorable and noble and trustworthy, all the things she cherished in a man. And he was kind and generous and protective of her and Raf and Gunlinghorn. He was all that and more. And she did not want him to leave.

Jenova sighed. She had a strong urge to tell him about her growing doubts where Baldessare was concerned, but she stilled her tongue. Henry might think she was telling him simply to keep him here, with her. He would know she was quite capable of looking after herself—she was the Lady of Gunlinghorn after all. But it was true, she was anxious, and she was beginning to think she had reason.

That reason was Alfric.

Earlier, he had managed a few words alone with her despite her machinations. Agetha had left to see to an errand—the girl no doubt believed herself to be helping her hero—and Alfric had begun a long speech about loving her above all others. Jenova had stopped him and reiterated her former declaration. "I will not change my mind. I am sorry, Alfric. Forgive me if I have hurt you."

His face had paled. "I may forgive you, but my father never will. He will force us into marriage, lady," he had added, urgently. "Believe me, 'tis better if you wed me of your own free will. You will not like my father's way of doing things."

Jenova had stood up, staring down at him. "Are you threatening me, Alfric?"

Alfric had shaken his head, his eyes bright with tears. "Nay, my lady, I am trying to *help* you." Without another word, he had also risen to his feet, bowed, and left her.

Jenova had remained standing, feeling increasingly uneasy. She still felt uneasy, many hours later. It sounded as if Alfric thought Lord Baldessare would force her into marriage with his son. He could not be so foolish. And yet Alfric had seemed to think he would—he had looked sick with fear.

Jenova shifted restlessly, causing Raf to murmur in complaint. Why had she said she would marry Alfric in the first place? What had she been thinking? She had seen enough of what marriage could do to women who were unhappy in their choices, or the choices made for them. Foolish, foolish Jenova. She had thought to revenge herself on Mortred's memory . . . instead she had put herself and all who depended upon her at risk.

"Jenova?"

Henry was leaning toward her, his blue eyes curious. "You look so serious," he said. "What is wrong?"

"There is nought wrong." She shook off her introspection, determined to put on a brave face. "Do you like the mummers?"

Henry glanced at the players dressed in their outlandish costumes. They were meant to be Saracens, but they looked more like bundles of rags. His brilliant gaze came back to her, seeming to delve into her very soul.

"I like the mummers. I like everything about Gunlinghorn."

Did he mean it? Was he no longer pining for London? She thought he did mean it—there was an openness in his face. Mayhap Gunlinghorn had wound its spell upon him at last. But was it strong enough to hold him?

"Will the Baldessares return?" he asked her, interrupting her thoughts. "I thought they had gone for good last time. Have we really seen the last of them?"

He had not known of their visit until afterwards, and then he had appeared, outwardly at least, to be amused by Alfric's persistence. But now there was a spark of irritation in his blue eyes, a touch of impatience to his smile.

Jenova shrugged. "They are my neighbors. I cannot refuse them entry to Gunlinghorn just because they annoy me."

"Why not?" Henry declared. "Put a sign upon the gate; a list of persons not to be admitted because they are bores."

"Henry . . ."

Raf giggled. "You could put Master Will's name on it, Mama. He talks too loudly and doesn't listen to a word you say."

He was clearly repeating something Jenova herself had said, and she shook her head at him, biting her lip on her laughter.

"And Lord Baldessare. He stares about the keep as though he thinks he could do it better."

Jenova did not feel like laughing now. She had not realized Raf was so acute. For one so young, he saw much. Beside her, Agetha clicked her tongue in annoyance, refusing to make fun of Alfric's family. 'Twas a pity, Jenova thought, that Agetha was not as canny as her son. . . . All of a sudden she remembered something Rhona had said, something Jenova had been meant to pass on.

After Alfric had left her in the great hall, Rhona had returned, looking flushed and agitated and quite unlike her usual restrained self. Jenova had been so surprised by her change in appearance and manner that for a moment she had hardly heard what the other woman had been saying.

"Lady Jenova, my father sends Lord Henry a message. He says to tell him that they have a mutual friend. Someone who knows of *le château de Nuit.*"

"I beg your pardon? I do not under—"

"I must go." The other woman's eyes were quite bright and a little wild. "Will you deliver the message to him?"

"*Château de Nuit.* Of course. But what does it mean?"

But Rhona had gone, hurrying after her brother, leaving Jenova bewildered and more than a little upset.

Le château de Nuit? It was an odd name, a dismal sort of name, and not one she had ever heard from Henry's lips. It seemed odd that Baldessare was sending such a message to Henry, a man he hated. Perhaps it was to make mischief. Jenova contemplated the idea of not telling him at all, but she was not the sort of woman to withhold information that did not belong to her.

"Lady Rhona spoke of something when she was here, Henry. A place you might know. She says you and her father have a mutual friend."

Henry turned his blue eyes on her, smiling. There was a new tension in his body, a new tightness about his jaw. "Oh?"

"It is a little strange. The name of a castle."

"Probably some new estate he claims I have stolen off him. I see I will have to give him every acre I own just to be rid of him. What is the name of this castle, Jenova?"

"It is called *le château de Nuit.* Have you heard of it?"

The smile was still on his mouth, his eyes were still fixed on hers, but it was as if he was no longer there. His body was empty, a husk without substance. Henry was gone, apart from a muscle in his cheek, which gave a violent twitch.

"Henry?" she said sharply, reaching out her hand toward him. But the unsettling moment had already passed. Henry was looking down into his wine goblet with a little frown, his hair falling forward to hide his eyes.

"The name is not one I know, or if I ever did, I have forgotten it. Did Lady Rhona say where she had got it from?"

"I believe she said a mutual friend of both her father

and you. She impressed upon me that it was important, but Henry, she was acting very strangely. I think something had disturbed her when she—"

Henry shook his head, still staring intently into his wine. "Nay, it means nothing to me, sweeting." He looked up at her and gave a grin. "I did not think Baldessare had any friends!"

She laughed even while she was thinking, *He called me sweeting. He never calls me that in front of others. He must be rattled if he has forgotten to watch his tongue. What can it mean? What is this place, this* château de Nuit?

"Raf," Henry was speaking to her son. "Tell your Mama what Raven did today."

Raf's face lit up with the memory, and he began to tell her a long, rambling tale of the black stable cat and her kittens. Jenova pretended to listen, making the right sounds in the right places, but she couldn't help but wonder if Henry had changed the subject on purpose to give himself time to recover. Out of the corner of her eye, she watched him. His normally healthy skin was pallid, almost sickly, and his mouth was closed hard, so that deep lines were clearly visible, slashing through his cheeks.

For the first time since Jenova had known him, Henry appeared old and worn, as though his devils had caught up with him.

Jenova pulled herself up. Such thoughts were strange to her. Henry would never have done a thing so terrible that he was afraid to tell her of it. Henry had never pretended to be faithful, and she was aware that he had had many women. He was also a knight who had fought in many battles and killed many men. No doubt he held secrets with the king, matters pertaining to the kingdom and those who might wish to harm it.

Heavy secrets perhaps, but nothing to make him look so ravaged.

Le château de Nuit.

What did it mean? Henry was pretending he had never heard the name before, when it was perfectly obvious to Jenova that he had, and that it meant something very important to him indeed. Blast Baldessare! Why could he not leave them alone?

"Mama? You have stopped listening to me!"

Raf was tugging at her sleeve impatiently. Jenova apologized, promising to listen now, but when she glanced up to include Henry in the moment, she found he was watching her with a strange, bleak expression in his eyes. As if he were a stranger.

Or she were.

Henry stood on the roof of Gunlinghorn Keep and looked out across the lush paddocks and water meadows and woods that comprised Jenova's lands, all the way to the sea. He could not see the cold, heaving waves in the darkness—there were clouds across the moon—but he knew it was there. Just as *le château de Nuit* was there, at the back of his mind. Waiting, always waiting.

He had hoped that that particular part of his life was gone, but at the same time he had always feared it was not. That it would return when he least expected it and destroy him.

And now it seemed that Baldessare knew the name. Henry could not imagine where he had found it out, or who had told it to him. Aye, that was the big question. *Who?* What nameless creature had remembered him and unburdened his soul to others? Whatever the circumstance, Baldessare had the name, and the implied threat was that he would use it.

King William would distance himself from his friend. Henry fully understood what such revelations would mean to his comfortable life at court. It would be over. And yet, for some strange reason, it was not the king he thought of now. It was Jenova, and what *she* would think of him when she knew about that place.

She would never be able to touch him and kiss him, to smile at him with that same glow in her green eyes. When she understood that Lord Henry, the handsome, woman-izing, oh-so-clever Lord Henry, with his witty tongue and brilliant mind, was but a sham. A façade behind which the real Henry hid, the boy with the tear-streaked face and trembling lip, who crept through the woods sur-rounding *le château de Nuit*.

Jenova had never known that boy.

Henry had taken great care that no one would ever know him.

But now it seemed that Baldessare knew. Knew enough to make his veiled threats, anyway. Henry wondered if he could discover just how detailed Baldessare's knowledge was before he made his next move. And he needed to know exactly what Baldessare wanted, or if he was just enjoying tormenting Henry. Revenging himself for all the supposed wrongs and slights Henry had committed upon him.

Henry didn't think so. Baldessare never did anything without hoping to gain something material. It was greed and avarice that ruled that man.

There is nothing I can do but wait and see. And keep a watch over my shoulder. . . .

And hope he could stop whatever catastrophe was coming before it crushed him.

"He will kill us. I know it. We can never be free of him." Rhona looked over at her brother's slumped form—a shadow in the darkness—his frightened words echoing in her head. She tried to think of something comforting to say, just as she always had. For once her clever mind was blank, her cunning tongue silenced, and she realized she was as frightened as Alfric. So much depended upon her now. She wasn't sure if she was up to the task.

She remembered again how they had returned to Hilldown Castle, routed by Lady Jenova but pretending otherwise. Their father was in a rage, one of his white-hot furies that even Rhona could not dampen with sweet reason. She had tried, but before she had been able to utter more than a few words, she had realized that their father knew.

He *knew*.

He had a spy at Gunlinghorn, and that spy had heard and seen enough to understand that Jenova had refused Alfric utterly.

"Why have I been cursed with two such useless spawn!" Baldessare had screamed, shaking his fists in the air. "I ask one simple request! One . . . simple . . . request . . ."

Alfric had whimpered and covered his head, knowing what was coming. His father had promptly thrown a goblet at him, and then another, and then the wine jug after them. Sour wine had dripped from Alfric's hair and clothing. The castle dogs had begun to bark with excitement and fright, circling him, not understanding that this was no game.

Baldessare had stood, panting, his face puce, and Rhona had closed her eyes and waited for him to begin to use his fists. And then she had heard it. Laughing. He was *laughing!* Her eyes had opened wide and she had watched, uneasy still, as the color had faded from his raddled face and his cold eyes had lost some of their craziness. Alfric had continued to huddle in the corner, rocking himself and moaning, but the dogs had begun licking at him—evidently the wine had been to their taste.

Mayhap it had looked funny, but Rhona had not been able to laugh. She had felt too sick at heart. The thoughts had run crazily through her mind. Was this to be her life? To be forever afraid of this man and what he could do to her, or have done to her. She could not live thus. She *could* not. . . .

As if he had read her mind, her father had turned and stared at her.

Remembering it now, Rhona shuddered and hugged herself, but at the time she had found herself frozen to the spot. Years of living with terror had taken away her ability to run, and even if she had run, where could she have gone? Jesu, where *was* there to go?

"Help me to destroy Lord Henry, and wed Lady Jenova, and you can have whatever you wish, Rhona."

Help you? She had licked her lips and swallowed, trying to find her voice. For a moment his words had made no sense. "Help you?" she had managed. "I have tried to help you, my lord. What more can I do?"

"That is for you to decide," he had said, as cold as he had been boiling with rage a moment earlier.

"If I help you, can I . . . can I have my freedom, my lord? A house in Normandy, mayhap? A life there."

He had stared at her, his face unreadable, and then he had smiled. A slow, savage smile, with a touch of pride in it. As if he'd seen a part of himself in her. "Away from me, you mean? Aye, why not. Get me what I want, Rhona, and I will have no need of you anymore. You can do what you like."

Her legs had trembled so badly that Rhona had thought she might have fallen over, but she'd locked her knees and stood straight. Her face had been deathly pale. "You say you want the Lady Jenova, my lord, but do you want her for my brother . . . or for yourself?"

He had stilled, arrested by the thought. It clearly had not occurred to him before. And if Jenova was to wed Baldessare rather than Alfric, then Alfric, too, would be free of his father.

Both of us to escape this monstrous place, and the monster within it. . . .

Her eyes had remained fixed on her father. All manner of emotions had passed across his face, and she'd noted each one. Excitement, lust, anticipation and greed. Oh, especially greed. Greed for Jenova's lands and her wealth, greed for her spirit and her beauty, greed for her body. Baldessare would enjoy breaking Jenova into one of those sniveling creatures he preferred.

Rhona had planted a seed and it had taken root, and with any luck it would grow into a tree that would shelter both her and her brother. That was all that mattered, she had told herself. That was all she must consider.

Abruptly Baldessare had nodded. "You are right, as always. I want her for myself, Daughter."

Rhona had nodded slowly, refusing to feel pity for the other woman. This was a matter of life or death, her own life or death. "Then I will get her for you," she had said, as if it were the simplest thing in the world.

Her father's eyes had flicked to Alfric, and a spasm of his earlier rage had crossed his face. "Get him out of here."

Rhona had not needed to be told twice. She'd hurried to Alfric's side, shooing away the dogs and lifting him with trembling arms, murmuring in his ear. He'd leaned heavily against her as she'd led him from the hall and the scene of yet another humiliation.

"I hate him, I hate him!" he had wept, his face con-
torted like a child's, stumbling along by her side. "I want
to use it now, Rhona! Let's use it now, and run away!"

"It" was the sleeping potion that they had been keeping hidden, to use at such a time they needed to run from
Hilldown Castle. But the time had never been right, and
they had always known that, once he woke from his stu-
por, their father would pursue them.

Rhona's arm had closed tighter, a warning. "So do I,"
she had whispered. "But what good is a sleeping potion if
he will wake and find us? Do not despair yet, Alfric. I will
take you to your room and you can rest there. I have a
plan that I believe will set us free."

He had looked at her in disbelief. "Free?" he'd spat.
"We will never be free."

But they would, Rhona thought now, gazing again at
the huddled form of her brother. They would be free, finally free. And she knew just the man to help them.

The winter dawn was a pale wash of blue and pink on
the horizon. Reynard, on his way to the stables to see
Lord Henry's horse readied for his morning ride, paused
to stare. There was beauty in that sky, but a cold, bleak
sort of beauty. He preferred warmer climes himself, a hot
yellow sun and a blue sea and bright-colored houses
along the foreshore.

"Reynard!"

One of the grooms was slouching toward him, wiping
a sleeve across his nose. It was Formac, the man who
used to work for Baldessare. Reynard suspected he was
still Baldessare's servant at heart.

"I have a message for you, Reynard." Formac put a finger to his lips in the childlike gesture for secrecy, but his
eyes were hard and knowing. "A certain lady has asked

that you meet her after the midday meal, at Uffer's Tower. Do you know it? It's a ruined castle or somefing, in the woods, on the border of Gunlinghorn and Hilldown."

Uther's Tower was a falling-down pile of timber and masonry that had acquired a certain reputation among the local folk. A place of assignation for lovers, so the rumors said. But Reynard did not allow that to raise his hopes.

"A certain lady?" he asked nonchalantly, but his breath quickened and his body tensed.

Formac reached into his tunic and scratched about. "I was given somefing for you . . . ah, here 'tis."

He brought out a small square of cloth and unwrapped it. A lock of hair, gold as the summer sun Reynard had just been dreaming of. He stared at it, then realized Formac was holding it out to him. He reached to take it in his big hand.

"The lady said to tell you she agrees to your terms."

Reynard nodded, ignoring the other man's curious glance, standing long after Formac had stumped away about his own business. He opened his hand and stared again at the smooth, golden lock of hair that lay within. It seemed to him that he could still smell the scent of her on it. A sweet, elusive perfume.

Lady Rhona. She had agreed to his terms. Her body for his soul.

He should be gleeful, rubbing his hands together in anticipation. He had won, after all. He had a foot in the enemy camp, and a chance to bring down a proud, stuck-up Norman lady. But despite that he felt as if he were wading into a swirling sea, tugged by unseen currents and well out of his depth.

Chapter 14

Jenova grimaced as she threaded her needle, listening to the chatter of her ladies about her. Torn and worn garments and bedding were spread about them, and although one or two were working upon finer items, most were intent upon the tedious task of mending.

Her "ladies" ranged in age from eleven to seventy, and Jenova had the care of them all. It was part of her duty as Lady of Gunlinghorn, but normally she found it no chore. Today, however, her ladies were intent upon a subject she would rather have left untouched.

Henry.

"He is so handsome," little Yolande sighed. "His eyes are bluer than . . ." But an item for comparison eluded her.

"Bluebells?" someone else suggested. "The sea in July?"

"He looks upon you very warmly, my lady," said Gertrude, seemingly intent upon her work, but making mischief as always. "He is very fond of you, I believe."

"We are friends," Jenova replied levelly. "We have known each other since we were children."

"I wish I had a friend like Lord Henry," Yolande said wistfully.

"He is like a father to Master Raf," Gertrude went on, very daring today.

Agetha frowned. "That is enough chatter. Lord Henry is not Master Raf's father and never will be."

Gertrude smirked. "And neither will Lord Alfric, now. I am glad he is gone. I did not like him."

Agetha's face flamed, but Jenova intervened before something was said or done that might embarrass them all. "Your likes and dislikes are of no interest to us, Gertrude. Look, you have an uneven stitch. Unpick it and do it again."

Gertrude's mouth set mulishly, but she did as she was told. For a moment silence reigned in the solar.

"Will Lord Henry be staying at Gunlinghorn?" Yolande was not to be diverted.

"His life is in London," Jenova said, and though her voice did not betray her, she felt a prickling behind her eyes. She did not want him to go, but how could she stop him? Henry had his own life, and she had hers. It had been understood between them from the beginning that he would leave eventually.

"Mayhap you should ask him to stay," Gertrude murmured. "Sometimes men need to be prompted in these matters. Mayhap he does not know you will miss him so much, my lady."

Jenova blinked in startled amusement.

"Thank you, Gertrude," Agetha retorted. "When Lady Jenova needs your fourteen-year-old wisdom, she will ask for it."

Their voices went on, bickering gently, joking and giggling. Jenova let them wash over her. *Ask him.* She did not know whether she could do that. He might refuse, or worse, laugh at her presumption that he might wish to stay here at Gunlinghorn when his life in London was so much more exciting.

And what of this place, this château? *Le château de Nuit.* There was a mystery there she had yet to unravel.

Jenova sighed. In the old days, when they had been merely friends, things had been easier. She had not been afraid to say anything to him then. Now it was different. She felt as if her words could be misconstrued, or worse, that Henry might see past her barriers and into her heart. He could hurt her now far more than he could before.

Ask him to stay.

She would be risking her feelings, but if she did not ask, she would never know his answer. Mayhap Gertrude was right, mayhap Henry didn't realize how much she would miss him.

I will then, she told herself, fingers trembling as she tried to sew. *I will ask him to stay, and if he refuses, then I will laugh and pretend I do not mind. But if he agrees . . .*

Jenova smiled to herself.

"Sea holly," she said abruptly. "His eyes are the color of sea holly."

And then blushed when all her ladies turned to gaze at her as if she had gone mad.

Rhona peered down through the mist that hung about the lower parts of the hill, winding through the trees like skeins of wool, clinging with damp fingers to their trunks and bare branches. Everything was so still, so silent.

She tried to subdue the flicker of fear inside her, the

doubts. Oh, she did not doubt that she would be able to carry off this exchange with Reynard. She had done it before. Her doubts were more to do with whether she would be able to save Alfric and herself, fulfill her bargain with her father, and buy their freedom from him forever. For once they reached Normandy, Rhona knew she would never return to Hilldown, nor would she ever allow him to reenter their lives.

Uther's Tower was behind her, amongst the trees, a mishmash of stone and timber, some falling down, some in remarkably good condition.

So here she was, in the freezing damp wood, alone in the mist. Lady Rhona, whose grace and manner portrayed her as a lady of highborn Norman blood, whose garments and jewelry were exquisite. But it was a sham. Beneath it all, Rhona knew she was nothing but a prisoner of her gender and her father's cruelty.

This morning, Rhona had sat and watched Baldessare gorge himself on cold meats and bread, washing it down with gulps of ale. He had seemed in a good humor, though Rhona had not known why. Unless it had been because he had dreamed last night of being wed to Lady Jenova. The thought had made her shudder, but she'd pushed it aside, and with it the knowledge that she was responsible for this change in direction. She could not afford to think of what would happen to Jenova—she had herself and Alfric to save.

Baldessare had slammed his ale mug down on the trestle table, making her jump. "I wish I could tell *Lord* Henry that his privileged life is coming to an end. That he will no longer be the king's favorite, his pet. Aye, I will make him sorry for all the humiliations and defeats he has made me suffer."

"If anyone can make him sorry, then it is you, Father."

Baldessare had fixed his cold eyes upon her. Rhona had returned his stare calmly enough, though inside her rib cage, her heart had been pounding like a warning drum.

"Do not fail me in this, Daughter." He had said it so quietly, but it had been no less of a threat.

Rhona had smiled. It had been the bravest thing she had ever done. "I never fail, my lord."

She hadn't told him about Reynard and this meeting; she had paid that thief Formac twice as much as usual to deliver the message and keep the details quiet. It had seemed safer somehow to keep as much as possible to herself.

A bird flapped up from the undergrowth, wings whirring. Rhona shifted her seat on her mount, feeling her feet going numb despite the fur-lined boots.

"My lady."

His voice was deeper than she remembered, with a rich timbre that set her senses quivering and humming. Rhona jerked her horse around, wondering how he had snuck up on her like that, without a sound. He was walking toward her through the trees. A heavy cloak covered him from shoulders to heels, but his head was bare, his dark hair damp from the mist.

"Reynard."

He came closer, looking up at her, his dark eyes flattering her squirrel-lined cloak and the red wool gown beneath it. She had left off her veil, braiding her hair and laying the long plait over one shoulder. She knew her skin was white from the cold, her nose pink, her lips rosy red, but Reynard did not seem to find fault in any of that—in fact he looked as if he could devour her on the spot.

Her breath came faster. This was a contract, she reminded herself. A way to get information, to get what her father wanted. It meant nothing personally. She must remain cold and in control, whatever Reynard might do to her.

He was watching her from heavy-lidded eyes. "You asked to meet me here, my lady, and here I am."

"So you are."

Suddenly he smiled, his rather harsh face warming, and held out his gloved hand to her. "Let us go inside before we freeze to death. I have built a fire."

With a sense of abandoning herself to the fates, Rhona held out her arms and slid down to the soft, snowy ground, and into the warmth of Reynard's embrace.

Again she was struck by how very big he was, and yet, strangely, she knew she did not fear him because of it. Being a small woman, she had never felt entirely comfortable in the company of big men, and she had expected it to be no different with Reynard. But it was. Here, now, standing within his muscular arms, she felt safe, protected, as if she did not want to leave them.

Rhona made herself step away, until she was once more solitary. Alone. For good measure she threw him a cold and haughty look. He raised an eyebrow back at her, as if her manner amused him. As if he knew very well what she was really feeling.

He *cannot* know, Rhona reminded herself firmly, pressing back a sense of panic. He is a man, a servant, not a seer. I must not give him a power over me that he does not have.

"A fire?" she said evenly, as if her feelings were not in rebellion. "In Uther's Tower? I did not think there was enough of it left to keep out the rain, let alone sit in in comfort."

"You will see. Come, and we will talk."

Talk? Only talk?

She hesitated a moment more, but her feet were beginning to turn into lumps of ice and she had lost the feeling in her hands. Even her teeth ached. She wanted to be warm. Besides, she was tired of mistrusting everyone, of being afraid. With a proud lift of her head, Rhona allowed him to lead her back into the mist-swathed trees toward Uther's Tower, trailing her horse behind them.

When they reached it, Reynard pushed open the stout door and entered, stooping his head beneath the lintel. Gratefully Rhona followed. It was a single room, dim and small but weatherproof. The fire Reynard had built in the center of the floor did little to help the murky atmosphere, but Rhona was willing to put up with a little smoke if she could be warm. She hurried across and held out her hands, trying not to groan with the pleasure of it. It might be close and smoky in here, but actually it wasn't as filthy as some of the huts of the serfs and villeins she'd seen on the Hilldown estate. Lord Baldessare was not a man who wasted his gold or his compassion upon those who could not help him further his ambitions.

"I will put your horse with mine, under shelter," Reynard said. "Sit down and warm yourself, my lady, while I am gone." The door closed behind him, and she was alone.

He had set a stool by the fire, and she sat upon it, arranging her skirts and pretending she did not feel awkward and ill at ease. He was being so kind. Rhona was not used to kindness. In fact, she was far more used to unkindness than to this tender care that Reynard was displaying.

Now that her eyes had adjusted somewhat, and her hands and feet had thawed out, Rhona looked about her. The room was clean, with firewood stacked neatly in one corner and straw heaped in another. Enough to make a bed for two. She shivered and hastily looked away, and again she wished she had not chosen this place to meet.

Suddenly she did not want to be here. She did not want to give her body to Reynard, coldly, in payment for his informing on his master. It felt wrong. Her stomach roiled at the idea of it, as if she had eaten something rotten. Instinctively, Rhona gathered her skirts in her hands, preparing to rise to her feet and leave.

But it was already too late.

Reynard had stepped back into the room, accompanied by a swath of mist, and he closed the door firmly against the cold. The fire flickered and settled back into a steady glow. For a moment he stood looking at her, noting her tension, the grip of her hands on the red wool cloth, her wide eyes staring into his.

"There is no need to go," he said quietly, and brushed the snow from his hands. "I won't hurt you, my lady."

"I am not afraid of you," she retorted. It was the truth—she wasn't afraid of Reynard. Only of herself.

Something was happening to her. She was allowing her feelings to interfere with her plan. And such strange feelings . . . feelings she had never allowed herself to experience before.

There was a wooden bench against the wall, and he dragged it across to the fire, so that it was to one side of her. Then he sat down, drawing his cloak about him in a graceful movement and stretching his hands toward the flames. His gloves were thick and mended and his boots were also worn, but of good-quality leather, the toes damp from the snow. His tunic was the Lincoln green one, and his breeches clung to strong muscled thighs and trim hips. He was broad across the shoulders and chest, and he sat a little hunched over, relaxed.

He was unlike any man she had ever met or known or

seen before. She could not stop looking at him; she did not want to. Suddenly he turned his head sideways and looked up at her with a rueful grin.

"So here we are, my lady. Just you and me in Uther's Tower."

For a moment, Rhona was tempted to grin back. She felt like a child, a little girl, confronted by something new and wondrous, and she wanted to partake of it.

"Just you and me, with a bargain to seal," she said now, drawing herself up proudly, reminding herself why she was here. "Let us get it over and done."

She went to rise to her feet, wondering as she did so whether her legs would hold her. But he reached out and caught her hand, preventing her trying. Rhona went still, staring into his eyes, wondering what he meant to do. She saw compassion in the dark depths. Did he actually dare to pity her? A churl, a servant, pity a Norman lady! Her face hardened as the anger swept through her, and she was grateful for it.

"I have done this before, Reynard. Do not think I am a poor maiden sacrificing herself for you. I am a Norman lady and I can well look after myself!"

"Now do not tear into me, my lady," Reynard said wryly, but still he did not let her hand go. His fingers were warm and strong and rough from work. In the midst of her fury, Rhona wanted to cling to them for dear life and never let go. "I want you," he went on, "believe me I do. If I were truly a churl, I would show you that part of me that wants you the most. But I do not want to lie with you here. Not hastily and without feeling, as if we were beasts. I want to enjoy you, my lady, but for me to do that, *you* must enjoy *me*."

She felt frozen, her hand still clinging to his.

No. No, no, no! We made a bargain. I agreed to his

terms and now he has changed the rules. Enjoy him? I cannot allow myself to enjoy him, or to enjoy being with him. I cannot allow my feelings to become engaged. That is not how it works. If I were to ever feel while I were paying my debts, I would curl up and die. If I were ever to take a long, hard look at what I have become, then I would want to die.

And yet Rhona realized, with a surge of dismay, that that was exactly what she did want. She wanted to have Reynard take her with feeling, with joy, with meaning. That was why she had felt ill at the idea of consummating their bargain in cold blood. When she looked at Reynard she did not feel cold; she felt hot. And it was only in heat that he and she should come together.

"My lady," he murmured, "Rhona." His tug on her hand brought her back to herself, just as he pulled her up from the stool. Her knees gave way. She tumbled into his arms. He caught her easily, settling her on his lap, enfolding her against his chest, pressing her head to his shoulder. And she sat there where he had placed her, stiff as a board, as unresponsive as it was possible for her to be, and yet inside her all was turmoil.

She should not feel like this. For her own sake, she must not. Rhona had learned long ago that to care for someone was to invite pain into one's heart. To survive in this harsh world one needed to have a heart of stone.

"I told you my father was a shipwright," Reynard murmured in her ear.

"You did," she said, her voice husky and small, as it had been in the garden at Gunlinghorn Keep. "What of it?" she added, more forcefully.

"I did not tell you he was also a navigator. He could read the stars. When he was younger and more carefree, he traveled to distant lands and saw many strange sights. Lands that were covered in ice the whole year round, and others that were hot and baked and made of sand."

Rhona wanted to make fun of him, to scoff at his words, but they evoked a longing in her that had never been there before. To escape, to travel far away, to be free of her old life. Was such a thing really possible?

"I would like to see those places," Reynard went on.

"Why haven't you, then?" she asked. Her body was growing warmer, and softer, relaxing in his arms. She felt herself molding to his shape, her breasts brushing his tunic, her hands, still resting in her lap, twitching to stretch up and touch his face, twine about his neck, pull his mouth down to hers.

"It seems . . . melancholy to go alone. I would like a companion. Someone to turn to and say, 'Look there!' or to laugh with me when I was happy, or weep with me when I was sad. But to go alone, my lady," he shook his head, "I would rather not go at all."

Rhona took a deep breath. He was spinning her wits like a spider's web. She could not think straight. They had come here to speak of Lord Henry and Lady Jenova. She had much to do, and he was delaying her with foolish tales of icy lands!

"Tell me about your master," she said harshly and pulled away, seating herself once more upon her stool. She straightened her cloak, tossed her golden braid back over her shoulder, and glared at him. "*That* is what you have come to tell."

Reynard smiled, a rueful smile, as if she had caught him out. But he didn't really seem to mind, and he linked his hands between his knees and did as she asked without argument.

"Lord Henry has a fine house in London, with a mistress he changes often, and many powerful friends. And yet he does not want to leave Gunlinghorn."

"And why is that, do you think?"

"Mayhap it is because he is fond of Lady Jenova, and she of him."

"More than fond," Rhona said, "if he has all that awaiting him in London and has not returned."

"She and he are old friends."

"Very old friends."

Reynard lifted his head and looked across at her. "Nay, lady," he was saying earnestly. " 'Tis not as you think. They grew up together in Normandy, and have always been close. Lady Jenova sent word to Lord Henry to come and offer her advice on her marriage to your brother. I do not think Lord Henry advised against it, but the lady decided on her own that she did not want to go ahead with the wedding."

"My father does not believe that, and neither do I."

"I do not think your father wants to believe it."

That was true enough. "Has your master spoken at all of leaving, of returning to London?"

"Aye, he has spoken of it, but he does not wish to leave Lady Jenova while she is at odds with your family. He fears for her safety."

With justification, thought Rhona bleakly. If only Henry and Jenova knew just how dangerous her father was, and that Rhona herself was working against Jenova! Henry would flee to London in an instant and take the lady with him. Perhaps he had thought of that? Rhona knew that if there was any sign of them leaving, she must act to prevent it. She could not let it happen, for if Jenova left, all Rhona's hopes for freedom would go with her.

"I want him to leave, not her," she said coldly, hiding

her fear. " 'Tis in all our interests if Henry leaves as soon as possible, and Lady Jenova remains at Gunlinghorn, alone."

"I see. So, with Lord Henry gone, Lady Jenova will be unprotected and open to your father's persuasions? Is that what you want, my lady?"

Her eyes focused on Reynard, and she found that he was studying her, reading her. How clearly he had seen through her just then! Her heart gave a little flutter. It was best if he did not know what she was planning. She must be careful, very careful. . . .

"I sent a message to your master through Lady Jenova. Le château de Nuit. Did he get it?"

"He got something. He has been like a wounded wolf, snapping and snarling at me, though he pretends to Lady Jenova there is nothing amiss."

Rhona raised her eyebrows. "Really? I did not realize it was so powerful a message. My father says he has a friend who knows a dark secret, something that Henry will do anything to keep hidden."

"And do you know who this friend is, my lady?"

"Nay." Her eyes narrowed suspiciously. "You are very curious, Reynard. I thought 'twas you who did the spying for me, not the other way around."

He reached out his hand and brushed his finger down her cheek, stroking the soft, pale skin with a reverence that took her by surprise. But the glow in his eyes was far from reverent as he said, "I am eager to do well in your service, lady, and receive my reward."

Her breath caught with just a few words and a glance. The dark gleam of his eyes made her body suddenly want to turn all warm and melting in his arms. She was the one in charge of this situation, not he. It was too important for her to lose her wits now.

"There was another reason I asked," he was saying. "Lord Henry is not a trusting man. He will never be completely convinced your father knows anything about this hidden secret until he has more proof. You must give him the name of this friend if you are to master him."

His tone was persuasive, and his words made sense. But more proof? That would mean she would have to speak to her father again, wangle the name from him somehow. It was not something she relished. However, Rhona nodded brusquely and stood up, the fire flickering from the movement of her skirts. "Very well, Reynard, I will find out. Will we meet here next time?"

"Not here. The Black Dog, at Gunlinghorn Harbor. We will be safe there, and it will be more comfortable. Send me word when you are ready to join me there, my lady."

Was it Rhona's imagination, or did he mean something more than just her readiness to hear further information? Nay, she did not think it her imagination—there was that gleam in his eyes again. She pretended not to notice.

"The Black Dog. Very well."

Reynard smiled into her eyes. "Remember," he said softly, "I want you to enjoy me as much as I will enjoy you." And then he turned and led her from the hut. Rhona found herself stumbling behind him, confused, angry. Outside it seemed colder than before, and Rhona waited while he fetched her mount, trying to still her trembling. As she moved to place her foot into the stirrup, Reynard caught her about the waist before she could protest, and tossed her up into the saddle.

Rhona steadied herself and turned, grasping the reins, feeling breathless and flushed. He must not know how he affected her. He must not realize how close she was to admitting the truth. That she would like nothing better than to lie in his arms and lose herself in the kisses of a churl.

"Farewell, Reynard."

"Adieu, my lady." He bowed, but not before she once again caught the dark gleam of his eyes and the teasing smile curling his mouth.

He knew.

God rot him! God curse him! Rhona cantered away from Uther's Tower, her anger keeping her warm. But by the time she reached the bottom of the hill, her bad temper was forgotten and she was daring to dream of the next time.

Thoughtfully, Reynard walked back toward Uther's Tower. Lady Rhona had shown remarkable candor; clearly the need to have Lord Henry leave Gunlinghorn was of much importance to her. Rhona, and through her, Baldessare, wanted the Lady Jenova alone and vulnerable. Reynard frowned, feeling the anger he had been holding back begin to burn. He could guess what that monster planned to do, and it was not pleasant.

Would Henry go? Reynard did not think Henry was the sort of man who would leave a woman defenseless to save his own skin. Besides, Henry would not go anywhere until he knew the name of his enemy, this friend Baldessare had spoken of. Rhona had promised to get that name for him, but he had seen the spark of fear deep in her eyes. Even Baldessare's own daughter was afraid of him, he thought with disgust.

Mayhap she can be turned to our side?

The voice in his head gave him pause. Mayhap she *could* be turned. Reynard did not think she was evil at heart. She was proud, aye, and she had been hurt, and if half the stories about her were true, she had few scruples.

But beneath her chilly exterior was a flesh-and-blood woman. He had held her, felt her tremble, seen the confusion in her beautiful face.

Lady Rhona was very troubled.

Was Reynard the man to save her from herself?

Chapter 15

Far beyond the keep, the sea pounded against the cliffs, white spray caught on the wind and tossed up onto the wharf at Gunlinghorn Harbor. The weather had deteriorated during the night, and although Henry had paid it little heed with Jenova wrapped in his arms beneath the warm furs, early this morning word had come to the castle that another ship had gone aground, a coastal trader seeking shelter from the storm.

"I am worried," Jenova said, and her green eyes were candid as they met Henry's. "Not for the seamen, thankfully they are safe. I am worried that my harbor will fill with silt and be no more. I had such plans, Henry!"

It was a very real fear. Many thriving, busy ports along the coast formed bars or spits that prevented craft from entering, and in some places the deep channels had silted up entirely. There were villages now where once, a hundred years ago, the sea had ebbed and flowed.

"Do you wish me to take a look, sweeting?"

Jenova was very proud of her position as lady, and Henry was careful to not assume more than she was offering. But this time she seemed so woebegone, so in need of help, that he reached out and touched her cheek, his fingers sliding back into her long, curling hair.

She leaned into his palm, nuzzling against him with perfect trust. Like Raf. It made his heart hurt, and the bitterness of his own unworthiness tasted like ashes in his mouth.

"That is generous of you, Henry. I know . . . I know you must have been wishing yourself home in London for many weeks now."

Her dark lashes swept down, hiding her eyes, and she bit her lip. Henry caught his breath. He wanted to take her in his arms and hold her, breathing in the scent of her, feeling the softness of her body, experiencing being with her. He wanted to tell her he would stay with her at Gunlinghorn forever, if she would let him.

But he did not; he dared not.

How could he, when he did not know what secrets Baldessare held? It might not be possible for Henry to stay. Tomorrow, he might be gone, riding north, leaving all this behind him. Leaving Jenova behind him. And yet . . .

"I would do anything for you," he said quietly, and meant it with all his heart.

Jenova looked up at him, pleased surprise widening her green eyes, her mouth curving into a delighted smile. "Anything?" she asked, a little breathless.

Henry made himself smile back, made his voice teasing. "Well, almost anything. I refuse to empty Raf's chamber pot again."

Jenova's lips quivered and she put her fingers to them, her eyes sparkling with laughter. "Oh, Henry, he did not ask it of you?"

Henry sighed. "He did. He did not want Agetha to think he was a baby, needing to relieve himself in the night. I had to pretend the piss was mine."

Jenova gave a giggle, and then another. "Oh Henry." Her laughter faded, and she rested her brow against his. He felt her trembling. "You say you will do anything for me, and I ask you now, before I lose my courage. . . . Will you stay at Gunlinghorn?"

He went cold and hot, one after the other, and suddenly he was trembling as much as she. "Jenova," he whispered, "you know my place is in London. As much as I want to stay, I fear you would grow weary of me and be wishing me gone soon enough. I am . . . you do not know me so well as you think."

He swallowed, wondering if the lump in his throat was from misery or fear; mayhap both. She had asked him to stay, she wanted him to stay, and he should be shouting with joy. Except that she did not know, and if Baldessare let free his secrets and she found out what sort of creature he really was, she would hate him. He would rather not be here to see that in her eyes.

A tear ran down her cheek. "Oh Henry," she said again in a shaky voice. Another tear slid after the first.

This time Henry did take her in his arms, holding her. She dissolved into more tears, and yet he didn't ask why.

He didn't have to.

The sea rolled in, sullen and gray, matching the clouds above. The boat that had struck the sandbar had been dragged clear and now rested against the wharf, unloading its cargo. Master Will was much in evidence, casting his eye over everything, playing at being in charge. He nodded at Henry, but it was clear he was wishing him anywhere but here.

"Not a friend of yours, my lord?"

Henry smiled at Reynard without humor. "He blames me for his failure to swindle Lady Jenova. He does not realize she is far too clever to be swindled by him or anyone else."

Reynard gazed out at the sea. "So, what is it you intend to do here? The silt will continue to come, unless something is done to stop it."

"You are aright, Reynard." Henry cast his eye over the entrance to the harbor. "What we need is a sea groin, a narrow wall striking out into the sea, a barrier to stop the currents from washing the silt into the harbor entrance."

"There was such a thing here before, long ago."

Henry looked to him with interest. "How do you know that?"

"Matilda, my aunt, at the Black Dog. When the first ship ran aground she said her husband had told her that at one time there had been a timber and stone wall, running out into the sea. It was old, very old, and rotted even when her husband's father was a boy. Roman built, perhaps."

"The Romans have been busy at Gunlinghorn. Do you know where it was? Exactly?"

"I can find out, my lord. There will be signs still, and memories are long here."

"Then that is where we will build our sea groin."

Reynard nodded. "It will take many men, and much hard work, quarrying the rock and carrying it here. And we will need timber from the woods. Have we enough men for it?"

"We can bring in more from my estates. And it will be worth it in the long run. Gunlinghorn has the chance to grow rich on profits from this harbor. We cannot afford to lose it."

Henry heard the *we* too late to keep himself from saying it. *We*, as if he and Jenova were a pair. As if Gunlinghorn belonged to them both. She had asked him to stay, and he was too much of a coward to explain why he had to go. She had said she would forgive him almost anything, but Henry did not believe her. The cold, hard truth was that, deep inside, Henry honestly believed he was not worthy of a woman like Jenova.

"Then any amount of trouble is worth it," Reynard agreed. "And if it fails, then at least we will have tried." He did not seem to be aware of Henry's silence, or if he was, he was too clever to give himself away.

"Aye, sometimes one has to try."

He should tell her, but the very thought of opening that door to his past made him shake and tremble. The risks were too great. He could bear it if the king turned away from him, or if his friends scorned him, but not Jenova. If Jenova lost her faith in him, then Henry knew he would die.

The two men stood a moment, looking out to the sea, both deep in their own thoughts. The cold, salty air blew against Henry's face, clearing his mind. He would build the sea groin. Even if he did no more and was not here to see it finished, he would begin the task and order its completion. It would be for Jenova, something that would last for many, many years to come, long after Henry was gone. And mayhap, when she looked upon it, she would remember him kindly.

"Lord Henry?"

Reynard was still standing beside him, but he was no longer looking out to sea. He was gazing beyond the wharf and the timber buildings that lined it, to the narrow track that led across the sand dunes and up onto the clifftops.

Henry followed his gaze. There were a horse and rider coming swiftly in their direction. The wind was blowing the rider's cloak back behind him like a pair of large black wings. Beneath them he wore some sort of dark robe, a priest's robe, and his face . . .

He had no face.

"Jesu," Reynard whispered, crossing himself. Several of the seamen working close by also crossed themselves, as if they were in the presence of evil.

The man and horse reached the wharf, hooves clattering across the timber surface, before drawing to an abrupt halt only a few yards from where Henry and Reynard stood. Henry realized now that the man was not faceless, as he had first thought. Where his face should have been, he wore a cloth hood, with holes cut for his eyes and mouth. It was the sort of thing Henry had seen worn by lepers. Was that what this priest was? A leper? Or one who had worked among them, and then been taken by that dreadful sickness?

And yet there was something threatening about him that caused Henry to think this was not a friendly visit. "Who are you and what do you want?" he demanded loudly, resting his hand upon the hilt of his sword.

The priest settled his restive mount, his gloved fingers stroking the beast's neck. It was a fine animal, a black stallion, and more suited to a wealthy and powerful baron than a mere priest. He had lifted his face in Henry's direction, and although Henry could not see his features, he felt his stare. There was a stillness about him, a silence, that was entirely menacing.

Henry felt the hairs stand up on the back of his neck.

"Who are you?" Reynard repeated and also stepped forward, half drawing his sword from its scabbard.

"I am Jean-Paul. Father Jean-Paul."

He spoke in a husky voice. It was not one that Henry recognized, and yet . . . there was *something*. He began to tremble, deep inside, and his breath came quick and fast.

"I am Lord Baldessare's chaplain," the grating voice went on. It was impossible to see his eyes through the cloth mask, only dark holes where they should have been. The effect was unsettling. Henry wanted to tear the mask aside and see the face beneath.

"What are you doing here, Father Jean-Paul?" Reynard was sliding his blade back into the safety of its scabbard. "Have you come to buy wool or wine?" He nodded at the coastal trader.

"I have come to speak with Lord Henry of Montevoy."

"Then it is me you want," Henry said, taking a step forward, although the wharf seemed to be swaying beneath his feet. His eyes were fixed on that cloth mask with a mixture of longing and terror, and he was not certain if he wanted to gaze upon the face beneath.

Silence. The head tilted to one side, as though the eyes within were examining Henry's person, taking careful note of him. Henry's sense of foreboding grew. *This is not right, there is something very wrong with this priest.*

"I have a message for you."

"From whom?"

"From Lord Baldessare."

"Deliver it then. You are wasting my time." That was better; some of his usual authority had returned to him.

The priest's shoulders shook slightly, although he made no sound. He was laughing! Anger spiraled through Henry. By God, he would remove this man's hood and see him for what he was! But just as he moved forward to do so, that husky voice came again, sly and intimate, and stopped him in his tracks.

"Baldessare knows the truth about you, Lord Henry.

He knows about *le château de Nuit*. He will spread the story of your past among your powerful friends, and I have no doubt it will soon reach the ears of the king. What will become of you then, Lord Henry? Who will stand by your side then?"

He couldn't breathe. Henry could not breathe. And then suddenly the air whooshed back into his lungs, filling them, making him cough. Jesu, he knew! Baldessare knew! It was exactly as Henry had feared. Baldessare knew, because someone had told him. Someone else had survived that appalling place. Someone who was prepared to hurt Henry, to destroy him, for some secret purpose of his own.

Henry took another breath. "No," he said, and wondered if that was really his own voice, trembling like an old man's. He closed his eyes, gathering his strength, reminding himself of who and what he was. He was a phoenix, raised from the ashes. He was a great and powerful lord. He had no reason to be afraid of Baldessare and his *friend*.

"No." He repeated it more firmly. "Baldessare knows nothing of me. You lie. If he means me mischief, then I will deal with him. Tell Baldessare that, sir priest. Tell him that he had best watch his back if he wants to start a war with Lord Henry of Montevoy."

The shoulders shook again in silent amusement. "And what of Lady Jenova, my lord? Will she believe you? Or will the doubt that is sown in her head be your destruction? You will lose her, and Gunlinghorn, too. You will never be able to return here. How will you feel then, Beau Henri?"

Beau Henri.

Henry felt the nausea strike within him and a sudden grinding pain behind his eyes, making his vision blur. He had not heard that name for a very long time, except sometimes in his nightmares. Now he lifted a white and ravaged face toward his tormentor and whispered, "Who *are* you?"

"I am the messenger, that is all," the voice went on, indifferent to his pain. No, that was not so, not indifferent. *Enjoying* his pain. Reveling in his pain.

The priest's cruelty steadied him; his realization that this man was his deadly enemy made him stronger.

"Baldessare would be generous," the priest continued. "He would give you a choice."

"What choice?" Henry said.

"You can leave here. Leave Gunlinghorn. If you do that, you can keep your reputation and your high place in the king's court. Nothing will be said of your past. But you can never return here, and you cannot take Lady Jenova with you. And before you go, you will persuade her that it is in her best interests to marry Lord Baldessare— my lord has decided he would make a better husband than his son, Alfric. The lady needs a stronger hand. Indeed, Lord Henry, he asks that you give them your blessing before you leave. My Lord Baldessare will do the rest."

For a moment the nausea was so intense that Henry thought he was going to be sick right there on the wharf, in front of the priest and the curious crowd. The priest wanted him to leave Jenova. Abandon her to her fate. Encourage her to marry that beast Baldessare. Not Alfric, who was weak but could be molded into an acceptable husband. Nay, not Alfric, but his father, who was good for nothing but savagery and inhumanity.

She wouldn't do it, not willingly. Jenova was no fool. But if Henry wasn't here . . .

He was being given a choice. A choice between keeping Jenova and keeping his present, comfortable position at the court. In short, he could have one or the other, but he could not have both.

But it was far more diabolical than that. Baldessare was not just asking for Henry to give up being Jenova's friend and lover; he was asking Henry to help make Jenova his prisoner. As Baldessare's wife, Jenova would no longer be the independent woman she now was, able to oversee Gunlinghorn and its people, to rule as she saw fit. She would no longer be able to stand in the role of protector to her son, to Raf, until he was old enough to rule for himself. That, too, would be taken from her, and Raf would undergo training as Baldessare saw fit. And having seen Alfric, Henry shuddered to think what Baldessare would do to Raf, or what he would become.

That was his choice.

"This is madness," he whispered.

"You have a week to think on it, Henri," said Jean-Paul, and there was an intimate note in his voice that had not been there before.

"A *week?*" Henry's voice trembled with sick fury, his chest rose and fell violently. "Tell me who I have to thank for this . . . this insanity? Who is colluding with Baldessare to destroy Jenova and me? Damn you, tell me his name!"

The faceless priest considered him: Henry had the sensation that he was savoring the moment. When he spoke, Henry heard again the satisfied smirk in his voice. "You have me to thank, Beau Henri. I am your worst nightmare come true. I hate you so much that I would do anything I could to harm you, and I have nothing to lose in doing it."

His voice wavered, grew tight with an anger that he was attempting to keep tightly reined.

"I have watched you, Henri, and I have listened. I have waited until the moment was right. I came to England, to Lord Baldessare, for a reason; because I knew he hated you almost as much as I do. And I knew he wanted Gunlinghorn. So I suggested he order his son to wed Lady Jenova, and then I placed before her a contract I knew she would find unpalatable. I knew she would not agree to Baldessare becoming her son's protector if Alfric died. I knew she would call upon her friend and adviser to come and help her.

"You, Henri! I knew she would send for you. I made you come here, so that I could punish you as you deserve. It is justice, don't you think? You see, I know how much Gunlinghorn and its lady mean to you. You feel safe here, you feel loved here. Without them you will be adrift. You will suffer. Just as I suffered when you took my home and those I loved from me. Oh yes, my Henri, I want you to suffer. As I have suffered."

Henry stared at him, openmouthed. *Who is he?* This man who hated him enough to tear his life to shreds. Again.

But the question came too late, as did the chance to unseat him and rip the mask from his face. The priest turned the stallion around, and in a moment they were clattering away, back toward the cliffs, his cloak flying behind him.

"What is it, my lord? What did the priest mean?"

The urgent questions came from Reynard. His man had moved close to his side, one eye on Master Will, who was hovering curiously. Henry did not know how much time had passed. It was as if his life were running by him, out of control. The priest had spoken true; Henry felt as if he had stepped into his worst nightmare.

Slowly, carefully, he took a deep breath, and then another. Enough. He must not allow this to prevent him from thinking straight. His intelligence, his clever mind, was his greatest asset. If he was to conquer this monster, whoever it was, and save himself and Jenova, then he must use his mind to do it.

"Baldessare has sent me a message, Reynard. You heard what that . . . creature said. If I do not want my secret revealed to the whole of England, I am to leave for London in a week and abandon Lady Jenova to her fate."

Reynard leaned closer, his big body a bolster against the wind, his dark hair whipping about his swarthy face. "I do not understand. What is this 'secret,' my lord? What can be so bad that a man would think of abandoning Lady Jenova to something like Baldessare?"

"The destruction of all I have tried to make of myself. Of all I now am. That is bad enough, Reynard. And it could happen. Aye, it could very well happen."

"Lord Henry—"

"I should never have come here. If I had not come to Gunlinghorn, Jenova's fate would not now rest in my hands."

"But, my lord, you came because Lady Jenova was planning to wed Lord Alfric. If you had not come, the wedding would probably have gone ahead, and then she would still be trapped in this maze. At least now you have been forewarned of what Baldessare means to do. You can stop him. You can tell her. You can arm yourself against your foe."

That was true enough, to a point. But how did one arm oneself against a foe that had no face?

And what of this choice that lay before him? Henry knew he could not return to London and see her destroyed, just to save himself. It was impossible, and it was not an option, despite what would become of him if he stayed. If he hurt Jenova, he might as well throw himself into the sea right now.

The priest knew that. It was part of his game. He had given Henry a choice that was in fact no choice at all. . . .

"My lord?" Reynard's hand was warm against his shoulder. "Tell me what it means. What hold does Baldessare and this priest have over you? Is the answer at *le château de Nuit*?"

"What do you know of that place?" Henry turned, his voice sharp and suspicious. For a moment he wondered whether even Reynard, whom he thought loyal, was part of this plot against him.

"My lord, I will tell you all I know, I swear it. But first I would ask that you answer."

Henry gave him a wild stare. Confusion overwhelmed him; he felt lost. His usually quick mind was fogged with terror. He had just begun to realize how much Jenova and Gunlinghorn meant to him, and now he would lose all. He had always feared this would happen, always dreaded it; there was almost a sort of light-headed relief in his fears being finally realized.

"I have a dark secret, Reynard," he said at last, in a voice dulled by pain. "I did not think there was anyone left to tell it, but Baldessare, it seems, has found someone. The priest, whoever he is, says he knows. That name he called me, Beau Henri. It is a name from my boyhood that I had hoped forgotten. Now he wants to hold my secret over me like a hangman's noose, until I am forced to do as he wishes. And if I do not . . . then the noose will tighten."

"Tell me this, my lord: Have you done aught wrong? Why are you so afraid of them telling, if you have not done wrong?"

He had done wrong, that was the problem, but he was

not about to be specific. His wrongdoing was not for Reynard's ears, although he could tell him a little. . . .

"*Le château de Nuit* belonged to King William's uncle. His name was Count Thearoux, and the king has fond memories of him. Long ago, after I had fought with William at Hastings, and he had rewarded me and become my friend, he spoke to me of Thearoux. He told me the story of Thearoux's death—all false, but I did not tell him so. He told me that one day he would discover the killer of his favorite uncle and see him punished. And all the time, as I sat there, listening and nodding, it was I. I was the one he was seeking."

"You?" Reynard frowned. "But—"

"I was there when Thearoux died. He was evil, Reynard. A detestable man. He was not the jolly uncle the king believed him to be. There was a fire. . . . I remember little of that night—but if someone wanted to point their finger at me, how could I cry innocent? One thing is certain, the king will never look at me as his friend again when he knows . . . that I was there. Probably he will not publicly punish me, probably he will say that he understands my version of events—after all, he would not want to look like a fool for having me as his friend all this time. But the fact will remain that I did not tell him the truth ten years ago. I kept silent. And that alone will make me guilty of disloyalty in his eyes."

It was not all strictly true, but true enough for Reynard to understand his predicament.

"So you will lose your favored position?"

"Aye. Everything will fall down about me. Everything I thought I had achieved will be destroyed."

"Unless you leave Lady Jenova and return to London in a week."

Henry laughed a bitter laugh. "I will not leave her. The

priest says he knows me, and if that is true, then he knows that I will stay and protect Jenova, no matter what. Our faceless Jean-Paul does not need to soil his hands; I will be tightening the noose about my own throat."

Henry had thought that Reynard would press him for more detail, ask him questions he did not want to answer. Force him to relive memories he did not know if he could face. But Reynard did not; he stood in thoughtful silence, as if considering the situation from all angles. It occurred to Henry that Reynard might be just the kind of man he needed at a time like this. Intelligent and strong, and with a hefty dash of cunning.

"There is something I must tell you." Reynard was watching him, and his face was very grave. "I had planned to tell you anyway, when I had a little more to say, but now it seems all the more . . . pressing. Lady Rhona approached me. . . ."

He went on speaking. The tale was a surprising one, but Reynard told it simply and with the occasional note of dry humor that had Henry smiling despite the seriousness of the situation. It was true that Reynard had taken much upon himself, but Henry could not fault him, and he believed him. Henry had dealt with many men, and he recognized an honest one. Reynard was on his side, and just as well. If they were to defeat Baldessare, they would need a pair of eyes and ears at Hilldown Castle.

"So, it seemed wise to agree to spy for Lady Rhona. At least then I would know what was happening. While she is using me, my lord, I will be using her."

Despite his relaxed manner, Henry could see Reynard was nervous. He had set himself up for a fall, and if Henry was of a mind to, he could shout betrayal and have him punished or dismissed. But Henry knew a good thing when he saw it; he trusted Reynard, and he was desperate for some lever to use to turn this situation to his advantage.

"Using her in more ways than one, aye," Henry agreed quietly. He met the other man's dark eyes. "You have done well, Reynard. I have no bone to pick with you on this matter."

Reynard blinked with relief. "I thank you, Lord Henry. I will not fail you." Then, with a thoughtful frown, he added, "But would the king really allow Lord Baldessare to force Lady Jenova into marriage with him? She is a favorite with him; surely he would never turn away from such a blatant disregard of his wishes? Lord Baldessare must know he would be punished when King William set foot once more in England?"

"Baldessare probably believes I will smooth things over with the king in my own self-interest. They could hold this threat over me for the rest of my life—have me dangling like a puppet on their strings." Henry shook his head, thrusting such a nightmare away. "Aye, the king will not be pleased if he finds Baldessare has taken Jenova against her will, but then again he may see little point in making a fuss if the deed is already done and Baldessare leads him to believe Jenova is well pleased with the arrangement. He may doubt, but if there are other more important matters requiring his attention when he comes home again, matters that could see the fall of his kingdom . . ." Henry shrugged. "It is likely the king may find himself putting down a rebellion, and he will have no time to deal with Baldessare."

"Aye, I see the dilemma."

"It will not happen, Reynard," Henry said quietly, and his blue eyes were very blue as he looked at the other man. "I will not let it happen. Baldessare and his priest can say what they like; I am not leaving Gunlinghorn undefended."

Reynard nodded, and a flicker of anticipation mingled with excitement in his own dark gaze. Reynard, thought Henry with an inner smile, liked a fight.

"When do you meet with Lady Rhona again?" Henry asked, moving ahead.

"In two days' time, at the Black Dog."

"Try and find out from her who this priest really is—the name Jean-Paul means nothing to me. And why he hates me so much that he has joined forces with Baldessare in order to destroy me. He is someone from *le château de Nuit*, I know it. But who . . . who? . . ."

"The castle of Night," Reynard echoed. "It sounds grim."

"Just a name, Reynard. Names cannot hurt us." *But people can,* Henry thought bleakly.

"And what will I tell Rhona, my lord? She will be expecting something in return."

Henry considered. "Tell her I am preparing to go home to London. Let her think her father has won. It should ensure she is more eager to speak to you."

"Aye, I will do as you ask. Will you explain to Lady Jenova what is happening?"

Henry didn't want to. His hope was that he could sort out this problem and have it solved before Jenova learned anything about it. Then she would never have to know. "Leave Lady Jenova to me, Reynard."

"As you wish, Lord Henry."

Reynard's footsteps gritted across the sand on the wharf, and Henry was alone. Alone with the cold, gray ocean. He let his eyes sweep over the wide horizon, narrowing them against the sting of the salty wind. Pray God that soon they would have this matter resolved and Jenova would be safe. And so would his secret.

He closed his eyes and pictured her, her calm beauty in the great hall, her wild beauty in his arms. He had discovered of late that if he did not look at her often, a hollow would open up within him. A sense of loss. He needed to see her. He needed to hold her.

When Jenova gazed at him she had a certain look in her eyes, a certain expression on her face. She looked at Henry and saw a man who was handsome and strong and honorable, a man she trusted and looked up to. The illusion kept him alive. He had not known it before, but he knew it now. Jenova's vision of him was all he had.

If she learned of his shadowy past, she would want him gone. Henry knew that. She would not tolerate him near her when she heard of the things he had done. He felt frozen inside just thinking of the expression on her face, the look in her green eyes. He could not bear it, and yet if he left now she would be in grave danger. He was damned either way.

Who was his enemy? Who was the faceless priest?

He did not know, but he knew of any number of persons it *could* be. It was just that he had believed them all dead. Thearoux, that monster. Could it be him? And the others, their faces hidden in the past, their memories pushed aside in order for Henry to continue living. The burden had been just too great, and to survive he had had to try and forget. At times he actually did forget, sometimes for days and weeks at a time.

He had been more resilient than he thought. More resilient than his friend Souris.

The Mouse.

The memory felt stiff and rusty, like chain mail not kept properly oiled and cleaned. Souris slipped from the creaky shadows in Henry's mind, his pale narrow face and sharp nose, the brown hair flopping over his brow, and his eyes full of glee. Souris, the Mouse, his only friend in a world where survival depended upon doing unspeakable things. But Souris had died with Thearoux, on that long-ago night, when the fire had burned *le château de Nuit* to the ground. Burned it to ashes, and with it the screams and sorrows of all those who had dwelt within it, and all the wretched souls they had stolen.

As far as Henry knew, he had been the only soul to escape.

Then who was it? Who?

Henry squeezed his hands into fists. He must find out. Not just for Jenova, but for himself. For the sake of his own sanity, he must know the truth!

And Jenova?

Even before this happened, Henry had not wanted to leave Jenova. He had wanted to stay here with her at Gunlinghorn. Whatever life he had built for himself in London was nothing to him, not compared to what he could have here. He had been pretending otherwise, but now the charade was at an end. *This* was his home, *this* was where his family resided. This was where he had placed his heart in safekeeping.

His enemy, whoever he was, had known this even before Henry. Had known exactly what would cause him the most anguish.

And now he was using it to destroy him.

Chapter 16

Jenova stood in her stillroom, surrounded by her herbs and potions, the silence a balm to her wounded heart. She had asked Henry to stay and he had refused. He had held her tenderly as she'd wept and he'd kissed the tears from her cheeks, and yet he had refused her.

She must move on from this, she must accept and live for the moment. And yet it was so *painful*. . . .

Jenova took a shaky breath, pushing away her sadness. And then she did something she often did when she was low or sad; she remembered a moment from her past. A time, long ago, in Normandy, when she and Henry had been close. He had been a strikingly handsome boy, with his blue eyes and perfect features, and his smile a little crooked and a little wicked, even then.

Jenova smiled now, remembering. He had asked her if she had ever been kissed, and she had told him no, a little shyly, a little coyly. Henry had taken her hand in his, his fingers strong and warm, and they had walked in the meadows, braving the bees that supped upon the flowers there.

After a time, he had kissed her. Gently and tenderly, innocently. They had lain in the grass and kissed for a long time, and Jenova still remembered the blue sky above and the white clouds gliding past. If she closed her eyes now, the scent of those flowers came back to her and the feel of Henry's lips on hers and his arms about her innocent girl's body.

When they'd returned to the keep, her mother had been angry, her eyes searching them as if she'd thought to find some sign of sin upon them. Jenova had been upset and hurt by her mistrust, but more by the fact that her mother had not understood how special those moments had been. There was no sin, surely, in holding a boy you loved, and who loved you?

Henry had left shortly afterward, off to yet another distant relative who did not know him and probably did not want him.

For a time, Jenova's heart had felt broken, but it had healed. They had met again, some years later, and she had looked at him in wonder, hardly believing she had ever thought they were destined to spend their lives together. He'd been a handsome, charming courtier, and he had not been for her.

But she had not understood that beneath that intoxicating exterior the old Henry had remained—he was still there. He had been waiting for her all this time, and she wanted to take him into the meadow again, hand in hand, and kiss him beneath a blue sky. And love him, as she had loved him long ago.

Jenova bowed her head. There must be some way in which to bring them both a happy ending! She would find it, she would. . . . She must.

* * *

"Well?"

Jean-Paul studied Baldessare a moment, taking in the other man's obvious hunger for news of Henry's pain. He was twitching with impatience, but Jean-Paul made him wait. It was a form of torture, and added to his enjoyment.

"Henry is frightened, and so he should be. He pretends to be brave, of course, but that is his way. He would never run at once—that, too, is his way. Perhaps he will sneak off in the dead of the night, and leave the lady to fend for herself? But he is beaten, my lord, you can be sure of that. I have convinced him that we mean what we say."

Baldessare smiled a most unpleasant smile. "Good. Very good. Let him quiver with terror. I want him to suffer as I have suffered. And I want him to know who is responsible for his downfall."

Jean-Paul nodded sympathetically, but he was secretly amused. As *he* had suffered? Did Baldessare have any conception of what real suffering was? He didn't think so. Baldessare was no different from all the other greedy Norman barons who believed they had a right to take that which belonged to others. Baldessare would have made a fine Viking, rampaging and marauding throughout the country, stealing anything shiny he liked the look of and slaughtering those who stood in his way.

Jean-Paul despised him.

He had used Baldessare to punish Henry, though Baldessare believed he was using Jean-Paul. Baldessare did not particularly like the fact that Jean-Paul had given Henry a choice—he did not understand that the choice was part of Jean-Paul's torture. It was a game. He wanted Henry to believe that it was within his power to decide his fate. But the truth was, Henry was trapped. Whatever path he now took would end in misery. If he chose to go back to court, leave Jenova to Baldessare, then he would suffer. If he chose to stay here, and the truth became known, he would suffer for that, too.

Jean-Paul smiled a satisfied smile. Whichever way Henry turned, he would be blocked, and as he sought a way out he would become more and more frightened and desperate. Until he realized it was a trap and he was caught firmly in it. With no escape.

Baldessare, who had been watching him, looked away uneasily. For so brutal a man, the baron was very squeamish when it came to his chaplain's ruined face. Jean-Paul found enjoyment in that, too. Baldessare's squeamishness gave him more power, more control. Oh yes, the baron might think he was in charge of the situation, but Jean-Paul knew differently.

"Oh, he will suffer, my lord. You may be certain of that."

"And he will hand Lady Jenova over to me? To save himself? That is what you said would happen?"

Sacrificing Jenova, thought Jean-Paul, was what Baldessare would have done in Henry's position. He would not understand self-sacrifice; it was beyond his limited imagination. "Undoubtedly," he lied in a soothing voice. "He will abandon the woman he loves to save himself. Why would he not?"

But perhaps Baldessare heard a hint of the scorn he felt in Jean-Paul's voice, because now his eyes narrowed in suspicion and warning. "I hope you do not mean to deny me Lady Jenova. I have decided she will be mine, and I want her, willing or not."

"Do not worry, my lord. Even if Henry balks at using his skills of persuasion to send the lady into your arms, even if he proves difficult, I have someone else to fall back upon. A friend within Gunlinghorn's walls. Not the groom who spies for you, but someone else, someone close to the family. So you see, my lord, you will have the lady, one way or another."

"A friend?"

Jean-Paul could see this was news to Baldessare, and that it didn't particularly please him. But Baldessare could do and think as he liked, that was not Jean-Paul's concern. It was Henry he cared about, and as long as Henry was punished, then Jean-Paul would be content.

Beau Henri.

Jean-Paul had suffered for him. *Oui*, many times he had tried to spare Henry from Thearoux's wrath. Many times he had brought him water and food when he was locked up and beaten. And many times he had hidden the fact that Henry did not do as he was told. What had Henry done in return? Jean-Paul had been left, abandoned in a burned-out shell. *Le château de Nuit* had been the only home he had ever known, and he had belonged there.

Jean-Paul clenched his fists, hard, and tried to calm himself. This was not the time to grow angry. Sometimes, when he was angry, he lost control of himself. He thought of Henry's face, as he had stood on the wharf. He had changed, grown older, but he would still have known him anywhere. Henry, as handsome as ever, his eyes that strange violet-blue. Henry, turning white with shock when Jean-Paul had laid his future before him.

Henry had known that Jean-Paul was someone he knew, someone from his past, but he had not recognized him. But he would. Oh yes, he would. Jean-Paul wanted to save that unveiling until the end. Let Henry wait and suffer more. Let him understand just how it felt to have everything you loved taken from you. Until you were left, alone, with only your hatred for company.

* * *

Outside the door, Rhona held her breath. She had come upon the two men by accident and had stayed, lurking near the doorway, listening to their conversation. She had not realized until now that it was Jean-Paul who was Lord Henry's enemy, and although it came as a surprise, she was not altogether shocked. She should have known—she had never trusted the disfigured priest. Although he had pretended to be her friend, she had never believed he would champion her if it were not in his own self-interest.

She wondered why he hated Lord Henry so much. Rhona could understand her father's hatred, because she understood his vicious character, but whatever Lord Henry had done to Jean-Paul was a mystery, though one she was keen to solve. How that would help her and Alfric escape their father's clutches she wasn't sure, but at least this new information would be something to tell Reynard.

Today she was to meet with him.

Rhona could not believe how much she was looking forward to it. To seeing him, hearing his voice, being close to him. There was something about him that lifted her spirits, even when she was upset with him. And she was often that. He was a stranger and yet he was beginning to mean a great deal to her. Mayhap it was his manner, his confidence in himself and his future, his dreams of traveling to strange and distant lands. She wanted to go to those lands with him. She wanted to sail with him beneath the stars.

Rhona was so tired of being afraid. She was so tired of always trying to think ahead, of trying to say and do the things that would please her father and not stir up his temper. Always plotting and planning, even while she slept! She wanted to live a life where such things were unnecessary. She wanted to be happy. . . .

She stopped and took a breath. Happy? *Ridiculous!* How could *she* ever hope to be happy? Survival was the thing. Staying alive long enough to escape her father's grasp, to save Alfric, who depended upon her, to save herself. And yet, some days, she had the horrible sensation that she was turning into him—Baldessare. Plot and plan and scheme though she might to escape him, the very act of doing so was making her more like him. So even if she did escape, it might already be too late.

Some days it felt so hopeless.

A sob rose in her throat. Rhona choked it back. The sound she made was faint, but she froze in place, praying that no one in the room had heard her. If she was caught listening, she would be locked in her room, and then she would not see Reynard today.

And suddenly Rhona knew she could not bear that.

Seeing Reynard was the only thing that was keeping her from despair. He offered her hope, though of what she was still uncertain. Perhaps just the fact that a man like him was in the world, and interested in her, made her think she could make a better life. That she deserved something better than this. . . .

"What was that?" Her father, his voice a low growl, like a savage dog that smells blood.

She would run. If he came toward her, she would run, and hope to reach safety before he caught her. . . .

"It is nothing. Just a mouse." Jean-Paul laughed softly, as if he had made a joke. "Do not worry yourself, my lord. All is in hand to see Lord Henry destroyed. Utterly."

There was tremendous satisfaction in his harsh voice.

In her listening place, Rhona, tense and frightened, wondered what Lord Henry had ever done to warrant such terrible enmity.

"Lord Henry?"

The voice was high pitched and impatient. Clearly Raf had been calling him for a while now without response. Henry blinked and looked down with a smile, taking the boy's hand in his own. With time such gestures had become natural, but he still had a sense of wonder when it happened. Here was a child who trusted him, liked him, smiled at him without guile. Henry couldn't bear to think of a future when he might not have the opportunity to do something as simple as hold Raf's hand.

"What is the matter, Raf?"

"Mama has said I may ride outside the castle gates. If you are with me."

Raf's eyes shone, and his cheeks were pink with excitement. Raf had been working on his mother for some time now, trying to persuade her that he should be able to ride beyond the castleyard, and that it was her duty to allow him to do manly things. Henry had enjoyed listening to them—Raf's stubborn determination to have his way and Jenova's stubborn determination to keep him safe. Raf had finally worn her down.

"Mama, I have told him!"

Henry looked up and found Jenova approaching them down the length of the great hall.

For a moment he simply watched, enjoying the vision. Her dark blue skirts swirled about her, the bejeweled girdle resting upon the swell of her hips, the pale fur decorating the hem and sleeves and neckline shining silver in the candlelight. She had a gold circlet holding her veil in place, a red stone shining at its center. She looked like a

queen. His queen. With her green eyes fixed upon him
and her pink lips curled in a faint smile, she was everything he had ever wanted.

That was when Henry accepted that he would do anything for her. Give up anything, become anything, just to
keep her safe.

Even if it meant he could never see her again.

"I will look after him," Henry said now, nodding
down at Raf, who was dancing anxiously up and down,
still clinging to his hand.

"I know you will." She smiled as she said it, but her
eyes were gentle and warm, as though she believed in him.
God help her, thought Henry bitterly and looked away.

"We can ride up the hill," Raf was saying. "The one
above Gunlinghorn that looks down upon all my lands."

"So that you can see how much you will have to look
after when you are grown?" Henry teased.

"I am grown now," Raf replied, looking seriously displeased that Henry should suggest otherwise.

Jenova laughed, and Henry's eyes twinkled—until it
occurred to him that they probably looked just like two
proud parents.

"You will grow bigger than this," Jenova said, placing
a gentle hand on the boy's head. "Taller than me, if I am
not mistaken."

Raf stilled, thinking about that. "Taller than Lord
Henry?" he asked, eyeing Henry speculatively. "Will I be
taller than Lord Henry?"

"Possibly," Henry said. "You will be your father's son,
and he was as tall as Lord Radulf."

Raf's eyes seemed to glaze over with the vision that
conjured. "Tall as the King's Sword," he whispered, as if
the thought of equaling the size of this legendary warrior
was hardly to be borne.

"Aye, you will be your father's son," Henry assured him, and laughed as Raf, spying Agetha, took to his heels, shouting, "One day I will be as tall as the King's Sword!"

Jenova's hand closed on Henry's arm, her slender fingers warm. He looked down at them, feeling himself tense, beginning to harden. Jesu, had he no self-control left where she was concerned?

"Not quite like his father, I pray," Jenova said quietly, her face turning sad as she looked after her son.

Instantly Henry was ashamed of his carnal thoughts. She was remembering Mortred's betrayal, of course she was. Jenova had loved her husband, and to learn he had not been the man she'd thought him had struck her deep. She would find it hard to trust again. And that was just as well, because one way or another Henry would betray her, too. It was inevitable.

"Raf is also *your* son," he reminded her levelly, ignoring the urge to take her fingers in his. "He will be a fine man. If . . . when the king calls him to court, I will make certain that he does not become corrupted."

Jenova glanced at him sharply, and her hand fell away from his arm. "Will you? You think you will still be at court then, Henry? In . . . oh, ten years' time?"

He knew what she was really asking. He could not answer her; he did not know. "Where else would I be?" he asked politely, but his eyes weren't smiling, and he saw her own narrow, a flicker of pain in the green before she looked away.

"Where else indeed?" she said brightly, as if it didn't matter to her at all. Mayhap it didn't, mayhap she would be glad to see him go. Only if he went, she would be at Baldessare's mercy. She just didn't know it yet.

"Jenova." He hesitated, wondering if he should even ask his questions—there was so little time. A week, the priest had said. A week to save himself, to redeem himself, to make all well again. It wasn't long enough.

"Henry? What is it?" There was anxiety in her voice now, their discord forgotten. "What *is* the matter? I know there is something wrong, and I won't be fooled by your pretending otherwise."

Tell me! Jenova's eyes were saying, but Henry did not believe she meant that he should tell her everything. Still, he found himself speaking, the words tumbling out.

"I met Baldessare's priest when I was at Gunlinghorn Harbor. He wore a . . . a mask over his face."

"Jean-Paul? His face is badly damaged. A fire, I think. The skin is scarred and puckered . . . awful. He wears the mask when he goes out so as not to frighten people. Why was he down at Gunlinghorn Harbor?"

Now, there was a question, Henry thought, but it was not one he intended to answer. At least, not honestly, and not now. He imagined her face changing as he told her the story, imagined her eyes growing cold, her skin pale with disgust. No, he could not tell her—he was not brave enough.

"He is no fool," she went on, seeming not to notice his silence. "Jean-Paul, I mean. He is a clever and educated man. 'Tis a cruel thing to say, but he seems wasted upon the Baldessares. He would have made a fine cardinal, except . . ." She pulled a face, catching Henry's gaze. "I do not trust him. There is something there that he hides well. He tries so hard to pretend he has no feelings; even when people slight him because of his face, he shrugs it off. But you just know that, inside, he is like a boiling pot, bubbling and seething."

"You describe him very well, sweeting."

"Why did you ask, Henry? What did he say to you? Tell me, I want to know."

Tell me . . .

"He asked if I would . . . persuade you to marry Alfric." No need to frighten her yet with talk of a bridegroom like Baldessare. "I said that decision was yours alone."

Jenova's eyebrows rose, her smooth brow creasing. "I am surprised. I did not think such a matter as my marriage to Alfric would concern him."

"Is his whole face ruined? I mean—"

"You mean, what did he look like before he was disfigured? A sweet face, I think. Not so much handsome as appealing. Pale eyes and long lashes—one of his eyes is still so, the other one is blind. I do not know how old he is, 'tis difficult to tell."

Henry nodded. She had just described several of his companions at *le château de Nuit.* And yet in his heart, deep, deep in his heart, he already knew who *he* was. The *he* who could hate him enough, who was patient enough, cruel enough, to do this thing to him. Betrayal, that was what was at the heart of Jean-Paul's game.

Henry's betrayal.

"Stay away from the priest," he said with quiet urgency. "Do not be alone with him, Jenova, and do not let Raf near him. I do not like him. He is dangerous."

Jenova eyed him uneasily. "Of course I will be careful, Henry, although I know I am perfectly safe here, on Gunlinghorn land. You would . . . you would tell me, if there was anything more, wouldn't you, Henry? You know you can trust me, don't you?"

Henry smiled into her eyes, but his heart was bleak. Trust her? Jesu, if only he could believe she could make all right again! But he feared even Jenova did not have that power.

Jenova wanted to force him to tell her what was in his mind. Something had happened, something more than his meeting with Jean-Paul. He was acting oddly, as if he were looking inward even as he smiled and chatted and lathed her with his famous charm. She knew him too well to be easily deceived—didn't he know that? Whatever it was, it was clear Henry did not want to share it with her.

Why had he spoken of court again? Even though it had been in the context of helping Raf, something for which she should be grateful, the mere mention of it had soured her joy. She didn't want him to go. She had half thought, hoped, that he had changed his mind.

She had learned from Mortred how painful it was to give oneself wholly to a man. She must try and keep her distance. And her heart in one piece.

Then why was it already feeling like it was too late?

"Jenova?"

He was watching her, his eyes so very compelling. Something in her own eyes must have betrayed her, for he caught her fingers in his and squeezed them tightly, as if for comfort. The moment stretched out. "Jenova," he murmured again, his low voice skimming her skin and her senses. And suddenly she was intensely aware of his body, his warmth, the scent of him. Desire flooded through her, quickening her breath, heating her blood.

Just like that, she was ready for him.

"Henry," she breathed, and looked into eyes blazing with ardor.

His face was rigid with his need of her. He stepped closer, and his warm breath stirred her veil. "I want you," he said, his lips almost touching her skin. "Now."

She laughed, as if she had drunk too much wine. "Now? Before my entire household?"

He glanced over his shoulder, as if only just realizing they had an audience. "Go to your solar," he said, as softly as before. "Go now. Make some excuse. I will follow."

"Henry—"

"I need to be inside you." He said it as if it were the most important thing in the world, and gazing into his eyes, Jenova knew that for him, it was. Her own body trembled with an equal need.

"Very well," she whispered. Stepping away, she began a pantomime of looking for her brooch and then deciding, aloud, that she had left it in the solar. She hurried toward the stairs, not looking behind her, wondering if she were completely insane. This was not the sort of behavior of which she would ever have imagined herself capable. She gave a stifled giggle, and then gasped.

Oh dear God, Agetha would be in the solar. . . .

Jenova went to turn, to go back down the stairs and tell him not to follow, when a strong hand closed on her arm and drew her into the narrow, shadowy landing.

Henry, his body all but touching hers, was gazing at her with his chest heaving, as if he was finding it impossible to get enough air. Jenova reached out to touch his face. "Agetha is in the solar," she said. "We cannot go there."

"What about here, then?" He pressed his body against hers, and she felt the hard ridge of his manhood through their clothing.

"Here?" Her eyes widened. Despite her shock at his words, she leaned her hips harder into him. Wanting him. "Henry, surely we cannot—"

"It is quiet, and we are alone. And it can be . . . exciting to make love so close to discovery."

Exciting? Jenova did not know if that was the word. Her body tingled, urging her to agree, but caution was a part of her, too. She teetered on the knife edge, then Henry pulled her fully into his arms and began to kiss her.

It was not a gentle kiss. His mouth devoured hers, his tongue thrusting deep. He pinned her against the wall, his body hard and heavy, and desire crashed over her like a wave.

She knew she had no intention of struggling or pulling away. She didn't want to. In her heart she might be afraid of their being caught, but Henry was right, there was a sort of excitement in that. She was, in truth, more afraid of being emotionally hurt. That did not make her want him any less. She didn't know how much longer they might have together. A day, a week, a month? This desperate moment with Henry could well have to last her for the rest of her life.

Desire, longing and anguish drove her, a heady mixture, as her mouth clung to his and her hands tangled in his hair. His body was hers, every hard line of it, every curved muscle. Her eager hips lifted to fit the bulge of his erection into the apex between her thighs, and she felt the first tentative ripples of her release, simply from that contact.

But it wasn't enough.

She needed more. She needed to become a part of him. She needed him inside her.

Henry's palms slid around her and down, clasping her bottom, and raising her up. Settling her more comfortably against him. Jenova curled one leg about his hips, pressing still closer, every one of her senses crying out for more. Her breasts ached. He bent his head, and his breath was hot through her gown as he opened his mouth against her, sucking at her through the cloth. Jenova reached up to tug at the laces at her throat, pulling them open, dragging the neckline down over her shoulders.

Her breasts were full and swollen, the nipples aching for his touch. Henry groaned and began to lave her with his tongue, sucking on them, pulling them into his mouth. Jenova moaned and arched against him, forgetting where she was, who she was. Or perhaps she just didn't care. Feelings like this were beyond her comprehension, too powerful to be denied. She had always believed herself a strong woman, but what she was feeling now was stronger.

"I want you," Henry growled and looked deep into her eyes. "I need to be inside you. Now."

She gave a laugh that was more like a sob and began to tug at the fastenings on his breeches. In a moment he was free, hot and hard in her hand. She stroked him, feeling him quiver, as helpless as her. He had rucked her skirts up, his hands gripping her thighs, closing again on her bottom, drawing her up, angling her just right. Jenova caught her breath, rubbing her body against his, delirious with the feel of him at the threshold of that most intimate part. The head of his erection brushed her swollen flesh, and his mouth was hot against her throat as her head fell back.

"Now," she groaned. "Oh, Henry, now."

He thrust into her, the full length of him, stroking her deep, deep inside.

Jenova gasped, a blossom of heat starting low in her belly, trembling in her thighs. She lifted her head, and Henry gazed into her eyes, his own still blazing.

She was beautiful. A siren. A goddess. He filled his vision with her, making it last. Her veil had come loose and with it her braid, and now her hair fell about them in waves. Her mouth, reddened from his kisses, curved upward, and her dark lashes drooped over the passionate gleam in her green eyes.

"Oh yes," she breathed.

Henry withdrew and thrust again, deep, knowing it would never be deep enough. He wanted to devour her, merge himself into her. He wanted her to swell with his child, and then he wanted to do the whole thing over again. And again. For how ever long they lived. And still it would not be enough.

He drove deep once more, and his mouth closed on hers, drowning out her cry of completion, echoed by his own. Their bodies clung together, shuddering. From far away servants' voices hummed, a dog barked, a soldier shouted training instructions. Life went on, and they were but a part of it. It was the same and yet it was different. Henry took several deep breaths, trying to understand what it meant.

Jenova managed a shaken laugh, releasing him, letting her skirts fall to cover herself. With fingers that trembled, she reached to lace up her gown. Henry gently pushed them aside, tying it for her, intent upon the knot. His throat was dry, his heart pounding. He felt as if he had died and gone to paradise.

He needed her. He had to save her from Baldessare. He had to protect her, even if she didn't want him to, even if he wasn't here at Gunlinghorn. He had to be in a position to do all these things, and there was really only one way to go about it.

He had to wed her.

The words were in his head, beating like a drum, and he was not even sure he had said them aloud until she froze beneath his hands. When he stepped back and looked up, she was gazing at him as if he had grown horns, hooves and a tail.

"Henry? Did you just ask me to marry you?" Her voice was hardly more than a breath.

"I think I must have."

She swallowed, eyes wide and disbelieving. She did not look exactly pleased. More bewildered, confused, uncertain . . . There was an anxious crease between her brows. Her hands went to her hair, twisting it back into some sort of order.

"Henry, you must not feel . . . you must not think that . . . I do not expect you . . ." She took a breath. "Before I asked you to stay, and you said you could not. Why are you now asking me to marry you? I do not understand."

Henry gave a shaken laugh. " 'Tis not personal, Jenova, 'tis—"

Her face went blank. "Oh?"

"You are in danger. I want to protect you. If I am your husband, I can do that far more easily."

The words sounded sensible to him, reasonable. And yet the silence that followed was long and heavy.

She closed her eyes. When she opened them again, the green had turned hard and cold and distant. "No, Henry. I do not need your protection. I suppose your offer is kindly meant, but I can manage very well on my own. I am sorry if my asking you to stay gave you the impression that I was clinging to you for protection. It is far from the truth. Now, if you will excuse me. . . ."

It was ridiculous. They had just made rough, passionate love on the stair landing, and she was asking to be excused. He laughed, sick at heart, longing for things to be different. And yet he understood her point of view. Jesu, he even applauded it! There was no reason for her to trust him. He was not a man to lean upon, and things were far worse than she imagined.

"Jenova," he whispered. "Jenova, *please* . . ."

She didn't look back. Her midnight blue skirts flicked around the corner and vanished up the stairs. Her footsteps faded into the general hum of castle life. Henry was alone. He had asked Jenova to marry him—his first ever proposal—and he had botched it.

The words had come from nowhere, surprising him as much as Jenova. Perhaps he had hoped for her to smile, and weep a little, and say yes. Then again, perhaps he was secretly glad she had refused him. What could he offer her, after all, but disgrace? If the truth became known, she would learn to loathe him.

It was a bad bargain for Jenova.

Henry rested his brow against the wall where a moment ago Jenova's head had rested. Smelling her scent, breathing her in, he wondered what he was going to do.

Chapter 17

"**P**rotect me?" Jenova muttered to herself, flinging open the door to her solar and finding that Agetha wasn't there after all. She slammed it shut behind her. "If he is my husband he can *protect* me far more easily?" She strode to the shuttered window, then to the warm brazier, then back again. " 'Tis not *personal*?" Her clothing was in disarray, her hair tangled down her back, her body still throbbing from Henry's lovemaking.

And she was angry. More angry than she had ever been. Angrier than she had believed it was possible for her to be.

Henry had asked her to marry him. To be his bride. And she hated him for it.

"Jesu! He doesn't want me because he cannot live without me by his side. He doesn't want me because he worships the ground I walk upon. Not because our bodies sing together. Not because he *loves* me. . . ."

Nay, none of that. Henry wished to marry her because

he was worried that she was in danger from Baldessare. He wanted to protect her with his name, so that he could gallop off back to London with a clear conscience. For even Baldessare would not dare lay a hand upon a lady who was wed to the great Lord Henry of Montevoy!

She was panting. There was a piece of embroidery folded upon a stool—painstaking stitches, beautifully arranged. She threw the cloth at the wall. A goblet followed, and a pair of slippers. The violence relieved her somewhat of her fury, but it still roiled within her like the sea in a storm. Fury with lashings of intense disappointment.

Jenova had told herself she would never marry again. Look at what had happened with Mortred. She had given him all of herself, opened her heart and soul to him, and she had expected the same from him. Instead he had betrayed her, humiliated her, wounded her so deep that she had struggled to recover.

And then look what had happened?

Because of Mortred, in the need to reassure herself and mayhap to revenge herself upon a dead man, in her loneliness, she had begun to look favorably upon Alfric. Alfric had seemed perfect for all her needs. Instead he had been another mistake.

Now Henry wanted to wed her and clear his conscience. Then he would leave her, and she would be no better off than she had been before. Worse off, because she had grown used to him being there, used to the sound of his voice, and his warm morning kisses. It would be like losing Mortred all over again. Only much, much worse.

She could not do it. She *would* not do it. For the sake of her own bruised heart, she would not marry Henry. It would be a terrible error of judgment. A sort of prison for both of them. For him, who clearly preferred to be away from her, and for her, who only wanted him by her side.

Jenova remembered again Henry's face when he had blurted out the question. That in itself had been odd— Henry losing his fabled charm and easy way with words—but at the time she had hardly noticed. He had looked ill. And shocked. As though the words had been forced from his unwilling mouth. As though he had not wanted to ask them but had felt obliged. As though he had been offering her some sort of payment for what they had just done on the landing.

Those moments together, when they had forgotten all else in the need to consummate their passion, had been some of the most exciting of her life. The possibility of being discovered, the wild behavior so out of character for her, and the sheer desperate need to join his body to hers. Aye, it had been wonderful.

Exciting and wonderful.

And then Henry had spoiled it.

Jenova felt hot tears fill her eyes and spill down her cheeks. He should have fallen in love with her. He should want to marry her for love. Oh, she knew marriage was a business contract, something arranged for land and money and bloodlines, but she had always hoped . . . she had always dreamed . . . Jenova swallowed back the girlish fancies she had thought long gone. Well, even if Henry could not *love* her, he had seemed so happy these past weeks, so content. He had seemed to enjoy the challenge of the tasks she had set him, although he had always deferred to her as Lady of Gunlinghorn. In short, he had been the perfect lord. A helpmate, a companion, and a lover. Everything she had ever wanted in a man.

Henry, her dearest friend Henry, was the perfect man for her. She should be the perfect woman for him. But

Jenova very much feared that her love was a threat to him, despite the fact that she had not stated it aloud.

For she did love him.

She loved him more and more each moment she spent with him. Jenova admitted it to herself, the tears rolling down her cheeks. She was a weak and foolish woman, because although she had vowed never to love another man after Mortred, she had. She did. She loved Henry.

She lay down upon her bed, hearing the rustle of the horsehair mattress, feeling the soft furs beneath her, and she cried until her chest ached and her face was swollen and she could cry no more. *This* was what she had feared from the start. That with the excess of joy would come an excess of pain.

"My lady?" It was Agetha, her voice tentative, her knock gentle upon the door. "Are you well, my lady?"

Jenova took a shaky breath and sat up, wiping her face. She was a mess, but there was nought she could do about that. Besides, what did it matter, she thought, calling for the girl to enter. Agetha was her friend, and she needed her friends about her at this difficult time.

Agetha's already rather protruding eyes bulged. "My lady? What is the matter? You . . . you have been crying!"

Jenova sighed. "I have. Can you please comb my hair and braid it again? It is making my head ache."

The girl hesitated, plainly wanting to ask more questions, but Jenova closed her eyes. She felt weak and drained from her weeping, but at least it had made her see things more clearly. After a moment, she felt Agetha move behind her and begin taking the long brown tresses in one hand, while drawing the comb carefully through them with the other. Jenova drifted, allowing herself to enjoy the attention.

She could not marry Henry. It would be disastrous. If,

she thought bleakly, she was unhappy now, then she would be even more so if they were bound together with ties of marriage and living far apart. Nay, her future had already been written. She would remain alone, and she would rule Gunlinghorn as wisely and well as she could, until Raf was old enough to take over. And then she would while away her days being as useful as she could, helping Raf, caring for her people, and when her grandchildren came along, she would take pride in them and try to guide them away from the same pitfalls that had beset her.

That was not such a bad life for a woman.

"My lady?" Agetha asked sharply. "Are you crying again?"

"No, I . . . just a sniffle. I am well, Agetha. Truly."

"Hmm," the girl made a suspicious sound but continued to comb Jenova's hair. Soon she was braiding it neatly. "'Tis Lord Henry who has hurt you," she said at last, her voice stony. "Do not deny it, my lady, for I know 'tis so."

"Agetha—"

"He is a man who enjoys women, and they enjoy him." It sounded as if Agetha was blushing. "He does not stay with one woman for very long. He can love none of them. I knew he would wound you, Lady Jenova. He does not deserve to touch the hem of your gown, let alone . . . well!"

"This is not your business, Agetha. Please stop."

"You know, you would not have been hurt if you had agreed to wed Lord Alfric. He is gentle and kind, he would never do anything to upset you. My lady, I am sure 'tis not too late if you—"

"No, Agetha! I do not want to wed Alfric or Henry or anyone else. I am content as I am. Now please, please, say no more."

To her credit, Agetha was silent, although Jenova sensed she was sorely tempted to carry on. But the girl quietly finished her task, and at Jenova's request, she sent for hot water for a bath. Jenova let her fuss and boss the servants about, supervising the bathing, making sure the addition of scents and perfumes was just as Jenova liked it. Agetha pampered Jenova like a child, and for once Jenova was content to let her.

Afterwards, warm and dry, she felt much better. The need for tears was gone, and she had made a decision. She would insist that Henry go on his way north as soon as possible. She had been hurt enough, and he had made it clear he had no real interest in her. Aye, it was much better if he did not stay longer. The sooner he left, the sooner she could get on with her real life. Besides, she did not think she could bear it if he was at Gunlinghorn another moment.

She would command him to go, although she did not relish the thought of telling Raf. Her son had grown very fond of Henry, and Henry had grown just as fond of Raf. Mayhap, when the sadness and loneliness were faded, she could remember that one thing. And treasure it.

Henry rode hard, sending Lamb pounding across the sodden ground, up hills and down again, through woods and out the other side. He did not realize, until he went many, many miles, that the snow was melting. It sloshed under Lamb's hooves and dripped monotonously from the tree branches. And the air, though still cold, felt a little less biting.

The thaw was upon them and, soon, the spring.

He would have liked to have seen Gunlinghorn in the spring. He would have enjoyed watching the new crops sown, and the new animals born, and work beginning on the sea groin. And, most of all, being with Jenova when the world was reborn in a cloak of fresh green leaves and sweet white blossoms.

How could he bear not waking up to her kisses and her soft body beside his, not seeing her smiles or hearing her laughter? These were losses he could hardly begin to contemplate—there was a terrible ache in his chest when he imagined being without her. A burning pain of emptiness and grief. He had never felt that before for any woman. He didn't know what to do about it. Clever and handsome Henry didn't know what to do.

Marry her.

The words rang out in his head, startling him from his depression. *I tried that,* he thought. *She refused me. What more can I do?*

Tell her the truth.

Aye, and what then? He would not only destroy his chance to marry her but he would also ruin whatever friendship still remained between them. She would send him away, and when she was all alone, Baldessare would strike.

"No!"

Lamb, startled by his cry, jumped sideways and nearly unseated him. Henry clamped his mouth shut and hung on grimly, drawing the big stallion to a halt and settling his ruffled nerves.

"Your master is a fool," he said, rubbing his hand over Lamb's rough winter coat.

And so he was. He could not let Baldessare hurt Jenova. He could not let Jean-Paul send him back to London with his tail between his legs, leaving Jenova to her fate. The solution was to marry her, do it in haste, before his enemies could do aught about it. Then, if Jean-Paul wanted to tell Jenova the truth, let him. She would no longer want anything to do with him, but at least Henry would be her husband and in a position to protect her. Whether she willed it or not. Even if he fell out of favor, Henry thought feverishly, he would still have that power. The king would not take everything from him, surely?

So you would wed her in deceit.

"For her own good. For her safety, hers and Raf's. It is I who have brought this danger upon them, and now it is I who must save them from it."

It sounded plausible enough. Lamb tossed his head in agreement, bringing a grim smile to Henry's lips. He turned him for home. *Home*, there was a bittersweet word. He had never felt he belonged anywhere, until now. Home was Raf, with his trusting smile, and Jenova, warm and pliant in his arms. Home was this place and its people. Aye, Gunlinghorn had become his home.

But instead of basking in the joy of his new discovery, Henry was facing the possibility of losing it all.

"Who are you, Jean-Paul?" he asked himself aloud, sending Lamb galloping down the slope toward the castle. "Why do you want to destroy me?"

All these years he had tried to forget. He had put the past behind a door in his mind and kept it shut fast. Sometimes at night he would dream, but during the day he had made a different life for himself. Risen up anew from the dreadful ashes. Now all that was under threat, and he had no idea how to stop it.

Perhaps Reynard would find out for him today, when he met with Lady Rhona? Surely there was some clue, some whisper, something! He must discover who Jean-Paul was. Although how that would help him, Henry did not know. Maybe it was just that knowing his enemy would make him seem less threatening, more beatable, than the faceless priest he had met upon the seafront.

Souris.

The name was a whisper in his head. Souris, clever and bright, his friend, and companion. Souris had saved him more than once, Henry admitted that. At the time he had been grateful. But Souris had not been trustable, he had had his own agenda. Henry had always known that Souris would never have helped him escape *le château de Nuit*. The château had been Souris' home, and he had had no intention of leaving it.

Souris would have seen Henry's leaving as a betrayal.

It would fester in him, it would become hate. Souris, damaged and yet fiercely intelligent, would find an especially cruel way to make Henry suffer.

Aye, *that* made sense.

If anyone had the ability to torture, to torment, to shut off any remaining spark of love or compassion, then it was Souris.

The Mouse.

The midday meal was being served. As Jenova passed through the great hall, toward the kitchen, the noise made her head ache. She ignored it. Just as she had ignored Agetha's worried and accusing glances. The girl had not given up on Alfric, but Jenova had refused to hear another word from her on the subject. Thankfully, Agetha had known when to stop, at least for the moment.

Henry, it seemed, was not so intuitive.

Jenova knew he was watching her. Ever since she had come downstairs, his gaze had followed her. She had the uneasy feeling he was like a wolf, just waiting for the right moment to pounce and pin her to the ground.

But, she told herself, she was ready for him. He would not take her by surprise again. If necessary, she would refuse to see him. Her heart was still too sore from their last encounter. . . .

A hand came out of the shadows and caught her arm. Henry! The entrance to a storeroom was close beside her, and as Jenova gasped and tried to pull free, she realized that Henry had been lurking in there, waiting for her. Lord Henry of Montevoy among last year's dried apples. It might have been amusing if it had not been so infuriating.

"Jenova."

"Go away, Henry." Her teeth were gritted, her fists clenched.

"I must tell you—"

"I mean it. Go away. Go home to London. I do not want you here anymore. You came to offer me advice— well, you have given it. Now go." She faced him, forcing herself to meet his eyes, wanting him to understand that she meant what she said.

He stared back at her, his gaze caressing her features, delving into her brain. She could already tell that he wasn't going anywhere; this was Henry, after all—he was simply rethinking his strategy.

"You don't understand, Jenova. You must marry me. You will not be safe until you do. As your husband I can deal with Baldessare and protect your interests. You must not think I will prevent you from doing just as you wish. I would not be a jealous husband, or a possessive one. Far from it, I swear to you. You can continue to rule Gunlinghorn as you will, do as you wish. Can you not see that?"

Jenova shook her head in bemusement—was this meant to persuade her or send her screaming to her solar?

Henry smiled, reaching to touch her shoulder. He must

have thought he had convinced her. "Jenova, you *do* see. You must do this for Raf's sake—"

"Enough!"

Oh, she was angry now. How dare Henry use Raf to turn her to his wretched point of view! He truly was misguided if he thought he could bully her by using her son as bait. She would have none of him or his squeamish conscience. Let him go home and forget her, as she would forget him.

"No, Henry. I say again, no, no, no! I can take care of my son and myself. I am used to doing so. Mortred, as you know, was never here and I was alone. I am *used* to being alone."

"Jenova," he tried again, but now there was desperation in his eyes, and a hint of something she had not seen there before. Some terrible pain had him in its grip, and suddenly Jenova had had enough. Damn the man!

"What is it, Henry? Tell me what is amiss. Something has happened, I know it. You must tell me—"

"No." Jesu, he looked pale and sick, yet even now he half turned away, as if to hide from her.

"Henry, how can you ask that I wed you, put my life in your hands, and yet refuse to tell me what is wrong?"

"There is nothing to tell."

She met his eyes and saw beyond the smiling blue to something else. A child, locked in a small, dark place without hope of rescue. Jenova sighed. Very well. It had come down to this. If he would not tell her, she would not have him at Gunlinghorn. The choice was his.

Her voice was flat and cool. "If you have nothing to tell, then I want you gone by tomorrow. Do you understand? You will say your good-byes and go."

He shook his head. "No, I won't." His mouth closed in

a hard line. Here was Henry the warrior, about to engage in battle. "Not until I know you are safe, Jenova."

Exasperation filled her, and a strange urge to laugh. *No?* Previously it had seemed as if he could not leave soon enough; now he was refusing to leave Gunlinghorn. Infuriating man!

Mayhap he noticed the change in her face, or mayhap he just decided to try another tactic.

"I think the reason you want me to go is because you are afraid of me," he said, and there was a wicked note in his voice, and a wicked gleam in his eyes.

She knew that look. Its power was not to be underestimated. Already Jenova felt her toes curl inside her calf-skin slippers. "That is nonsense," she retorted, giving her voice a rousing note. "I don't fear you in the least. Why should I?" But, just in case, she took a step back.

"Because you know in your heart that I will eventually persuade you to do as I want. Because you can't resist me."

He reached out and caught her hand, giving her knuckles a gentle nip before she could react and pull it away again. His mouth burned her skin. She felt her body respond, softening, readying itself for his. No, no, this was not the time to be ruled by her desire!

"I can resist you perfectly well," she retorted, trying not to sound breathless.

He smiled, that so-handsome Henry smile. And yet he was different. . . . That was when Jenova realized that his hair was a little tousled, his tunic a little rumpled. Henry, who was always immaculate, was far from it. And when had he last asked for hot water, for one of his daily baths? Jenova, who had longed to see him mussed, realized with despair that it only added to his appeal. It gave him a vul-

nerable air that made her want to take him in her arms
and comfort him.

Jesu, what was she going to do with him?

"Can you resist me?" he said. "Let me see." He came
closer, but she edged away. "I only want to kiss your lips.
They are so sweet, Jenova. They taste of wild fruit. The
sweetest and juiciest berries, all lush and red. But wild at
heart and wanton, like you in my arms. I want to kiss
them, and then I want to kiss your—"

"Henry . . ." she breathed in anguish, wanting to look
away, wanting to stop listening. Knowing that every word
he spoke was drawing her deeper into love with him.

"You are not like any of the others, Jenova."

He sounded as if he meant it. His mouth was still
curved in that irresistible, teasing smile, but his eyes were
serious and his gaze unswerving. She might almost have
thought it a vow.

Jenova honestly didn't know what to say, how to fight
him. She only knew that her head was pounding and she
longed to be alone.

"Please, Henry," she began again, trying to make her
voice firm. She could order her garrison, why not a single
man? "Please, leave Gunlinghorn. It is no use you staying. I will never marry you. I will never marry anyone. I
have made my decision."

"Never is a long time," he replied, lifting his eyebrows. "Marry me now, and if we don't like it, we don't
have to see each other very often. Once a year, on the
stair landing—"

With a cry of angry frustration, Jenova turned and left
him. She half thought he would follow and continue to
pester her, but he did not. He must have known he had
said enough. What was she going to do with him? She

could order her garrison to throw him outside the gates, or arrest him and lock him up in her dungeon. Mayhap just tie a gag about his mouth so that he could not speak.

It was a ridiculous situation.

Jenova had thought Henry had had more pride than to linger where he was not wanted, especially when she had refused him so often and so finally. Mayhap that was the reason he was staying; his pride. She had dented it badly by turning him down—Lord Henry, the handsomest man in England—and now he meant to repair the damage by making her beg. *Please marry me, Henry, please.* . . .

"I cannot bear it," she murmured. "I cannot bear to have him here. I do not want him for my husband when it is all for duty and consideration! When there is something very wrong and he will not tell me what it is."

I love him, and I want him to love me.

The words were on the very tip of her tongue. Jenova was afraid that, if she was not careful, she would say them aloud. Somewhere Henry could hear her. How he would smirk then, how he would laugh! His pride would be restored to its previous hard shine.

But Jenova's would be in tatters.

She straightened her back. No, she would not let him hurt her like this. There was something amiss. She knew it; deep inside, she sensed it. Henry was hiding something from her, and it was making him miserable.

With new determination and energy, she vowed she would make him tell her what was wrong. Aye, somehow she would wheedle his secret out of him . . . or else it would truly be the end between them.

Chapter 18

The Black Dog was a single-story building, with a warehouse on one side and a bakery on the other. A board painted with a rather ferocious-looking dog sat outside, otherwise Rhona doubted she would have known where to go without asking. As she dismounted her mare, her legs were shaking, and it was only with great effort that she walked toward the low doorway.

The last two days had been fraught with fears that her father would somehow prevent her from coming. Alfric had kept to his room much of the time, sullen and hollow-eyed. Rhona herself might have felt as depressed as her brother, but she'd had her plan to buoy her up. The chance to be free.

And then, this morning, when she had overheard Jean-Paul and her father . . . mayhap she was losing her courage, but she had been afraid then. Something in that husky voice had frightened her, so that all she had wanted to do was turn and run.

Now, in hindsight, Rhona considered that it might not have been a lack of bravado that had caused her to want to escape at that particular moment. Maybe she had simply been living this uncertain life for too long, and she had reached a point where she could not go on. Surely everyone came to such a moment in their lives, when it was too difficult to take another step forward? Then again, not everyone had to live the life Rhona did.

She felt sickened, by herself as much as by her father and Jean-Paul. Even Alfric's whining sickened her, though she pitied him. Aye, she loved him even as she wished she were not the one responsible for him. They must get away! If they did not get to Normandy this time, Rhona had a real fear that they never would.

Inside the door there were voices and smoke. The smells of ale and food and other, less savory, odors. Rhona stood, blinking, trying to get her bearings. She jumped when a voice piped up at her side.

"Will I stable your horse, me lady?"

A boy, peering up at her through a thatch of red hair, his eyes as blue as summer.

"Yes, thank you. Tell me, is Reynard here?"

The blue eyes narrowed, grew sly. "Aye, me lady. He's over there, by the fire." And then he was gone, and she was left to try and see through the gloom to where the boy had pointed.

Something big moved, shifted in the shadows, and came toward her. Rhona did not retreat, although she felt like it. Reynard's face and form took shape from the murk, his eyes gleaming down at her.

"My lady," he said, and she felt like his. *His* lady.

"Reynard," she replied, her voice deliberately cold and mannered.

He reached out and took her arm, his fingers stroking

the yellow wool of her sleeve and the warm flesh beneath it. "You are like a beam of sunlight," he said, and when he said it, it did not sound trite. "There is a private place at the back," he added quietly, ignoring the interested looks they were getting. "Come with me."

She would have gone with him anywhere, she acknowledged to herself as she followed him down the narrow alley beside the building and into the yard at the back. He had twisted her around his big little finger, taken her cold, wounded heart and made it beat again. And Rhona did not know whether to be grateful to him or fear him the more because of it.

At the back of the inn, there was a wooden ladder leading up into a loft set in the roof above the smoky room she had just seen. She negotiated the ladder without any mishap, and Rhona was already sitting up above, upon a pile of straw, when Reynard's head rose through the doorway. He sat down beside her—the roof was too low for him to stand—and turned to look at her.

His eyes searched her face, which was pale, she knew, from lack of sleep, while she sat, avoiding his gaze, wondering what he was seeing, what he was thinking.

Reynard sighed. "There is something wrong. Tell me, so that I can help you."

He would help her? It was as if a warm light pierced the sense of aloneness that had begun to swallow her up.

She would not cry. She would not cry.

"How can you help me?" she asked him, her voice husky with emotion. "I am beyond it."

Reynard touched her cheek with his finger, gently brushing her skin, leaning in so close to her that his breath warmed her. "Nay, you are far from that, lady."

She wished it were so. But he did not know her, not really. Rhona sighed. "I am what I am because I have had to be, in order to survive. Things are not . . . easy in my father's keep, Reynard. I learned long ago that I must be strong for my brother as well as myself. And now there is a chance," she said as she looked at him sideways, beneath her lashes, wondering just how much she should tell.

"A chance?" he prompted.

"A chance to escape forever. To Normandy. My father will let us go if I help him to gain Lady Jenova."

Reynard paused a moment. "And by 'gain' you mean that she should marry your brother?"

"Nay, not Alfric. We have gone beyond that. Wed my father."

Their eyes met. She saw no particular reaction in Reynard's—did he already know? Well, he may as well know the rest.

"It was my idea."

Now there was disgust before he masked it. Rhona told herself she was not upset or insulted, for it was only what she felt for herself. "I cannot be squeamish," she went on quietly. "I cannot afford to be. I have my brother and myself to think of. My father has said he will let me sail for Normandy if I gain him Lady Jenova, and I hope to take my brother with me. I cannot take him if he is wed to Jenova. If I must sacrifice her to achieve our freedom, then I will do it."

Reynard nodded, slowly, as if he truly understood. "Do you believe your father will grant you this freedom? Do you trust him?"

Rhona smiled a bitter little smile. "I *want* to. I have to. I have no option."

Again he nodded. "Do you trust me?" he murmured in a deep voice.

"I don't know," she managed, her eyes staring into his. What did she see there? Darkness, desire, faraway places.

He kissed her, a gentle brush of his lips to hers. Her lips parted on a sigh, and he kissed her again, more firmly, their flesh clinging, melding together. Rhona leaned into him, her arms slipping about his neck, and it felt right. Entirely right.

"Lady," he breathed against her cheek. "You know I want you, but only if you want me."

She caught her own breath, leaning back a little to see his eyes. She could drown in them, she realized. Sink deep into their heavenly darkness, floating in a midnight sky. "I want you," she said, and wondered if he even realized what she was saying. She didn't just want his body, although that was a part of it; she wanted *him*.

He smiled and gently pushed back her hood, smoothing his hands over her fair hair, kissing her brow like a benediction. "Good," he said. "Very good."

Rhona reached up to undo the ties of her cloak, but he caught her fingers and held them, stilling her. Confused, she tried to read his expression.

"You do not want to . . . you do not wish me to . . ." she stumbled.

He shook his head, his fingers caressing hers, sending a wave of heat through her trembling body. "Then it would be like the others. I want it to be something, somewhere, special. A proper beginning for two people who mean to spend their whole lives together."

"Reynard, we hardly know each other," she began reasonably.

"Oh, we know each other, lady. I need only to look into your eyes and I know everything I need to know about you. Your beauty, your pain, your strength, your bravery."

Tears filled her eyes, and she bowed her head. "You cannot know," she whispered, "what my life has been."

"It will be different from now on." He placed a finger under her chin and tipped her face up, using his thumbs to smooth away her tears. "Trust me, Rhona. I will help you to free yourself." His mouth closed on hers in a deep kiss.

She kissed him back, losing herself in his embrace, knowing this was all new to her. Never had she wanted a man as she wanted Reynard, never had she allowed her mind to be subjugated by her feelings in a situation such as this. It had always been too dangerous, but now . . . now, she did not care.

His big hand slipped beneath her cloak and closed over her breast, cradling her, her nipple hard against the flesh of his palm. Passion ripped through Rhona like lightning. Every sense came alive, turned molten.

Reynard tucked her in closer against him, his hand squeezing gently, his mouth hot and open on hers.

Voices, down in the yard. The boy from the inn, and another, younger voice. Rhona went still, trying to clear her head, trying to pull back from the mindless desire she had been indulging in. Reynard, too, had drawn away, turning his head to see down from the loft without being seen. After a moment the voices retreated, and all was quiet again. He looked back at her, surveying her swollen mouth and glittering eyes. His own mouth was reddened from their kisses, and deep in his dark eyes desire still lurked. But he had tucked it away for now, and she admired his control.

Rhona cleared her throat and smoothed her hair back, for it had come unbound and fell in ringlets about her face. As if he sensed her discomfort, Reynard reached out and twisted a curl about his finger, letting it bob free. He smiled, his smile broadening when she blushed.

Rhona shifted away from him, trying to regain something of her businesslike manner. There were things to say, and things to hear. Secrets to share between them.

"Tell me. What have you heard at Gunlinghorn these past two days?"

He seemed content to let her bring him back from daydreams to cold reality.

"Your chaplain, Jean-Paul, came to see Lord Henry when he was at Gunlinghorn Harbor. He wore a mask over his face. He told Lord Henry that he would give him a choice. The first was to leave Gunlinghorn and return to London, and if he did this, then Jean-Paul would not reveal whatever it is he knows about Lord Henry. But he would only be allowed to do this if he could persuade Lady Jenova to wed your father. The second choice was to remain at Gunlinghorn and face the consequences of his secret being told to everyone. In short, of having his life destroyed."

Rhona nodded. It was much as she had guessed when she had overheard her father and Jean-Paul.

"And what did Lord Henry say to that?"

"Not a great deal. He was taken by surprise."

"What will he do?" she demanded impatiently.

Reynard met her eyes, and he hesitated. Rhona wondered why she felt as if he was deciding between telling her the truth or a lie.

"He does not want to abandon Lady Jenova to such a fate," he said at last, "but neither does he want his secret to become known. Jean-Paul gave him a week to make up his mind."

"He will stay," she said with despair. "He is not the sort of man to leave the lady in peril. He will stay, and Jean-Paul will expose his secret, and Jean-Paul probably knew that that was what would happen when he gave Henry the choice. It is part of the Purgatory he is forcing Henry to undergo." She looked into Reynard's black eyes, searching their depths. "I think he has something else planned. Another plot that Lord Henry does not know of. I overheard him and my father this morning. Jean-Paul said he had a friend at Gunlinghorn, but he meant a spy."

"The groom," Reynard said quietly.

"Nay, not the groom. Someone else, someone close to the family."

Reynard puzzled over this for a moment with a frown. "You are aright, my lady. The priest will not let things rest where they are now. He knows Lord Henry will destroy himself rather than abandon Lady Jenova to Baldessare. He hates Lord Henry. I could hear it in his voice. That degree of hatred will not be satisfied with mere threats. He will want to carry them through. He will want to be sure that Lord Henry is helpless to prevent his lady's suffering."

"Believe me, he is the sort to force Henry to watch them in the bride bed."

"Jesu, he is a monster!" Fury narrowed Reynard's eyes.

"No more than my father," she said quietly.

"I pity Lady Jenova."

Rhona watched him a moment, thoughtful. "Does she know? Has Lord Henry told her the change in bridegroom?"

"Nay, I don't think so. I know he has said nothing of whatever it is Jean-Paul knows of him."

"He should tell her," Rhona said urgently. "If she loves him, she will understand, whatever this secret is. Women are far stronger than men think them; they have to be."

Reynard smiled. Rhona realized then what she had said. Had she forgotten which side she was on? Her freedom, and Alfric's, depended on Lady Jenova's downfall.

She must not forget that, she must not grow squeamish now. . . .

Reynard turned his attention once more to Jean-Paul. "Do you know who he really is? Do you know anything at all about him?"

"I think he is truly a priest. He knows too much to be playing a part. He has been with us a year now, and I am surprised he's stayed so long, for he is a clever man. I think he could do far better than Hilldown Castle. It is as if he chose us on purpose, for some reason of his own."

"Perhaps he did."

"Aye, perhaps. His disfigurement comes from being badly burned. The scars are old. I have heard they cover most of his body. 'Tis a miracle he survived."

"A miracle indeed. And you do not have another name for him?"

"Nay, only Jean-Paul." Rhona twisted a ring restlessly upon her little finger. "He . . . he is not a man with whom to have a pleasant conversation. I have never felt entirely comfortable with him. There is something in his eyes . . . eye. As if he is secretly laughing at me. Even when he is being sympathetic, he is laughing. And the laughter is not kind, Reynard."

The words spilled from her; she could not stop them. It was as if all her reticence, all the walls she had built to keep herself safe, had come falling down.

Reynard covered her hands with his, squeezing gently. He could feel her bones through the flesh, so fragile. She was a small woman, and could be so easily hurt. He did not want her to return to Hilldown Castle, to her father and Jean-Paul, but he knew he had no choice but to allow it.

Allow it? He smiled to himself. As if she would let him

boss her about! Lady Rhona was very much her own woman, used to taking command. Could he persuade her to change sides? It was one thing to show signs of regret, but it was a big step from that to betraying her father and throwing in her lot with Lord Henry. Reynard did not believe that Baldessare would set her and Alfric free—they were his, and he was too greedy of his possessions to ever let them go.

Voices again, this time his aunt, scolding one of the lads who fetched wood for her. Reynard glanced at Rhona and gave her a reassuring grin. "It is only the innkeeper, Matilda. Do not fear, she will not betray you."

Rhona gave him a suspicious, sideways look. "You seem to know her well, Reynard."

He hesitated. "She is my father's sister," he said.

She appeared startled. "Oh."

"She wasn't always as you see her now. Once she wore fine clothes, like you, and rings upon her fingers. She was a merchant's wife in Bruges and very proud. But he lost his fortune and died in debt, and left her to grow old in poverty."

Rhona looked away, as if she didn't want him to read her thoughts. "That must have been difficult for her."

"Aye. I have helped her when I can. I am only sorry I cannot do more."

Now she did look, and there was a wondering expression in her eyes. "So you help her? You haven't abandoned her because she is poor and of no use to you?"

Reynard felt pain, an aching jolt in his chest, that she should think such a thing, that her life with Baldessare had led her to believe such actions were the norm. "Nay, lady, I would not abandon her," he said gently.

She gazed at him a moment longer, as though trying to read his thoughts, and then she nodded her head. She

looked down at her hands, folded in her lap, and gave a
sigh. It was a deep sigh, a sigh of longing, and suddenly
Reynard knew he wasn't making an error of judgment in
trusting this girl. His instincts were correct. She was
worth saving.

He reached over and covered her hands with his. She
started, but did not remove them.

"I want to help you to be free," he said quietly and
reached up to caress her cheek, her throat, exploring her
soft, vulnerable flesh. She was so beautiful. He knew he
would never tire of touching her, of looking at her.

Her lashes fluttered down, dark against her pale
cheeks. "Do you, Reynard?"

"You have suffered, Rhona, but that can change. I can
spring the trap you are in."

"If only you—"

"Will you travel with me to faraway lands, lady? Will
we see all the world has to show us, you and me?"

She looked up then, her eyes ablaze. "Oh yes. Yes,
please."

His lips brushed hers, teasing, testing. Then deeper,
drawing her against him, until she softened, molding her
curves to the hard planes of his body. Her arms tangled
about his neck and she hung on, her tongue dueling with
his, her mouth hot and wild and willing.

Reynard was sure he had found paradise.

And then she pulled away.

Her breasts beneath the yellow gown were rising and
falling, almost as wildly as his own heart was beating.
She put a palm flat against his chest, as though to hold
him back, but he wasn't moving.

"You must know . . . you should know that what you
said about me was true. My maidenhead was given as an
inducement to a man who had land my father wanted.

And there were other times, times when I had to . . . when I . . ."

"I don't care."

She blinked, as if she couldn't quite accept what he had said. As if she was certain he had some other, crueler meaning he meant to hurl upon her.

"I don't care," Reynard repeated softly, so she could not mistake him. "Your past is nothing to me, and I hope mine does not influence you. We are two lonely souls, and we have found each other. Let us be grateful for it."

Tears filled her eyes, her mouth trembled, but she managed to answer him. "I am grateful. Help me, Reynard. If I can escape my father, if I can save myself and my brother, and Lady Jenova, too, then I will! But I cannot do it on my own."

"I know, lady, and I will help you. We will win through."

He kissed her, feeling the need in her, holding back. Now was not the time. When he had freed her, when they were together, then he would be able to love her as he wished, as she wished. Until then, they must wait.

"'Tis cold as a witch's heart out there," Matilda said, looking up as her nephew sat down on the bench beside her.

Reynard laughed. "What do you know of a witch's heart?" he mocked gently.

The old woman grumbled into the pot she was stirring over the coals. Hare stew, the same hare Reynard had brought with him. It smelled good.

"She is a fine lady," she said now, refusing to meet his eyes. "Too fine for you, Reynard. The Normans are too proud a race to look beneath their own."

"Perhaps she is tired of her own race. Perhaps I can give her something they cannot."

"I saw her, in her velvets and her furs, her fingers heavy with jewels. How can you compete with that, Reynard? Nay, 'twill be only unhappiness you find with her."

Knowing his aunt's own background, Reynard could understand her need to preach caution. But she didn't understand Rhona as he did. She did not see her pain and her hurt and her need for the simple, valuable things he could give her. Kindness, gentleness, compassion, but most of all, love.

"I will be careful," he said now, sniffing appreciatively at the hare stew. "Don't worry about me. I know what I am doing."

She gave him a narrow, sorrowing glance. "I have heard many men say those words in my long life, Reynard, and none of them did. Not in the end."

Rhona's horse flew over the stony ground, leaping half concealed branches and logs and dangerous dips in the ground. She was being reckless, and she didn't care. She had never been so happy. She had thought to find a spy in Reynard, someone to use in her plot, and instead she had found love, and a man who was everything she had ever wanted.

Of course he was a servant. A mercenary. The son of a shipwright and navigator. Doubts circled her, but she pushed them away and rode on. This was beyond any considerations of wealth and blood and power. Her father might believe such things were all that mattered, but Rhona no longer did.

They would be together.

Just how, she did not know. Reynard had sworn to

meet her again tomorrow, at Uther's Tower. Mayhap he would have thought of something by then. She knew now that Lord Henry had no intention of placing Lady Jenova into her father's hands. He would die rather than allow that to happen. But Jean-Paul must have known that, she realized, just as he seemed to understand so many other aspects of Lord Henry's character.

He must have another plan.

She must learn what she could, and then tell Reynard. Together they would thwart Jean-Paul, and her father. And then? Her father would not simply be furious with her. If he found out, he would kill her.

"The king will not be pleased to hear what Baldessare has been up to," Reynard had said, holding her in his arms, his deep voice filling her senses. "The king will punish him, possibly he will strip him of his lands and his wealth. How will you like being just Rhona, a simple, freeborn girl?"

Rhona had expected to feel regret. There was none. It would not matter to her, she realized in surprise. She would still have the thing that mattered to her most. She would have Reynard.

But she might not be able to wait until the king returned to England. She might have to run as soon as Baldessare's plot began to go wrong. And so she had told Reynard.

"Come to Gunlinghorn," he had replied. "You will be safe there."

Come to Gunlinghorn. As if it were the simplest thing in the world. As if it were not partly her fault Lady Jenova was in this predicament.

But Rhona knew that if it became necessary, she would do just that. Come to Gunlinghorn. And pray she had a welcome there.

The walls of Hilldown Castle came into sight. She rode through the postern gate, nodding at the guard on duty. He had been given a coin for his trouble and would say nothing about her slipping out for so long. Rhona left her horse with one of the grooms and hurried into the keep and up the stairs to her small room—no more than a corner in the tower. She would straighten her clothing and comb her hair, and go downstairs to play her part. There was much to be done, and she needed to be brave. . . .

As Rhona opened the door, someone rose from the seat by the window.

It was Jean-Paul.

Chapter 19

"Did she say what he looked like beneath that accursed mask?"

Henry was rubbing his jaw, making a grating sound as his hand passed over his unshaven skin. It was the first time Reynard could ever recall seeing Henry at this hour without his face being cleanly shaven. His tunic, too, looked creased, as though he had picked it up off the floor and put it back on. His hair needed combing, and it was matted at the back.

Reynard experienced a strong feeling of unease. Was it a good thing or a bad thing that his lord seemed to have lost his peace of mind? When he had first come into Henry's service, he had thought him the most composed man he had ever met. Nothing had seemed to upset him, and he had been in full control of his life. Now it was as if a different man altogether had stepped in and taken Henry's place.

"His burns are extensive," he said, trying to bring his

thoughts into line. "It is difficult to tell what he used to look like, or even how old he is. And he has someone here at Gunlinghorn, my lord. A spy. It is someone close to the family. I think he means to fool you into thinking he is planning one thing, and then he will do another."

Henry slammed one fist into his palm in frustration. "Mayhap it's all a game! Perhaps he will not do anything at all!"

"Can you take that risk?" Reynard reminded him.

Henry went still, and Reynard, looking into his eyes, realized just how shaken Henry was. Rattled completely from his normal state of mind. He knew he would have to destroy himself for Lady Jenova's sake, and he was going to do it. He must love her very much. . . .

Henry closed his eyes, and when he opened them again, they were burning with fury. "I know what I would like to do. Ride to Hilldown Castle and find this Jean-Paul. If he has his way, I will have no friends or supporters. All it will take is a seed of doubt, Reynard, to bring me down."

"Lady Jenova will stand by you, my lord."

Henry laughed, but there was no humor in it. "Will she? You do not know what she will do when she knows what I did, what sort of life I lived, what horrors I took part in. Women, in my experience, prefer not to be troubled with such things. It is easier to find someone else."

"Lady Jenova is not like that. You know she will be your friend whatever happens."

Be my friend? Perhaps. But my lover, my wife? I doubt it.

And how could he blame her for that? He was not worthy of such a woman; he did not deserve her. He had no right to a happy life here at Gunlinghorn, with Jenova and Raf.

Henry cleared his throat, aware that Reynard was still watching him, still waiting. "If I had an army, we might have a chance of taking Hilldown Castle, but as yet Baldessare has done nothing wrong. Can I lay siege to a man who has done nothing apart from threaten me?"

If only Jenova would agree to marry him! He could protect her then, and even if the truth was disclosed, he could bear the disgrace because she would be safe.

Tell her the truth.

Could he risk it? He felt as if he were standing on the edge of the cliffs above Gunlinghorn Harbor, about to jump. All his life he had chosen women he could not love and who did not love him, and now he knew why. Now he understood what would happen to him if he found that soul mate, only to lose her. He *had* found her, and soon she would turn her back on him and walk away. . . .

"My lord?"

Henry blinked at Reynard's watchful face, for a moment hardly recognizing him. His head was aching, and he felt dizzy. When had he last eaten? The days and nights had melded into each other, full of questions and memories. He must pull himself together!

"What is it, Reynard?"

Reynard hesitated a moment, and then he plunged in. "Lady Rhona is mistreated by her father. I want her to leave. I want her to come here, to Gunlinghorn, where she will be safe."

Henry looked at him blankly, and then he laughed. "You want to bring Lady Rhona here? Against the wishes of her father and her brother? As if things were not bad enough, Reynard! Do you intend to start a war now?"

Reynard's jaw clenched. "If I have to."

Henry gave another wild laugh, then shook his head. "Jesu, I thought I was the madman!"

"She is—"

"I know, I know. Her life is a misery. You wish to save her." A wry smile twisted his mouth. "Aye, all right. If she will agree to it, then bring her here, Reynard. We may as well annoy Baldessare as much as we can. When do you see her again?"

"Tomorrow."

"Then meet with her tomorrow and see how things are, then make your decision."

Reynard released his breath. "Thank you, my lord." When he left, there was a spring in his step.

I have made him happy, at least.

In the yard, the Gunlinghorn garrison were training— the professional soldiers and the villeins, who were required to do garrison duty every week. Henry, after receiving the permission of Jenova and Sir John, had been giving their captain some instruction on training methods. From the look of the men training now, they were doing extremely well. Give them another month or two, he thought, and they would be good enough to beat off anything that Baldessare could pit against them.

But he had forgotten. He did not have that long. He had but a week, less than that now, and his life would be over. And if Jenova did not wed him, then he would not even be able to save her.

Henry had been standing in the castleyard for a long time now, oblivious to the cold or the soldiers who were trying their hardest to win his approval. He looked as if he were in a dream. Jenova sighed and asked herself what Reynard had said to him to make him so pensive.

She smoothed the mulberry-colored wool she had been so carefully stitching. It had been meant as a late Christmas present. A new tunic for Henry, a special present for her oldest and dearest friend. Now it was something she would give him when he went away—a good-bye gift. She had it almost finished, but as she watched him standing so still, she wondered if she could bear to give it to him. Although she had told him to go, Jenova knew that no gift could sweeten his leaving. She would be bereft. She would miss him so much that it would be as if a part of herself were gone.

If only it hadn't happened this way! If only their passion could have faded, as it was supposed to, instead of burning brighter every day. And turning, for her part at least, into a love so strong and glowing that it could outshine the sun.

Suddenly, as if he had sensed her watching him, Henry looked up. Jenova was still standing at the window, and she felt the shock as their eyes met. There was a connection between them, and it sent a tingle down her spine and a shiver over her skin. For a long moment he stood, staring up into her eyes, and then abruptly his jaw tensed, his face hardened, and he took off at a run toward the keep.

Uneasily, stumbling a little, Jenova backed away from the solar window. What was wrong with him? What was he thinking? And why did she suddenly feel like she wanted to bar her door before he got here? Because she knew very well that this was where Henry was headed.

The door was thrown wide, and Henry strode in.

He was nearly out of breath, and his eyes were alight with some inner quest. Oh God, she thought, what now? That was when Jenova realized how much he had changed. Henry hadn't shaved. She blinked. His clothing was in disarray. There was a stain on his tunic. He had the wrong rings on the wrong fingers. Even his boots looked grubby.

Was this her perfect Henry? What had happened to him?

Dismay took the strength from her, and she dropped the mulberry wool at her feet. "Henry!"

"Jenova," he said, and his voice was low and powerful. "I need you to marry me. You were right, I didn't tell you the entire truth before. You see, 'tis Baldessare who means to have you for his wife. Not Alfric, Jenova, but Baldessare, and he will have you, willing or not. Marry me, now. You must. You no longer have a choice."

She sat down on the window seat, carefully, composing herself. His violet-blue eyes were blazing as if they had a torch behind them. He looked dangerous. She had never seen Henry so wild, so uncontrolled, so totally lacking in all the attributes that made him Henry. Clearly this was a moment to choose her words very carefully.

"Henry, we have already spoken of this—"

"Baldessare wants you, Jenova. Take heed, he will not give up easily."

"I have dealt with Baldessare before. You know that. Besides, if he tried to marry me against my will, the king would punish him. Even Baldessare is not such a complete fool as that."

"Baldessare believes he can do whatever he wants. By the time the king returns to England, the marriage will have been accomplished."

She frowned, about to argue, but he went on.

"Do not think the king is not fond of you, Jenova. He is, and he has been more than generous to you, when it was within his power to force you into any number of marriages for his own benefit. But if Baldessare makes this union between you, and then promises to behave, the king will be inclined to listen to him. Especially if he has other matters to deal with—there is much unrest in England at the moment, and he will be concerned with that when he returns. Baldessare will have many months to persuade you to tell whatever lies he wants of you."

Jenova thought she might explode; her face was flushed, her hands had clenched into fists, her green eyes were dark with anger as she looked up at Henry. "No one can force me to do anything I do not want to do, Henry. You should know that. I am no feeble woman. I am the Lady of Gunlinghorn."

"Baldessare has a spy in your keep, Jenova. He has someone you trust working against you."

Her thoughts scattered. "I don't believe it. All my people are loyal. Who told you that?"

"Reynard."

"And who told him, Henry!"

Henry hesitated, and then shrugged, as if he had decided it was safe to tell her the truth. Her anger rose another notch. "Lady Rhona."

"Ah."

"What do you mean, 'Ah'?"

"I mean I do not trust Lady Rhona. Possibly she tells Reynard lies to help her brother's cause."

"How can the telling of such a thing help her? 'Tis more likely to put her at outs with her father. I would not want Baldessare angry with me, would you?"

He seemed so sincere. Jenova could see it in his eyes. He wanted her safe, and he saw marriage as the way to do it. She believed that about him; she even believed that he was fond of her. If she were *fond* of him, then she would not mind marrying him. They could live apart and be perfectly happy seeing each other only occasionally. But Jenova *loved* him, loved him with her heart and her body and her soul, and it was just not enough anymore to have him as her comfortable friend.

She would rather not have him at all.

Her decision confirmed, Jenova patted the seat beside her. "Sit down, Henry."

He eyed her narrowly, impatiently, but he came and sat beside her. Jenova decided he looked even worse at close quarters, with his unshaven face and shadowed eyes, and the hint of self-mockery about his mouth.

"Mayhap you do not understand how it is for a woman in my position, Henry," she said in a carefully moderated voice. The voice, she realized guiltily, she had used in her conversation with Alfric not long since. "I am better off alone."

"You do not trust me."

He said it evenly, as if it didn't really matter, but she saw something in his eyes, something hurt, as if she had struck him with a closed fist. *Henry, hurt?* It was almost impossible to believe. Henry, a man with an iron shield of confidence, with an easy, smiling charm? She found it difficult to believe anything she said to Henry could pierce that armor. And yet, looking at him now, she did not see much of that old Henry at all.

Jenova wondered if she could have wrought this change. Was this her fault? But no, how could it be! Whatever had happened to Henry, he was keeping it locked away inside. For her to help him, he must trust her.

"I trust you," she said carefully. "Far more than you trust me. I have said this before, but I think . . . I *know* you are keeping something from me. There is more to your concern about Jean-Paul, and probably about Baldessare, too, more than you are telling me. But if you will not tell me, then I cannot give your wishes proper consideration. And I do not wish to marry you under these circumstances. I am sorry, Henry."

"So you need no help with all of this? You can defeat

Baldessare, hold off his army, discover the spy in your keep, and protect your lands until the king's return? There seems little point in me remaining here, then. I am merely in your way."

He was angry with her, and his words gave her a pain in her heart that was as sharp as a needle. But she kept it at bay—there would be time to feel later.

"I never expected you to stay at Gunlinghorn forever," she said quietly. "Of course I will miss you. You know I will. I . . . I am used to you being here, Henry. Raf will miss you, too. But I am fully aware that your real life is elsewhere; you have never led me to believe anything differently."

Now was the time, if he wished, to tell her what was troubling him. To trust her. To throw himself open to her healing love. Henry stared at her and said nothing. There was a fine sheen of perspiration on his face, and when he leaned back against the window embrasure, his body was as tense as iron. Jenova watched him sadly, eyes fixed on his profile, the perfect line of nose and brow and bearded jaw, the fall of his hair, the hard soldier's body. Something was eating him alive, but he would not share it. And Jenova knew she could not bow to his wishes. He must tell her the truth—as much as she loved him, they could not live together otherwise.

"You are very understanding, Jenova," he said at last, and there was little emotion in his voice—perhaps a hint of dry mockery.

"We are friends, Henry. We were friends before and we will, I hope, be friends after." It was costing her a great deal to be so reasonable and so calm. To pretend her heart was not breaking.

"Aye, friends." There was bitterness beneath the surface, but she ignored it. He might be suffering from hurt male pride because she wouldn't accept his help, or irritation because she had not needed him to ride to her rescue. Or mayhap he was simply annoyed because she had put him into a corner. But Jenova could not escape the sense that, deep inside, he needed her most desperately.

"Raf is expecting you to take him riding tomorrow," she said, holding on to her composure by a thread.

He nodded, not meeting her eyes. "I hadn't forgotten. Will he really miss me?"

Now there was vulnerability in the line of his mouth, an uncertainty that had never been there before. Jenova felt tears sting her own eyes, and she had to look away and pretend to smooth her sleeve. "Of course he will, Henry. You are his hero."

Henry smiled back, but the pain in his face had not gone away. "I am glad I am someone's hero then, sweeting. If you do not mind, I think I will go and speak to your scribe. I have some plans for him to draw up, for your harbor. That will be safe, at least."

"Thank you, Henry."

He took her hand as if to kiss it, then changed his mind and let it go. Jenova smiled, but he had already gone through the door. It was best, she told herself. Her heart was breaking, but he would never know it. She would allow him to go back, without guilt, to the life he loved without feeling he needed to stay on for her sake.

This was her gift to him, and it was of far greater value than any tunic.

"Jean-Paul?"

In the moment after opening her door, Rhona had time to gather her wits and smooth her features into the mask she usually wore when she was in his presence. That he was in her room at all was frightening enough, but there could be an entirely innocent explanation for it.

"Where have you been, my lady?" That single pale eye raked over her, taking in the wrinkles in her clothing, her untidy hair, her bruised lips. Ticking off each damning piece of evidence against her.

He knew. Somehow he knew, and Rhona was experienced enough to realize she would be foolish to pretend otherwise. But she could bend the truth, make it work for her. She had done it before.

"I have someone in Lord Henry's camp who tells me things. I was meeting with him, Jean-Paul. Furthering the interests of my father and Alfric."

His gaze was still upon her, his disconcerting face in shadow. "Who is this 'someone'?"

"Lord Henry's manservant," she replied without hesitation. "He is enamored of me," she added, with a laugh and toss of her head, as if it mattered not at all. "I'm sure he would do anything for me, if I asked it of him."

"Is that why you were listening at the door this morning, my lady? I thought he was the spy, not you."

Jesu. "I-I could not help but overhear, but I would not repeat what I heard. Why would I? I lingered because I was eager to learn what was in my father's mind, so that I could help him to secure Lady Jenova as his bride."

"She is ours anyway," the priest replied matter-of-factly. "Your father will tame her."

Rhona couldn't help it; she flinched. Horror uncoiled in her belly. Lady Jenova, beautiful and calm Lady Jenova, beaten into submission by Baldessare. She had tried not to think of it, tried to put it out of her mind, but now it was there, in all its terrifying detail. And she knew at last what her heart had been trying to tell her all along.

She could not do it. She could not be a party to this thing. Reynard was right; she belonged with him, at Gunlinghorn.

Mayhap he saw that in her face. Mayhap her mask slipped long enough for him to read what she was thinking. His voice dripped satisfaction.

"Your father still has need of you, my lady. Do not think that because he will wed Jenova he will no longer require you to help him in his dealings. We both have plans for you."

Somehow she stayed upright. She even lifted her chin as he rose and came toward her, his long robes brushing the floor. He smelled of incense and something rancid, as if he did not wash himself very often. She met his one good eye as he paused before her, staring down at her.

"You are very lovely and very brave, *chérie*," he whispered. "Too bad. Do not leave the keep again. If you try, I will have you locked in. Do you understand?"

His mouth was curved with satisfaction, but it did not disguise the cold savagery in his ruined face. The fire might have damaged the outer shell of this man, Rhona thought, but others had survived such trauma. No, it was the inside that was rotten. And perhaps that had always been so.

"As you say," she replied coolly.

When he had gone, she sank down onto her bed and stared at nothing until the trembling eased. She was alone, more alone than she had believed possible, or perhaps it just felt worse after being with Reynard.

Nothing had changed.

She had had such hopes, and now nothing would ever change. She would remain the spare arrow in Baldessare's quiver, to be used for his benefit. Forever. The only thing different was inside her, the change in her, and that was because of Reynard. She was changed because of him, he had given her hope of a better life, and now she would never see him again. He would wait for her tomorrow at Uther's Tower, but she would not come.

And he would never learn why.

Mayhap she could get a message to him, through the groom, as she had before? But they would know. Jean-Paul and her father would be watching, now that they no longer trusted her. A message wasn't worth a beating. And it wasn't worth dying for.

A tear ran down her cheek.

She had been so happy as she'd ridden home. She had even begun to think that maybe she had a future. And now it was all gone, all destroyed. She was back to being what she had always been, something to use, something whose feelings were never taken into account. Whose feelings simply did not matter.

"Rhona, are you there?"

It was Alfric. He tapped upon her door, his voice whispery so as not to be overheard. Had he been told to stay away? Obviously he did not want his father to know he was there, but it was brave of him to have come at all, and Rhona knew Alfric was not very brave when it came to facing up to Baldessare.

"Yes, I am here," she called softly, but she did not get up.

There was a pause, and then his voice came out in a rush. "Rhona, I am afraid. I-I-I know you will s-save us both, but I am still very afraid."

Save them both. She must have been insane to think such a thing. She was alone against the combined evil of her father and Jean-Paul.

"I am resting, Alfric. I will talk with you later."

"Oh." He hesitated, knowing something was wrong, but helpless to ease her pain. Finally, his steps retreated. Rhona lay down and closed her eyes, and pretended she wasn't there.

Chapter 20

In his dream Henry could hardly see where he was going. At first he had thought he was at Gunlinghorn, but the shadows were so deep and the passages twisted and turned. He was soon lost.

It was night, but there were no torches upon the walls, although there was an old smell of ashes. He stumbled along, hands outstretched, trying to see his way. There was no light, none at all. Nothing to tell him whether or not he was going in the right or the wrong direction.

Jenova. He needed to speak to Jenova, but he had to find her first. She had rejected him again. He had meant to keep persisting until he had worn her down, but he did not think he could bear that. He had his pride, after all, and she was slicing it to pieces with her kind, sad smile.

He had meant to tell her, today in her solar, that he was happier at Gunlinghorn than he had ever been before, anywhere in his life. He had meant to tell her that he felt part of a family for perhaps the first time in his whole life. The abandoned boy, shunted from relative to relative, never belonging to anyone. He had always been afraid to give too much of himself, in case it was taken from him. But now the need was greater than the fear.

Jenova was his life. If he left her behind, if he left Raf and Gunlinghorn, he would feel like that abandoned child all over again.

He had meant to tell her all these things, but somehow the moment had slipped away from him. Faced with the reality of her, the possibility of rejection, he had been too much a coward to speak the words. She would ask him all the questions he so feared. And turn away from him, the disgust plain on her face.

Henry didn't think he could stay and see that.

He was only a man, after all, not a saint.

Beau Henri.

Henry stilled, his outstretched hand touching stone, roughly cut and crumbling stone. Beyond him, in the darkness, he could hear breathing. He wasn't alone.

There was a smell. A mixture of despair and terror, pain and misery. He knew them all. He knew that smell.

That was when he realized he was back in *le château de Nuit*.

He woke with a sob.

Jean-Paul had been waiting, standing like a shadow in the woods beyond the meadows, only his breath to betray him. Gunlinghorn Castle rose bulkily against the sky, dark apart from the occasional flicker of torchlight from the patrolling watch. There seemed more on guard than usual, as if they were preparing for a possible enemy attack.

He smiled to himself.

They thought the danger would come from outside

Gunlinghorn. The truth was, it was already lodged safely within.

A figure was approaching on foot, its cloak flapping behind, an inner agitation causing jerky movements. And fear. Jean-Paul recognized the emotion instantly—in his youth, he had seen many people running through fear. It had been his job to catch them and bring them back; his and Henry's.

"You are late," he said and moved out into the figure's path.

It jumped and gasped and clutched its chest. "Oh, you frightened me! I did not see you—"

"Have you news?"

A deep breath, a resigned huff at his bad manners. "Lady Jenova will marry none. Not even Lord Henry."

"Not even Henry . . ." Jean-Paul considered that, enjoying the idea of Henry begging Jenova to marry him and her refusing. Had he told her about his past yet? Had he shared that with her? Did he dare? Jean-Paul almost hoped he would, so that he could suffer even greater depths of despair.

"What do you want me to do?"

Jean-Paul turned and stared at the face within the hood, considering it. "You must be very brave. If we are to give Lady Jenova and Lord Alfric the happy ending they deserve, then we must now take an action some may consider . . . extreme."

"What action?" The voice was shrill, too loud.

"Hush!" said Jean-Paul impatiently. "Do you want the watch to hear you? It is only extreme because it is unusual, but it is necessary. Completely and entirely necessary. You trust me, don't you?" He fingered the cross on his chest, letting the starlight catch it, reminding her of what he was.

The head within the hood bobbed respectfully. "Of course I do, Father Jean-Paul. I know you want only what is best, as I do. Sometimes others are blind to such things, and they must be shown the way. Prodded, gently, in the right direction."

His own words, come back to him from another's lips. He smiled. "That is so true, my child. Very well, I will tell you what I want you to do. Listen carefully and be brave. It will all soon be over."

His voice went on, softly, urgently. At first the figure gasped and shook its head, but gradually, as his words washed over it, acceptance came. By the time they parted, it was nearly dawn, but his persuasion had had its effect.

Jean-Paul's will would be done.

This morning the air was chill, but the sky had lost its ominous look. Henry led Raf up the slope through the trees, turning back to smile at the boy's flushed and excited face beneath his furry hood. Jenova and Agetha had bundled him up so much that he resembled a round bladder rather than a skinny little boy.

"Not much farther."

Raf grinned back, urging his pony faster. It lumbered along behind Lamb, making hard work of the slope. Jenova had not wished to join them, although both Henry and Raf had asked her—mayhap Raf had been the more sincere of the two. They had around half a dozen men from the castle as guard, but so far Henry had not sighted a single soul besides themselves.

It was too early and too cold.

Last night's dream had stayed with him, an unpleasant sensation. As if someone was standing behind him, unseen and yet with eyes fixed upon him. Henry had lain awake the rest of the night, trying to put the nightmare out of his mind, but it was as if Jean-Paul, whoever he really was, had released the past from its locked room and now he could not put it back. Flashes of memory, pictures from long-ago days, came and went in his waking mind, and he was unable to stop them.

"Hurry up, Henry!" Raf called, and Henry looked up to see the boy racing ahead, the little fat pony's legs a blur. They reached the top of the hill together and stopped, catching their breath, horses snorting and puffing. The guard had dropped behind, but Henry did not worry. Up here it was as if they were all alone in the world.

Gunlinghorn was spread out before them, just as it had been the day that Jenova had brought him up here. The day that had started it all. The river was moving sluggishly, still half frozen, the woods were dark and bare, but soon they would be green and lush. Gunlinghorn was ready to burst into life.

"Is all of this really mine, Henry?" Raf's voice was small, as if the thought of so much good fortune overwhelmed him.

Henry nodded, a serious nod. "All of it, Raf."

Raf's small, pale face swung slowly from side to side as he took in the hills and the vale. " 'Tis very big."

"But you will get bigger, too, Raf. You will be a good lord, just as your mother is a good lady. And the people of Gunlinghorn love you. But always remember, love comes with a price. In return for the love of your people, you must always do your best to protect and look after them. And you must rule them wisely and well."

Raf nodded solemnly, but his sideways glance was anxious. "But you and Mama will help me, won't you, Henry?"

There was that now familiar ache in his chest. Henry

ignored it. "Your Mama will always help you, Raf. And so will I. When I can. But I may not always be here, you see. The king might need me again, and I have to help him, too."

Raf thought about that for a moment. "You must be very important if the king needs your help," he said at last.

Henry couldn't help but smile. "I've learned I am not as important as I thought I was. The king can always find other men to help him if I am not there." *But where will I find another Gunlinghorn? How will I ever restore myself with Jenova when I have let her down so badly?* "Are you ready to go back now?"

Raf ignored the question, set upon a quest of his own, and Henry knew from experience that Raf would have his answers. "Mama will be sad if you go. She has smiled much while you are here. You make her laugh, Henry. You would not . . ." But he hesitated, doubtful.

"Ask your question, Raf. I will answer it if I can."

Raf nodded and took a breath. "You would not think to take us with you when you go, would you, Henry?"

Those green eyes, so like Jenova's, looked directly into his. Henry had the urge to promise the boy anything, just to make him smile, but he held it back. He had learned enough over the past weeks in the child's company to know it was not kind to promise things he could not provide. Much as he wanted to say yes, Henry well knew that Jenova would say no.

"Your Mama will not want to come, Raf, and you are too young to go alone. When you are older, though, I will be pleased to have you come and stay with me whenever you wish."

Raf frowned in thought, and then he shook his head. "I could not come without Mama," he said at last. "But I do thank you, Henry, for your kind offer."

Henry grinned. "My pleasure, Raf."

He did not tell the boy that there would come a time when he would be more than happy to leave his mother here at Gunlinghorn and spread his wings. The boy's love and devotion did him credit, much of it due to Jenova, Henry was sure. He wondered what sort of man he might have been if he had had a loving mother, if she had not left him to the care of strangers. . . .

"Lord Henry!"

The shout startled him, and he drew his sword before he realized it was Reynard, riding to meet him. The big man came up to them, bowing his head to the boy and following it up with a smile.

"Master Raf, you are looking very fine."

"My pony is old, but he is determined," Raf replied. "One day I will have a stallion like Lamb, but not yet."

"No, you are wise to wait. Lamb can be a handful some days, even for me." Reynard turned to Henry, and the good humor dropped away from his rugged face. "I am off to Uther's Tower."

Henry moved closer, lowering his voice so that the boy could not overhear. "Bring her back if you can, Reynard. I think you are right. She is not safe where she is. I have decided I will ask Jenova's permission to send for Lord Radulf's men. He has an army to the west. If I have to leave . . . well, Baldessare's greed might overcome his fear of the king, but he would be a fool to fight the King's Sword."

Reynard nodded his agreement. "Send for them anyway, my lord. Lady Jenova need not know until they are here, and then she will hardly turn them away."

Henry laughed. "Aye, I will take your advice, my friend. Very well. Go and keep your meeting. Master Raf and I are ready for home, eh, Raf?"

"Aye." Raf smiled and then gave a little shiver.

The boy was cold. What was he thinking to keep him sitting here so long? Henry urged Lamb down the hillside, carefully, keeping an eye on Raf at his side. The pony was favoring one of his forelegs, but only slightly. The boy was cold, his beloved pony injured, well done, Henry! He gave a grimace. Pray God it didn't get any worse.

Before long the gates of Gunlinghorn were before them, and once inside, Henry lifted Raf down from his now badly limping pony. "There, go inside and warm yourself. Your mother will not be very happy with me if you have caught cold."

Raf, looking a little flushed, retorted that he had so many clothes on he was hot, not cold. But Henry could see the worry in his face when he looked upon his faithful mount.

"He may have bruised himself. I don't think it's serious," Henry said, nodding to the pony. "If you like, we could put a poultice on that leg. I will show you how."

Raf seemed happy with the offer, and some of the concern left his eyes.

"Then go and do what you must, and then come back to the stables. I'll be waiting."

When he had gone, Henry led Lamb back to his stall, while the groom took the pony. He tried to spend time with the big horse every day, and often brushed him and spoke with him. Sometimes he swore that Lamb understood every word he said and was far more sympathetic than most people.

Today he was more concerned with Raf's pony. Henry had always had a way with animals, apart from that early run-in with the destrier. It was something else he could teach Raf before he left.

Reynard was right. He would send for Radulf's army now, and at least stay until they came. If he could not persuade his stubborn lady to marry him, then at least he would know she was safe. He would feel better then.

But not happier.

"I am already too hot!"

Raf stuck out his lip mulishly, on the verge of rebellion. Agetha clicked her tongue impatiently but gave in. She folded the warm cloak over her arm and took Raf's hand in hers.

"Very well, then, but you might need it later. Come on, or we will be late."

"Late for what?" Raf demanded. "Lord Henry is expecting me in the stables. My pony has a bruised foreleg." But, still, he went with her, used to obedience where Agetha was concerned. They hurried down the stairs and through the storerooms and the wine cellars, the smell of grain and wine and salted food heavy in the gloomy, dry air. A cat sprang out of the darkness, trapping a mouse. There was a horrid squeaking, and Raf pulled at Agetha's hand.

" 'Tis Raven! Raven has caught a mouse for her babies' supper!"

"Hush, Master Raf."

"But I promised Gertrude I'd show her and—"

"Come with me!"

Raf gave up and let her tug him along. He was tired from the ride on his pony and confused as to where he was going. Agetha had said something about a friend and that she would explain it all in a moment. He felt he should ask her more, but he knew her and trusted her, and although sometimes she was impatient, she was also kind. Well, most of the time.

There was a door. Agetha drew the bolt and tugged at it, pulling it open with a gasp. More stairs, down into the darkness. Someone had lit a torch, and Agetha took it from its sconce and held it up to show the way. It was a tunnel, and at any other time Raf would have been excited, but now the damp shadows made him nervous. Then at last another door, and Raf realized that this door led out through the wall of the castle. They had passed through a tunnel between the keep and the wall, and now they were outside.

"Agetha!" he gasped, but he had no time for more. She was pulling him down a slope and into a tangle of bushes, almost running, as if she was afraid of being seen by one of the guards above. When he looked back over his shoulder, Raf could see that they were at the back of the castle, where it looked over the river. Usually the water was enough to deter would-be invaders.

The tangle of bushes gave way to marshes, and Raf saw a boat tucked away there. Agetha lifted him into it and then climbed in herself, using the oars to row them along, under the shelter of the bank.

"Where are we going?" he asked, but his voice was small. By now Raf realized that there was something very wrong. Agetha should not have had him out here. He'd known, but he had trusted her. He was beginning to think that had been a mistake.

"Nearly there," she panted. Her face was red, and perspiration ran down it. She was not used to rowing, he thought smugly. He hoped her arms were aching. And then the boat ran into the bank and Agetha climbed stiffly over the side and pulled it up a little, so that it would not float away. She reached in and half carried, half dragged Raf to the shore.

"Ouch!" he complained. "I want to go home!"

"Well, you cannot," she retorted breathlessly. "Not until your mother sees sense."

He did not understand. As he made to answer, he heard a sound and turned, just as Agetha gave a cry of relief. There were men in the trees. Not Gunlinghorn men. Men he had never seen before in his life.

"Who are you?" he asked them imperiously, though his knees were shaking.

"I am Jean-Paul," one of them said, and Raf saw with a shock that the man had no face, just a smooth piece of cloth over his head with holes for the eyes and mouth.

Raf stumbled back, into Agetha's skirts, and she gripped his shoulder. Her fingers hurt, but even in his own fear he understood that it was because she was frightened, too. And then Jean-Paul came to take him and he could think no more.

Chapter 21

Jenova listened as her steward took her through an inventory of Gunlinghorn Castle. It was almost time for the evening meal, the day was waning, and they were seated in a small alcove off the great hall. They had been dealing with the important matter of what food stores they already had, and what would be needed for the year ahead. Jenova's head was swimming with figures, from the number of dried apples still edible, to the amount of sour wine still to be drunk.

"Of course Lent is almost upon us," she said with a thoughtful frown. Lent meant fasting, and as this was the time of year—late winter shifting into spring—when food stocks were running short and the new season's crops were yet to be edible, a lack of sustenance could conveniently be turned into piety.

"Most of the fields are plowed," the steward went on, naming them, ticking each meadow off on his fingers. "And the tree and vine pruning is complete."

"All is in readiness then," Jenova agreed. "I think we will reach the Easter feasting comfortably, if we are careful."

Her steward smiled. "Aye, my lady, roasted beef and good French wine! I can hardly wait for Easter!"

Jenova smiled back, but inside her feelings were very different. If Henry was not there, then what did she have to look forward to? Her life would be incomplete because there would be something vital missing.

"My lady?"

It was Gertrude, one of her young ladies, her eyes wide and her hands twisting in her skirts.

"My lady, 'tis Master Raf. I went to his room so that we could go and see the kittens together. But he wasn't there and though I looked, I-I can't find him."

Gertrude could be naughty, but she was a good girl at heart, and Jenova knew she would not think a prank such as this funny. Besides, there was nothing in her round face but anxiety. Jenova felt a curious hollowness developing in the pit of her stomach. "He went out riding with Lord Henry," she said, trying to calm herself as well as the girl.

"Aye, he came back from that, my lady, but now he's nowhere to be found. 'Tis not like him, my lady, not when he promised to show me Raven's kittens."

"He must be hiding, or . . . or with Lady Agetha?"

The girl shook her head. "Lady Agetha says she hasn't seen him, my lady. I've sent the cook's boy to all the places he knows Master Raf likes, and I've called and called. . . ."

The hollowness inside Jenova deepened. Where was he? Had Henry told him he was leaving, and Raf was so upset that he had found some secret place to be sad in? It did not make sense. If Raf was upset, he would come to her. He was not the sort of boy who would run off and hide.

"Where is Lord Henry, Gertrude?"

"In the stables, Lady Jenova."

"Fetch him to—No, no, I will go myself!"

She hurried through the great hall, hardly noticing the startled looks she was receiving. Where was Raf? It must be a mistake. Something completely innocent. And yet, considering the turmoil in other areas of her life, she could not quite believe it.

Outside the last rays of the sun were shining weakly, and there was a promise of warmth in the air that had not been there only days before. Spring was coming, and Jenova did not even notice it. She fairly flew across the yard and into the stables. Grooms were forking hay and dung. Farther down the aisle, Reynard was standing, leaning against one of the stalls, speaking to someone on the other side.

As Jenova drew closer she heard him say, "She didn't come. I thought to stay and wait, but it will be dark soon and I know she won't set out so late. I am fearful for her, my lord."

Henry's voice, muffled, from inside the stall, answered. "If I were the devil's advocate, Reynard, I would say she has taken you for a fool. That she has pretended to be what she is not. Are you certain that is not the case?"

Reynard ran an agitated hand through his hair. "Nay, she is not like that! There is something amiss. I can feel it inside."

Henry stood up just as Jenova reached them. His eyes widened at the sight of her, and he came forward to open the stall door, setting aside the poultice he had been using on Raf's pony and wiping his hands on a rag.

"What is it?" he demanded.

Jenova felt suddenly breathless. She put a hand to her chest, struggling to find her voice. "Raf," she gasped. "We cannot find Raf."

Henry put his hand firmly on her shoulder, and the

warmth, or just the contact, did bring a stillness to her.

"Be calm, Jenova," he said quietly. "Raf is here some-where." Then with a frown, he turned to Reynard, who shook his head in bewilderment. "I was seeking him my-self, earlier," Henry admitted. "He said he would like to help me with his pony—the old chap has a bruised fore-leg. He seemed keen at the time, but when I couldn't find him I thought he must have found something else to do."

"You are his hero, Henry!" Jenova cried. "If you wanted him to help you, he would never let you down. Don't you know that?"

Henry stared at her, as if stunned by her words. Had he only just realized how much Raf loved him? But perhaps he had, Jenova thought wildly. After all, Henry had come from a childhood where love had been a rare commodity.

"He came back with you, Henry, didn't he?" she went on. "You did bring him back to Gunlinghorn?

Now Henry looked incredulous. "Of course I did! I don't have him in my pocket, Jenova, if that's what you think. I brought him back, then Agetha came to fetch him and took him away. I have not seen him since."

"Agetha says she has not seen him since that time, either."

They were silent, both caught in their own private fears.

"Did you tell him that you were leaving us?" Jenova asked abruptly, not caring if Reynard overheard her, only intent upon getting to the bottom of this mystery. "Was he upset?"

Henry tried to remember. "I said something about the king eventually needing me back at court. He wanted . . . he asked if I would stay at Gunlinghorn. I didn't want to promise something I could not . . ." He cleared his throat, not meeting her eyes. "He wasn't upset. I did not upset him. He understood. The ride was enjoyable, and he was a little tired, but that is all."

Of course Henry would not upset Raf. Jenova knew it. Just as Raf loved Henry, Henry loved Raf. Loved him like his own son. In the midst of her pain she realized something else about Henry—his willingness to forsake Raf rather than tell her his secret must mean it was something very terrible indeed.

Something she might not want to hear.

Tears stung her eyes, and she blinked them away.

"Raf? Where is Raf?" she whispered. "Henry, where is he?"

Fear and doubt and then anger flared in Henry's eyes, and suddenly he was all action. He turned to Reynard, giving orders in a confident and sure voice. "Get some men together and search every inch of Gunlinghorn—keep and yard, stable and storerooms. Everywhere. And ask everyone—*Everyone!*—when they last saw Master Raf. We need to discover where he went after Agetha left him."

"Aye, my lord." Reynard was gone, taking big strides, his shouts ringing through the yard as he reached the door.

Jenova stared after him, not knowing what to do. After a moment she turned and found Henry watching her, the pain in his eyes mirroring her own. "Be reassured, my love. He will be found," he said quietly. "We will find him."

She nodded, then nodded again. She felt lost, as if she were drifting. Suddenly everything that had seemed so important to her a moment ago meant nothing. She needed her son; if he was not safe, then nothing else mattered.

Jenova swallowed. She must not break. Henry would find him—Henry might not trust her, but she trusted Henry. He was strong and clever, and he would find her son for her and return him to her arms. She was made of stronger stuff than this, and it was time to show it.

Jenova straightened her back. "Thank you. I will go and speak with Agetha again. If you want me—"

He nodded, grim-faced. He knew better than to take her in his arms.

Jenova walked away, keeping herself upright with an effort. She felt fragile, close to shattering. If he had touched her again, reached for her, she would have fallen into pieces. She had never felt so alone, and she did not like it.

She found Agetha in the solar, folding clothing. The girl straightened up, her face flushed from bending over the trunk, the scent of lavender drifting about her. "My lady!"

"Agetha, my son . . . I am sure it is nothing, but it seems my son is not to be found. Have you seen him?"

Agetha shook her head, her eyes wild. "Nay. Not since he came back from his ride with Lord Henry. He was weary, so I brought him to his room to rest. When I looked in later, he was gone."

"Gone? Gone, where? Where could he have gone?"

Agetha seemed startled by Jenova's aggression. "I . . . I don't know, my lady."

Jenova went to the window, her skirts swirling about her, and opened the shutters, uncaring if the air was bitter. It suited her mood. The sun was almost set, the shadows were growing long and blacker. It would be night soon. Cold and dark. How would they ever find one small boy?

"My lady, I am sure that everything will end well," Agetha said in a tentative, anxious voice.

But Jenova did not hear her.

"Is this the man?"

Reynard nodded. Both he and Henry stood a moment beyond the door, staring at the thickset young man who was waiting, shifting nervously from foot to foot, in the guardhouse. As if he sensed their eyes upon him, the man glanced up and saw them, and stilled. By the single candle it could be seen that his round and honest face was pitted with old scars, and his eyes were apprehensive.

Reynard entered the room. "You know who this is, Cecil?" he asked, nodding to Henry, close behind him.

Cecil bowed his head at Lord Henry and spoke in French with a strong English accent, "Aye, sir, I do."

"Lord Henry would hear what you have to say. Tell him again what you told me."

Cecil gave another jerky bow, but the eyes he raised to Henry were clear and honest. "I were in the storeroom where the wine is kept, me lord. I were counting how many barrels were left, for the steward. He and Lady Jenova were taking a tally of them, before the beginning of the Lent fast."

"Yes, go on."

"I were down on the floor, because it looked like one of they barrels had sprung a leak, and I had to get down to see. Then I heard steps passing me by, hurrying steps, two pair. And I heard voices, soft voices. I thought, 'Now who could that be? There's no one supposed to be down here but me.' So I got up and looked, and I could just see the back of them, through the barrels like. Her and him."

"Tell us, man, for God's sake!"

He took a deep breath. "'Twere Lady Agetha, my lord, and she had Master Raf with her. I heard him say he were tired or some such thing and she were telling him to hurry on and be quick about it. Something like that. Then they were gone, out through the other storeroom, and I heard no more. I thought it were odd but it isn't my place to question the ways of my betters."

Reynard thanked him and handed him a coin, which Cecil examined carefully before he placed it in the cloth purse attached to his belt. When he had gone, Henry stared at Reynard in bemusement.

"Agetha? Where was she taking him? Have the store-rooms been searched?"

"At least three times. But I have learned something more, my lord. There is a secret door in one of the rooms there, and a tunnel beneath the castle wall. It is known to only a few, which is why Cecil does not know of it. It takes you out of the castle and down to the river. I looked for myself, and found footsteps that could belong to a child in the mud along the bank. And there is a small boat, pulled up into the marshes. A boat big enough to hold a woman and a child."

Henry nodded as if he understood, but his head felt as if it was going to burst. Agetha had taken Raf. Taken him . . . where? Possibilities swirled around him, threatening to drown him. He took a breath and forced calm upon himself. Jenova was relying upon his cool head, and for her sake, as well as Raf's, he dared not let his fears overwhelm him.

"I see. She took him in the boat. But she is back here now, Reynard. Where did she go? And where is Raf now? It makes no sense—"

"But it does," Reynard replied grimly. "You know that Lady Rhona said that Jean-Paul claimed to have a friend at Gunlinghorn. Someone close to the family. What if he has made use of that connection?"

"Agetha?" Henry whispered. "But why take Raf? What can he want with a child?"

"Lady Jenova's child. For whose safe return she would do anything."

Anything? Even marry Baldessare? And Henry would be unable to stop her—how could he stop her? A boy he loved, too. A boy that he himself would do anything to save. . . .

"Jesu," he groaned and put his head in his hands.

"I have put a guard on the Lady Agetha's door, my lord."

Henry's mind was blank. Henry, who had always been good in a crisis, to whom the king looked for clear thinking, was beyond thought. Was this his fault? After all, it was he who Jean-Paul hated, he who Jean-Paul wanted to suffer. If it had not been for Henry, then Raf would still be here, safe in his mother's arms. Jenova, too, would be safe, and not under threat from Baldessare. But how could Henry have known, all those years ago, when he'd risen from the ashes, that it would mean disaster for those he loved?

"Is Lady Jenova still in her solar?" he asked.

"Aye, my lord."

"Then take Agetha there. We will question her together."

Reynard went to do his bidding, leaving Henry alone in the guardroom. The candle spluttered, and the silence crushed him. He thought of Raf's brilliant smile and green eyes, he remembered the conversations they had had, and the times he had taken him up upon Lamb. And Henry knew that if he had to batter down the doors of Baldessare's keep himself, if he had to raze it to the ground, he would save Raf. He would do whatever he had to do.

Jenova, seated on a stool by the brazier, looked up in surprise when first Henry, then Agetha, and then Reynard, entered the room. Agetha appeared pale and sullen, and no wonder, for Henry had an ungentle grip on her arm. The girl tried to shake him off, but he held her firm.

"Henry? What is happening?"

"My lady," Henry said formally, and pushed the unwilling Agetha forward, until she was standing before her mistress. "I have some news for you. We have learned that Raf left the castle with Agetha."

"With . . . with Agetha?" Jenova stared at him, then shifted her gaze to the other woman. Agetha quailed a little under the look in her mistress's eyes and said nothing. But Jenova read the truth in the girl's bowed head and stooped shoulders, and she knew a burst of rage such as she had never felt before. This woman, who had professed to be her friend, had taken her child. If Jenova had had a dagger, she would have killed her.

"Where is he?"

Agetha shook her head.

Slowly Jenova rose up from her seat, every line of her taut with fury. "Tell me, or I will give you to my soldiers to question!"

Agetha gave a wail. "Please, don't, don't. It will be all right. I tried to tell you before that everything will be all right. If you will just agree to marry Alfric, then Raf will be returned, and everything will be as it should."

The quiet was deathly.

"Marry Alfric?" Jenova whispered at last. "Is that what this is all about? You have given my son to Baldessare as a hostage?"

Agetha bit her lip, her eyes teary. "It was for your own good," she whispered, no hint of uncertainty in her voice. In her arrogance, the girl believed that she was right.

Jenova could hardly believe it. That Agetha, whom she had thought her friend, *Raf's* friend, could do such a thing. And yet, by that defiant cast to the girl's expression, it was clear she truly believed she had done what was best for them all. How could anyone be so utterly blind and stupid? It was time to close the shutters on Agetha's girlish dreams.

"Do you know what happened to Baldessare's last wife?" Jenova asked her, her voice icy. "He beat her to death."

Agetha blanched. "No, I . . . I meant you to wed Alfric. Alfric is gentle and kind and . . ."

"Alfric does not want to marry me, or if he does he would not deny his father. It is Baldessare who wants me now, Agetha, and you have given him the perfect way to have me, haven't you? He knows I will do anything to get Raf back safe."

Agetha was shaking her head. " 'Twas not Baldessare I gave him to," she whispered. " 'Twas the priest, Jean-Paul. A priest would not do anything bad to a child. He promised me. It was for the best. You must see, my lady. I did it for the—"

"The priest? But Jean-Paul is not to be trusted. He is the master and Baldessare his puppet. Just like you, Agetha."

"My lady, I did not . . . I am sure . . ."

"Get out!"

With a sob, Agetha bolted and slammed open the door on the startled guard outside. She gave a wail as he grabbed her arm and escorted her away.

Jenova knew she, too, should weep and rail. But it was as if all feeling had frozen inside her. She was numb. After a moment she felt the warmth of someone standing near her, and, turning her head, she found Henry. He looked far older, the lines on his face seemed to have deepened, and the unshaven cast of his jaw was quite dark. This was Henry as he might look in twenty years' time—careworn and sad. Jenova wondered if she looked the same, and then didn't care.

"Jenova," he said, and there was cool reason in his voice, despite his appearance. "Jean-Paul does not hate you. It is me he hates. This was all done to punish me."

He sounded reasonable, aye, but what he had said made no sense. She shook her head.

"It is a long story," he persisted. "I think you should know it. You have been asking that I tell you, and I have resisted. When you hear me out, you will know why. I know that perhaps this is not the right time, and I know that you have other things on your mind—and I do too, my love—but it is important to tell you now. So that you will understand the man we have to deal with. Jenova, do you think you can bear to listen?"

"What of Raf? Henry, what of my son?"

"This morning I sent a message to Crevitch, in the west, to Lord Radulf, to ask for as much of his army as he can spare. It will take nearly four days—three if they take little rest. When they arrive, we can besiege Hilldown Castle, or threaten worse. We can frighten Baldessare into giving Raf up. But for now I have sent Reynard to Hilldown Castle with a message for Baldessare, demanding that Raf be released at once. If he does that, then I have sworn no harm will come to Baldessare or his family. I have made mention of the king's anger when he hears what Baldessare has done. A man like that, blinded by his greed, will only listen if he thinks his land and wealth could be taken away from him. We must make him aware of how much he will lose by carrying through with his plan. As for Jean-Paul . . . Perhaps we can persuade Baldessare to turn against the priest in his own self-interest."

"What will they do to Raf?"

"Nothing. I am sure neither Baldessare nor Jean-Paul will hurt Raf; why would they? Their plan depends upon the boy remaining safe and well."

She tried to think over what he was saying. Radulf's army, coming to Gunlinghorn. Threats to Baldessare's wealth and power. Turning Baldessare against Jean-Paul.

Aye, his words were reasoned and sensible, and although she knew she should be angry at his high-handedness in sending for the army without her knowledge—to protect her, she supposed—she could not find it in her just now to feel anything very much.

What she really wanted to do was throw back her head and howl. And then she wanted to ride to Hilldown Castle and scream out her terror and her anger at the gates. She wanted to tell Baldessare that if he wanted her, then he could have her, as long as Raf was returned safe and unharmed.

Except that when Baldessare forced her into marriage with him, Raf would be in his power again. She would not have saved him; she would have doomed him to a life of hell.

Henry was still watching her face, waiting for her response. Jenova searched her memory. What had he said? That all this was his fault. It was nonsense. And then it occurred to her that he was talking about the secret she had known he was keeping from her. He was finally offering to share it.

Jenova looked at him, really looked at him. His blazing violet-blue eyes were dull, his mouth was held tight. Pain, a great deal of pain. And guilt. Henry truly blamed himself for all this. Jenova wondered if perhaps he had cause. She knew she must hear what he had to say. Strange to think she had been so desperate for him to tell her only a short time ago. Now she wondered if it even mattered.

"Jenova," he murmured and took a step closer. His hand was shaking as he placed it upon her arm, and then he leaned forward and rested his brow against hers, squeezing his eyes tight shut. "Jenova," he said, "I could not bear to tell you this before. You have a vision of me in your head, a picture of the man you believe me to be. I could not bear to soil it. I could not bear to destroy your image of me. Sometimes, I think your belief is all I have to make me feel worthy of being who I am."

Something in his voice, in his manner, broke through her indifference.

Jenova rallied.

"Tell me then," she said, and took his face in her palms, forcing him to meet her eyes. "Tell me why Jean-Paul hates you. Make me understand, Henry. And it must be the truth. I will not have lies. Do you understand me clearly?"

Henry gave a bleak smile and nodded. He drew away from her and sat down on the seat under the window. After a moment Jenova sat down beside him. And waited. Very soon he began to speak, his voice low and tentative, as if he were remembering an old, half-forgotten dream. As if it were something that had happened to somebody else.

"It happened at *le château de Nuit*. Aye," he grimaced, when she gave him a sharp look, "the place I said I had never heard of. Perhaps in a moment you will understand why I lied about that, Jenova. It happened many years ago. After I left your home, where I was so very happy, I went to *le château de Nuit*. I always think of it as walking from sunlight into darkness. For that is what I found at that cursed castle. The darkness of endless night . . ."

Chapter 22

The lumbering old wagon took him along roads that seemed devoid of all human life. Even when they passed through villages, there was not a single peasant or barking dog or waving child to be seen. All the cottages were shut up tight. It was as if the wagon were cursed, and him with it.

Henry did not know Count Thearoux. The count was a distant cousin by marriage of his mother's, but not one he had ever met before. As a boy who was constantly being passed about from relative to relative, Henry was used to finding himself in strange places with strangers. He managed. He was bright and confident and could normally find himself a niche somewhere. He had no choice, really, did he?

He would miss Jenova. She was like the other half of him, and she had wept when he'd left. Henry had wept too, but in private, for he was almost a man and it was not proper for men to cry. It was Jenova's mother who *had sent him away. She had disapproved of him from the beginning, and when Jenova had shown an equal wildness to his, she had used it to declare he was a danger to their daughter. Henry thought she was probably afraid Jenova would want to marry him in a year or two, when they were old enough. Jenova had already said she had no plans to marry anyone, not until she was an old lady, but her mother hadn't believed her. Henry smiled—well, her mother would soon find out just how stubborn Jenova could be.*

The wagon was climbing now. Above him, among the bare rocks and windblown trees, was a gray castle of thick stone with tiny windows. It looked like many other places he had seen, and he did not think too much of its repellent air until they reached the gates and passed inside.

The horse's clomping hooves echoed in the stillness. The wheels creaked. From somewhere above them, behind one of those little windows, a voice called out and was silenced.

For the first time Henry began to wonder what sort of place this château de Nuit might be.

The driver drew to a halt and, climbing down, went to lift Henry's trunk from the back of the vehicle. Henry, too, climbed down and stood there, at a loss what to do. As he gazed about at the apparent emptiness of the place, he heard a door open.

"Ah, Beau Henri! I have you here at last!"

Surprised, Henry turned and found himself facing a big man with a heavy paunch, his head shaven bare, his face ugly but creased into a beaming smile.

Cautiously Henry smiled back. "Monsieur?"

"I am Count Thearoux. You are welcome to my home. I am sure you will make many friends here."

Friends? What friends? There was no one else here.

The driver was climbing back onto his wagon, preparing to leave. Suddenly Henry did not want him to go. The man had been grumpy on the long journey, but he had shared his meager meals and seen that Henry was warm at night. He seemed like a last link with Jenova, and Henry had the embarrassing urge to cling to him.

"Come, Henri!" Thearoux was already turning away, toward the door in the keep. Henry followed, glancing over his shoulder as the wagon disappeared through the gate and back the way it had come.

Alone. He was all alone.

The door swung inward with a creak. Henry walked through and jumped as Thearoux slammed it behind him. It was gloomy in here; a single torch threw wavering shadows down a long passageway.

"I have you now," the count said softly.

Henry stared, thinking he had misheard, but the next moment the man gave a hearty laugh, making a joke of it, and Henry felt obliged to smile also.

"Are you alone here, my lord?" he asked tentatively, following Thearoux's swinging gait along the ill-lit tunnel of stone.

"Alone? Not at all. There are others here. They are sleeping now, but you will meet them soon. Much of our work is done at night."

Perhaps Thearoux was mad, Henry thought uneasily. Perhaps he had come to the home of a madman. What would Jenova think when he told her of this! But then he remembered, with an ache where his heart should be, that Jenova would not hear of it because he would never see her again.

There was a door open on the right. Thearoux did not stop or go in, he kept walking down the passage. But

Henry looked in, and then paused, blinking, trying to make sense of what he saw. There was a great wheel in the middle of the room, bound in iron, and there were spikes along the length of it. The walls were hung with what looked like blacksmith's tools. Strange long-handled pinchers, and lengths of chain, and other objects that made no sense.

"Come on!"

Thearoux was ahead of him, and still puzzling over that room, Henry hurried to catch up. They rounded the corner in what was, he realized, a passage that followed the inner wall of the keep. Ahead there were stairs, winding upward. As they climbed, Thearoux huffing and puffing, Henry began to hear sounds.

Soft moanings and groanings. A ragged breathing. Someone sobbing. And now there were doors, closed doors, bolted doors. What was this place? It smelled like . . . what was that smell? Henry wrinkled his nose. It smelled like the butchery at Jenova's parents' castle, the place where the animals were taken to be killed for the table.

It smelled like death.

They had reached the landing.

Thearoux was waiting there for him. His ugly face, which Henry had thought jolly, was full of gloating anticipation. The small black eyes fixed on his.

Henry hesitated on the stairs below, feeling the weight of that place about him, sensing that not many who came here ever left. "I want to go home," he said, and his voice shook like the adolescent boy he was, and for once he didn't care.

Thearoux watched him a moment, consideringly. And then he said, "Well, you're here now. May as well stay a while, eh? This is your room."

He opened a door. Inside, the room was hardly bigger than his trunk, in it a straw mattress and a candle and a bucket. A prison cell. A place of punishment. But what had he done?

Thearoux shoved him in and slammed the door. Henry heard the bolt slide home.

"Welcome, Beau Henri!" he cried, the jovial note back in his voice. "Welcome to le château de Nuit."

"Henry?"

It was Jenova. Jenova's sweet, melodious voice. It was like a balm, like honey poured upon a scold. The sound of it miraculously soothed the agony within him. Slowly, Henry turned his head to stare at her. He did not know how long he had been silent, how much time had passed. The solar was quite dark, and she had lit no candles. He could hardly see her face. He was not sure he wanted to.

"What sort of place was it? Henry, what happened to you there?" Jenova whispered, as if she did not feel it quite appropriate to speak loudly. As if the picture he had painted for her was far too horrible.

Henry cleared his throat, shifted slightly on his seat, rubbed a hand across his jaw and heard the scrape of his whiskers. When had he last shaved? Or changed his clothes? He could smell himself. He needed a bath. He had not realized that his life had begun to crumble about him like this, or perhaps he had just not cared.

He forced himself back to that place he had never wanted to remember again, but the memories were choking him. As if she sensed his despair, Jenova's warm fingers slipped around his and gripped, hard, giving him strength. After a little while, Henry found his voice again.

"It was a wolf's lair; savage and cruel. Thearoux lived

there with his men, and at night they rode out into the surrounding countryside. He called them hunters. 'We're going hunting!' he used to say, with such a look in his eyes. Their prey was anything they could find. Villagers, peasants from the surrounding countryside. Jesu, no wonder their doors had been locked when I rode past! They were terrified. They knew if they were caught out after dark they would be killed or raped, or taken back to the château to be tortured in that appalling room for the amusement of Thearoux and his men."

He blinked at her, his voice struggling past the lump in his throat. "Thearoux cared nothing for these people, Jenova. He and his band lived to commit their evil. And the night after I arrived there, Thearoux told me that I was now one of them, and that if I did not take part in their grisly hunt, then I would be their next victim. 'Tis remarkable how the conscience can be silenced when you are staring death in the face. It was I who gave the poor wretch we hunted the coup de grace that night."

"Oh, Jesu . . ."

Henry heard the shock in her voice, but he couldn't stop. He knew if he stopped now, he would not be able to go on. And he had to finish this. He had to tell her everything. It was like opening a vein; the blood would not be stopped once it had begun to flow out. No matter what damage it did to the patient.

"So I rode with them."

"Henry, poor Henry."

"No, not poor Henry," he reproved her.

"You were thirteen years old!"

"Maybe, but I was not the one to pity, Jenova. I was afraid, so I went with them and pretended I did not care. But that night I wept, sick to my stomach, and for many nights after. Aye, as time went on, I learned to pretend I was going to join in, and then I would hide myself away. Make out it wasn't happening. I was a coward. Sometimes . . . sometimes I couldn't hide and I couldn't pretend, and then I saw everything. Those memories are my worst. Have you ever seen a hunt, Jenova? Of course you have! We Normans love to hunt and kill. The chase, the baying dogs and shouting men, the victim brought down and torn to pieces, or else throat cut. The blood, the endless, warm gouts of blood. Aye, 'tis a sight not to be missed."

Silence. Henry closed his eyes. He had quieted her at last. He was doubly glad now that he could not see her face, that the room was in darkness. He could not bear to read what was in her eyes as the full impact of what he had done weighed upon her.

He cleared his throat, for he was not finished yet.

"Souris and I—he was another boy a little older than me—would sometimes be sent out to flush out the kill. Or to lure some poor creature from his or her home, and lead them to their death. I would try and save them, if I could. Once I hid a boy up a tree, and Souris knew, but he said nothing. He thought it was funny, Thearoux and his hunt riding around, seeking the boy, when he was right above their heads. It amused him. I amused him. But that was why I was there, for Souris' sake."

"Souris? This boy was as bad as the rest of them, then?" Her voice was a whisper in the darkness, her hand gripped his painfully hard.

"He was one of them. They called him Souris, the Mouse, because he was small and quiet. He was Thearoux's son by some woman in the village who had been kept at the château for his use. Souris had been spawned in evil and weaned upon murder. What could you expect him to be like? And I had been brought to the château specifically to keep Souris company. He wanted someone of his own age to play with. Thearoux had heard of me from my mother, and she had given him permission to take me in. So kind of them to arrange it between them, don't you think?"

"Oh Henry."

He did not stop, he could not stop. "My friend Souris was not like me. He did not have to pretend to enjoy the hunts, he loved them. The bloodlust shone in his eyes. Thearoux's blood ran true in him."

Jenova was silent a long moment. "Why . . . why did Count Thearoux do such things? What reasons could he possibly have for . . . for . . ."

"He enjoyed it," Henry said quietly.

He closed his eyes again, but the pictures were in his head. The dark trees and the moonlight, the running prey, the ragged breath, the yells and cries of the hunters and the howling of the dogs. And then the screams, the endless, endless screams . . . and worse, the silence.

And always that doubt inside him, that terrible fear that maybe he was just like them.

He put his hands over his face. "Jesu," he whispered. "I watched them kill so many, so many, and I did nothing."

Jenova did not answer. After a moment, he knew she was not going to answer. She must be wishing him gone; she had her son to worry about. Why should she care for his miserable tale? But he might as well tell the rest before he left. It was nearly over. If only he were not so tired. . . .

"There was a girl. Young, pretty, innocent. She made me think of you. Until then I had been able to go on, but seeing her . . . remembering what my life should be like . . . it was the end for me, Jenova. I tried to save her, but Souris had decided he wanted to see this one suffer. He liked to hurt—he liked to hear women scream. After that I . . . went a little crazy.

"I found my way to Thearoux's den. They were all there, drunk, sated on the murder of that pitiful innocent. There were plenty of weapons in the room—lots to choose from. I really can't remember what I picked up, but it made a mess. I hit him, hard, and the blood sprayed out. He stood up, roaring at me, and I hit him again. And again."

He took a shuddering breath, as if preparing himself for the worst.

"It felt so good, Jenova. Every time I hit him I laughed. Some of the others began to wake and I swung at them, too, and it felt even better. I knew then that they had made me into one of them. I was a murderer, too."

Jenova made a sound in her throat. Disgust, he thought, and he had to force himself to go on. Nearly there now, he told himself desperately. Nearly over . . .

"It was time to leave. I looked about me and felt sick and dizzy. Those I hadn't . . . hurt were still too drunk to do much. I told myself that these men didn't deserve to live—so I set about killing them. I made a fire—it was simple, really. It was as if I had only just thought about setting fire to some straw in the room with the wheel, and the next thing the fire was there, burning so quickly, so fiercely, that even if I had wanted to put it out I could not have. I suppose it was me who lit it, but truly I do not know for sure.

"The fire was well alight by the time I remembered Souris—I had forgotten about Souris. I ran to his room, but he was not there. I was choking, and the fire . . . I couldn't look any further. I-I always felt guilty about leaving him, despite what he was. He was my friend, sort of, and in a way he was a victim, too.

"I don't remember running, only that suddenly I was outside, a little hurt and a little singed, but well and alive. My head ached, with all the things in it I did not want to remember. I felt as if I had escaped from a dream, so for a time I let myself believe that was so. I walked and walked, stealing food, hiding from the peasants, until I reached a large town. No one knew me there. I stole some clean clothing and knocked upon the door of the local lord, and offered myself as his squire. Perhaps my sheer gall impressed him, for he took me in.

"During those days, I tried to put it all behind me. I thought of myself as a phoenix, risen from the ashes of *le château de Nuit*. I promised myself that I would do something with my life, make a success of myself. I swore I would not let Thearoux, that monster, stop me from living it the way I wanted to. I would make my survival worthwhile. It was remarkable that I was not hunted down, but I later learned that Thearoux's friends and family did not even know I was there—very few did. My mother said nothing. She must have known, but she took the secret of my escape to her grave. I suppose I can thank her for that, if nothing else.

"When I arrived in England with William, the past was long forgotten. Even I had forgotten it, or I told myself I had. And who would connect Lord Henry of Montevoy with the sniveling boy who had crept from Thearoux's château while all about him burned? I was safe. Until Jean-Paul came to Gunlinghorn."

Henry turned to look at the shadow of her face, and his shame and self-disgust filled him. And his guilt. He could see the shine of her eyes, like that long-ago girl, staring up at her tormenters and knowing she was about to die. And he had not been able to save her, just as he could not save Jenova and Raf.

"This is my fault. Jean-Paul wants to hurt me. He thinks he can do that by hurting you and Raf."

"Henry . . ." She was close to him, her breath fragrant and warm upon his cheek. "Who do you believe Jean-Paul is? I think you must already know, in your heart."

He felt light-headed. Too much, it was all too much. The faces from the past were ranged before him, accusing him, pleading with him, telling him he had not tried hard enough. *Murderer . . .*

"Souris. I think Jean-Paul is Souris. He knows too much for it to be otherwise. He knows *me* too well."

"But why does he hate you? Surely Souris was your friend."

"Because he thinks I left him to die. Because that place was his home and Thearoux was his father. I took all that from him, remember, so now he wants to take you and Raf from me. He wants me to hurt as he hurt, to suffer as he suffered."

He wondered, bewildered, why she was asking him these questions. Why was she still in the same room with him? He would have to make it even plainer for her, and then she would walk away from him. As he deserved.

"I enjoyed killing Thearoux," he said. "That's what I didn't want to tell you. Sometimes I even enjoyed the hunting. There was excitement in it, in the chase and the kill. I felt . . . powerful. Mayhap that was the real reason why I had to kill Thearoux and escape. Not because of that poor girl, but because I was beginning to like it too much. I was turning into one of them. I had to save myself before it was too late."

Jenova made a small sound in her throat. Her hand was limp by her side, but he lifted it up and gripped it, tightly, as if he did not mean to let her go. Although he had expected to drive her away, he found now that he did not want that. He knew he should be strong and walk away from her, but suddenly he did not feel strong. Henry felt like weeping.

"That day at Gunlinghorn Harbor, Jean-Paul gave me a choice, Jenova. I did not tell you that. I could not begin to tell you. He said he would inform the king about my past if I did not hand you over to Baldessare with my blessing. You see, Thearoux was the king's uncle. He will hate me for what I have done, and he probably will not believe that Thearoux was a monster. Why should he, it is only my word against his. And he will ask why I have taken so long to tell him my story. If I was innocent, wouldn't I have spoken of it before? I imagine that he will order me to my furthest estates—if he leaves me any estates after he has punished me. As for my friends . . . Once Jean-Paul lets it be known what I have done, and the king has cast me off, I will not have many friends left."

"You speak as though it is a foregone conclusion," she said huskily. "That you will stay here at Gunlinghorn and see your life destroyed."

"Leave Gunlinghorn? Of course not. You see, he knows me, Jenova. He knows I will never leave you unprotected against Baldessare. And he also knows I cannot bear you to know my secret. So I will stay, and you will find out—as you have done—and abandon me. And then I will have nothing, just as Jean-Paul has nothing.

"Except he has broken his word and taken Raf. He is a liar and a cheat, and we will not give in to him."

Jenova stood up then and lit a candle. The flame wavered, illuminating her face as she set it down on the lid of a trunk nearby. Her cheeks were wet with tears, her eyes reddened, as though she had been weeping, and yet he had not heard her. She had sat and listened to his story and wept, and he had not even known it.

"Look at me, Henry," she said.

Henry met her eyes. And waited. For the noose to tighten.

"I can understand why you would believe your London friends would desert you, although I am a little surprised you would think Radulf might do so. And I can understand why those women you share your body with would leave you—they are hardly in love with you, or you with them. But I am . . . angry that you would believe *I* would turn my back on you when I heard the truth. I would have liked you to tell me before, when you first realized who Jean-Paul was. I can understand why you would wish to forget it, but in not telling me you have allowed this man, this Jean-Paul, to work his spite upon us all. If I had known, then Raf would still be here."

She paused, thought a moment. "Well, maybe not. Agetha would still think Alfric a suitable husband for me if he had two heads. But you should still have told me. I suppose this is why you wanted to marry me? So that you could save me? Even though you believed I would hate you when the truth came out. Oh Henry, you are a silly, wonderful man!"

"But Jenova," he said, his voice hoarse with the effort to keep it steady, "I could not let Baldessare hurt you. I could not let another woman be degraded and hurt by a monster. . . ."

She felt sick. A wave of nausea washed over her. He *had* tried to save her. Just as she knew he had tried to save all those poor people, and he had only been a boy. A child. She imagined Raf in such a place and shuddered. She thought of Henry as she had known him back then, so vital and handsome, so alive. How could all that have been taken and twisted, just so that a monster could gain pleasure from it, and his son could have a *friend*. . . .

"Do you understand?" he was asking, and his voice broke, the pain in his eyes making her own heart ache. "Do you understand what I have said?"

"Yes, Henry, I understand. I know what you are saying, and what you fear. But you were not like them—you were a boy, alone, frightened, and you did what you had to do to stay alive. 'Tis necessary, sometimes, to do bad things to stay alive."

She squeezed his hand, but now it lay still and lifeless in hers. So she took his other hand, and then she moved to sit close by him and drew his head to rest upon her shoulder. He stayed there, but she could tell he would not let her comfort him. He was holding himself rigid, as if afraid to give in to her. In case she changed her mind and abandoned him after all, she supposed.

How could she have been so wrong about this man? She had believed he did not care enough, and in fact he cared too much. He had been hurt so badly that he'd kept his pain hidden, and never allowed anyone to prod it or poke it. He'd never allowed anyone close enough to understand, or to help take some of the burden from him. He'd felt he had to bear it all on his own.

Until now.

"Henry," she whispered, "oh my dearest Henry. Do you remember when we were young, and you asked me if I had ever been kissed? And I said no? You told me then that you would be the first to kiss me, and we lay together in the flowers in the meadow, with the sky blue above us, and we kissed. We kissed for a very long time. And I still remember it. That memory is such a joy to me. When my days were dark, I would remember those moments with you. So, please, please, let me comfort you. Let me bring some light to your darkness, my dearest love."

He stirred, but she would not let him speak. It would be just like Henry to deny himself comfort because he felt he did not deserve it. Henry, who had been willing to sacrifice everything he was, to stay and protect her. Henry, who would lay down his life for her and Raf, even though he expected to be abandoned all over again. How could she not have known that? She, who thought she knew him so well?

"I am appalled by what happened to you. I would like to kill that man, but you have done it for me. I am sure if we were to ask the villagers what they thought, they would weep their gratitude, Henry. I do not know what the king will say, and I do not care. You are my friend, my oldest friend, and I would never turn my back on you. Never."

He turned his face into her breast, and it was then she felt his shoulders begin to shake. He was weeping—silently weeping, because Henry did not cry. Jenova held him close and kissed his brow and shared his pain.

Chapter 23

There was a child crying.

Rhona could hear it, soft but definite, coming from the tower room above hers. It had invaded her sleep, making her wonder whether she was dreaming, but now she was awake and she could still hear it. A child, crying.

There were no children at Hilldown Castle. So, who was it crying?

Rhona rose, shivering, and pulled her cloak over her chemise. She slid her feet into her indoor slippers, curling her toes against the bitter cold, and went to the door. It opened at her touch, and she breathed a sigh of relief. Jean-Paul had threatened to lock her in, but her door was open. He probably thought she was beaten; she had not left her room since her visit to the Black Dog.

Reynard would be wondering where she was.

Was he the sort to wait long at Uther's Tower, or had he shrugged his shoulders and dismissed her and gone on his way? Perhaps he had not expected her to be there;

perhaps despite all he had said he had not believed anything she had told him.

Rhona bit her lip. Mayhap for his sake it was as well if he didn't, and yet she was weak. She wanted him to think well of her. She did not want him to believe she might have lied to him, or played him for a fool, duped him with false tears and sad stories.

But why not? She had done it to other men. Reynard probably thought he was just one of many. How could he know he was *the* one, that he was the *only* one. . . .

The crying sound was louder as she climbed the stairs. Outside the arrow slit in the wall the air was icy, and stars shone in a cold sky. They gave her enough light to see her way, as she continued to climb until she reached the door.

This one was barred.

The room was used as a storeroom, or sometimes for inconvenient guests. It was small and out of the way and, most of the time, forgotten. That someone was occupying it now, someone with a child, was very strange. Especially when, to Rhona's knowledge, no one had arrived at Hilldown Castle for weeks, and even then it had been one of her father's elderly cronies. Surely no one in their right mind would send a child to stay here!

She lifted the bar, her arms straining. It bumped and made a noise, and the sobbing halted abruptly. Rhona could almost feel whoever it was on the other side, straining, listening.

"Is someone there?" she asked softly and tried the latch. The door swung to with remarkable ease.

And a small, wild thing launched itself at her, catching her in the midriff and making her cry out in shock and pain. She wrapped her arms about it, wrestling a moment, and, more through good luck than any skill on her part, brought the creature to the floor. She fell on top of it, using her weight to hold it there.

It fought. It muttered. But it was pointless, and after a moment it seemed to accept that fact and gave up the struggle. Panting heavily, Rhona searched for and found a face. It was a child. A child with a mop of dark hair and a pale, damp, tear-streaked face. It sniffled as she half sat up, pulling it into the better light from another arrow slit. Pale skin, dark lashes and hair, and big, big eyes.

They stared at each other in the half-darkness.

"Lady Rhona?" the child said shakily. "Have you come to rescue me?"

It was Raf, Lady Jenova's son. With a horrible sinking feeling, Rhona thought she knew what had happened. Whoever it was who was Jean-Paul's spy at Gunlinghorn had brought him here, and now they planned to use him in their plot. They would force Jenova to their will with threats against her child, and Lord Henry would be powerless to stop them.

Suddenly Rhona had had more than enough. Oh, she had had enough before, but she had been content to stay in her room and cry and wail and wish for someone strong to come and rescue her. Now she was tired of that. She had waited long enough, and no one had come. It was time to do something for herself.

"I do believe I *have* come to rescue you, Raf," she said, answering his question. "Fetch your cloak and rug up. We are leaving this place and returning to Gunlinghorn."

Raf sat up and gave her the most beautiful smile she had ever seen. "Good," he said with a relieved sigh. "I was hoping you would say that. Agetha tricked me, you know. I would never have gone with her if she had told me the truth. I trusted her."

His eyes filled with tears, and Rhona gave him a quick hug. "She is a stupid girl, Raf. Don't worry, I am sure that Lady Jenova and Lord Henry will be very angry with her when they find out. She will be sorry for what she did then, won't she?"

Raf thought a moment, and then a small grin tugged at his mouth. "Aye, I s'pect she will."

Rhona waited while he put on his cloak, and then she took his hand, leading him quietly down the stairs. Alfric slept in a room off the great hall. Rhona placed Raf safely behind a tapestry and went to scratch on his door. It took some time for him to wake, but eventually his face peered at her through the opening, his eyes bloodshot.

"Rhona? Are you all right? I was so worried that—"

"No, I am all right, brother." She put her hand on his arm and squeezed to silence him, glancing over her shoulder. There was probably no one listening, but she had long ago learned never to take chances.

"You must help me. I have something I must deliver to Gunlinghorn. A small parcel."

His face froze. He blinked. He understood her, Rhona thought with a sinking feeling. He must know that the child had been brought here and held captive until Jenova agreed to marry Baldessare.

"Rhona," he groaned. "Do not say you are thinking to—"

"What is being done here is very bad, Alfric," she said in her sternest voice. "You know that I am right. And I am tired of being afraid. I am very, very tired of it. So I am going to do what is right for a change, and you are going to help me. We will use 'it,' Alfric. He will sleep for hours and hours. Jean-Paul is in the chapel—we will bar the door so he cannot get out. And we will both of us leave this place and never return."

Alfric swallowed. Then he blinked. "W-where will we go?" he whispered, sounding not much older than Raf.

"Gunlinghorn, first of all, and after that, wherever we wish. And we will never come back here again."

"What of our inheritance?" he asked, suddenly sounding more like his father's son. "I am heir to Hilldown Castle and my father's other estates. I am the next Lord Baldessare."

Rhona leaned closer and whispered in his ear. "When it becomes known what our father has done, the king will take everything he owns and throw him in jail. Do you want to join him there, and be heir to that?"

Alfric shuddered.

"Then help me."

She met his eyes in the light of the torch and saw his decision even before he spoke.

"I seek words with Lord Baldessare!"

The torches held by his men flared, and Reynard narrowed his eyes against the heat and the light. The walls of Hilldown Castle were a dark mass, interspersed with more torches and the shapes of moving men. He had ridden hard to get here, and now he waited.

And waited.

"We know," a voice called back. "My Lord Baldessare has been told."

"Perhaps he is grinding bones to make bread," some wit murmured behind him.

"As long as they aren't Raf's bones," Reynard replied bitterly, and there was an uneasy silence. More voices above—the mutterings of discontent? Mayhap. Reynard could not believe that all the souls in this place were happy with the way Baldessare ruled them. He had seen some miserable hovels on his way here, and some thin, starved faces. It did not seem as if Baldessare cared much for his villeins, but then Rhona had told him as much.

Rhona.

A part of his mind mocked and tried to make him believe she was watching him from behind these walls, laughing at him. That she had been a party to Raf's kidnapping, and she was as evil as her father. Or mayhap not evil—just desperate to please him, even to the extent of destroying Lady Jenova, so that he would set her free.

No.

Reynard did not believe it. He had tried, on his ride here, but there was another, larger part of him that simply refused to accept it. The woman he had held in his arms would never do such things. She had suffered, aye, but she was good at heart. Something or someone had prevented her from coming to him at Uther's Tower. Despite all the evidence to the contrary, he knew it. He knew it in his heart.

His Rhona was in trouble, and he was helpless to save her.

He should never have allowed her to return here; he should have taken her to Gunlinghorn when he'd had the chance, even if he would have had to kidnap her. Now 'twas possible he would never see her again.

"W-what is it you want?"

The voice came from above them, loud enough, but wavering up and down with fright. It was a voice Reynard knew. Lord Alfric's. What was he doing there? Where was Baldessare?

Reynard looked up, shading his eyes against the glare of the torches, trying to see Alfric's handsome face among those of the guards. But they all wore helmets and chain mail, and there was no way to tell them apart.

"I need to speak to your father, my lord," he called back. "I am come on Lord Henry's behalf and—"

"Is he afraid to come on his own?"

That got him a laugh. Alfric seemed to take courage from it, continuing in a more confident tone.

"My father does not want to speak to you. When he is ready, he will send word to Gunlinghorn. You will just have to wait."

"You have Lady Jenova's son."

Alfric was silent a moment, and a hush fell over the wall.

"You are mistaken. There are no children here."

"You lying swine! Let me speak to your father now!"

Then Alfric said something Reynard could hardly believe.

"Wait. You are obviously hard of hearing. I will come down and speak with you face-to-face."

Reynard turned and looked at his men. They were gaping back at him. It was a trick. It had to be. But no, soon enough the gate was opening, and a number of soldiers stepped out, all wearing chain mail or leather tunics and helmets. One of them came forward cautiously, and it was indeed Lord Alfric. Beside him, a decidedly tubby soldier waddled along, struggling to keep pace. Warily, they halted several yards from Reynard and his men.

"Reynard? I-is that your name?" Alfric asked. "Come forward, I want to see you."

"Don't go!" one of his men warned, but Reynard decided that if Baldessare's men had wanted to fire an arrow at him from the walls, they would have done it before now. He kicked his mount forward, tempted to run Alfric down. Except that that would solve nothing. Perhaps he could capture him and hold him for ransom? Although, having seen how Lord Baldessare treated his son, it was doubtful he would care.

Alfric was speaking in important tones, as if he were not saying the oddest things. "I have a man here, Reynard, who will go back with you to Gunlinghorn Castle. He will speak with Lord Henry in person and explain to him what we want in return for Lady Jenova's brat. Do not harm him, for he is important in this matter. Do you understand me?"

Reynard nodded in bemusement.

Satisfied, Alfric flicked his fingers at the soldiers behind him. "Come here."

The fat soldier waddled forward, puffing and panting. Beneath his helmet, his face was dark with grime and running with sweat. Alfric gave him a curiously gentle pat on the shoulder. "Do as we said and all will be well," he instructed. "I-I am forever grateful. And do not fear for me. I believe I have finally found my courage."

For a moment he seemed to waver, and then he quickly turned away, his men behind him, and the gate closed with a thump.

Reynard looked at the soldier and shook his head. He really was fat—a great round belly and only thin legs to hold it up. Dear God, how were they to get this creature up onto one of the horses?

"Will you hurry?" the lardy soldier said in a hissing wail. "I am about to fall down. And Raf can hardly breathe under this chain mail."

Reynard was down off his horse and at her side. It *was* she. It was Rhona, disguised under a wash of mud and the ancient helmet. Her chain mail tunic was enormous, big enough for two, and if what she had said was correct, there were two under it. No wonder she could hardly walk!

"Be careful," she whispered, her eyes eating him up. "One of my father's spies might be watching. The men are not all loyal to my brother and me, but there are more than we ever thought. We have sent my father to sleep with a sleeping potion, but it will not be forever. I thought Alfric would come with me, but now he wants to stay and take my father's place. He wants to hold him prisoner in his own castle. Dear God, my gentle brother Alfric to play the hero! He does it for me, so that I can get away to safety. He says it is for all the times I have saved him. Oh, Reynard . . ."

Tears streaked the mud on her cheeks. Reynard ached to hold her, but with all those watching eyes he knew it would not be wise. So instead he allowed himself a brief, searching look before he turned to his men.

"Come on, help me get this soldier up onto a horse!" he shouted. "And then let's go home."

They rode into the woods before he adjudged it safe at last to stop. Rhona was lifted down and her chain mail removed. Raf, who had been tied to her chest, was released, and he lay panting on the ground.

"I could hardly breathe, and the chain mail was so heavy," he complained. Then his lip trembled. "Where are Lord Henry and Mama?"

Rhona stroked his hair. "You'll see them soon. You were very brave and very quiet. They will be proud of you, Raf."

Reynard was watching her, and when she looked up, he saw that her eyes were filled with tears.

"I couldn't let it happen," she said, her lips trembling, too. "I thought I would rather us both die trying to escape than suffer what my father and Jean-Paul had planned."

"Rhona, you are a brave and wonderful woman. But I always knew it was so."

Her face crumpled. "I thought I would never see you again!"

He took her into his arms, holding her fast, feeling her body so soft and trusting against his. She *was* his, he realized in gratitude. He had been given another chance to take her home to Gunlinghorn, and this time he would never let her go.

Back at Hilldown Keep, Baldessare was stirring. First one eye opened, then the other. He blinked, sleepily, then with a growing alertness.

As he awoke, the rage awoke with him. Until it consumed him. *Alfric.* He would kill Alfric first, and then Rhona. A father deserved the loyalty of his children—he was a king in his castle, after all. Disloyalty was treason, and treason was punishable by death.

Chapter 24

⁓ ⚬⚬ ⌒

"**M**y lady, my lady!"

The voices grew louder, approaching up the stairs toward the solar. Shouting now, with an hysterical edge. Jenova opened her eyes. Somehow she had fallen asleep, here on the seat, enclosed in Henry's arms. Henry, who was already on his feet, and running for the door.

It was flung open before he reached it.

Reynard, the night damp clinging to his clothing and sprinkling his hair, his black eyes gleaming like stars. And in his arms, a small, pale boy with reddened eyes and a wobbling mouth.

"Raf!"

Jenova clutched him to her, beyond thought, beyond tears. Her body shuddered, and she carried him with her back to the window seat and sank down, still holding him. Behind her she heard Henry asking questions, but she didn't care what the answers were, not yet. It was enough that she had her son back.

357

Safe in her arms.

"Lady Jenova?"

This voice was not one that should have been in her so-lar. Perhaps it was the fact of it being out of place that pierced her abstraction. She looked up and blinked. Lady Rhona? Her face filthy, her clothing . . . Jenova's eyes narrowed.

"Lady Jenova," Rhona repeated, tilting her chin in her usual proud manner. But there was something new in her eyes, a hint of pleading. "I have brought your son home to you, and at great cost to myself and my brother. I am placing myself in your hands and asking that you allow me to stay within the safety of Gunlinghorn's walls. If my father finds me, he will kill me for what I have done. God have mercy on my poor brother."

She swallowed, and Jenova could see that she had been crying. Slowly, her gaze roved over the girl, taking in the bagging breeches and the enormous chain mail tunic. Her fair hair curled and straggled about her dirty face.

"Mama," Raf spoke in a husky voice, pushing slightly away from the comfort of her arms, but not too far. "Mama, Rhona saved me. She found me in the room they had locked me in, and she took me to her brother, and they made a plan to save me. They were frightened, be-cause her father isn't very nice, but they did it anyway 'cause she said it was the right thing to do. Please let her stay."

Rhona managed a smile, her gaze meeting Jenova's a little defiantly. "I admit I have not always thought in such terms, my lady, but there have been . . . reasons for that. I think there comes a time in all our lives when we must face the consequences of what we have done or what might be done if we sit back and do nothing."

"And you had reached that point," Jenova replied levelly. She was thinking of Henry, that he too had found the point where he could go no further. A question occurred to her. "What of Jean-Paul? Where is he?"

Rhona's smile widened, strangely childlike on her grubby face. "I locked him in the chapel and put a guard on the door. He cursed me, but I laughed and told him to pray to God for his freedom."

"Let us hope God has better judgment than Lord Baldessare."

"Let us hope so, my lady."

"Mama?" Raf tugged impatiently at her sleeve. "Can Rhona stay? You have not said yet."

"Then I will say now. She can stay, Raf," Jenova said. She took a deep breath, meeting the other woman's eyes. "You have my everlasting gratitude and protection, Rhona. If I can do anything to help you, I will."

Rhona's eyes widened, and she glanced at Reynard, and blushed beneath her dirt. "Thank you, my lady. I think . . . I think I have all I need, now."

Then Henry came and lifted Raf from Jenova's arms. She released him a little reluctantly, but secure in the knowledge that her son was as safe with Henry as he was with her. She knew that Henry, too, would die to protect him. He was a remarkable man, the more so because of the travails he had suffered and conquered along the way.

"I am very glad to see you again, Raf," Henry said quietly. "I have missed you very much."

"I missed you, too," Raf replied in a little voice. "Will you stay at Gunlinghorn now, Henry? Will you stay forever?"

Henry did not glance at Jenova. "I will stay until you are safe again," he said. "I will protect you and your mother as long as it is necessary."

"Until I am big and strong and can protect her myself," Raf added, and he gave a sigh and cuddled into Henry's shoulder. "I am very tired," he announced with a jaw-cracking yawn. "Can I go to bed now?" Then, as another thought struck him, he lifted his head, his eyes widening. "But not if Agetha is still here. I do not like Agetha anymore."

"Agetha is locked away," Henry assured him. "She has been bad and must be punished. Perhaps we can talk about Agetha in the morning."

Raf seemed content with that, and within moments he was fast asleep in Henry's arms.

Baldessare barely glanced behind him at Alfric's bloodied body. The boy had fought hard, harder than he had expected—Baldessare felt a sting of pride through the red haze of his anger.

He pushed through the doorway, Alfric's sword in his hand. Where was the priest? This had all been Jean-Paul's idea—Baldessare would have been just as happy to have forgotten the subtleties and taken Gunlinghorn by force. Jean-Paul had talked him out of it—the king must not be angered, he had said. You must not break his laws, he had said, but you can bend them.

Bend them! Well, Baldessare would *bend* Jean-Paul. . . .

"Where's the priest?" he bellowed.

Armored men backed away, their eyes fixed nervously upon him.

"Where is that monstrous priest!"

"In the chapel, my lord," someone was brave enough to finally give him the answer he wanted. "He's barred in there. 'Twas Lord Alfric's orders—"

Baldessare fixed them all with a furious look, just to remind them who was really in charge of this keep. When he turned toward the chapel, no one said a word.

In truth Baldessare still felt foggy from whatever potion his foul offspring had given him. His eyes narrowed. Rhona; it was she who was behind this, and she would feel his wrath. Perhaps, he thought as he reached the chapel, he would give her to the garrison as punishment. Aye, she would be more pliable after they had had their use of her.

"Priest! Are you there?" Baldessare's fist crashed against the thick wooden door.

A step sounded from inside, and that harsh, husky voice came to him, slightly muffled. "Baldessare? Let me out."

"Oh, I will," Baldessare muttered, gripping the bar across the door, lifting it and tossing it to one side. "I'll let you out, Priest, and then I'll kill you."

All his pent-up anger and loathing where Jean-Paul was concerned flared in his eyes as the chapel door swung open. The priest stood there, dark against candlelight. Even as Baldessare lurched forward toward him, bringing up his sword, he felt a cold droplet of terror spill into the boiling cauldron of his fury.

"My lord, predictable as always."

That harsh voice was the last thing Baldessare heard before the knife blade entered his chest and pierced his heart.

"Henry?"

He looked around. She was standing on the roof of the tower behind him, a shadow against the predawn sky, her cloak wrapped about her, and the torchlight in her hair. Henry took a final glance at the peaceful Gunlinghorn countryside and walked toward her. As he drew closer, he saw that her face was pale and tired, but the anxiety that had drawn lines upon it had gone.

She was as beautiful as ever.

"What are you doing out here?" he asked her, taking her arm and leading her inside, down the stairs. The castle was at rest, its young master home and safe, and everything had returned to normal. Well, almost.

"I was looking for you."

"I am making sure we are protected, Jenova. I promised to do that, and that is what I am doing."

They had reached the landing on the stairs, the same place they had made love and he had blurted out his proposal. He didn't dare imagine he would ever hold her like that again; he was still coming to terms with the fact that she had so readily accepted his time at *le château de Nuit*. And yet maybe this was a night for taking chances. . . .

"What will happen?" she was asking.

"I am hoping the army from Crevitch will arrive soon, and I have sent a messenger to the Regent, Archbishop Lanfranc, to explain to him what Baldessare has been up to. He will not escape punishment, Jenova, not this time. I will make certain of it."

Jenova hoped he was right. She did not know how she would continue to live here, with such a man on her border. Especially if Henry was not here to support her, to stand behind her like the wonderful man he was. She had thought, after the maelstrom of the night, that he would never leave. But now, after what he had said to Raf, Jenova was no longer sure.

"Jenova," he said softly. He still hadn't shaved. Soon he would have a beard like a Saxon. "I will only ask this once. I know how unworthy I am, and I do not think I have the courage to ask again. And I am tired. So very tired. I want to rest. I want to sleep for a hundred years, and I want you in my arms when I awake."

His eyes met hers, so somber, so vulnerable.

"My lord!" They both looked up, startled, memories

of the past hours resurfacing with a sickening lurch. Jenova went pale, and Henry slid his arm about her, holding her against him as Reynard thrust his way onto the stairs below them.

"What is it, man! You will wake Raf."

Reynard had the grace to look sheepish, but the urgency in his eyes didn't go away. "My lord, I have Master Will in the hall below. He has come from Gunlinghorn Harbor. He says that the priest has taken passage on one of the boats about to leave—"

Henry was gone, pushing past him down the stairs and into the great hall.

Sleeping bodies lay on benches and mattresses; it was early yet. Outside, a cock began to crow. Master Will was standing by what was left of the fire, and he turned eagerly as Henry strode toward him.

"My lord, the priest . . . I know he is no friend of yours—I was there at the harbor when he rode down to speak with you. He is back there now, at the harbor. He has taken passage on one of the Channel traders. He came not an hour ago, with plenty of money to buy himself a place aboard."

"And they gave it to him?"

"At first the captain was hesitant—the priest wants to take that accursed black stallion with him. But the priest offered him a goodly amount, and the captain has agreed."

"When do they leave?"

"Now, my lord. That is what I came to tell you! The tide is on the turn now, and they leave with it!"

Henry spun around, spying Reynard behind him and Jenova hurrying for the door. "You will take charge while I am gone, Reynard," he said, already moving away. "I will stop him if I can." He kicked at some of his men as he passed, waking them, shouting for them to get up. The rattle of swords and shuffle of boots followed him out.

Reynard and Master Will looked at each other.

"You did well to bring this news to us," Reynard said. "Lord Henry will be grateful."

Master Will nodded, his pale eyes gleaming. "I know. I trust he will be grateful enough to think of me when Gunlinghorn Harbor grows fat and rich."

Reynard shook his head. "Lord Henry prefers men who think of the common good, my friend. Remember that."

Master Will snorted and turned away to find some wine and food to compensate him for his journey. Reynard, watching him go, felt a warm hand on his back. He smiled before he turned.

She had bathed, and now her golden hair was damp and smooth, and she was wearing one of Jenova's blue gowns, which was much too long for her. She had tucked it up around her girdle to prevent herself from tripping on the hem.

"My lady," he murmured and bent to kiss her mouth.

She clung to his neck, stretching up onto her toes, with her body pressed to his. "Reynard," she breathed against his cheek and smiled. "I am ready," she added.

He leaned back to look at her, a question in his dark eyes.

"You said you would enjoy me when I was ready to enjoy you. I am ready."

His breath came a little faster. "Rhona, are you . . ."

She put her fingertip to his lips. "I know what I am saying," she told him firmly. "I have never been more sure."

"I wanted to love you on a warm beach, with the blue sky above and the sea whispering against the shore."

Rhona laughed softly. "You are a poet, my Reynard.

You can love me there, if you like, but I know a soft warm bed which would be just as wonderful." She hesitated, doubt in her eyes now. "Perhaps I am too bold. I have never . . . this is the first time I have ever lain with a man I truly love. A man I want so much it makes me ache."

He groaned softly and kissed her again. "You must show me to your bed, my lady," he said, "but not yet. I would wed you first."

Rhona blinked, taken by surprise, and then she smiled. "Aye," she whispered. "I would like that . . ."

Henry had run to the stables to saddle Lamb, and he found Jenova there before him. She was ordering the stableboys about, her brown hair loose about her shoulders, her green eyes wide and shadowed with anxiety. She turned as he reached her, and she moved close to him, her hand upon his chest.

"Henry, be careful."

"And you, my love. I will be back as soon as I can."

She gazed into his eyes as if she would memorize them, and he felt a jolt straight to his heart.

"I love you, Henry," she said, oblivious to his men, who were beginning to gather about them, and the stableboys rushing to saddle horses. "I cannot live without you. There, I have said it. I have opened my heart to you, just as you did to me. Mortred hurt me, so that I thought I was afraid to love again, but then you came and . . . I could not stop it, no matter how I tried."

Someone cleared his throat, but Henry did not notice. He bent his head and kissed her, his lips soft and serious against hers. A pledge.

"Jenova, my sweetest love, will you let me stay at Gunlinghorn? Will you marry me and let me live with you here, until I am so old I am no longer of use to you or anyone else? This is my home, and you and Raf are my family, and I cannot go. If I go I will be nothing, my life will be nothing. I love you." He suddenly looked lighter of spirit, and some of the shadows had left his eyes. "I love you," he said again. "You are everything to me."

Jenova felt herself smiling so broadly that it hurt. She put her hands up, one on either side of his face, and held him still. He was rumpled and untidy; so unlike Henry. She had broken through his handsome armor and found this man, who was weary and worn, a little afraid and very vulnerable, and who had suffered terribly. No doubt he would soon resume his charming, handsome façade, but now she knew that this was the real Henry. And she loved him.

"Oh Henry, of course I want you to stay with me always. I was worried you would be bored with us here, that you would long for your old life back again. I could not bear it if you grew weary of us," she whispered, tears filling her green eyes.

"Weary?" he said, and laughed with sheer joy. "It is my old life that wearies me. You are everything to me, Jenova. I have been adrift for so many years I had forgotten what it was like to belong, perhaps I was afraid to belong. If I gave too much, then I thought I would be hurt. But now I know that the pain is worth it, if I can have you. I will never leave you."

She kissed him resoundingly, and there was a muffled cheering and more throat clearing. Realizing they had an audience, Henry glanced up and noticed several of his men surreptitiously wiping tears from their eyes. It was a moment to be long remembered.

However, Jean-Paul was about to escape, and Henry knew he must try and stop him.

"I have to go."

Lamb was ready, and Henry climbed into the saddle with graceful ease. Jenova looked up at him, still smiling, her green eyes shining.

"Come back to me," she said.

"Always."

And he was gone, leading his men from the stable and out into the bailey. The gate opened as they approached, and they were soon pounding away from Gunlinghorn Castle, heading for the harbor.

"Keep safe," Jenova whispered. "My dearest love."

The dawn had arrived in truth now, the gray sky washed with pale light. Henry put his head down and rode hard, feeling the wind on his face and knowing that same wind would soon be filling the sails of the boat that could take Jean-Paul far beyond his reach.

How had he escaped? But then Jean-Paul seemed to have a miraculous ability to escape justice.

It had been an eventful night.

He had told Jenova the worst about himself and she had not turned away from him. She had understood. It did not matter to her that in the end he had failed to save those poor souls; she had thought he was brave and strong. You were only a boy, she had said. She'd forgiven him, when he had had such difficulty forgiving himself, and her forgiveness had helped him begin his own healing.

She loved him.

After all these long years, Henry had found his place in the world. Not at court, where he had imagined that taking a new woman as his mistress every month was a good sort of life. Now he knew differently. He had not allowed himself to feel, probably not since he had left Jenova's home in Normandy all those years ago. Now he knew what he had been missing, and he meant to hold on to it. Tightly.

"My lord! There it is!"

They were upon the clifftop, and Henry could see down to the harbor. There was the boat, one of the clumsy-looking traders, but it was still tied up to the wharf. Although the captain and crew were clearly preparing to leave, there was a problem, and Henry could see what it was.

The stallion.

Jean-Paul's stallion resented being forced to board the vessel via the narrow boardwalk set from the wharf to the boat. One man was presently holding the reins as another was attempting to coax the animal from behind, while Jean-Paul moved back and forth, trying to urge his horse aboard through sheer force of will.

At that moment the stallion lashed out and the man behind fell, screaming, to the ground. The animal reared, clearly terrified, while Jean-Paul tried to calm it, his black robes flapping in the wind.

Henry took the track down, riding dangerously fast, feeling Lamb's powerful body beneath him as they flew over stones and bracken and uneven ground. When he reached the sand dunes, he could see that the stallion was back on the wharf and Jean-Paul and the captain of the vessel were in close conversation. Henry pushed forward again.

The crew saw him. He could see the faces of the seamen lift in his direction as they paused in their work. Somebody shouted and pointed. The priest turned and went still, his black cloak drawn close about him, faceless behind his cloth mask. And then in an instant he had thrust his foot into the stirrup and mounted upon his stallion's back.

"Halt!" Henry called.

Jean-Paul let the stallion dance nervously beneath him, but Henry wasn't fooled into thinking he would not try to escape. "Henri, of course," Jean-Paul sneered. "We meet here, at the end of the story, as is only right. Did you know that Baldessare set me free? He wanted to kill me. Why was that, do you think?"

"Souris? It is you, isn't it? I know it is you."

The priest tilted his head. "You know nothing." His voice was harsh. "You understand nothing, Henri!"

"I took away your father, and you hate me for it. But I looked for you, Souris, even after you hurt the girl, I looked for you. I could not find you in your room."

Henry was closer now. He saw Souris' shoulders shake. Damn him! Why did he think it so funny? "I wasn't in my room," he said, his voice surprisingly clear, despite the wind and the mask. "I was with *her*. The girl. She was nearly dead, but I wanted to be sure. I wanted to see if I could make her scream one last time. I was with her when you murdered my father and burned down my home."

Henry was chilled, sickened. He knew then that Jenova was right. He was not like Souris, he never had been. The horrors he had seen had, for a time, numbed him into thinking he did not care. Into thinking he was like Thearoux's band, enjoying cruelty and pain for their own sake.

But he wasn't.

As he stared at Souris, unable to answer, the priest removed his hood. The scars were obscenely stark in the bright morning air. Far worse than Henry had imagined, they distorted the face that should have been. It was

Souris, and yet not. And then the priest turned his head, and the other side of his face became visible, and it was untouched.

Henry knew him. With a dizzy wave of recognition, he saw the boy he had hated and feared, and yet who had been his friend in all those awful months at the château.

"I was burned," Souris said. "I thought I would die. I lay in the ruins and thought I was dying, and that you had left me to die. I knew you'd gone. Henri the avenging angel! Only you could have done such a thing as burn down *le château de Nuit.*"

"You should have died." There was no pity in him for Souris, not now.

Souris held his stallion firm. The ship's crew had finished their work, and the vessel was ready to leave. "Ho, Priest!" The captain stepped nearer, eyeing the horse warily. "We must go. If you still want to take passage with us, then you must board now. I will take you, but the beast must stay—he has injured one of my men."

Souris gave him a bleak look. "I will not leave my horse. He is my friend."

The captain shrugged indifferently and turned away, calling to his men to cast off.

Henry tried again. "Souris . . ."

Souris turned to him, and his ruined mouth was working. "I would have! I would have died! Do you know how I was saved? Oh, you will laugh, Henri, when I tell you. The villagers came, those poor creatures whose lives we had tormented for so long. They came creeping about the ruins of *le château de Nuit,* thinking to make certain everyone was dead. And then they found me.

"I was burned too badly for them to know my face— and I do not think they knew it anyway. But they saw that I was a young boy, and they thought I was you, Henri!

Their friend, who tried to help them, who had saved quite a few of them from my father and his hunt. I let them believe it. I thought it was prudent. They took me back to their village and nursed me, and told me that God had saved me because I was a saint. They sent me to the monastery to be a priest, because they thought me a *saint*." He was nearly choking on his laughter. "*Now*, do you see what is so funny, my friend?"

Henry shook his head, even more sickened. "You should have used your good luck to change your life for the better, Souris. As I did. Instead you have wasted it in bitterness and hate."

"Not wasted. I have enjoyed our encounter again after all these years, Henri."

"You must come back to Gunlinghorn with me, Souris. This time you must pay for your crimes."

Souris smiled. The wind wrapped his black cloak around him. A sinister figure. A sad figure. They stared at each other in silence, and then Souris threw his hood up into the air. It was caught on the breeze and flew over Henry's head, like a dark bird.

"If I must die, then let it be as myself," he shouted. Then, before Henry could stop him, he turned his black stallion and, driving it with heels and hands and knees, made for the end of the wharf.

Shocked, Henry started after him, but he was already too late. Souris reached the end and the stallion leaped out, into nothingness. Briefly they seemed to hang in the air, the powerful animal and the cloaked man, and then they hit the gray water with a splash.

Shouting, Henry dismounted, running to lean over the edge. Both man and horse had surfaced, floundering in the icy sea. But even as he started to believe the situation might be saved, that the small boat the captain had launched might reach Souris in time, he saw the flash of a knife. And the blood in the water.

In a moment the weakened horse sank below the waves, and the man clinging to its back went too. And there was nothing but the roll of the gray sea.

Henry stood up and wiped the spray from his face. It was over. *Le château de Nuit,* and all it meant to him, was finally gone. It was time for Henry to take up his life anew.

At Gunlinghorn.

Epilogue

The chapel at Gunlinghorn was awash with wild roses and honeysuckle. The scent hung heavy in the small space, making Henry's head swim. Or mayhap it was sheer happiness that did that. He was marrying his one true love, the only woman he had ever loved and would ever love.

Jenova.

Beside him, Reynard shuffled his feet. Henry glanced at him, and saw that he was exchanging looks with Rhona. They had been wed at Easter and were leaving Gunlinghorn after Henry and Jenova's wedding. They didn't seem very clear on where they were going, but they were so much in love they didn't care.

Alfric had survived his father's attack and was still at Hilldown Castle. When she had heard of his wounds, Agetha had turned into a harridan, demanding to be taken to his side. She had nursed him back to wellness, and now to everyone's surprise—apart from Jenova's—

Alfric and Agetha were to wed. Henry was not sure what sort of neighbors they would make, but they could only be better than Baldessare.

Baldessare, who was dead, murdered by Souris. So Henry's secret could still have been a secret if he had wished it so. But he had known he could not be completely healed until he had completely cleansed himself. King William had returned to England after Easter, angry with the news that the earls had been plotting against him. But by then Lanfranc had already put down the short-lived, rather small rebellion. Henry had told William the truth one night, late, while drinking some good French wine. William had seemed to understand, but he had already been predisposed to forgive Henry—Henry had just helped him defeat two hundred Danes who had arrived, rather late, in support of the rebellious earls. Thus, so far, everything was well.

A murmur rose at the back of the chapel, capturing his attention. Henry turned to look at what was causing the stir, just as a small boy, resplendent in a tunic and breeches of moss green with gold trimmings, led the way toward the front of the chapel. As he drew nearer, Raf gave Henry a wide smile, his face alight with happiness. Henry smiled back and gave him a wink. Then he looked beyond Raf, and all coherent thought left his head.

Jenova was dressed in white velvet.

The most expensive cloth in England, the most difficult to procure. And she looked breathtakingly beautiful. She looked like a queen.

The velvet clung like skin to her lush curves. The neckline was cut low, outlining full breasts, following her trim waist to her hips, and then flaring out in heavy, shimmering folds to brush the stone flags as she walked. Her entire body seemed to gleam, and then Henry realized that the cloth had been sewn with hundreds of tiny pearls.

Her hair was unbound, curling about her back and shoulders, and more pearls shone among the warm, brown tresses. Her lovely face was aglow with happiness, just like her son's, and her green eyes were fixed on Henry's. Loving him.

Henry had not known it was possible to feel like this. Now that he did, he would never look at his friends with puzzlement and envy again. Jenova was his life, and he knew he would never regret leaving behind the gaudy emptiness he had once thought so important. Here at Gunlinghorn, he had finally found home.

She had reached him. Dazed, he saw now that there were flowers, as well as pearls in her hair. A cascade of cream and gold honeysuckle. She smelled of spring, a new beginning. He wanted to take her out to the meadows, as he had long ago in Normandy. Only this time he would not end the day with a kiss. His gaze slid over her white velvet gown, lingering, wanting to undress her slowly, taking his time.

"Can I kiss my bride?" he asked her, the old wicked glint back in his blue eyes.

Jenova leaned forward and said breathily against his ear, "In a moment you can kiss your wife."

He smiled. "Even better."

Hiding his own smile, the chaplain began to say the words that would join them together.